"In the stultifying world of 1960s suburbia, four women discover that their seemingly perfect lives are missing something essential. Bound by a shared sense of longing and dissatisfaction, they form a book club that will challenge their assumptions, ignite their ambitions, and forge an unbreakable bond of sisterhood. A powerful tribute to friendship and self-discovery, this captivating novel celebrates the power of women to find their voices and create a better future for themselves, one page at a time."

—CHRISTINA BAKER KLINE, *NEW YORK TIMES*
BESTSELLING AUTHOR OF *THE EXILES*

"No one writes female friendship like the luminous Marie Bostwick. When a group of friends decides to read Betty Friedan's blockbuster, *The Feminine Mystique*, the words on the page serve as a rally cry to action for Margaret, Viv, Bitsy, and Charlotte. Long before women were recognized for their contributions and talents, Bostwick carves an unforgettable path for her characters in *The Book Club for Troublesome Women*. At its heart, this is a novel about ambitious women and the mentors that inspired them to excellence. This story is a time capsule of what was, which shows us who we are today."

—ADRIANA TRIGIANI, *NEW YORK TIMES* BESTSELLING
AUTHOR OF *THE GOOD LEFT UNDONE*

"In *The Book Club for Troublesome Women*, the talented Marie Bostwick says this, 'Acquaintances abound, but true friendships are rare and worth waiting for,' capturing the essence, and the heart, of this story. If you love stories about friendships, strong women, the 60s, and the power of the written word, this is the book for you."

—MARYBETH MAYHEW WHALEN,
AUTHOR OF *EVERY MOMENT SINCE*

"I loved this book! Touching, timely, and introspective, Marie Botswick's *The Book Club for Troublesome Women* transcends decades to explore the bonds of women's relationships, both with husbands and with the friends without whom we cannot reach our potential. While the novel is set in 1963, it is incredibly relevant to today's women who are expected to work like they don't have a family and run a home like they don't have a job. A perfect book club read!"

—SARA GOODMAN CONFINO, BESTSELLING AUTHOR OF
DON'T FORGET TO WRITE AND *BEHIND EVERY GOOD MAN*

"I've fallen in love with these troublesome women! Marie Bostwick has written an irresistibly funny, thoughtful story about Margaret, Viv, Charlotte, and Bitsy. During one tumultuous 1960s year these four suburban housewives discover the power of sisterhood and the sometimes dangerous truths about their own formidable talents. Prepare for the potholes, or crevasses, along the way. And clear your calendar to avoid missed appointments!"

—STELLA CAMERON, *NEW YORK TIMES*
BESTSELLING AUTHOR

"In 1963 picture-perfect suburbia, expectations for women are clear: the house is clean, the children are well cared for, and dinner is on the table at 6 p.m. sharp. But when Margaret, Viv, Bitsy, and Charlotte read Betty Friedan's seismic new book, *The Feminine Mystique*, for their book club, fault lines in their own lives shift and a new path forward for each of the women gapes open. In a 1960s world Bostwick expertly describes as equal parts hilarious, frustrating, and challenging, these four women form a bond that changes their lives forever as they each explore what it means to be a woman and a friend."

—ELIZABETH BASS PARMAN, AUTHOR OF
THE EMPRESS OF COOKE COUNTY

The Book Club for Troublesome Women

The

BOOK CLUB

for

TROUBLESOME
WOMEN

A Novel

MARIE BOSTWICK

HARPER MUSE

The Book Club for Troublesome Women

Copyright © 2025 Marie Bostwick

Published by Harper Muse, an imprint of HarperCollins Focus LLC.

Library of Congress Cataloging-in-Publication Data

Names: Bostwick, Marie, author.
Title: The book club for troublesome women : a novel / Marie Bostwick.
Description: Nashville: Harper Muse, 2025. | Summary: "Margaret Ryan never really meant to start a book club . . . or a feminist revolution in her buttoned-up suburb"—Provided by publisher.
Identifiers: LCCN 2024043464 (print) | LCCN 2024043465 (ebook) | ISBN 9781400344741 (paperback) | ISBN 9781400344758 (epub) | ISBN 9781400344765
Subjects: LCSH: Book clubs (Discussion groups)—Fiction. | Women—Fiction. | LCGFT: Novels.
Classification: LCC PS3602.O838 B66 2025 (print) | LCC PS3602.O838 (ebook) | DDC 813/.6—dc23/eng/20240923
LC record available at https://lccn.loc.gov/2024043464
LC ebook record available at https://lccn.loc.gov/2024043465

Printed in the United States of America

25 26 27 28 29 LBC 7 6 5 4 3

This book is dedicated to the original Margaret, my Margaret, my mother, who inspired this journey by her example and with these words: "I don't know if I ever told you, but that book changed my life."

On February 19, 1963, a troublesome, imperfect, controversial woman named Betty Friedan published a troublesome, imperfect, controversial book titled *The Feminine Mystique*.

The book didn't solve the problem.

But it did put a name to it, shining a light that helped women who felt isolated and powerless find one another, and their voices.

That has been the start of every revolution.

CHAPTER I

Members of the Club

March 1963

On a Wednesday morning in March 1963, twenty-five miles and yet a world away from the nation's capital and the rumblings of change that were beginning to be felt there, in a northern Virginia suburb called Concordia, so new that the roots of the association-approved saplings were still struggling to take hold, and so meticulously planned that when the first wave of residents moved in the year before, the shops, library, and church opened on the very same day, as if God smote the ground and a fully formed suburb had erupted from the crack, Margaret Ryan stood in a sunny kitchen with appliances and matching Formica countertops of egg-yolk yellow, trying to decide what to serve the three women who would be coming to the first meeting of her new book club.

Beth Ryan, eleven years old and the eldest of Margaret's three children, peered over her mother's shoulder, shaking her head at the small mountain of recipes Margaret had torn from her extensive collection of women's magazines.

"Why so many? Why not bake oatmeal cookies and be done with it like any normal mother?" Beth snatched a recipe clipping from the stack. "Anchovy and cream cheese canapés? If that's dinner, I'm eating at Melanie's."

Every family has its smart-ass. Beth was theirs.

With her strawberry-blond hair and enviably long lashes, Beth was the image of her father. But her cheek was pure Margaret, and a payback, Margaret was sure, for the sins of her youth. When her own mother was still alive, she had cursed Margaret countless times, saying, "When you grow up, I hope you have a daughter that's as fresh as you are. *Then* you'll know."

Now she did know, and it wasn't so bad. Margaret liked that her daughter knew her own mind and wasn't afraid to speak it. It was an underappreciated quality in women, one that often faded with age.

At age seventeen, Margaret had sworn that she would grow up to be nothing like her mother. After a promising start, the fruit of her early efforts had shriveled. Now, at age thirty-three, Margaret sometimes wondered if every woman was destined to become her mother eventually. Recently, however, things had started to shift.

And not just for Margaret.

As with any seismic occurrence, the impact would be felt more keenly by some than others, and responses to it would vary widely. Some would embrace the change. Some would decry it. Some would avert their eyes and pretend nothing had happened. It didn't come all at once, of course. Meaningful change rarely does. There would be more rumblings, more waves, more altercations in decades to come. But in the fullness of time, no one could deny that landscapes and lives had been irrevocably transformed.

Nevertheless, Margaret didn't fully appreciate that yet. Neither did she understand that the impulses she'd given in to over the last three months and the secrets she kept—including the presence of the rented seafoam-green typewriter she'd hidden in the far reaches of the linen closet—would alter her family, her future, and her sense of self. Today she was just excited about the book club, thrilled to be the point of connection for the other three women who had agreed to take part, some more reluctantly than others, and determined to make their first meeting memorable.

Without the assistance of an alarm, Margaret's eyes had flown open promptly at five that morning. Walt hadn't come home from the VFW until well after midnight, so there was little chance of disturbing him, but she slipped quietly from bed and tiptoed down the hall to the bathroom anyway. Why risk endangering her good spirits with some pointless confrontation?

Half an hour later, she emerged with her chestnut hair curled and sprayed into a shoulder-length flip, wearing lipstick, heels, and a black watch tartan jumper over a cream-colored blouse, as polished and pulled together as any magazine model. Coming downstairs for breakfast, the kids had hovered on the kitchen threshold, confused to see her looking so smart so early in the day.

"Is it Sunday?" six-year-old Susan whispered to Beth, who shook her head but didn't budge from the doorway. Bobby, eight years old but already the tallest in his class and perpetually famished, broke the spell. "Mom? Can we have waffles? And bacon?"

"Waffles are for Saturdays," Margaret said, chewing her lip as she scanned an ingredient list for turkey and mushroom roll-ups. "Have some cereal. There was a new kind at the market."

Bobby trotted to the cupboard and let out a whoop.

"Cap'n Crunch! That's the one from the TV! You are the best mom *ever!*"

He threw his arms around her waist. Margaret patted his back. He was so easy to please.

"Slice some banana on top," she said. Despite the cereal company's claims about vitamins, feeding her brood a sugarcoated breakfast with a cartoon captain spokesman didn't make her *feel* like the best mom ever. Tomorrow she'd make scrambled eggs.

"Suzy," she said, noticing the child had missed a button on her cardigan, "come here."

Susan, who most closely resembled Margaret in looks, hopped up from the banquette. She stood perfectly still when Margaret knelt to rebutton her sweater, examining her mother's face.

"How come you're so dressed up? Are you going to the doctor?"

"My book club is tonight, remember? It's our first meeting, so I'm excited."

"You don't look excited. You look nervous."

"Well . . ." Margaret picked a pill off Susan's cardigan. "It's always a little scary, isn't it? Getting to know new people, letting them get to know you? So, yes. I am a little nervous. But also excited."

"Like I felt on the first day at our new school?"

"Something like that. Go finish your breakfast."

Beth tilted her chin toward a bright-red book lying next to the coffee percolator that Walt and Margaret had received as a premium for opening a new checking account.

"Is that what you're reading?"

"Uh-huh." Deciding that Beth had a point about anchovies, Margaret moved the canapé recipe to the reject pile. "It came out just last month."

Beth picked up the book, lips moving silently as she sounded out the title.

"What does *mystique* mean?"

Margaret hesitated. Their bookstore order had been delayed, so she'd only had time to read the first few chapters. Even so, the declarations she encountered there were electric, jolting a shrouded, dormant part of her brain to life with ideas that seemed utterly fresh but also uncannily familiar. Reading about the strange stirrings and unnamed problem, knowing she wasn't the only one who had wondered why "having it all" somehow wasn't enough, had left Margaret awash with relief and an unexpected sense of vindication, akin to the moment she'd first spotted Charlotte Gustafson in the drugstore—a complete stranger who still barely qualified as an acquaintance—and somehow known they were in sympathy.

Charlotte had called the book groundbreaking. Margaret agreed. Would the others feel the same? As if they'd been unburdened of a shameful secret? Reprieved from a long, lonely, and unjust exile?

"Mom? Mystique?"

"It's . . . a kind of aura, a sense of mystery or power, a sort of magical reputation attached to a person or group. But I don't think that's really what the author meant here. I think she's saying a mystique can be a lie, or even a kind of diversion."

"Sounds boring." Beth tossed the book aside. "Who's in the club?"

"So far, it's just me, Viv, Bitsy, and Mrs. Gustafson."

"Mrs. Gustafson? The new neighbor? People say she's an oddball."

"You shouldn't be listening to what people say. Or repeating it," Margaret said. "Anyway, Charlotte's not an oddball. She's just different, artistic, a freethinker. Heaven knows we could use a few more of *those* in Concordia."

Beth frowned. "What's wrong with Concordia? I like it here."

"Nothing," Margaret said, smoothing her daughter's hair. "I like it too. It's just that sometimes the people here can be a bit . . ."

Margaret searched for a word to sum up the conflicting emotions she felt regarding their new home, but her lifelong facility with language, which she'd honed to an even sharper edge over the previous three months, failed her. How could she explain her love-hate relationship with Concordia to her little girl when she didn't really understand it herself?

✳ ✳ ✳

Later that same morning, thirty-nine-year-old Charlotte Gustafson put a Newport between her lips, leaving a fire-engine-red imprint on the filter. She tilted her chin and exhaled, watching the smoke drift to the ceiling of Dr. Ernest Barry's office.

His practice was located on the ground floor of a three-story redbrick townhouse in Alexandria, Virginia. Charlotte had to drive forty minutes each way for her twice-weekly appointments because there weren't any psychiatrists in Concordia and she'd been referred to Barry's practice by her old doctor in New York. She didn't mind. Alexandria wasn't Manhattan, but it had a few good antique shops, a decent shoe store, and a certain charm. Dr. Barry, who had a pompous attitude and an excess of nose hair, was considerably less charming. But anything to escape the mundanity of suburbia.

Charlotte took another drag and crossed her feet, clad in Italian leather pumps the same shade of sapphire as her sheath dress and matching swing coat, trying to get more comfortable.

"Charlotte, I've asked you before not to smoke."

"Dr. Gould always let me smoke."

"Dr. Gould doesn't have asthma." He held out an ashtray. Charlotte took a quick puff and stubbed out the cigarette butt. The doctor picked up his pen. "Did you dream this week?"

"I told you before, I don't dream."

"Everyone dreams."

"Fine," she said, clutching the fingers that should have been holding her cigarette into a fist. "I don't *remember* any dreams."

"All right. Let's move on. What was your week like? Anything new?"

"Same old, same old." She shrugged. "The mutual loathing Howard and I feel for one another continues unabated. My father still prefers him to me, treats my husband like the son he never had and me like a titian-haired, addlebrained idiot. Denise won't take her nose out of her books to speak to me, or anyone else, and is still set on going to Oxford after graduation. I don't blame her for wanting to escape, but why England? It rains incessantly, there's no central heat, and the men have terrible teeth. Why not go someplace hip, with good weather and good-looking people? Why not escape to Rome? Or even Los Angeles?"

Charlotte craned her neck to the side, as if actually expecting a response. The doctor made a note on his pad. Charlotte sighed, wishing she'd worn her watch so she'd know how long it would be until the end of the session and her next cigarette.

"I suppose Junior is doing fine at the military academy, but he hasn't written in weeks, so who knows? Laura and Andrew are still sweet, but at twelve and eleven, you'd expect that. Of course I was an early bloomer, but I don't think most people start despising their parents until they hit their teens, do you? Let's see . . . What else is new?" She drummed her fingernails against the brown leather of the therapy couch, which was really more of a chaise.

"Oh yes! Another gallery turned me down. This time the owner phoned *personally* to say he found my paintings amateurish and derivative. Good of him to make the effort, don't you think? But that's about it. Nothing new to report.

"Oh, wait," she said, and snapped her fingers. "There is *one* thing. I joined a women's book club."

"A book club?" Barry scooted forward in his burgundy wingback chair. "Well, that's excellent, Charlotte. Do you know these women?"

"Just one, Margaret Ryan. She showed up at the door unannounced with a plate of cookies and invited me to join."

"Excellent. Making connections with other housewives can be very therapeutic and help you adjust to your role. Do you think you can become friends with this woman?"

"We'll see," Charlotte said, squishing her lips together. "She may be too nice. Her taste in literature is *much* too nice. I only agreed to join because she let me pick the book."

"And what book is that?"

Had Dr. Barry been able to read Charlotte as well as he thought he could—something she was determined to prevent him from ever, *ever* doing—he would have seen the bow of her lips and known it was the smile of a woman who took pleasure in baiting hooks and seeing the barbs swallowed whole.

"*The Feminine Mystique* by Betty Friedan," Charlotte said sweetly. "Have you read it?"

Barry's bristly white brows became a disapproving line. "I've heard about it, and that's quite enough. Therapeutically speaking, Charlotte, I don't think—"

"Oh, but you *must*," she interrupted, rolling onto her side and fixing him with her emerald-green eyes. "I found chapter five, 'The Sexual Solipsism of Sigmund Freud,' *particularly* enlightening. I'm sure you would too. Would you like to borrow my copy?"

"No, thank you," Barry said stiffly, and scribbled another note on his pad.

Charlotte's purse was sitting next to the couch. She reached inside for her cigarettes.

"Sorry," she said when he shot her a look. "It's beyond my control. Oral fixation. You understand." She pushed herself to a sitting position and lit up. "I believe our time is up for today. But I think we've made real progress, don't you?" She stood. "Oh, one more thing? I'm going to need a new prescription. The one Dr. Gould wrote for me is about to expire. Doesn't have to be today though. I can get it at my next appointment.

"See you then," she chirped, giving a little wave as she headed to the door.

* * *

The late afternoon sun was shining in Rock Creek Park, turning the newly unfurled leaves of the trees that lined the horse trail an even brighter shade of green.

As the end of the bridle path came into sight, Bitsy Cobb—whose hair, worn in a pageboy held back from her face with a narrow red velvet ribbon, was as black and shiny as the coat of her mount—loosened the reins, letting Delilah canter for the final hundred yards. Though the same age as her twenty-three-year-old rider, the horse moved well.

"You've still got it, don't you, girl?" Bitsy said as they approached the stable and Delilah slowed to a walk.

The horse, spotting a well-dressed woman of middle years

standing near a fence, perked up her ears and picked up her pace, jogging toward the woman, who murmured affectionately when Delilah stopped in front of her.

"Beautiful girl," the woman said, pulling half an apple from the pocket of her well-cut tweed jacket and offering it to the horse. "You're aging better than I am, aren't you?"

Bitsy climbed down from the saddle.

"Mrs. Graham, have you been waiting? I'm sorry. I didn't know you'd planned to ride."

"No time today, I'm afraid. Two dozen editors, plus wives and girlfriends, are coming for dinner. Tomorrow it's freshman congressmen—Democrats *and* Republicans. I'm putting the summer slipcovers on early in case blood is drawn," she said, then laughed.

Katharine Graham was an heiress, the wife of Phil Graham, publisher of the *Washington Post* newspaper, and one of Washington, DC's, most influential hostesses. Though Bitsy had only been working at the stables for a few weeks, she'd found Mrs. Graham to be unpretentious and kind.

"I just dropped by to say hello to my girl," Katharine said, stroking Delilah's neck as the horse munched the apple. "She was a wedding gift from my father, did I tell you? I was far more excited about Delilah than I was about those eighteen place settings of Limoges, believe me." Mrs. Graham smiled. "Thank you for taking such good care of her."

"Oh, it's nothing," Bitsy said in a soft Kentucky drawl. "Sometimes I can't believe how lucky I am, getting *paid* to ride horses. Honestly, I'd do it for free. Don't tell my boss though."

"It'll be our secret. But you do a lot more than just ride the horses. You curry, water, and feed them, too, among other less savory jobs." Mrs. Graham shifted her gaze to a nearby manure shovel. "And always with unflagging dedication, I've noticed."

Unaccustomed to much praise, Bitsy felt her cheeks go warm. "Well, I grew up with horses. My daddy was barn manager at Prescott Farms for thirty years before he passed."

"In Lexington? You don't say. They've produced some fine thoroughbreds, quarter horses too. Delilah's grandfather came from Prescott Farms. You should be proud."

Bitsy beamed. "Yes, ma'am. I am. Ever since I was this high," she said, flattening her palm just above her knee, "I'd tag along behind Daddy, helping in the barn. Mother wanted me to be a lady, but the only thing I cared about was horses and books."

Delilah nudged her shoulder, and Mrs. Graham stroked the animal's nose. "I thought as much. I didn't suppose that as the wife of a successful equine vet, you took this job for the money."

"Well, he's still building his practice," Bitsy said. "But yes, we're comfortable. We bought a house in Concordia. It's nice, but different from Lexington. I'm the youngest woman in the neighborhood and the only one without children, so I don't quite fit in. King is older than I am and anxious to start a family—I am, too, naturally—but no luck so far.

"Anyway . . . ," she murmured, fearing she'd shared too much and remembering Mrs. Graham had things to do. But instead of making an exit, Katharine nodded.

"It's a lot of pressure, isn't it? You know, nearly three years passed before Phil and I had our first child. My mother called every single day to ask what was taking so long."

Bitsy gasped. "Mine too! She doesn't even say hello now, just, 'Well?' It's unnerving!"

When their shared laughter faded, Mrs. Graham patted Bitsy's arm. "Things have a way of working out when and how they're meant to. You'll see. As far as the women in your neighborhood, don't turn yourself inside out trying to make everyone love you. Instead, be on the lookout for two or three like-minded souls who'll take you as you are and stand by you no matter what. Acquaintances abound, but true friendships are rare and worth waiting for."

"I just joined a book club," Bitsy offered. "Maybe I'll find friends there. We're reading *The Feminine Mystique*. It's interesting."

"And controversial." Mrs. Graham nodded appreciatively. "I like these women already."

"Me too. So far."

"Give it time," Katharine said, then glanced at her wristwatch. "Speaking of which . . ."

Bitsy led Delilah toward the stable, and Mrs. Graham walked to her waiting sedan. After turning on the ignition, she pulled the car up alongside the fence and rolled down the window.

"Bitsy?" she called out. "When your mother phones, tell her that not only is it possible to love horses and books and still be a lady, but Katharine Graham says it's practically *required!*"

* * *

After laying the teasing comb on the counter and giving her blond bouffant a final coat of hairspray, forty-one-year-old Vivian Buschetti cranked up the volume of the bathroom radio, hoping the sound of Eydie Gormé blaming it on the bossa nova would drown out the noise of her six children, whose argument over the television set was reaching a fever pitch.

Knowing she had only moments before the kids would start pounding on the bathroom door and demanding justice, Viv applied her eyeliner and pulled a black nylon and lace slip over her head, tugging to clear her full bosom and generous curves. There was a knock.

She turned down the radio. "Do not make me come down there," she warned through the locked door. "If I do, *nobody* is watching *anything* for a week. Vince? Andrea? You hear me?"

"Loud and clear. But it's not Vince. Or Andrea."

Viv smiled and blotted her pink lipstick with a tissue. "Who is it?"

"The man of your dreams. But don't tell your husband. I hear he gets crazy jealous."

Viv opened the door. After eighteen years of marriage, the sight of tall, dark, and handsome Anthony Buschetti in his crisply pressed naval uniform, with his melting-chocolate eyes and teasing smile, still made her a little weak in the knees.

"You're an idiot," she said, shaking her head.

"*You* are a bombshell." Tony's eyes traveled over her body. "Va-va-voom!" He stepped across the threshold and locked the door, backing her up against the countertop and nuzzling her neck.

"Stop, honey," Viv giggled. "We can't. The kids."

"They're fine. I told them to go outside and wait for the pizza delivery guy."

"You ordered pizza?"

"Uh-huh." Tony's lips moved from her neck to her décolletage. "So you can get ready for your hen party without having to worry about making dinner. Ain't I a prince of a guy?"

"Yes. But it's a book club, not a hen party. And I still need to get ready, Tony. Really."

"Seriously?" he asked, lifting his head and groaning in response to her nod. "Well . . . okay. But try to come home early. Because you look amazing, absolutely irresistible."

She turned to the mirror to fix her lipstick. Tony sat on the counter and watched her.

Viv sighed. "I don't feel irresistible. I feel bloated, cranky, and tired. If I didn't know it would hurt Margaret's feelings, I'd skip tonight. I only agreed to join because she was so excited about it and because that stupid doctor made me so mad," Viv said, her irritation rising. "The nerve of that man! Refusing to write me a prescription for the pill unless *you* show up to sign off on it. As if I'm a child instead of a grown woman. And as if an officer assigned to the Pentagon has time for his wife's doctor appointments!" She stabbed the air with an eyebrow pencil. "If he wasn't the only gynecologist in Concordia—"

"I know," Tony said. "But let it go. I'm taking Tuesday off. We'll see the doc, get the prescription, and that'll be that. Play your cards right, and I might take you to lunch after."

She smiled. "You know something, Anthony Buschetti? You really are a prince of a guy."

Tony spread out his hands. "What do I keep telling you?"

Their kiss was interrupted when their eldest, seventeen-year-old Vince, rapped on the door to say the pizza had arrived. "Be right down," Tony called, then peered into Viv's face. "You really are tired, aren't you? Maybe we should rethink the idea of you going back to work."

"No!" Viv smacked her eyebrow pencil down on the counter. "We always said I'd get back into nursing once the kids were in school. It'd only be part-time. With Vince starting college next year, we need the money. And I need . . ."

"You need what?"

Tony pulled her close, resting his hands on the swell of her hips. Viv pressed her lips together. When she spoke again, her voice was hoarse.

"I need to feel important again. I was a good nurse, Tony."

"Best on base. Best in the whole damned European theater," he said. "The CO threatened to bust me a rank for taking you away from it. You *are* important, Viv. You're the glue that holds this family together." He traced a finger on her cheek. "You know that, right?"

Viv bobbed her head. She did know. Viv loved being a mother and was proud that they'd raised six terrific, respectful, clean-cut, all-American kids—Vince, Andrea, Mike, Nick, Mark, and little Jenny. Not a delinquent in the bunch. But now she wanted more.

Viv had never been much of a reader, and that book Margaret had talked her into reading for the club was so boring that it practically put her to sleep. But one part—an interview with a housewife who reported realizing one day she'd already hit all the expected milestones of the feminine achievement and had nothing new to look forward to—sounded a deep chord within her.

Tony tucked a blond strand that had somehow escaped the hairspray behind her ear.

"You know what? I think you need a break. On Saturday I'll make pancakes for the kids so you can sleep, then drop them at a matinee and come back to join you. How's that sound?"

"You, me, and the house to ourselves for two whole hours? Like heaven."

"Good. It's a date."

Tony went downstairs to pay for the pizza, leaving the bathroom door slightly ajar. Viv opened a package of pantyhose she'd ordered from Sears, her first. She perched on the toilet seat to don them, amazed at how light they felt compared to a girdle. Would they hold her in as well? Probably not. But who cared? Margaret said she ought to give them a try, and she was right. They were so comfortable!

Viv got to her feet to pull them up. The sound of happy, hungry children digging into boxes of pizza wafted through the air, along with a powerful smell of greasy pepperoni that assaulted Viv's nose, and then her stomach, making her gag. She spun toward the toilet, doubled over, vomited twice, then sank to her knees, overcome by an old, all-too-familiar weakness.

"No, no, no," she murmured, her voice choked and rasping. "Not again. Not now!"

"Viv?" Tony's voice boomed from below. "You coming? We saved you some pepperoni."

Pepperoni. Even the word sickened her. She screwed her eyes shut and swallowed bile.

"That's okay," she called. "Let the kids have it. I'm not hungry."

She went to the sink, pulled a flowered paper Dixie Cup from the wall dispenser, and rinsed out her mouth. A minute later, Tony appeared in the doorway.

"Are you okay?"

"Of course," Viv said, screwing the top on the toothpaste tube. "Why wouldn't I be?"

"You said you weren't hungry."

"So? I'm running late, that's all. Don't wait up."

She turned sideways, trying to squeeze past. Tony put a hand out to stop her, frowning.

"Yeah, but honey—you love pizza."

"Tony," she laughed, "could you possibly be any *more* Italian? Just because a person isn't hungry doesn't mean something's wrong. I'm saving my appetite for the book club, that's all. I bet you anything that Margaret's been cooking since dawn, trying to make things special. Remember what happened at Christmas? I know she tried to laugh it off, but I think that whole thing with Walt really hurt her feelings. She's been acting funny ever since, like she's keeping a secret or something."

Viv dropped her gaze, speaking more to herself than to her husband.

"Margaret is my closest friend in Concordia, my only friend. I just can't stand to see her disappointed again."

CHAPTER 2

Consequential Christmas

Late December 1962 – Three months before

Walt said she was going overboard. Maybe she was. But it was their first Christmas in the new house, and she wanted to make it memorable. Was that so terrible?

"It's a day like all the rest of them, Maggie," Walt reminded her when she brought home kits to make needlepoint Christmas stockings for all three kids. "Don't you think it might be a mistake, getting yourself worked up like this?"

His concerns were not unfounded.

The things Margaret set her heart on almost never came to pass. And if they did, they turned out to be less satisfying or meaningful or lasting than she'd imagined. Just less. Building up expectations was almost always a prescription for being let down, and never more so than at Christmas.

But it didn't *have* to be that way.

Christmas of 1945, the celebration of which her mother had postponed until January 11, 1946, the day Dad mustered out of the military, lived in Margaret's memory as a perfect day, a singular happiness. Had she been forced to choose one day to live over and over, that would have been it.

They didn't have two nickels to rub together. Mom had been laid off from her job at National Cash Register, which had retooled to make fuses, gunsights, and airplane parts during the war. But everybody was strapped in those days; the postwar economic boom didn't really get rolling until the 1950s. Sugar was still being rationed in '46, but had it been otherwise, they wouldn't have had money to buy it or much of anything else. There were a few presents, the kind that prove it really is the thought that counts, but nothing expensive. Her gift from Dad—a wooden bird whistle he'd carved from the branch of a German linden tree—still sat on Margaret's dressing table. And even after all this time, the scent of freshly cut spruce still summoned memories of the fresh garlands and Christmas wreaths her mother had twisted together by hand on that one perfect day.

How that Christmas *felt*, how they felt about one another, was what mattered most. For four uncertain, troubled years, everybody had done their job and their share, pulling in the same direction even when they were apart, and had come out on the other side, united in purpose and together again, a family.

It didn't last, of course. How could it?

When Margaret sat down to brush her hair at night, her fingers would light upon the touchstone of her father's gift. Looking into the mirror, she'd see the earnest eyes of a fifteen-year-old girl who was certain she could recapture the moment once more and hold on to it forever if only she worked hard enough, did enough, *was* enough.

That was why, two days before Christmas, when driving home from the poultry farm with a special-order turkey stowed in the passenger side footwell and spotting a stand of spruce trees fifty yards from the road, Margaret had slammed on the brakes, bailed out of the station wagon, and climbed over a barbed wire fence to cut some branches. Her sweater snagged on the fence and her shoes were coated with mud, but the car being filled with evergreens was worth it. Christmas was going to be magical. A holiday they would always remember.

Turning right onto Laurel Lane, Margaret spotted their house, a center-hall Colonial with white siding, forest-green shutters, and two scrawny birch trees in the front yard. She would have preferred blue shutters and flowering dogwood trees, but Concordia had covenants for everything, which meant no blue shutters and no dogwoods, nothing that wasn't pre-approved in the master plan.

Still, in so many ways, it was a dream neighborhood and a dream home.

Margaret loved her house. After a decade of run-down rentals with water-stained ceilings, what she most loved was the *newness* of it—the fact that she'd been the first one ever to put a bottle of milk in the refrigerator, and that the wall-to-wall carpet gave off a faint chemical scent, like Pine-Sol and motor oil, when she ran the vacuum.

When crossing the threshold for the very first time, footsteps echoing through bare rooms that smelled of paint, Margaret had been filled with a bright, breathless anticipation. She envisioned the house that *could* be, how the naked living room would look furnished with new sofas and chairs, imagined sparkling conversation with interesting friends taking place around a teak dining table she'd seen in a magazine. Mentally she had already papered walls and accessorized rooms, creating a warm, welcoming, and stylish home.

It wouldn't happen overnight, but that was all right. She could be patient.

She worked with what she had—painting bedrooms herself and placing potted plants by the windows. She built shelves from cinderblocks and boards, filled them with borrowed library books and shopworn volumes purchased from the discount table in Babcock's Best Books, as well as one pristine copy of Anne Morrow Lindbergh's *Gift from the Sea* that she bought on her first visit to the bookstore, the same week they moved in. It was a splurge, but Margaret couldn't resist. Buying that book felt like making a down payment on the life she hoped to have.

But now, nearly a year after the move, those hopes were still frustratingly unrealized.

Every time Margaret hinted about replacing the secondhand furniture they'd inherited from his parents, Walt shook his head. "Buying the house wiped out our savings. We shouldn't undertake any unnecessary expenditures until we build it up again."

She knew he wasn't wrong. And it wasn't as if they were the only family in Concordia who had emptied their bank account to buy a house they couldn't afford to furnish. But she and Walt hadn't always had such different ideas about what was and wasn't necessary.

They'd met during her freshman year at Ohio State. Margaret and Walt were enrolled in a class titled Great American Novels, along with seventy-plus former servicemen.

When the war ended, men like Margaret's father, who was thirty-one when he was drafted and had been working at the factory for years before Pearl Harbor, went back to their old jobs. Younger veterans had a harder time finding work. Thanks to the GI Bill, ex-soldiers flooded college campuses to earn degrees in lucrative fields they hoped would support a family.

They were an impatient generation. War had interrupted their lives, so they were anxious to make up for lost time and eager to tick off the courses required for graduation, including a mandatory 200-level literature class. They were good men, hardworking and focused, but most of them didn't give a fig about great American novels, or *any* novels.

Walter Ryan was the exception.

He had questions, *so* many questions. His hand was always the first to go up, so often that other soldiers-turned-students would groan at the sight of Walt's waving arm. He had observations too. Some were more insightful than others, and not all of them related to the material at hand. Sometimes he tried the professor's patience. But no one could doubt that Walt was curious about literature, and life in general.

Margaret didn't really notice him until she walked into the cafeteria one day and spotted him alone at a table, surrounded by books and about fifty packets of saltines, which were free for the taking from the condiment table. He opened the packets one by one, dipping the crackers into a shallow paper cup of tomato ketchup, munching as he pored over a copy of Margaret Mead's *Coming of Age in Samoa*.

He must have felt her eyes on him because he lifted his head.

"Sorry," Margaret said, feeling the color rise in her cheeks when his slate-blue eyes met hers. "Didn't mean to disturb you. I can see you're cramming."

"Cramming?" He blinked, then closed the book. "Oh no. This is just for fun."

"You're not an anthropology major?"

"Was. Then I switched to philosophy, but only for a semester. After that it was political science. At the moment, I'm undeclared, but I'm thinking about English literature. Or maybe European history. I can't decide. Do you want to sit down?"

Margaret wasn't sure. He was such an odd young man but better-looking than she'd realized at first glance.

In an era when tall, dark, and handsome was considered the ideal, Walt was middling of height and slender of frame, muscular but lithe, and had fair skin and reddish-blond hair. He *was* handsome, she decided—when he smiled, he reminded her of the actor Van Johnson, his face lit up with a kind of joyous, boy-next-door charisma—and undeniably intriguing.

Margaret set down her cafeteria tray and took a seat. Walt brushed cracker crumbs from the table, as if trying to make things more presentable.

"What's your major?" he asked.

"I haven't declared yet, but probably English. Not sure what I'll do with it. Teach, I suppose, unless I happen to—"

Margaret took a quick drink of milk to mask her near fumble, grateful she'd stopped herself from saying that teaching would be her fallback position if she didn't meet her husband before graduation. Even if she'd been interested in him, which she absolutely wasn't, a girl didn't want to look too eager. Margaret put down her milk carton.

"What year are you?"

"Sophomore. I should be a junior. But . . ."

"You keep changing majors," Margaret said, laughing and finishing his sentence for him. "But you'll decide eventually, won't you? I mean, you can't just be a student forever."

"No, you're right," he said, ducking his head in a way that made Margaret wish she hadn't laughed. "I'll have to graduate and go to work eventually, but when will I ever have another opportunity like this? The chance to think and study and explore ideas and . . . well, live. Really live."

There it was again, that earnest, boy-next-door sincerity and enthusiasm. But Walt Ryan was a boy who had already seen a lot.

"I joined up in forty-three," he told her. "Two days after my seventeenth birthday, me and a bunch of my friends from high school. The recruiting officer knew we weren't old enough but was willing to look the other way. A lot of us didn't make it back. Some that did won't ever be the same. Guess I'm not either, if I think about it. I was never much of a student—valedictorians don't lie about their age to join the army, you know? But now, I just . . ."

He spread his arms to encompass the books piled around him like the walls of a fortress, while smiling and turning his head from side to side as if greeting old friends.

"Well, I just want to read everything and learn everything and do everything. Don't know if I'm doing it for myself or the guys who never got to. I only know things are different for me now. Doesn't make sense, I guess. But there it is."

Walt shrugged, dunked a cracker into the pool of ketchup, and took a quick bite, as if suddenly afraid he'd said too much. But Margaret understood. The war had changed a lot of people. And there were worse things than returning from combat with a hunger for life and knowledge. Margaret held out half of her ham sandwich.

"Here."

"You sure?" he asked, accepting the sandwich when she said she was. "Thanks."

Most everybody at Ohio State was on a budget, and Walt wasn't the only student to take advantage of the free crackers and condiments. But Margaret had never seen anybody make a meal of them and supposed he must be well and truly broke. She nodded toward the empty cracker wrappers. "End of the month?"

He shook his head. "Saving up for a guitar. If I only eat one meal a day, I'll have enough by the end of the term."

"You play the guitar?"

"Not yet," he said, grinning as he wolfed down a bite of the sandwich. "But I will."

She married him two years later, when she was twenty and he was twenty-five.

The guitar was still with them, stashed in a corner of the garage. But Walt never played it or read for pleasure anymore, and the curious and handsome young man who smiled easily and talked too much was gone. She was grateful for the man he'd become, of course, and the life he'd made possible for them. If not for Walt's cautious self-discipline, they'd still be renters.

But sometimes she missed the boy—the odd, hungry, indecisive, far-too-impulsive boy.

✳ ✳ ✳

Margaret swung open the station wagon's rear gate and began pulling out branches just as Viv, whose blue, split-level ranch house stood kitty-corner, was carrying out the trash.

"What is all this?" Viv asked, coming to stand beside her after jogging across the street.

"I'm making garland!"

"How much? You've got enough greenery to decorate the whole neighborhood."

"I'm just going to wrap the banisters. It always takes more than you think."

"Maggie, I don't know where you get the energy."

"Don't be too impressed," Margaret said, piling more boughs

into her arms. "Not yet anyway. I'll have to get a wiggle on to finish before the kids get home from school. Hey, can I borrow your punch bowl? *Ladies' Home Journal* had an eggnog recipe I want to try."

Viv ran ahead to open Margaret's door and stepped aside so she could pass.

"Homemade garland? Homemade eggnog? Tell me you baked a gingerbread house, and I'll slash my wrists with a rusty frosting palette. How are the rest of us supposed to compete?"

Margaret frowned and turned sideways, squeezing through the doorway.

"It's not a competition. I just want things to be nice. For the kids. And Walt."

"No, I get it. I feel the same way. But sometimes I wonder . . ." Viv tilted her head to the side. "Do you think anybody really notices?"

❄ ❄ ❄

As it turned out, no one did.

Later that afternoon, moments after the kids got home from school to start the Christmas vacation, Suzy vomited onto the freshly waxed parquet floor. All three of them came down with the flu. Margaret spent the holiday bouncing between their bedrooms, bringing crackers and ginger ale, buckets and mops, and words of comfort. There'd been no time to cook Christmas dinner, which was probably just as well. In her rush and enthusiasm to make the garlands, she'd forgotten the turkey and left it sitting in the station wagon for hours. The bird might have been all right, but it wasn't worth taking the chance, so she tossed it into a pot, boiled the bejeebers out of it, and made soup.

After the kids fell asleep on Christmas Day, Margaret and Walt ate the soup with some of the corn bread she'd planned to use for stuffing, then sat down on the sagging sofa they'd inherited from his parents, careful to avoid the sprung coil in the center, to exchange gifts.

Margaret gave Walt a new cigarette lighter and a set of gold-plated cuff links. She could have used her weekly household allowance to buy them, but that felt like cheating, as if Walt would have been paying for his own present. Instead, she traded in her hoard of S&H Green Stamps, the underground currency of American housewives. Every purchase at a participating store or filling station earned stamps that could be pasted into booklets and traded in for all manner of merchandise—dishes, toys, appliances, sporting goods, and even furniture.

"Weren't you saving for lamps?" Walt asked, slipping the links through his cuffs.

Yes. One more book would have done it.

"The lamps can wait," she said, proud of her small sacrifice.

"Well, these are great." He raised his wrist to admire his gift. "Makes me a little embarrassed about my present though. Didn't have time to wrap it. Hope you don't mind."

When Walt pulled the envelope from his jacket, Margaret felt a thrum of excitement. Because what else could it be besides money, or maybe a check, to buy furniture? What *else* would one put in a plain white envelope at Christmas? She worked her finger under the flap, then pulled out a postcard printed with the image of a delighted-looking woman wearing heels and a polka-dot housedress, and effusive red script that said: "A Gift! For YOU!"

"I know how you love your magazines," Walt said. "I spotted this one in the dentist's waiting room and thought you might like it." He shifted his weight to one side and pulled an issue of *A Woman's Place* out from under the sofa cushion, where he'd hidden it. "This'll hold you over till the subscription starts. It's only been read a few times."

As Walt talked—seemingly oblivious to her disappointment—the empty, vacuous sensation that spread through her upon opening the envelope balled into a hard, heavy, and palpable ire, a stone she could not help but throw.

"You shouldn't have," Margaret said.

"The dentist won't care. He's got plenty more." Walt slid a Pall Mall from a pack stored in his shirt pocket. "Anyway, you're welcome. It'll be like getting a present every month."

He flipped open his lighter and positioned the cigarette tip in the flame. Margaret stared at him, resentment growing as she counted the seconds it took him to feel the smoldering heat of her gaze, finally look at her, and see how badly he'd blown it.

"Walt," she said, her voice brittle. "You *shouldn't* have."

He thought she was being ridiculous and ungrateful and small.

"When I was growing up, Christmas was for kids. In forty years, my parents *never* exchanged gifts! Why can't you give me a little credit? At least I got you *something*! And you like magazines!"

Yes, but that wasn't the point. His gift seemed like an afterthought. Was she an afterthought too? Had he not been stuck in the dentist's waiting room, would he have gotten her anything at all?

Walt stormed off to sleep in the den with a bottle of Jack Daniel's to keep him company. Margaret climbed the stairs and slammed the bedroom door, feeling furious but also foolish.

And yes, small. Lonely and small and less. Just less.

❋ ❋ ❋

The day after Christmas, Walt went to work early, mumbling something about "last hired, first fired." Margaret phoned the pediatrician, then went to Mayer's Drugstore to pick up a prescription.

Barb Fredericks was coming out as she was going in. "Grab a magazine," Barb advised, knotting her scarf under her chin. "Must be twenty people in line for the pharmacy. Half the town is down with the crud."

Barb was new to Concordia—everybody was. Yet she seemed to know everyone in town, and their business.

"Clark, Wilkerson, Trowbridge," she said, ticking the names of infected families off on gloved fingers. "Bitsy and King are okay, but you'd expect that, wouldn't you? No kids, no germs.

Oh, guess what? I saw a moving van parked in front of that new Nottingham model. Think I'll pop over later, invite her to the coffee klatch. Well, I should scoot. Happy New Year!"

After wishing her the same, Margaret entered the drugstore, walking to the center aisle and sighing at the length of the line. She didn't like leaving the kids alone for very long, but there was no help for it.

Margaret took her place at the end of the queue behind a bare-headed woman with a mass of reddish curls who was smoking a cigarette and wearing an exquisite mink coat that fell to her ankles. Fur coats were a status symbol, the sign of a man's success and a woman's too. They measured her ability to support his career so well that he could afford such luxuries, and please him so thoroughly that he wanted to spoil her—at least that's what the ads said. A few of her friends had minks, but none as fine as this, and they'd never have worn one to run errands, not even on a cold day in December. Margaret moved close enough to feel the silky luxury of the woman's pelt as it briefly brushed her forearm. It was so soft!

Oblivious to Margaret's presence, the woman let out an impatient sound, somewhere between a growl and a sigh, and reached for a copy of the *Atlantic Monthly*. For a moment, Margaret considered plucking the same issue from the rack and sparking a conversation. But Margaret got the feeling this wasn't the sort of woman who was in the habit of chatting with strangers.

She chose a copy of the *Saturday Evening Post* instead, flipping past ads for Longines watches (The World's Most Honored!), the Famous Artists School (boasting a faculty who "DREW Their Way from Rags to Riches"), and a purportedly in-depth study of the American woman. Margaret started reading a profile of Eleanor Courter, a housewife who, in many ways, could have been her doppelgänger.

Eleanor was thirty-four to Margaret's thirty-three, and also had three children. Eleanor, too, lived in a middle-class suburb near Washington, DC, but Maryland instead of Virginia. They shared similar attitudes toward religion; Eleanor said faith was important to her, and Margaret felt the same. Walt slept in on Sundays, but Margaret and the children went to church every week. Eleanor Courter was blond and Margaret brunette, but both had athletic, slightly boyish figures, blue eyes, and snub noses sprinkled with freckles.

That was where the similarities ended.

Eleanor was happy and fulfilled, satisfied with days spent cleaning, cooking, and driving kids to scouts, declaring herself to feel useful and "proud of her role." According to the *Saturday Evening Post*, she wasn't alone. In a survey of eighteen hundred married women, thirty-nine percent reported themselves as being "fairly happy" in their marriages. Fifty-seven percent said they were "extremely happy." Adding up the figures and realizing she was part of a very small minority, Margaret felt a hole open up inside her.

What was wrong with her?

There had to be something, didn't there? Some flaw in her character, biology, or background? If ninety-six percent of women in the survey were contented and fulfilled and *normal*, it could only mean she was—

Feeling a catch in her throat, Margaret blinked quickly and reshelved the magazine, then grabbed the one next to it, which happened to be *A Woman's Place*. The copy Walt brought home from the dentist's office was months out of date. This latest issue sported a glossy photo of Mrs. Rose Kennedy, the president's mother, wearing pearls and a beatific smile. Margaret had to admit it looked like an interesting magazine. But until she started reading, she never could have guessed how interesting.

Between a recipe for hula chicken and the interview with Mrs. Kennedy, Margaret saw an announcement for an essay contest with a top prize of one hundred dollars.

One hundred dollars? Just for writing an essay?

Though she'd barely picked up a pen in years, Margaret had done quite a lot of writing in college. More than one of her professors had complimented her work, said she had talent. A hundred-dollar prize would attract countless entries, but the third-place prize—a pair of brass lamps that were just as nice, if not nicer, than the set she'd been saving her stamps for . . . That might be possible, mightn't it?

"Don't you think it might be a mistake, getting yourself worked up like this?"

Just as Margaret was about to agree, the echo of Walt's voice in her mind was interrupted by another voice, very sharp and very real, a voice that eschewed caution and authority.

"What do you mean? I've been taking it for *years*."

Margaret looked up, surprised to find herself at the front of the line. The woman in the mink was standing at the counter, impatiently puffing a cigarette and talking to Mr. Mayer in a New York accent that sounded more uptown than down.

The druggist pushed his glasses up the bridge of his nose. "Yes, but perhaps you shouldn't. There's been concern about addiction. Some studies suggest that meprobamate—"

"Oh, please." The woman puffed, tilting her chin and blowing smoke upward. "Are you trying to impress me with your mastery of pseudo-Latin names made up by drug marketing teams? Miltown," she said flatly. "Call it Miltown. Everybody else does. Everybody else *takes* it, too—Lauren Bacall, Milton Berle, *Lucille Ball* for heaven's sake! If there was something wrong with it, you think they'd let Lucy take it? People love Lucy! They made a whole damn show about it. *Everybody* loves Lucy!

"Well, everybody but me—I thought her character was an idiot," the woman said, puffing and tilting and blowing again. "But that's beside the point. *My* doctor, Alvin Gould, prescribes Miltown all the time. He has an office on Fifth Avenue, a medical degree from Columbia, and privileges at New York Presbyterian. *That's* the man who wrote my prescription. Now. Are you going to fill it or not?"

Pushing the magnificent mink aside, the woman planted a fist on one hip and an elbow on the other, with her arm bent at an angle and her cigarette clamped firmly between her fingers, striking a pose that said she was willing to stand there for as long as it took. The beleaguered druggist glanced toward the line, which was getting longer, then shoved a white paper bag across the counter. The woman tossed a few crumpled bills onto the counter and pivoted toward the door, clutching the paper sack in her hand.

"Keep the change."

Margaret's eyes followed as the woman flounced down the aisle, the scent of cigarette smoke and Chanel No. 5 hanging in the air as she passed. Approaching the exit, she stuck her arm straight in front of her, flattened her hand, and gave the door a mighty shove, as if intent on leaving a palm print on the glass to mark her departure.

"Mrs. Ryan? Mrs. Ryan, can I help you?"

"Hmm? Oh, sorry." Margaret stepped forward. "Bobby woke up with an ear infection. Dr. Babcock said he'd call in the prescription?"

"Yes, yes, I remember. Just give me a minute to find it."

While the harried druggist searched the shelves, Margaret turned toward the front of the store and the door the woman had disappeared through. A sunbeam shone through the glass, illuminating a faint but visible handprint. Though they hadn't exchanged a word, Margaret was certain she wasn't part of the ninety-six percent either. But there was something admirable in the way she refused to be cowed, how she stood her ground till she got what she wanted. What must it feel like to be like that, a woman who wasn't afraid to make demands or stir up trouble? Margaret found it hard to imagine herself doing something similar, but in the fleeting moment when she *did* imagine it, her pulse picked up and her skin tingled.

Mr. Mayer returned with the pills. Margaret fished money from her purse to pay for the prescription. The druggist nodded toward the magazine she'd abandoned on the counter.

"Are you taking that too?"

* * *

Fat, wet snowflakes were falling, drifting to the bare pavement and melting, or landing on the slushy piles shopkeepers had shoveled earlier. With the folded copy of *A Woman's Place* peeking from her purse, Margaret hurried through the town center, trotting past shops still decked out in holiday finery, while thinking about the woman in the drugstore. Though it would have been a shame to interrupt such a triumphant exit, she wished she'd stopped her as she swept past, asked her name, and confessed that she'd never loved Lucy either.

The wind picked up. Margaret shivered and clutched her coat closer around her body. An icy gust whistled down the alley. Margaret whipped her head to the left to avoid the blast. That's when she noticed the typewriter in the shop window and a placard shouting, "Sale!"

"What is it?" Margaret asked the salesman. "I've never seen a typewriter like it."

He grinned, rubbing his hands together. "*That* is an IBM Selectric, best electric typewriter on the market. It has a type ball instead of individual keys, which you can easily change out if you want a different font." He went on a little longer, explaining the machine's many advantages. Margaret was less interested in the details than one crucial question.

"How much?"

"Regular price is $350, but the sale price is $299."

That was more than their mortgage payment.

"Oh. I see. Thank you."

Margaret buttoned up her coat, hearing Walt's voice chiding her for getting herself worked up, yet again, over things that were unattainable. But as she approached the door, the image of the fur-clad woman who wouldn't take no for an answer popped into Margaret's mind. Margaret turned around.

"I don't suppose you have any other models on sale? Something more affordable?"

The salesman nodded. "Everybody wants electric now, so we're phasing out some of the manual models. I can sell you a nice portable Royal for $140. That includes the case."

"Oh well. Thank you anyway."

"You can rent by the month, you know. And after two years, it's yours to keep."

"How much?"

"Eight dollars a month."

Margaret's purse held seventeen dollars and change, earmarked for groceries and household expenses. It had to last until Walt replenished her allowance. Was it right to feed her family tuna casserole for the next week just to rent a typewriter and peck out an essay that would probably end up unread on a pile of entries from hundreds of other hopeful housewives? What would Walt say if he found out?

Of course, if he never did . . .

"Can I take it home today?"

The salesman beamed. "I'll carry it to your car."

CHAPTER 3

What the Neighbors Think

February 1963

When Margaret first saw the contest announcement, six weeks had felt like more than enough time to write one little essay. But the task turned out to be more challenging, and more invigorating, than she'd imagined. Handing the envelope with her entry to the postal clerk filled her with fluttering excitement and a sense of accomplishment she hadn't known in years.

Upon exiting the post office, she drove to the stationery store to return the typewriter.

"Are you sure?"

The clerk cocked an eyebrow in a way that made Margaret think he somehow knew she'd come to think of the machine as a friend, that she'd even given it a name—Sylvia—and that the clackety-clack-clacking of the keys and spritely ding of the return lever lifted her spirits like nothing else.

"Tell you what," he said, clapping his hands together, the same gesture he might have used to trap a fly midflight. "How about I drop the rent to seven dollars, and she's yours after twenty months? What do you say to that?"

Margaret couldn't say she wasn't tempted. But seven dollars was still seven dollars, and the contest was over. Why spend money she didn't have on something she'd never use again?

Margaret bit her lip. "I really shouldn't."

The clerk stared at her, waiting.

Margaret opened her purse.

✳ ✳ ✳

During college Margaret had been the kind of student who made other students groan when they spotted her on the first day of class because they knew her presence would skew the curve and torpedo their chances for an easy A. Had she stayed on for her final year instead of marrying Walt, she would have graduated with high honors. Even so, the fact that she took to academic life so readily surprised no one more than Margaret herself.

She'd grown up in a modest neighborhood favored by blue-collar families who worked in Dayton's factories. Though she maintained a B+ average in high school, the idea of going to college never occurred to her, nor to most of the girls in her graduating class. Those with boyfriends scheduled summer and fall weddings. Those without planned to take jobs and live at home until they found a husband, Margaret among them.

Then, a week after Margaret graduated from high school, her mother died.

Instead of finding a job, Margaret spent the summer keeping house and caring for her younger siblings, stepping into her mother's shoes so her father could continue working. Things might have gone on like that had not her best friend, Ethel Chenault, phoned in late August, sobbing and furious, to report that she'd caught her fiancé, Cliff, necking in the back row of the movie theater with Cherry Schaffer, the town tramp.

"Cherry Schaffer! Can you believe it?"

Margaret could. Cliff was the type who winked at every passing skirt. But what can you do when your friends fall in love with the wrong people?

"I poured my Coke over his head and told him that was it— the wedding is off!"

"Oh, Ethel. I'm sorry."

"Better I found out now rather than later, right?" Ethel sniffled, sounding less than convinced. "Anyway, I wanted to let you know before you bought the fabric for your bridesmaid's dress."

Too late. Margaret was stuck with four yards of peach chiffon she now had no use for.

"Is there anything I can do to help? When my dad gets home from work, maybe we can go do something fun to get your mind off things. Not the movies, obviously, but . . ."

Ethel sniffled again but also laughed, as Margaret had hoped she would.

"Thanks, but I'm packing. I can't stick around Dayton after this. I just got off the phone with the admissions office at Ohio State. They said all I need to do is drive over and register for the fall semester, so Mom is driving me to Columbus. Why don't you come too? It'll be fun!"

"What? You mean to college? I can't do that."

"Sure you can! Why stick around here and marry a mechanic when there's a campus full of eligible college men less than a hundred miles away? Come on, Maggie! Don't you want to get away from here? See the world?"

Seeing the world was beyond the boundaries of Margaret's imagination—she'd never traveled farther than Indianapolis. But yes, oh yes, she very much wanted to get away from Dayton, the house permeated with grief, and the small, ordinary future that was mapped out for her. All these years later, Margaret still felt guilty about deserting her post. But her father understood.

"Just come home weekends," he said when he dropped her at the bus station in September. She promised she would but rarely did, and felt guilty about that too.

But she had loved college, especially the fact that she was surrounded by strangers; no one, apart from Ethel—who was impregnated by an engineering major in the spring semester and dropped out to get married—knew anything about her or her family. She loved her classes, too, signed up for the toughest courses she could talk her way into, and worked hard, giving her full concentration to topics that were weighty and wonderfully impersonal. Her moral analysis of *Mansfield Park*, arguably Jane Austen's least readable novel, was heavy lifting, and her A was well deserved. But did the musings of a nineteen-year-old girl on a 135-year-old novel matter in the here and now?

Not a bit. Well, apart from the grade.

Collecting top grades was something else Margaret loved about college, revealing a competitive streak she'd never known she had, which had reemerged the moment she handed the clerk at the stationery store eight dollars for the first month's typewriter rental.

She hadn't told anyone about the essay contest—not even Viv, whom she normally shared everything with—furiously tapping out drafts while the kids were in school and Walt was at the office. The rules stipulated that submissions must be typed double-spaced, no more than twelve hundred words in length, and titled "A Holiday to Remember." The Christmas debacle gave her plenty of material to work with.

Her writing muscles had atrophied considerably since college, but day after day she kept at it. She went through half a ream of paper over a period of weeks before producing a draft that shone a bright light on her feelings about Christmases past and present, linking them in ways that surprised even herself. It was a fine piece of writing, poignant and honest, infused with longing for things just out of reach. But once her subscription started showing up and Margaret began studying the magazine's content more intently, she realized that poignant honesty wouldn't make the editorial cut at *A Woman's Place*.

She started all over again, leaning harder into humor, setting the tone with a few paragraphs about the hopes and heroic efforts she'd put into creating a magical holiday that quickly went off the rails, something she thought most women could relate to.

The middle section was a mostly accurate depiction of how things unfolded, including the part about leaving the turkey in the car and turning potentially poisonous poultry into soup. In hindsight, it really was pretty funny. Then she took a turn from comedy to romance, altering the ending to make it sweeter, because who wants to read a Christmas story about harsh words and a husband sleeping in the den?

Instead, she gave it a sort of "Gift of the Magi" twist, in which she sacrificed her precious cache of Green Stamps to get Walt a new bag for his golf clubs, and Walt sold his clubs to buy Margaret lamps *and* a maple dresser, ending the piece with a kiss in front of a crackling fire that just happened to coincide with the ringing of distant church bells and a gentle fall of snow.

Margaret felt better about this version. Not because the writing was better than her earlier attempt. She knew it wasn't. But she wanted to do more than write well; she wanted to *win*. Of course the money would be great. But wouldn't it be something to see her words and name printed in a national magazine? One read by thousands of women?

❆ ❆ ❆

Margaret was the last to arrive at the coffee klatch. If she hadn't known that Barb would have called later, sweetly but persistently probing for an explanation, she might have skipped this week. It wasn't that she disliked Barb, or any of the neighborhood women. When she first moved to Concordia, she'd been grateful to meet women she had so much in common with and who, like her, were eager to launch new friendships. Lately, however, she'd begun to think they might have too much in common. All they ever talked about was kids, husbands, recipes. And Margaret was as guilty as any of them.

What had happened to her? She used to be an interesting person.

The front door had been left ajar. Margaret entered a wide foyer papered with navy-blue toile. Danish modern was all the rage, but Barb's taste leaned to Virginia Colonial, lots of florals and dark wood. Margaret hung her jacket on a hall tree and headed toward the crowded, overheated living room. It smelled of burned coffee, stale cigarettes, and Shalimar.

"There you are!" Barb said, raising the coffeepot in a sort of salute as Margaret entered. "We were starting to wonder what happened."

"Sorry. There was a line at the post office."

"That's all right. Sit down, let me get you some coffee. Ellen, Dorothy, Iris," she said, addressing the three women seated on the sofa, "scoot down to make room for Margaret."

Margaret had been disappointed to discover it was Iris Rasmussen, and not the intriguing woman from the drugstore, who had moved into the Nottingham right after Christmas. Two months later, she was still disappointed. Iris was too anxious to be liked, almost obsequious in her attempts to gain approval and make friends. But in a way, weren't they all?

Viv, the only woman Margaret truly counted as a friend, was the lone exception. Perhaps because she was a military wife and had herself served during the war, Viv had a plainspoken quality that Margaret appreciated. "An ounce of pretension is worth a pound of manure," she often said. And who could argue with that? Next-door neighbors were kind of a lottery; you got who you got. When it came to Viv, Margaret felt like she'd won the jackpot.

Viv was sitting in one of two crimson wingback chairs that flanked Barb's fireplace, pinching a smoldering cigarette between her fingers and balancing a plate of cookies on her knees. The second chair was vacant, but that was where Barb always sat.

Bitsy Cobb, so nicknamed because she'd been a petite child before an adolescent growth spurt shot her up to a willowy five feet nine, sat near the window in a velvet barrel chair that was too small for her frame. Bitsy was the youngest and quietest member of the group, so Margaret knew her even less well than the others. But it occurred to her that Bitsy always sat with limbs pulled in tight, as if she wanted to take up as little space as possible. Margaret walked to the crimson-and-cream-plaid sofa. Iris stubbed her Pall Mall out in the ashtray and shifted to make space for her.

"Are you comfortable?" Iris asked. "I can scooch down a little more."

"I'm fine. Plenty of room."

Barb handed Margaret a cup, then gestured toward a three-tiered tray of cookies on the coffee table, saying she should help herself.

"Let's get you caught up. Iris's dining room table is back-ordered. Tom told Dorothy that he wants his mother to move in with them. And Ellen's baby *still* isn't sleeping through the night." Barb clucked sympathetically. "Seriously, Ellen, try feeding her some rice cereal at bedtime. It worked on all three of mine."

"I will," Ellen said, yawning. "If the pediatrician doesn't approve, then *he* can come over and do the three o'clock feeding."

Barb carried her cup to the wingback chair and took a seat. "Viv volunteered to head up the cookie sale for Andrea's Girl Scout troop and says we all have to buy at least four boxes."

"I'm not kidding," Viv said, holding up a handful of forms when the women laughed. "Nobody leaves without placing an order."

Margaret grinned and took a lemon bar from the tray. Viv leaned forward to tap cigarette ash into the ashtray and gave her a wink.

"Your turn, Margaret." Barb paused to take a sip of coffee. "Anything new?"

Half of Margaret's brain was jumping up and down like a six-year-old with a secret, shouting, *Yes, yes, yes! I wrote an essay for a contest! If I win, then thousands and thousands of people will read it!* The older and wiser half of her held her tongue.

"Not really. I tried a new meat loaf recipe—you replace half the hamburger with ground lamb." She shrugged. "Walt didn't like it."

"Give it to me later, will you? Jim loves lamb." Barb turned her eyes toward the chair near the window. "Bitsy? How was the tennis tournament? Did you make it to the finals?"

"Oh . . . um, I didn't go after all."

Barb tsked. "Don't tell me: King decided that tennis is too much for you?"

Kingsley Cobb, nicknamed King and nineteen years Bitsy's senior, was an equine veterinarian building clientele among Virginia's horsey set. Bitsy had met him in Lexington and married him only weeks after her father's death. King, perhaps understandably considering his age, was anxious to start a family. During a recent equestrian weekend in Loudoun County, he had forbidden Bitsy to gallop, illogically afraid that it might keep her from conceiving.

"Bitsy," Barb said in a flat, authoritative tone, "you're young and healthy. A little tennis won't stand in the way of your getting pregnant. King should know that, being a medical man."

Bitsy, looking adorable in a Mary Quant dress with big white daisies on a black background, fiddled with her hem. "No, I know. I mean, he does. But that's not—"

"Men. Always overthinking," Viv interrupted, waving her cigarette in Bitsy's direction. "You and King just need to buy a cheap bottle of Chianti, put on some Sinatra, and let nature take its course. Works every time, whether you want it to or not. After six kids, I should know."

Ellen shook her head. "Not always, Viv. Stan and I tried for three years before Debbie came along. Honey and cinnamon," she said confidentially, leaning toward Bitsy. "Two tablespoons right before bed. That did the trick for us."

"And don't get up right away," Iris advised. "Hold your knees to your chest for thirty minutes after. I read that somewhere," she said when Viv shot her a look. "Can't hurt to try."

Like Viv, Margaret thought Bitsy and King just needed to calm down, but she didn't say so. Instead, she turned her gaze toward the willowy figure in the too-small chair, who was twisting her napkin between her palms with the same motion one would use to wring a chicken's neck. Couldn't everyone see how embarrassing this was for her?

Knowing it would end any discussion of Bitsy's sex life, Margaret considered spilling the beans about the essay contest. But then Bitsy blurted out an announcement of her own.

"I got a job!"

The awkward pause that followed Bitsy's exclamation threatened to douse the spark of enthusiasm in her bourbon-brown eyes. Margaret was first to break the silence.

"That's great, Bitsy! Congratulations! What kind of job?"

Barb interrupted before Bitsy could answer.

"Why would you start working? Are things not going well with King's practice?"

Bitsy seemed a little confused by the question. "No, it's nothing like that. But since I don't have anything to do during the day, I might as well work."

"Oh, well, that makes sense," Dorothy said. "I had a part-time job as a bank teller after Brian and I married. Of course I quit as soon as I got pregnant. But as long as you don't have kids to chase after, no reason not to bring in some extra money."

Iris bobbed her head. "I worked full-time at the phone company for a while. We wanted to get a little nest egg going before we started a family. It was *supposed* to be two years. That was the plan. But you know how that goes," she said, giggling. "Sarah made her appearance eighteen months to the day after the wedding."

"Where will you be working?" Ellen asked, lighting another cigarette. "Part- or full-time?"

"Part-time. At the Rock Creek Park stables. I'll be grooming and feeding the horses, cleaning out stalls, and even doing a little training."

Barb's frown was bewildered and disapproving. "You're taking a job as a *stable hand*?"

"Yes," Bitsy said. "The same work I did back in Kentucky when I was helping my dad. I've always been good with horses. In fact," she said, lifting her chin and locking eyes with Barb, "sometimes I prefer them to people."

Barb blushed. Margaret clamped her lips to keep from laughing. When Viv caught her gaze, she knew they were thinking the same thing. Bitsy had a spine! Who knew?

"I didn't mean anything by it," Barb said, recovering her composure. "I was just surprised, that's all. What does King have to say about all this?"

"He's all for it."

"Well, why wouldn't he be?" Viv said, dunking a piece of shortbread into her coffee. "Bitsy will be rubbing elbows with some of the richest folks in the area. If their horses need a vet, she'll know just who to recommend, right?"

"Exactly," Bitsy said.

"Smart plan," Margaret said, smiling at Bitsy before changing the subject. "Barb, we haven't heard from you yet. Anything new? Did Jim get that new Florida route?"

Barb's husband, Jim, was a pilot based out of the recently opened Dulles airport.

Barb sighed. "Still waiting. But I do have news. Someone moved into the new Oxford."

There were only twelve models of homes in Concordia, all named after English villages—York, Rye, Exeter, and the like—so the women knew exactly what house she meant. Oxfords were by far the largest available, even bigger than Barb's Cambridge model.

"Odd that they'd move in the middle of the school year," Ellen said, frowning. "Do they have kids? With that big place, I suppose they must. Six bedrooms, isn't it?"

"Well, if they don't," Viv said, lighting another cigarette, "I'd be glad to lend them a couple of my kids. Not a thing wrong with any of them that being an only child wouldn't cure. Will you invite her to join the coffee klatch?"

"Don't think so," Barb said primly. "I've *heard* things about her."

"Such as?" Margaret asked.

"Such as she's spent time in the loony bin. And I believe it, too, after seeing her." Barb leaned in, scanning the eyes of her rapt audience before going on. "When I drove past, she was standing in the driveway, directing the movers, wearing a full-length mink coat. Mink! In the middle of the day!"

Barb's eyes went wide.

"I mean, honestly! Did you *ever*?"

＊ ＊ ＊

Less than two hours later, Margaret was trotting down the street holding a plate of warm cookies. What she'd meant to be snicker-doodles had turned into sugar cookies because, in her excitement to meet the new neighbor, she'd left out the cream of tartar.

It *had* to be the same woman! How many daytime-mink-wearing women could there be in Concordia?

There had been a moment, while she slipped cookies from the baking sheet, when the words *loony bin* echoed in Margaret's mind. She knew for a fact the woman was taking Miltown, so Barb could be right about her purportedly shaky mental state. But she also might be passing on unfounded rumors. It wouldn't have been the first time.

Besides, Margaret's college psych professor had posited that nearly everyone suffered from some type of maladjustment, with women especially being susceptible to all sorts of neuroses and nervous disorders. It wasn't something people talked about, but Margaret wouldn't have been a bit surprised to find out that some of her friends took tranquilizers.

Like the woman had said, *everybody* was taking Miltown.

And why should wearing a fur during the day make someone a social pariah? Was it so terrible to be different, even eccentric? In Margaret's book, that was a plus. She was tired of stale conversations, the company of generic women who made her feel like she had to swallow her opinions and camouflage her personality.

Turning the corner, Margaret saw a three-story house that looked almost baronial, with dark faux Tudor beams and mullioned windows. She jogged up the sidewalk, smoothed a hand over her hair, and rang the bell. After a long delay, the door opened to reveal a tall woman with a head of unsprayed red curls.

It *was* her.

The cigarette was still in her hand, but she was minus the fur, dressed in a black turtleneck that clung tightly to her large breasts, and black cigarette pants that made her slim hips look even slimmer. The look was a little bohemian for Concordia but not completely out of the ordinary. Since *Breakfast at Tiffany's* had come to the big screen, more than a few women were taking their fashion cues from Audrey Hepburn—but there was more to it than that.

Her whole outfit, and even her hair, was spattered with dozens of colors of paint, as if she'd been showered with confetti like the grand marshal in a ticker-tape parade. Even her feet, which were bare, were splattered with blobs of blue, orange, apricot, and ocher.

Margaret was more intrigued than ever. Was she an artist? Or had she decided to repaint the interior of every room in the house, each in a different color?

"Yes?" the woman said, breaking the silence and Margaret's wide-eyed stare.

"Oh . . . hi! I'm Margaret Ryan. I live down at the far end of Laurel, the white Stratford with the green shutters. I just wanted to drop by and welcome you to the neighborhood."

Margaret held out the plate. The woman stared at it for a few seconds, then looked Margaret up and down. She took a quick puff of her cigarette before accepting the offering and setting the plate down on a nearby box.

"I'm Charlotte Gustafson."

"Like the Brontë sister!" Margaret chirped, inexplicably delighted to know her name. "Welcome to Concordia, Charlotte. Do you have children?"

Charlotte narrowed her eyes and put her cigarette to her lips. "Two girls and two boys."

"Is that right? How old are—"

Charlotte blew out a column of smoke. "Thanks for the cookies. I'm sure the kids will love them. But if you'll excuse me, I've got boxes to unpack."

"Oh, right. Of course. Moving is such a nightmare, isn't it? Once you're settled, I hope you'll join our weekly—"

Margaret had been about to say "coffee klatch" but interrupted herself before the words got out. Charlotte Gustafson didn't seem like the coffee klatch sort.

"Our weekly . . . ?" Charlotte prompted, twirling her cigarette in the air.

Margaret chewed her lip.

"Book club!" she said at last. "I've decided to start a book club."

"Have you now?"

Charlotte wrapped one arm across her body and propped her elbow up on her fist, a faint smile tugging at her lips.

"What's the book?"

Margaret still set aside time to read, making it her goal to finish one new book every month. So this should have been an easy question. But something in Charlotte's tone made Margaret's brain seize up for an agonizingly long moment. Finally, a title popped into her head, and she blurted out the name of one of her all-time favorites.

"*A Tree Grows in Brooklyn*. It's a wonderful book about a young girl coming of age in New York before the First World War. Have you read it?"

"Yes. Back in high school. *Everybody* read it in high school and loved it. But . . ." Charlotte shrugged. "That was a thousand years ago. What would be the point of reading it again?"

"Oh. Well, I just thought it might be—"

Charlotte lifted her hand. "Listen, Margaret. That's your name, right? Margaret? Listen, Margaret. It was nice of you to drop by. But the thing is, I've never been much of a joiner, and I can't see—"

She stopped short, gave Margaret a considering sort of look, and sniffed.

"Hang on a second, would you? I'll be right back."

She was gone more than a second and even more than a minute, leaving Margaret with ample time to stand awkwardly on the stoop, shuffling her feet and feeling foolish. Finally, Charlotte returned carrying a book with a red cover that she thrust into Margaret's hands.

"*The Feminine Mystique*," Margaret murmured, reading the title. "Is it good?"

"It is brilliant," Charlotte declared. "Groundbreakingly, earth-shatteringly *brilliant*. At least so far. It was just released, so I've only read the first few chapters, but . . ." She waved her cigarette over her head, wreathing her curls in a coronet of smoke. "If your little book club wants to read something important, something like *this*, then okay. I might be interested."

Charlotte took the book from Margaret's hands and stepped back from the doorway.

"Otherwise, what's the point?"

CHAPTER 4

Taking the Cake

March 1963

Margaret made four different appetizers for the book club: turkey and mushroom roll-ups, chicken salad in toast cups, pickled asparagus wrapped in ham, and smoky salmon cream cheese spread—a bright pink concoction with the consistency of library paste that she molded into a fishlike shape and decorated with slices of pimento-stuffed olives, overlapping the edges so they looked like scales. Since she still had Viv's punch bowl, she made punch too.

At the last minute, Margaret decided they needed dessert and baked a coconut ambrosia cake—white layer cake with a pineapple filling, frosted with clouds of fluffy meringue, and decorated with shredded coconut, canned pineapple rings, and maraschino cherries. Walt came home from the office just as she was finishing the decorating.

After tossing his navy jacket over the back of a kitchen chair, he loosened his tie and came to stand next to Margaret, wrapping an arm around her waist as she painstakingly placed cherries into the exact center of each pineapple ring. "Wow! If that's dessert, I can't wait to see dinner. Pretty fancy for a Wednesday night."

Walt's embrace threw off her balance, causing her to drip cherry juice onto the coconut. Margaret pushed off his arm and leaned closer to the cake, squinting and picking off garish pink shreds with her fingers.

"It's for the book club," she reminded him. "They'll be here at seven."

Walt took a step back, taking in the platters she'd just removed from the refrigerator. They were ringed with green parsley hedges and red radish roses that were planted with frilled toothpicks to keep the Saran wrap from touching, like poles under a cellophane circus tent.

"I hope you're not expecting me to eat finger food for dinner. I'm starving."

"There's a cheese sandwich and some apple slices in the fridge. The kids already had theirs. Plate's right in front of you," she said when he opened the refrigerator door, impatience creeping into her voice as he stood there, gazing into the depths of the appliance with unseeing eyes and a grim expression. "Right there. Next to the milk."

"A cheese sandwich. Gee. Hope I didn't put you to too much trouble, Margaret."

He reached into the refrigerator, bypassing the sandwich and pulling out a beer bottle. Margaret stepped back from the cake, tossing the frosting palette she'd been using to camouflage the pink blotch against the countertop, where it landed with a clatter.

"Oh, for heaven's sake! Just this once, will it kill you to have a sandwich for dinner? I've been working all day, trying to get ready for this party—"

"And do you know what I've been doing all day, Margaret? *Actually* working. Clocking another ten-hour day so we have money for the mortgage and the car loan and everything else around here, including food to feed a bunch of gossipy housewives who have nothing better to do with their time than sit around on their asses, eating cake and whining about how terrible men are!" He yanked open a drawer, pulled out a bottle opener, then wrenched the cap off his beer and tossed back a furious swig.

The crack about "actually working" plucked the string of Margaret's already taut nerves. She felt like reciting a list of all the thankless, boring, unremunerated tasks she undertook on a daily basis, everything from washing his underwear and ironing his dress shirts to waxing the floors and defrosting the freezer. But the petulance in his voice and his outrageous statement about a book she knew he'd never even read pulled her up short. Was he serious?

"You're throwing a temper tantrum because of the *book*?" She rolled her eyes. "Wow. And you've got the nerve to say women are the whiny ones? For your information, it's not *about* you! Of course I shouldn't be surprised, because men always think everything is about them. But this time it's not.

"It's about *us*, housewives, women just like me," she said, softening to near supplication. She pressed her open hand to her chest, afraid she'd been too harsh, and wanting her voice to make him understand. She moved closer, placing her body between Walt and the still-open door of the refrigerator. "It's about the things we long for and have been denied, the soap we've been sold and the lies we've believed, and the way we've been—"

As she spoke, he reached past her and pulled out the sandwich plate. Then he marched across the room and dumped the food into a trash can with great ceremony, his posture ramrod straight, his face icily devoid of expression.

Margaret gasped, then shouted, "Dammit, Walt! Why are you acting like such a child?"

Giving no response, he pivoted on his heel like a sentry performing an about-face and walked away, leaving her ignored and unheard, abandoned. Margaret followed him, feeling a cold flutter of anxiety as fury and frustration were replaced by the fear that she'd gone too far.

"Where are you going? Walt?"

He smacked his beer bottle onto the kitchen table and grabbed his jacket from the back of the chair. "The club. Don't wait up."

"For the third time this week?" she said, hating the neediness in her voice but relieved he was speaking to her again. "Walt, please. Don't be like this. I'll make you something hot, all right? How about scrambled eggs?"

He shook his head wordlessly and stuffed his arms into his jacket sleeves, frowning slightly when his hand touched his pocket and he felt something inside.

"This came for you," he said, tossing the envelope onto the table and retrieving his car keys. "If it's another ad for a magazine subscription, the answer is no. We get too damned many as it is."

Walt drained his beer and Margaret tore open the envelope, heart pounding and fingers trembling, quivering with anticipation and dread that made her feel almost sick. Only vaguely aware that Walt had walked to the refrigerator to get another beer for the road, she pulled a thrice-folded sheet out of the envelope, staring at the back side of the creamy stationery for a long and breathless, almost prayerful moment before unfolding the letterhead.

Had intensity of longing been enough to bend the universe in the direction of desire, Margaret would have seen her own name written in the salutation of that letter, followed by words of congratulations and perhaps even a check with her winnings.

But that is not how the world works.

After scanning the "Dear Contestant" greeting and generic rejection, Margaret screwed her eyes shut and took a moment to berate herself for forgetting that. There was little time for self-pity, and none at all for tears, because her guests would be arriving any minute. Thank heaven she'd resisted the urge to tell anyone what she'd been up to. She didn't want anyone, especially Walt, to know she'd wasted time and money on such a quixotic endeavor. Margaret crumpled the letter into a tight ball, swallowed hard, and opened her eyes.

Walt was gone.

He'd left the refrigerator door half open and a frosting-smeared knife on the counter. Before walking out, he'd hacked off an asymmetrical triangle of cake, leaving a litter of crumbs and coconut on the plate and a cherry-red gash in the snowy-white icing.

CHAPTER 5

Truth Serum

By 7:40 that evening, it looked as if the book club would be yet another of Margaret's disappointments.

At least the food was good. Charlotte, who said she never ate sweets, had a piece of the cake and declared it divine. Margaret had done a quick repair job, sweeping away the crumbs and cutting an even wedge that showed off the filling, like they did in the magazines, as if that had been her intention all along. So there was some comfort in that.

But everything else about the evening seemed just a little . . . off.

Bitsy was even quieter than usual and looked so wan that Margaret wondered if she might finally be pregnant. She didn't ask, of course. Anything could happen early on, and she didn't want to jinx it. Viv seemed subdued too. Or distracted? When Margaret asked if everything was okay, Viv said everything was just peachy, smiling as she nibbled a turkey and mushroom roll-up, which seemed odd. Viv wasn't a nibbler; Viv was an eater, and sometimes a gobbler, a woman of voracious appetite and strong opinions. But not tonight. Tonight she had very little to say. This was frustrating to Charlotte.

"You can't just say you don't like the book. You've got to explain *why* you don't like it."

Charlotte, wearing a cream-colored skirt of wool and silk and a matching jacket with navy-blue trim, an ensemble that Margaret was sure she'd seen in an ad for the House of Chanel, paused to take a drag from her cigarette. She sucked so hard on the filter that her cheeks sucked in too, as if she were trying to slurp a thick milkshake through a paper straw.

"The whole purpose of a book club is to discuss the book. So let's try this again, shall we? *Why* didn't you like it?"

Charlotte's strident tone, the way she sat there staring at Viv, eyes like arrows and body arched like a bow as she waited for—no, demanded—a response, was making Margaret nervous. She, too, was disappointed that the discussion wasn't going anywhere. But did Charlotte have to be so pushy? Viv could be pushy too, if the situation called for it. Margaret braced herself for a cutting retort from Viv and the subsequent fallout, which might mark the first and last meeting of the book club.

But instead of returning Charlotte's barb, Viv simply sighed.

"I just couldn't relate to it. I didn't have six kids because my husband is stealthy and I'm a heavy sleeper, you know. I *wanted* to be a wife and a mother."

"Fair enough. I love my kids too." Charlotte shrugged. "Well, most of the time—it was easier when they were little. But why is marriage and motherhood expected to be our entire existence and North Star, the center of our satisfaction? Didn't you ever want more? An accomplishment that's all your own, based on your brains and not just your biology?"

"Well, sure," Viv said. "But I had that. I was a nurse during the war, deployed with a field hospital. We served in Tunisia, Italy, France, and Germany."

"Really?" Charlotte sat up straighter, looking at Viv with renewed interest. "Driving kids to Little League and cleaning the oven must seem pretty dull by comparison. Don't you miss it?"

Viv slouched into the sofa, puffing her own cigarette with a morose expression.

"I thought we were here to discuss the book, not our personal lives."

Charlotte rolled her eyes. "Examining thoughts and ideas that can impact your life is the whole *point* of reading, especially a book like this. It's not *Wuthering Heights*. It's a treatise on the conditions and suffocating boundaries of American woman-hood," she said, snatching her copy off the coffee table and holding it aloft like a tent revival preacher brandishing a Bible. "Both of which have deteriorated considerably since you risked your life to serve your country during the war. You don't think that's personal?"

"I don't want to talk about it," Viv said, slumping even more deeply into the sofa.

Charlotte puffed her annoyance and turned to Margaret.

"Well? What did you think?"

"Oh, I think it's amazing. At moments I felt like Betty Friedan was reading my mind. The part about women's magazines re-ally struck me. They really have changed over the years, haven't they?" Margaret said in the earnest tone of someone who had just woken up to something incredibly obvious and couldn't understand why she didn't see it before.

"I used to read my mother's magazines when I was little, be-fore the war. There were articles about politics and world affairs, things you almost never see now. I wasn't interested as a girl, but I loved the stories. The characters were brave, had exciting jobs and lives and adventures. These days, nearly all the magazine stories are straight romance, and almost none of the heroines have a career. If they do, they give it up so they can marry and be happy."

"Exactly!" Charlotte said, tossing up a hand in an "at last some-body gets it" gesture. "The magazines sell women soap, appliances, and girdles. But they're also selling the idea that there is *one* path to ultimate female fulfillment, and it starts and ends at the altar. We all buy into it, but by the time you realize marriage isn't what they sold you, you're stuck! Am I right?"

"Oh, I . . . I don't know about that," Margaret stammered. "I mean, every marriage has its ups and downs, don't you think? After all, no man is perfect. No woman either."

"Speak for yourself."

Charlotte's haughty tone, the tilt of her chin, the way she circled her lips into a bright red O as she blew smoke, all reminded Margaret of what had so intrigued her when she first saw her in the drugstore. Charlotte was quick and confident, so self-assured.

But . . . was she really? Would a truly confident woman need a Miltown refill?

It didn't sound like she was very happy in her marriage. Of course Margaret couldn't say she was either, certainly not today. But it wasn't always like that. She meant what she said about ups and downs. Lately there seemed to be a lot more downs, but Margaret wasn't about to share that with the group any more than she'd tell them about the essay contest, admitting that her weeks of hard work and hope had come to naught. She couldn't let herself think about it right now, but the first thing she planned to do after saying good night to her guests was to go up to her bedroom and have a good cry.

"What about you?" Charlotte asked, swinging her gaze to Bitsy, who was sitting in a side chair with her arms wrapped close. She wore a white turtleneck and green tartan kilt that made her look more like a schoolgirl than a wife.

"You went to college, right? Biology major? After all the time and effort you invested in getting an education, is it fair that society says you're supposed to forget it ever happened and spend your life changing diapers and making meat loaf?"

"No. But . . . somebody has to have the babies, don't they? I mean, if they can?"

Bitsy swallowed hard and blinked even harder. Margaret had suffered a miscarriage early in her marriage, and it suddenly occurred to her that Bitsy's wan appearance might not be due to pregnancy but because she wasn't pregnant *anymore*. Margaret laid a hand on her shoulder.

"What's wrong, Bitsy? Did something happen?"

"I really can't talk about it. King wouldn't like me to."

"Oh, for shit's sake! Isn't anybody going to talk about *any-thing*?" Charlotte ground her cigarette butt into the ashtray and got to her feet. "I need a drink."

"The punch!" Margaret exclaimed, popping up from the sofa. "I almost forgot!"

She scurried into the kitchen, then emerged a minute later carrying Viv's punch bowl. The punch was neon red and had orange slices and an ice ring of frozen cranberries floating on the surface.

"You are *all* about garnishes, aren't you?" Charlotte angled a skeptical eyebrow as Margaret set the punch bowl down on the table. "What *is* that?"

"I found the recipe in a magazine ad," Margaret said, ladling the liquid into dainty crystal cups. "It's cranberry juice, frozen orange juice concentrate, 7 Up, and white rum. The recipe didn't call for rum," she admitted, "but I decided to put in a little, only half a cup. I thought it might help ease the getting-to-know-you awkwardness. Try it."

Charlotte took a sip and made a face.

"Oh, for the love of . . ." She plunked the cup onto the table. "Where's the bar?"

"We don't have one. I store the liquor in a cabinet over the stove."

"Do you have vodka? A shaker?" Charlotte asked. "What about crème de menthe?"

"Maybe?" Margaret felt like she was failing a pop quiz. "Walt's the bartender in the family. But I can look and—"

"Never mind. I'll find what I need."

Charlotte headed toward the kitchen. Viv's eyes followed her.

"What are you making?"

"Truth serum."

✷ ✷ ✷

Charlotte reappeared a few minutes later, carrying a tray of four martini glasses that brimmed with chartreuse-colored cocktails. She set down the tray, picked up a glass, and held it out to Viv, who shook her head.

"I'd rather not."

"Oh, come on," Charlotte said, making no attempt to hide her exasperation. "The color is a little strange, I'll give you that. But they're good. At least give it a try. Apart from reservations, vodka stingers are the only thing I know how to make."

Truth serum really might have been the better name for the concoction. Because when Charlotte thrust the glass under Viv's nose, she blurted out a confession that none of them expected.

"It's not the color. It's the smell." She screwed her eyes shut and whipped her head to the side like a toddler refusing spinach. "It's just so strong and I . . . I'm pregnant."

The other three women gasped. Viv started to cry.

"Oh, Viv." Margaret perched on the sofa arm and patted her back. "Are you sure?"

Viv bobbed her head and said she was, blubbering. Bitsy handed her a paper napkin.

"How far along are you?"

"Not very," Viv said, dabbing her eyes. "Maybe a month."

"Well, then you don't know for sure, do you?" Margaret said. "It could be a false alarm. The doctor won't order a test until you've missed two periods, and then you'll have to wait a few days to get the results and see if the rabbit dies."

"Oh, the rabbit *always* dies," Bitsy said earnestly, laying her hand on Margaret's arm. "Even if the test is negative, the rabbit still dies. It's barbaric. If I'm ever pregnant, I'm just going to wait until I start showing, no tests. But Margaret's right," she added quickly after Margaret shot her a look. "Maybe you're just coming down with something."

"I'm not," Viv said. "After six times at the rodeo, I *know* what pregnant feels like."

Charlotte looked Viv up and down. "How old are you anyway?"

"Forty-one," Viv said, then broke into a fresh wave of weeping. "Forty-*one*!"

"Wow," Charlotte deadpanned. "Not a record, but right up there. Are you *sure* you don't want a drink? What about straight vodka? It doesn't smell like anything."

Viv sniffled and swiped her nose with the sodden napkin. "I don't like to drink when I'm pregnant. I don't think it's good for the baby. When I worked in a hospital maternity ward before the war, it seemed to me that the babies of the mothers who drank were smaller and not quite as healthy."

"What are you talking about?" Charlotte asked, scoffing. "My doctor says a drink or two is good for expectant mothers, helps them relax. When I showed up at the hospital three weeks early to have Andrew, they gave me vodka and orange juice to try and help stop the labor."

"Well, forgive me if I'm just a little skeptical about doctors right now," Viv said, setting her jaw. "If that idiot MD I went to see last month had given me the prescription I asked for instead of insisting that my husband take a whole day off work, come to an appointment in person, and sign off on letting me have birth control pills, maybe I wouldn't be in this mess!"

"Have you told Tony?" Margaret asked.

"Not yet. The second people hear you're pregnant, they start treating you like an invalid." Viv sighed, shoulders drooping. "With Jenny in school, I was going to get back into nursing. But now . . ." She looked up, scanning their faces. "You won't tell anybody, will you?"

"Your secret's safe with me," Bitsy said, holding her hand up flat to seal the oath.

Margaret did the same, nodding. "I won't say a thing."

"Neither will I," Charlotte said. "But that doctor! What an arrogant SOB!"

She tossed back a gulp of stinger, handed fresh glasses to Bitsy and Margaret, then picked up the book again.

"But don't you see, Viv? That's why good old Aunt Betty's book *is* relevant to your life, to all of our lives. Because at some point, every woman has been a Betty, roadblocked by biology, or society, or the whim of some damn man. Look, I'm not saying you have to agree with everything that's in here. But we all know there's a problem. If we can't be honest about that, how is anything ever going to change?"

"Well, Tony has never tried to stand in my way," Viv said. "Not even once. But big picture? I get it. You should have met my commanding officer." She raised her eyebrows meaningfully and took the book from Charlotte's hand. "Maybe I'll give it another try."

"Atta girl." Charlotte lifted her glass. "To Betty," she said.

The others picked up their glasses, even Viv.

"Just one sip," she said, pinching her nose, then clinking her rim against theirs. "To Betty. And the Betty Friedan book club."

* * *

Viv took over bartending duty. As the stingers continued to flow, so did the secrets. It only took half a cocktail for Bitsy, who'd once been grounded for a month when her mother caught her sipping champagne at a cousin's wedding, to spill the beans.

"King got a referral to a fertility specialist from Johns Hopkins," she said, cradling her cocktail glass like a chalice as she sipped. "He told me tonight."

Viv refilled Charlotte's glass. "Well, maybe it's time. At least this way you'll know."

"Couldn't agree more," Bitsy slurred, lifting a hand as if casting a vote. "In addition to studying biology at the University of Kentucky, I grew up on a stud farm. I know how breeding works. However, Mr. Kingsley Cobb has informed me that only one of us will be seeing the doctor, and that would be me—Mrs. Kingsley Cobb."

"What? Why?" Margaret frowned. "The issue could just as easily lie with him as with you. You went to college, but are you sure King did? Maybe you should ask to see his diploma from vet school. Because that's about the stupidest thing I've ever heard."

"Stupid," Charlotte agreed. "But typical. Take Henry VIII. After six wives, wouldn't you think it crossed his mind that *he* was the problem? But no. It *had* to be the women. Off with their heads!"

She thrust her glass into the air, sloshing green droplets over the rim. Bitsy lifted her glass to her lips for another drink.

"Nope. I really am the problem."

Viv set down the cocktail shaker. "You don't know that."

"Oh, but I do," Bitsy said, moving her head slowly from side to side, like a very old and very weary tortoise. "Turns out that King has already fathered a child. Ten years ago, he had a fling with a married woman and got her pregnant. She lost the baby, but her military husband was stationed in Korea, so King knew it was his. And since he's 'not shooting blanks,' as he so delicately informed me, our failure to conceive must be *my* failure."

Margaret, as upset with King's tactless blame casting as she was with Bitsy's acquiescence to it, smacked her empty glass down on the table.

"Stop that right now. You are not a failure!"

"I feel like one."

"Well, you're *not*," Margaret said. "Lemme tell you about failure."

She reached for the shaker, then proceeded to tell them all about the contest, the rented typewriter, the hours she'd spent writing and rewriting, her ridiculous hopes, the fight with Walt, and the crumpled rejection letter, which she passed around for inspection and referred to as Exhibit A. "Incontrovertible proof of my status as an A1, first-class, bona fide loser."

"Oh, puh-leeze," Charlotte said, stretching her legs out long and crossing her feet at the ankles. "You're not even close to A1.

"In the ten years since I took up painting, I've sold exactly two pieces, both to people who hoped it'd give them an in for business deals with my father. Also, my work has been rejected by every major gallery in New York, and most of the minor ones. When you've been failing for a decade, *then* we'll talk about status. Viv? The shaker is empty. Can you mix up another round?"

"Don't you think you've had enough?"

"Why settle for enough when you can have *more* than enough?"

Margaret and Bitsy mumbled their support, telling Viv not to be a party pooper. She picked up the shaker and headed toward the kitchen. "You're gonna have one helluva headache in the morning."

"Let's worry about that tomorrow, shall we?" Charlotte rocked forward to retrieve her nearly flat pack of Newports from the coffee table and lit one up. "Now that we're an official book club, I suppose we should set some ground rules, work out a structure."

"Such as?" Bitsy asked.

"Such as," Charlotte said, pausing to inhale. "Is this it? Or should we expand our ranks?"

Margaret shook her head. "I already asked the other women in the neighborhood. Not interested. I think it's just as well. They're definitely not Bettys."

"All right, we shall remain exclusive. No non-Bettys allowed." Charlotte slipped off one of her blue spectator pumps and used it to gavel in their decision, rapping the heel against the coffee table. "We'll meet monthly, every third Wednesday. Since not everyone has finished the book and we didn't get very far this evening," she said, casting a gimlet eye toward the kitchen and Viv, "I move we continue our discussion of *The Feminine Mystique* to next month."

Everyone agreed this was a good idea.

"But how do we decide what to read after that?" Bitsy asked.

The kitchen telephone rang in the background. Margaret called out to Viv, "Would you mind getting that? If it's Walt, tell him I've moved." Margaret turned back to the group. "Why don't we get some suggestions from Babcock's and vote?"

"I love that bookstore," Bitsy said, nodding. "Mrs. Babcock is so nice, and she really knows her stuff. She'll have some great recommendations."

Charlotte tapped her heel on the table again, declaring the motion adopted. Viv appeared in the doorway, holding the telephone receiver. The bright yellow coil that tethered the phone to the wall prevented her from entering the room.

"Maggie? It's for you."

Margaret rose reluctantly from her seat, stretching out her hand to take the phone.

"His name is Leonard Clement," Viv said. "He sounds older, and grouchy."

Margaret frowned. The name didn't sound familiar. She pressed the receiver to her ear.

"Hello? This is Margaret Ryan."

"This is Leonard Clement." Viv was right, he did sound grouchy. "With *A Woman's Place* magazine."

Margaret groaned. She should have told Viv to let it ring.

"Isn't it a little late for sales calls? Besides, I already have a subscription, which I intend to cancel as soon as possible."

"I'm not a salesman," he said, sounding offended. "I'm an editor."

The stinger buzz was beginning to fade, and the headache Viv had predicted was arriving ahead of schedule—so Margaret was feeling pretty grouchy herself.

"Well, if you're calling to let me know that I didn't win the essay contest, you're too late. The rejection letter came today. So if you'll excuse me—"

"Not calling about the contest, *Mrs.* Ryan," he said, making the honorific sound more like an insult. "I'm calling to offer you a job. But hey, no skin off my nose if you're not interested. None of this was my idea, believe me."

The quick, sharp shake of Margaret's head was slightly painful and wholly involuntary, a reflexive response to a sentence she was certain she'd misheard.

"Wait. Did you say a job? Doing what?"

CHAPTER 6

A Woman's Place

For the first few miles of the journey from Washington to New York, the Pennsylvania Railroad Legislator snaked through squalid swaths of urbanity, past warehouses with rusty roofs and dirt-filmed windows, and sooty brick row houses with listing back porches overlooking stingy yards that sprouted little but weeds, rocks, and corroded oil drums.

Charlotte, who had taken the seat opposite Margaret, was in a buoyant mood, animated and talkative. But when human habitation gave way to farms and fields and the train picked up speed, she popped a pill from the small brown bottle she carried in her purse, draped her mink coat over her body, and fell asleep.

The stylish ensemble Charlotte wore under her fur, a purple Dior day dress with chocolate-brown buttons, a silk taffeta bow, and kid gloves of the same shade, had caused Margaret some consternation. Though Margaret was wearing her best, a green bouclé knit suit with a pencil skirt, asymmetrical collar, and oversized buttons aligned on the left side, she felt like a country cousin by comparison. If everybody in New York dressed like Charlotte . . .

Staring sightlessly out the grimy train window, Margaret reminded herself that she was going to a business meeting, not a society luncheon, and that looking capable was more important than looking stylish. Besides, the lack of a designer wardrobe was the least of her worries.

When Mr. Clement said he was calling with a job offer, Margaret's heart leapt with the kind of joy that marked life's pinnacle moments—finding her name on the college honor roll, seeing Walt pull an engagement ring with a twinkling chip of a diamond from his pocket, learning she was pregnant with Beth, getting the keys to the house, driving home from the stationery store with a rented typewriter stowed in the trunk.

But Margaret had lived long enough to know that pinnacle moments are exactly that: pulses of joy that usually don't last and are frequently accompanied by unforeseen complications. Leonard Clement's call was no exception.

Still, things could be worse. At least the kids were all right with it.

After Margaret explained that dinner would be ready at six like always, that she'd continue to drive Bobby to scouts, Suzy to ballet, and Beth to confirmation classes, and that she'd write her columns at home while they were at school, the children had taken the idea of her working in stride. Beth seemed genuinely impressed.

"You'll be a girl reporter like Brenda Starr," she said, referring to the heroine of her favorite cartoon.

"Not quite. It's a funny, slice-of-life column for housewives, not actual news."

"But they're paying you actual money, right?"

"Twenty-five dollars an issue. Assuming they like my work," Margaret added, giving herself an out.

"They will," Beth said with a forgone-conclusion confidence that Margaret wished she shared. "Hey, when they pay you, can I get a new bike?"

"Let's not count our chickens just yet, okay?"

During the call with Mr. Clement, Margaret learned that her essay *had* been a top pick among the panelists charged with choosing the winner but was eliminated due to its topic. The winning essays would be published in the Easter issue, and a Christmas-themed story didn't fit. However, someone higher up on the editorial food chain loved Margaret's piece and had ordered Mr. Clement to hire her as a columnist. As he'd said, it wasn't his idea.

"I don't care if it is only a women's magazine. Writing should be done by writers."

Winning Clement over wasn't going to be easy. That's why Charlotte had urged Margaret to make this quick trip to New York and the magazine's offices.

"It's a lot harder to dismiss someone once you've met them face-to-face," Charlotte advised her the next day, when she'd invited the Bettys over to see her paintings. The oversized abstract canvases were bursting with color and chaos, a description that could just as easily have been applied to her house. The cavernous rooms were cluttered with books, projects abandoned midstream, and scores of cardboard boxes that, a month after the Gustafsons' move to Concordia, had yet to be unpacked.

"I mean, just look at us," Charlotte said, smirking as she dug mismatched coffee cups from a box. "I assumed you three would be as thick as gravy and as provincial as my mother's bridge club. But after meeting you in person, it seems possible that I might end up liking you. Who'd have guessed?"

"Well, the jury's still out on *you*," Viv said, giving Charlotte a wink, then turning to Margaret. "But she has a point. And why would you pass up a trip to New York? I can pick your crew up after school and watch them until Walt gets home from work, if that's what you're worried about."

"And I'll come over and help babysit just as soon as I get home from the stables," Bitsy offered. "King's working late these days. He won't mind."

"See?" Charlotte said. "Everything's covered. Leave your husband a bowl of kibble or a meat loaf or something, and you'll barely be missed."

Margaret thrust her hands in front of her, as if to push away their proposal. "This is crazy. I can't just show up at the man's office unannounced."

"Why not?" Charlotte asked. "Bring him a plate of cookies. It worked on me."

Margaret shot her a look and Charlotte smiled.

"I'm kidding! You can't just waltz in without an appointment. Call ahead, tell him you'll be in the city and want to drop by for fifteen minutes to get his guidance about the column."

"Oh, he'd never go for that." Margaret bit her bottom lip. "Would he?"

"Trust me, he'll eat it up with a spoon. Men love nothing as much as explaining stuff to women." Charlotte tapped her cigarette on a nearby ashtray. "And since it's your first trip to New York, I'll come along to chaperone. Show you Grant's Tomb, flag down taxis, that sort of thing. I'll even pick you up and drive you to the train station. How's that sound?"

"Like an awful lot of trouble just for one day," Margaret said. "There won't be time to see Grant's Tomb or anything else. I'd have to go right back on the afternoon train. And what would you do while I'm in my meeting?"

"Oh, I'll keep myself occupied—drop in on my parents, see old friends, maybe pop into Bergdorf's and wreak my revenge on Howard for making me move. Don't worry about me. You just focus on marching into that office and making Leonard Clement fall in love with you."

Margaret laughed. "Oh, is that all?"

Just getting him to tolerate her would be a tall order, forget about falling in love. And Clement wasn't the only one who was less than thrilled about Margaret's new job.

"I don't understand," she said the night after Mr. Clement called, as Margaret and Walt were getting ready for bed. "You're the one who's always saying we should be saving more, complaining about our spending—"

"It's not complaining," he interrupted. "I'm simply stating fact. We spend every dime I earn, sometimes more."

"That's why I thought you'd be happy that I'll be bringing in a little money!"

"*Little* is the word, all right." Walt spit toothpaste into the sink. "How long did it take you to write the first story? The one they *aren't* publishing and *aren't* paying you for?"

"About a week," Margaret said, drastically deflating the timeline.

"An entire week? To write one essay?"

Margaret picked up her hairbrush. "Probably less. It's hard to say for sure."

"Okay, so do the math. Minimum wage is a buck and a quarter. If it takes you forty hours to write a column, you'd be better off waiting tables. You'll spend half your paycheck on train tickets and taxis in New York, plus another seven bucks a month to rent a typewriter. At that rate, you're practically paying them, not the other way around."

Margaret raked the brush through her hair, wishing she'd waited for a paycheck before telling Walt about Sylvia.

"I'm sure I'll get faster once I get into the swing of things," she said, working to maintain a tone that was, if not pleasant, at least neutral. After the blowup about the cake, she'd made up her mind. No more squabbles or taking the bait. But Walt wasn't making it easy.

"And Sylvia—I mean, the typewriter—will be mine in another year and a half. Think how handy it will be once the kids are older and need to write term papers and such. And I'll only be going to New York the one time, to meet my editor and hopefully get on his good side."

She ran the brush through her now-shining hair one last time. Then she turned toward him, smiled, and rested a hand lightly on his forearm, hoping to get on Walt's good side as well.

"Honey, I realize it's a drop in the bucket compared to what you bring in. But every little bit helps, doesn't it? And who knows? Maybe it'll lead to something bigger down the road, a full-time job with a real salary."

Walt lowered his arm so that Margaret's hand slid off.

"You have a full-time job taking care of the house, the kids, and me. If you insist on doing this writing thing . . ." He shrugged. "As long as the kids don't suffer, I won't stand in your way. You can keep your pin money too. I don't need it. Save it for the new furniture you're always going on about. Just remember it's a hobby, Margaret, not a job. That's all it will ever be."

Insult flared in her like a lit match, threatening to singe her resolutions of peacekeeping. Before she could react, Walt took a step back, looking into her eyes with an expression that was tired, resigned.

"I'm sorry. That didn't come out how I meant it. I just can't stand to see you getting hurt, is all. Setting your heart on things that can never happen."

Walt was one of those men who tended to signal his regret through his actions—complimenting Margaret's outfit or hair to let her know he was sorry, doing chores he'd normally avoid rather than voicing an actual apology. So the fact that he apologized now said a lot, and doused the spark of Margaret's ire. She moved nearer, pulled him close, kissed him.

It was unusual for her to take the lead in lovemaking, not because Margaret was a prude but because she rarely needed to. Beneath Walt's starched, standard-issue accountant dress shirt lay a passionate man, a generous and confident lover. But something in his eyes and defeated tone filled her with tenderness and a desire to make him smile. She slipped the silky fabric of her negligee off one shoulder and lifted his hand to caress her bare skin, her eyes inviting him to remove the rest. Instead, he pulled his hand away, then palmed her cheek.

"Good night," he said, and kissed her forehead.

* * *

The Christoph Building, home of *A Woman's Place* and several other businesses, wasn't the tallest or most imposing structure on the street. But as Margaret stood in front of its double set of revolving doors, surrounded by a swirling river of hurried pedestrians, she felt paralyzed by a mixture of awe and intimidation. Charlotte squeezed her shoulder.

"We've come all this way. Don't lose your nerve now."

"*Lose* my nerve? What makes you think I ever had any to begin with?"

"You can't back out now. You've got an appointment with Mr. Clement, and I've got an appointment with Mr. Bergdorf. Go on," Charlotte said, giving her a little shove. "I'll meet you back at the station in front of the ticket counter."

"Our train leaves at 3:15. Don't forget."

"I know," Charlotte said, fluttering her fingers. "But really, would it be so terrible if we missed it? You still haven't seen Grant's Tomb. Or the Blue Bar at the Algonquin. They make the best martinis—four parts vodka, two parts atmosphere, and an olive. You'd love it."

"If Clement spends more than fifteen minutes with me, I'll be shocked. So maybe I will have time to pay my respects to General Grant. But we cannot miss that train, Charlotte. If I'm not home by nine, Walt will divorce me."

"Pfft. Husbands." Charlotte flapped her hand. "New York is positively dripping with them. Five minutes in the Blue Bar, and you'll find one you like as much as your current model, maybe more. He'd only be a loaner, but that might be a plus. What do you say?"

"Don't be late, Charlotte. I'm serious."

Charlotte sighed. "Oh, fine. Have it your way."

She walked off, waggling gloved fingers of farewell over her shoulder. Margaret watched until she reached the corner, counting the number of male heads that swiveled as Charlotte swept past, recalling the first line of *Gone with the Wind*, and thinking that Charlotte was a modern Scarlett O'Hara. Though Charlotte was not truly beautiful, men seldom realized it when caught by her charms.

A passing pedestrian bumped into Margaret, jostling her from her reverie and reminding her of the task at hand. She took a breath, closed her eyes, and propelled herself into the carousel of revolving glass.

* * *

Two hours later, Margaret was back on the street.

She walked quickly, feeling a little frantic and trying to remember if she needed to turn left or right to get back to Penn Station. After all her fussing at Charlotte, wouldn't it be embarrassing if she was the one who made them miss their train?

Margaret hadn't come close to making Leonard Clement fall in love with her. He'd looked exactly as he'd sounded on the phone—like a grizzled old newsman with leathery skin and a perpetual scowl. However, thanks to the sample column Margaret brought with her—and getting caught in a lie—it seemed he might be willing to give her a chance.

Clement liked the piece she'd written about using a mix to bake a favorite cake from her husband's childhood, trying to pass it off as from scratch, and getting caught when he took out the trash and spotted the empty Betty Crocker box. It was fun, fluffy, entirely fictional, and exactly what Clement was looking for. In fact, he'd only made one change, crossing a red line through what she'd felt was an innocuous query about why a man's stomach should be a more reliable route to his heart than, say, meaningful conversation.

"We're paying you to be funny, not philosophical," he said, putting down his red pencil and looking at her over the top of his black-rimmed glasses. "Otherwise, not bad. Not great, but not terrible. Give me more like that, and maybe this can work out."

Not quite a ringing endorsement, but probably as much as she could have hoped for. After spending another fifteen minutes brainstorming ideas for future columns, Margaret stood up, thanked him, and gathered her things.

"Where are you running off to?" Clement asked.

"Penn Station. I've got to make the 3:15 back to Washington."

He scowled for a moment, then threw back his head and barked out a laugh.

"Ha! You played me! You didn't come to New York to visit your aunt. You came here just to see me and try to butter me up, didn't you?"

Margaret stammered, feeling her face flush. Clement laughed again.

"Well, you're gutsy. I'll give you that." He stood. "Come on. The boss wants to meet you."

"The boss? But . . ." Margaret looked at her wristwatch. "My train."

"Doesn't leave for over an hour. You've got time," he said, then led her to the office of David Miles, executive editor of *A Woman's Place*.

Miles was as jovial as Clement was curmudgeonly, handsome to boot, and much better dressed. He greeted her with a smile and much praise, telling Margaret he was the one who'd decided to bring her on board. She was pleased but a little overwhelmed, especially after Miles gripped her hand and a photographer snapped their picture. The flashbulb was so bright it made her see spots.

"I want to introduce you personally in the next issue," Mr. Miles explained, "let readers know that an ordinary housewife, somebody they can identify with, is working at *A Woman's Place*. A magazine for women by women. Great angle, don't you think? Come on," he said, beckoning her. "Let me give you the nickel tour."

It *was* a great angle, she had to admit. And quite a number of women did work at the magazine. However, as the tour progressed through the photography studio, the test kitchen, and the editorial, art, and production departments, Margaret noticed that most of the women occupied low-level positions as secretaries and copy editors. She met a couple of women writers—including Selma Cantrell, author of the "Selma Says" etiquette column, whose tall sprayed bouffant practically qualified as a sculpture—but not even one female editor.

Still, it had been an amazing day, one she would never forget. Weaving through the phalanx of New York pedestrians as if she belonged there, Margaret couldn't keep from grinning. Clement had praised her for being gutsy, but Charlotte was the one who had pushed her into taking a chance. Miraculously, and against Margaret's better judgment, it had paid off. She couldn't wait to tell Charlotte about everything that had happened, and to thank her.

While idling impatiently at the corner of West Thirty-First and Seventh Avenue, waiting for the light to turn and marveling at the size of Penn Station, Margaret spotted a woman in a mink coat on the opposite corner, her back turned toward the crosswalk. Margaret was relieved. She'd been worried about finding Charlotte.

The light turned red, and the torrent of traffic came to a halt. Midway through the crosswalk, Margaret realized that Charlotte wasn't alone. A man with dark eyes and a shock of thick, gray-white hair swept back from his high forehead was standing next to her. Or perhaps she was standing next to him? The handbreadth distance that separated them suggested intimacy. The way Charlotte reached up to pick a bit of lint from the lapel of his blue-black wool peacoat confirmed it. It was such a personal, possessive gesture, the kind of thing a woman did only if she found a man attractive or was attempting to attract him to herself.

Margaret felt flustered, wondering if she'd witnessed something she wasn't meant to, then trying to decide if she should walk right past Charlotte and her companion and pretend she hadn't seen them. But Charlotte turned and waved, seeming not at all ruffled.

Margaret must have misread the situation. With his rumpled chinos and a denim shirt with an open collar under his coat, the man didn't seem like the sort of person Charlotte would know. But maybe he was a relative of some sort? A cousin or brother?

"You made it!" Charlotte exclaimed. "I was getting worried. Let me introduce you to Lawrence Ahlgren, the painter." Margaret nodded. The name was familiar, but she couldn't recall his paintings. "And Lawrence, meet Margaret, fellow inmate of the intellectual prison that is Concordia, a member of my book club, and my very oldest, brand-new best friend."

"A pleasure," he said. His handshake was firm, and he spoke with an accent Margaret thought might be Swedish. Or Dutch? She couldn't say for sure. Margaret smiled and returned the sentiment.

"Well," Charlotte said, sounding reluctant, "I suppose we must dash."

She rocked forward onto her toes, kissed Ahlgren on the cheek, whispered in his ear.

"All right," he said in a husky tone Margaret didn't think she was meant to overhear. "But don't make me wait too long."

They said goodbye to Ahlgren and headed to the station, passing rows of soaring stone columns to the entrance. When they reached the main door, Charlotte hesitated, looking over her shoulder to the corner. Margaret did the same.

Ahlgren was still standing there, watching Charlotte with a frank and hungry expression.

CHAPTER 7

The Definition of Fun

The trip to New York had been more successful than Margaret could have imagined. Not only had she made inroads with Leonard Clement, but she'd also received a backstage tour of a national magazine and star treatment from its publisher, all of which seemed to bode well for the future of her little column.

But that walking-on-air sensation she'd known upon exiting the building faded when she saw Charlotte pick that piece of lint from Ahlgren's lapel. And the ravenous, almost wolfish look in the painter's eyes as he watched Charlotte walk away left Margaret feeling unsettled.

They came very close to missing the train. Charlotte led the way, pushing through the morass of humanity churning through the grand concourse. The sound of their heels echoed as they ran through the elegant marble hall, then descended to the lower level in a less elegant stairwell that smelled of urine and axle grease. After running across the platform, they hopped onto the nearest car only a breath before the train lurched forward. Then they made their way through four other cars before flopping into their reserved seats.

Margaret was sweaty, out of breath, and relieved. But Charlotte seemed elated, almost giddy. Her green eyes glistened as she pulled a pack of Newports from her handbag.

"Well! That was fun, wasn't it?"

"Fun?" Margaret blinked. "Are you kidding? We were *that* close to missing our train."

"But we *didn't* miss it, did we? We made it! By the skin of our teeth, but we did. That's what fun *is*: putting yourself into a situation where everything could go horribly wrong, then somehow dodging the bullet."

Margaret rolled her eyes, and Charlotte laughed. "Oh, Maggie, you have *got* to loosen up. A drop of danger makes life more interesting!" She lit her cigarette. "And it was only a train. If you miss it, you simply catch the next one."

"I know, but Walt—"

"Stop," Charlotte said, blowing smoke and cutting her off. "Not another word about Walt. I only want to talk about you. How was your meeting with cranky Mr. Clement? I bet you charmed the pants off him."

"Not quite." Margaret's smile spread slowly. "But almost."

"Ha! I knew it!" Charlotte took a triumphant puff from her cigarette. "Tell me every little detail. Don't leave anything out."

Margaret didn't. Charlotte kept interrupting to exclaim her congratulations, ask questions, and press for more, so they were halfway to Philadelphia before she got through the whole story. Margaret, happy for an opportunity to relive the experience and cement her memory of it, didn't mind. But upon wrapping up, she thought of Charlotte and Ahlgren on the corner, and the unsettled feeling returned.

How long had they been standing there before she arrived? Had they run into each other by chance? Or had their meeting been arranged beforehand? Perhaps long before?

"Enough about me," Margaret said. "What did you do today?" She glanced at the empty seat next to Charlotte. "I don't see any shopping bags. Didn't see anything you wanted?"

"Not a thing," Charlotte said, shifting her gaze from Margaret's and lighting another cigarette, her fourth. "And as it turned out, I didn't have much time for shopping. I was standing outside

Bergdorf's, hailing a cab, thinking I'd try my luck at B. Altman. And who should step out of that cab but Lawrence!" Smiling, she took a quick drag, then rounded her lips as she exhaled. "He asked me to lunch, then insisted on coming to the station to see me off. Can you believe it? Such a crazy coincidence."

It certainly was.

Margaret couldn't guess the odds of two particular people running into each other in Manhattan on any particular day, but they had to be long. Still, it could have happened. Improbable wasn't the same as impossible.

"How did you meet him anyway?"

"Lawrence? Oh, gosh. It was so long ago that I can hardly remember. Let me think." Charlotte took another drag, narrowing her eyes. "As I recall, we first crossed paths at a gallery opening for some not very talented artist in the Village—eight, ten years ago? We got to chatting, and then he asked if I wanted a drink. We went to some horrible little dive—filthy, full of beatniks wearing turtleneck sweaters and earnest expressions—and talked until two."

"Two in the morning? What did your husband say?"

Charlotte tipped her head back, exhaling smoke and laughter.

"Oh, Margaret! You are precious. Don't look so scandalized. Manhattan isn't Concordia, you know. And Lawrence is just a friend, a dear old friend. I do think he's a little in love with me," she said, then shrugged. "But what can you do?"

For reasons she couldn't pinpoint, Margaret found herself blushing, which made her feel silly, afraid that Charlotte would laugh again, accuse her of being unsophisticated and provincial. Still, the situation didn't sit right with Margaret. It felt . . . not wrong necessarily, but unwise, even dangerous. Margaret liked Charlotte too much not to point that out.

After all, Charlotte was a wife and mother. Though she might think of flirting with danger as a bit of harmless fun, when mothers were careless or failed to think things through, it was children who bore the scars, sometimes for a lifetime.

"But Charlotte, if that's true, if this man is in—" Margaret stopped, unable to utter the word *love* because the look on Ahlgren's face told her it was the furthest thing from that. "If this man has feelings for you, was it really a good idea to go to lunch with him, and all alone?"

The green flame in Charlotte's eyes sputtered and went dark, cutting the connection between them. Margaret started to back-pedal but couldn't bring herself to drop the subject completely.

"I'm sure it was all perfectly innocent like you said. Still, don't you think you might be giving him . . . well, the wrong idea?"

Instead of answering the question, Charlotte crushed out her cigarette butt.

"I am *desperate* for a martini," she said, and got to her feet.

Margaret stood too, then followed her to the club car, which was filled with cigarette smoke and raucous, boisterous business-men who shouted over one another to be heard.

It was no place for conversation.

After the second martini, Charlotte popped another pill, slouched into a club chair, and slept for the rest of the journey. When they got back to Washington, she was still so groggy that Margaret took her keys and drove, arriving home a few minutes later than promised because she had to walk from Charlotte's house.

Walt was in the den, watching baseball on television. A bowl of popcorn and five empty beer bottles were sitting on the coffee table. He lifted another bottle to his lips as Margaret entered the room.

"Everything okay?" she asked, coming up behind the sofa and putting her hand on his shoulder. "Did the kids go to bed on time? Did Beth do the dishes like I asked?"

Without taking his eyes from the screen, he said they had but that Beth had left a roasting pan in the sink to soak.

"That's all right. I'll wash it in the morning. What about you? Did you have a good day? How was work?"

"It was work. Same as always."

Margaret stood there for a moment, waiting for him to ask about her day. She couldn't tell if he was mad at her for being late or for going in the first place, or was just absorbed in the game. It didn't matter. She took her hand from his shoulder.

"Guess I'll go to bed. You coming?"

"Later," he said, and tipped back the beer bottle.

* * *

Margaret was exhausted. She fell asleep almost as soon as her head hit the pillow, only to wake a few minutes later after hearing a strange noise, a crack like a gunshot, from below. She got up, thinking she should go downstairs to investigate.

But when she opened the bedroom door, instead of the upstairs landing that would have brought her to the wide staircase with its white-painted railing, she stepped into a small living room with low ceilings, a redbrick fireplace, and a wooden floor with narrow planks of honey-colored oak. The floor was clean and shining, as if someone had recently given it a good scrub and a fresh coat of wax. The sight caused Margaret's shoulders to tense and her jaw to clench. A tight knot of emotion twisted insider her—apprehension, dread, fear that verged on panic, and a desperate wish to be somewhere else.

She turned to leave, but the door she had just come through was now gone, replaced by a dark, narrow, and silent hall. She walked down the corridor, opened her mouth to call out a name, but found herself unable to speak. The cries were trapped in her throat, but they echoed in her brain, ringing louder with every step. They made her ears hurt and her heart race.

And then she was standing in a sparkling clean kitchen with white cabinets, dark green linoleum floors, and a squat, old-fashioned refrigerator. Margaret turned in a slow circle, searching, the unspoken name still ringing through her mind. Stopping in front of the white icebox, she felt the knot inside her tighten. She stretched out her hand, wrapped her fingers around the cold metal door handle, opened the refrigerator door, and looked inside. The strangled cry broke free from her brain, her body, her throat, flooding the room with shouts and anguish.

Then, suddenly, there was a bright light in the room, two hands on her shoulders, shaking her hard, a voice demanding she open her eyes. Walt's face was close to hers, frightened and frowning, telling her it was only a dream and that everything was all right, that she was all right.

Margaret blinked over and over, adjusting her eyes to the bright overhead light in the bedroom. She took three long, slow breaths to steady her pounding heart. Walt was sitting on the edge of the bed, his shirt untucked and the whites of his eyes tinged pink. He smelled of beer. Margaret looked up at him.

"Did I wake the kids?"

"No, they slept through it. Was it the old dream? The one you used to have?"

Margaret nodded. "So strange. I can't think of what triggered it. I haven't dreamed that dream in years."

"Well, I can. The stress of this job—it's too much for you. You never have that dream unless you're upset about something. This stupid column has brought back the nightmares."

Margaret pushed herself up into a sitting position.

"It's not that."

"Of course it is," he insisted, shifting his body backward, opening the distance between them. "What else could it be? Nothing else has changed around here."

"It's *not* the job. If anything, that's the *one* thing that's going right for me at the moment."

Walt stood. "What's that supposed to mean?"

"Nothing." She lay back down and curled onto her side, deciding it wasn't worth it. "Are you coming to bed?"

"The game went to extra innings."

"Fine," she said, then shut her eyes.

He stood his ground for a few seconds. Even with her eyes closed, Margaret could feel his presence, feel him watching her.

Then he turned away. His footsteps made soft whooshing sounds as his shoes brushed against the shag carpet.

"Would you mind turning out the light?"

The room went dark. She sat up, spoke to the husband-shaped silhouette in the doorway. "By the way, yes, I did have a great time in New York. My boss likes me, the publisher gave me a personal tour of the office, and it lasted so long that Charlotte and I nearly missed the train. It was lots of fun. Thanks so much for asking."

Walt shut the door softly.

Margaret grabbed a pillow and hugged it to her chest, crushing handfuls of cotton-encased feathers in her fists, wishing he'd slammed it.

CHAPTER 8

Art Lover

April 1963

With their journey to the city ending so awkwardly, Margaret was afraid she'd cast a chill over her barely bloomed friendship with Charlotte and possibly even damaged future prospects for the book club in the process.

After seeing the kids off to school and Walt off to work in the morning—neither of them acknowledging her nightmare or their testy exchange—Margaret went about her routine. But she was so distracted that she failed to notice that she tossed Suzy's red shorts into the wrong load of laundry and dyed Walt's underwear pink.

She put them into the sink to soak in a bleach solution, then fired up the vacuum, keeping one ear cocked for the ringing phone, fearing Charlotte would call to say she'd changed her mind about joining the Bettys. For two whole days, Margaret heard nothing, and the calls she placed to Charlotte went unanswered and unreturned.

On the third day, Charlotte did call, with an invitation.

"After completely striking out at Bergdorf's and never making it to B. Altman, I still feel compelled to buy *something*. I thought I'd try my luck at some of the shops in Alexandria. Do you want to come along? I mean, if you're not too busy."

At the time, Margaret had been reading the second to last

chapter of *The Feminine Mystique* titled "The Forfeited Self." She not only wanted to finish the book before the next meeting but planned to read the whole thing a second time. She had a hair appointment scheduled for the afternoon and needed to squeeze in some writing as well.

"I'm not doing a thing," she said, promising she'd write twice as much the next day.

Charlotte picked her up half an hour later, cheery as ever, behaving as if the incident on the train had been forgotten completely. Margaret was grateful, and relieved.

They had a wonderful time. Charlotte seemed to purchase about every third item she laid her eyes on. Margaret, who couldn't possibly keep up, contented herself with window shopping. But she soon realized that, even there, she had to watch her step. When Margaret admired a hat she couldn't afford, Charlotte offered to buy it for her and could only be dissuaded when Margaret said that, on second thought, the pink was too chalky, like Pepto-Bismol, and that veils reminded her of funerals and widow's weeds. At her words, Charlotte laughed so hard she almost cried.

"My mother adores veils."

Three days later—two weeks before the next book club meeting, which Charlotte had volunteered to host—she called again.

"Since I really can't cook, I've elected myself the official Bettys' bartender. But I really need to expand my repertoire beyond vodka stingers before the meeting, so I just mixed up some sidecars. Want to be my taste tester?"

This was a far more appealing prospect than cleaning the oven, and Margaret said she'd be right over. When she arrived, Charlotte ushered her through the house to the back patio.

"Promise you won't look," Charlotte said as they passed through the living room. "Everything's still such a mess."

Margaret couldn't help but look. This wasn't an instance of false modesty or a woman being house-proud; everything really was a mess. Open but full moving cartons were scattered everywhere, like picked-over boxes of chocolates that had been pilfered of nuts and chews. It didn't seem as if Charlotte had made any progress unpacking since the Bettys had come over two weeks before.

"I'll have it all sorted before book club," Charlotte said. "But you don't want to rush these things. Put something in the wrong spot and it's there for the duration."

Margaret believed in doing things right the first time, so this made sense to her. Still . . .

"You've got so many beautiful things," she said, which was true. Margaret had never seen a house so stuffed with expensive furniture, rugs, and accessories. Her own living room looked like an empty warehouse by comparison. "But it's a big job. Are you sure you don't want some help? I'd be happy to lend a hand."

"You're sweet to offer, but it's not as bad as it looks," Charlotte said brightly, handing Margaret a frosted cocktail glass with a thin wedge of orange perched on the rim. "Honestly, it's all but done. Shouldn't take more than two or three hours once I get going. I just need to buckle down and focus. Besides, Denise will help me."

Margaret had doubts about that.

She had already met Charlotte's children, all except Howard Jr., who went to a military academy—his father and grandfather's idea, Charlotte said, making her disapproval and desire to have her boy back home clear. Though Charlotte sometimes cracked sarcastic jokes about the "joys of motherhood," Margaret knew she adored her kids. The smile that came into her eyes whenever they entered a room made that obvious. The little ones, Laura and Andrew, were sweet as could be and clearly adored her right back.

But Charlotte's eldest was . . . different.

Denise was studious and reserved—Charlotte's polar opposite in everything except intelligence and a tendency toward irreverence, though without her mother's humor. The girl's eyes were solemn and her gaze was alert, as if she was taking mental notes about everything around her. Margaret got the feeling that she spent her life waiting for the other shoe to drop, which seemed odd in someone so young.

But it was the way Denise sometimes spoke to Charlotte that surprised her most, with an impatience that teetered on disrespect. More surprising still was the fact that Charlotte generally let it pass, because Charlotte never let anything pass.

Margaret understood better than most that mother-daughter relationships could be complicated and contradictory, but she couldn't imagine Denise helping Charlotte with the unpacking, not willingly. But, she reminded herself, it was none of her business.

Margaret lifted the cocktail glass to her lips, taking a tentative sip of her sidecar.

"Ooh, yummy. What's in it?"

"Lemon juice, orange liqueur, and cognac," Charlotte said, taking a sip for herself and then laughing. "Cognac always reminds me of Switzerland."

"Switzerland? I thought cognac came from France."

"Yes, but I had my first taste in Switzerland," Charlotte said, then went on to explain.

Apparently, after she was expelled from just about every private school in New York, Charlotte's parents shipped her off to a finishing school in Switzerland. Three days after arriving, Charlotte stole half a ham and a bottle of cognac from the school kitchen, then disappeared for two weeks.

"Hang on a second," Charlotte said, interrupting her story and jogging toward the door. "There's something I want to show you."

She returned a couple of minutes later carrying a framed photograph. It was a snapshot of her sixteen-year-old self, posing on an Alpine summit with the cognac bottle tipped to her lips. According to Charlotte, it was one of her most prized possessions.

"Two days after this was taken, Madame Bergé discovered my whereabouts, personally escorted me by train to Le Havre, and put me on the first boat back to New York." The slow spread of Charlotte's smile, like butter melting on toast, told Margaret this had been her plan all along. "I was finished, all right. Not quite the way my parents planned."

Charlotte was always cracking wise and sharing funny stories. But later when Margaret replayed them in her head, she'd sometimes hear an edge she hadn't picked up on the first time. There were times when she wanted to dig a little deeper with Charlotte, but she resisted the urge. Despite its short duration, Charlotte's friendship had come to mean a lot to Margaret.

Viv, of course, was the closest friend she had in Concordia, one of her closest friends ever, which made sense. They lived on the same block, moved in on the same day, and hit it off right away.

But the friendship really took hold about a month after the move, when Viv diagnosed the rash on Suzy's tummy as scarlet fever and advised Margaret to call the doctor right away. Scarlet fever could be dangerous if left untreated, and Margaret was so grateful that she baked a strawberry pavlova and brought it to the Buschettis as a thank-you. Viv insisted she stay and have some, and they ended up talking for over three hours. Having a nurse in the neighborhood was a boon. People were always asking Viv for medical advice, but there was more to it than that. Margaret and Viv shared similar working-class backgrounds and a practical, can-do approach to life. Naturally, they were friends.

By contrast, Margaret and Charlotte had almost nothing in common. Oddly, this was part of the attraction. Charlotte was intriguing and unpredictable. She did and said things that surprised and even challenged Margaret, making her brain light up with ideas that hadn't occurred to her before. Though Charlotte wasn't as forthcoming as Viv, the things she did reveal made Margaret curious to know more. However, the way Charlotte shut down when Margaret overstepped the boundary on the train had taught her to tread lightly. This first transgression had cost only a temporary silence, but a slammed door might never open again.

The impromptu cocktail hour on the patio marked a new phase in their relationship. They spent a lot more time together after that, talked on the telephone nearly every day, and met up in person a couple of times a week. They'd had chicken salad sandwiches and strawberry milkshakes at the soda fountain in Mayer's Drugstore, and Folgers and snickerdoodles—this time *with* the cream of tartar—in Margaret's kitchen.

And four days before the second book club meeting, Charlotte phoned to say she wanted to take all the Bettys on a field trip.

❋ ❋ ❋

Charlotte's sedan—a light blue Buick Riviera with white upholstered bucket seats front and back—was brand-new and equipped with every luxury, including air-conditioning. As they crossed the Memorial Bridge, Viv, who was sitting in the back with Bitsy, stuck her head through the cleft between the two front seats.

"Where are we going?"

"To DC," Charlotte said.

"I know. But where in DC? You said we'd be back before the school bus, remember?"

"And we will be," Charlotte assured her. "Provided we don't get lost. Margaret, check the map again. What's the best route to Dupont Circle?"

Margaret flipped the map to the back side, which had a more detailed view of the city.

"Let's see . . . Either Twenty-Third to New Hampshire, or Constitution to Seventeenth to Connecticut."

"I don't care. Just pick one."

Charlotte smacked the heel of her hand on the horn, then pressed the gas pedal, inching toward the bumper of the Oldsmobile in front of her.

Viv gasped. "Watch it! You're following too close!"

"*He's* driving too slow," Charlotte countered, but eased up on the gas just the same. "Speaking of too close—Vivian, would you *please* sit back? You're making me nervous."

Viv huffed but complied. Charlotte whipped her head toward Margaret.

"Well?"

"Take Seventeenth. We can get a peek at the White House as we pass."

"Too late. We already missed the turn."

It was a circle, not a turn; they could have simply gone around again. But driving in city traffic seemed to unleash Charlotte's inner New Yorker, so Margaret didn't argue. At this point, she just wanted to get to wherever they were going without causing an accident.

"Twenty-Third is fine. Here, right here."

Charlotte exited onto the street Margaret was pointing at, then immediately veered into the left lane, zipping past the plodding Oldsmobile. Bitsy, who had been quiet for most of the journey, leaned forward, but not as far as Viv had.

"Can we drive past the White House on the way back?"

"Why?" Charlotte asked. "Haven't you seen it before?"

"Yes. King and I spent a weekend seeing the sights when we first moved, but I'd like to go past again if we can. It's such a pretty day, maybe the First Family will be outside. Vice President Johnson gave Caroline a sweet Shetland pony, Macaroni, as a present. I saw a picture of her riding on the White House lawn with the president holding the reins to lead him."

"I'm pretty sure that was just a publicity stunt," Charlotte said, speeding through a light that was, if not righteously red, certainly pink. "But sure, we can drive past on the way back."

"Thanks!" Bitsy said happily, then leaned back into her seat and let out a startled yelp.

"What is it?" Charlotte shifted her gaze to the rearview mirror. "What happened?"

"I don't know," Bitsy said in an anxious voice. "I think maybe . . .

Maybe I did something to your car? I put my arm on the rest, and the window rolled down all by itself."

Charlotte grinned. "Don't worry, you didn't break anything. It's the power windows. You must have bumped the button with your elbow or something."

"Power windows? Wow, this car really has everything, doesn't it?"

"Well, unless it has a bathroom," Viv said, sticking her head between the front seats again, "we're going to have a real problem in about five minutes. I swear, this baby has decided to park itself directly on top of my bladder today."

"Not to worry," Charlotte said, pulling the sedan toward the curb. "We're here."

Margaret looked out the window toward a tall, gray, generic-looking building.

"Where is here?"

"The Washington Gallery of Modern Art," Charlotte said, switching off the ignition. "And before you ask—yes, Viv, they have a bathroom."

* * *

While Viv scampered off to the powder room, Charlotte paid for the tickets, insisting it was her treat. Margaret and Bitsy made their way into the first exhibit space.

The interior of the gallery was far more interesting than the exterior. Located in a large converted turn-of-the-century carriage house, it boasted soaring ceilings, vast white walls, and clean, brilliant lighting. The wide honey-colored floor planks were distressed enough to suggest they might be original, polished to a mirror glaze shine. The windows were clear, but the sun shone through them, casting tilted, rectangular grids of light onto the floor and giving the rooms a cathedral-like quality—spaces that demanded humility and hushed voices.

And indeed, during the hour that Charlotte served as their private docent, giving detailed explanations of the influences, themes, compositions, and techniques of the various works, her tone was uncharacteristically reverent. In fact, she made only one caustic comment the whole time they were at the gallery, while reciting names of some of the artists whose works were on exhibition.

"Ellsworth Kelly, Robert Indiana, Marcel Duchamp, Jasper Johns—an all-male roster. Alice Denney cofounded the gallery, and Adelyn Breeskin is the director, but art is still a boys' club. Girls are permitted to help pay the bills and keep things tidy, but they're *never* allowed to join," she said with an unmistakably bitter edge that she quickly covered with a smile.

"But we *can* visit, which is pretty terrific. As you can see," she said, stretching her arms wide toward the canvases on either wall, "there is some remarkable work here."

Viv turned her head left and right, then gave it a little shake.

"How can you tell? I mean, what's it supposed to be? Most of them look like something my Jenny could have painted, and she's only five."

The look that came over Charlotte's face in response to Viv's comments left Margaret with the same unease she'd felt when they'd started wrangling at the book club meeting. But she was happily surprised when Charlotte, instead of saying something cutting, took in a breath, held it for a count of about three, then let it out again and smiled.

"If that's true, I'd love to buy some of Jenny's work. Because, trust me, it'll be worth real money someday."

"Now, *there's* a thought," Viv said, grinning at Margaret and Bitsy.

"Modern art may appear simple at first glance, but there's real technique involved. As far as what it is . . ." Charlotte shrugged and turned out her hands. "Well, that's for you to decide. The point is less what you think it looks like than how it makes you feel. Good art, the best art, elicits a reaction of some sort, not always a positive one. It might make you feel peaceful or joyful or curious. But it could also make you feel angry or ashamed or afraid. The response will vary from person to person. But if the piece evokes something genuine, even raw, it has fulfilled its purpose.

"Just keep that in mind as you go through the gallery," she continued, scanning their faces. "Better yet, keep an *open* mind. You may find there's more here than you realized."

Though she wouldn't have said so aloud, Margaret's initial reaction to the gallery's collection wasn't all that different from Viv's.

What is it? What's it supposed to be?

But when she took Charlotte's advice to heart and kept herself open to what the paintings made her feel, she started to find them interesting, if not precisely enjoyable. By the time an hour had passed, Margaret noticed that all of them were lingering in front of the paintings, even Viv, giving them, if not outright appreciation, at least serious consideration.

Viv decided her favorite was a piece called *Red White*—a huge painting by Ellsworth Kelly, with a single bright red shape on a white background. When Charlotte asked what she liked about it, Viv shrugged and said, "Well, I've always liked red. And that thing in the middle reminds me of a pair of red shorts Vince had when he was little. He always looked so cute in them, with his stick legs and scraped-up knees."

Margaret was attracted to two works by Jasper Johns. The first, titled *Map* and painted with broad, seemingly hurried brushstrokes of blue, red, yellow, and orange, bore a rough resemblance to a map of the United States, but with the borders blurred and overlapping. The second, *False Start*, with chaotic, sharp-edged splotches of blue, red, yellow, gray, white, and orange, also had words for the colors stenciled atop the splotches but almost never in the same color as the word. Margaret wasn't sure what all that meant, but she liked the bright, happy colors. Though she wouldn't have said so for fear of offending Charlotte, she really did find them somewhat childlike—but that was what she liked most about them. There was a playfulness to them, the sort of unbridled enthusiasm that usually fades with age or becomes buried by disappointments.

Bitsy's appreciation of Johns was more nuanced.

"He's a trickster, trying to confuse our brains by painting the word in a different color, forcing us to look twice to make sure we got it right. Or a joker," she said, leaning closer to study the canvas, "a naughty boy who scribbles on walls because he knows he can get away with it. Or maybe a philosopher? Challenging us to confront the fact that borders are just arbitrary lines marked out by somebody who woke up one day and decided to put them there. Or possibly all three. Hard to say."

She took two steps backward, taking in both canvases.

"Whatever else he may be, he's certainly confident." She turned her head left and right, looking at other works by other artists. "They all are, don't you think?"

Margaret turned in a circle, scanning the walls, realizing Bitsy was right. No matter the mood, message, palette, or technique, every canvas in the room exuded confidence, as if not one of the artists ever doubted himself or questioned his right to be there.

What must that feel like?

Time passed quickly. They hadn't quite made it through all the rooms before Bitsy regretfully reminded them they should start heading back.

"The school bus, remember? And you never know about traffic on the parkway."

Viv decided she'd better visit the bathroom again before they left. Bitsy joined her. Margaret and Charlotte went to explore the last gallery together. There was a small painting in the corner, about the size of a piece of paper. Charlotte walked directly to it, bypassing the other pieces. Margaret followed.

The background made Margaret think of sour milk, curdled and grayish. The foreground had splotches of color, predominantly red, and myriad black slashes that, depending on how you looked at them, might have been disembodied faces, severed limbs, or your imagination. In the lower right corner,

also in black, was a small, sharp, arrogantly confident signature—
"L. Ahlgren."

Charlotte stared at the canvas for a long time, as she had the others. Though Margaret had never seen that expression on her face before, she recognized it. Ahlgren had worn the same look when he watched Charlotte walk away—a covetous, hungry, and lustful gaze, burning with desire for a thing beyond his grasp.

Margaret suddenly understood why they had come to the gallery.

That would have been the moment—just the two of them, the painting, and the empty room—for Margaret to stand next to her, eyes on the canvas instead of Charlotte's face, and quietly ask, "How do you know him?" By which she would mean, "*Why* do you know him?"

But she didn't.

When a friendship is new, precious, and perfect, sometimes there are things you'd rather not know.

CHAPTER 9

Help Wanted—Female

Viv's silver 1957 Bel Air sedan had the turning radius of a tank. Squeezing it into the only available parking space she'd been able to find, four blocks from where she was going, required five attempts. She turned off the ignition and sat behind the wheel, rubbing the neck kink she'd gotten from looking over her shoulder to back up, thinking this interview might end up being a colossal waste of time.

Did she really want to drive all the way into DC for a part-time job?

But it was too late to back out now, so she got out of the car, double-checking to make sure the doors were locked, and started walking.

The neighborhood wasn't rough, exactly, just different from the generic, rigidly regulated surroundings she'd become used to in Concordia. Houses with weedy yards, fences missing pickets, and sloping porches sat next to other homes that boasted fresh coats of paint, manicured lawns, and flower boxes at the windows. There was clearly no master plan in effect here, and no palette of approved colors, which was nice. It reminded her of the neighborhood she'd grown up in back in Tacoma, Washington. However, unlike her childhood home, the palette of Brookland's residents was as varied as its dwellings. People of every color passed her on the sidewalk, all minding their own business and not the least bit interested in her.

Crossing the street and entering a more commercial area, she saw her destination, a shop front in a low-slung brick building with a painted front window that read: "F. E. Giordano, MD, General Practice."

Dr. Giordano's waiting room was packed and very noisy, a cacophony of coughs, sneezes, crying babies, and conversations, some in English and some not. The receptionist was a thin, wiry woman in her late fifties with an understandably harried demeanor. When Viv gave her name and the purpose of her visit, the woman, who introduced herself as Dorothea Harris, smiled and said she'd let the doctor know she'd arrived.

The chairs were occupied, so Viv leaned against a wall to wait. A very young mother with a fussy, dark-eyed baby who kept tugging at his ear—Viv diagnosed an ear infection—sat nearby. After catching the little one's gaze, Viv lifted her hands to cover her eyes, initiating a game of peekaboo.

The baby stopped fussing but didn't respond for the first two peeks, watching Viv with a skeptical expression. Finally—on the third "boo!"—the baby let out a delicious laugh and pressed his fat fingers to his own eyes, taking lead of the game for three more rounds, until Dorothea popped her head in to tell Nurse Buschetti that the doctor would see her now.

✳ ✳ ✳

Minutes later, Viv found herself sitting on a plastic chair in front of a desk awash with folders, charts, and medical journals, being interviewed by her prospective employer, Francesca Elena Giordano, MD.

Dr. Giordano was a bit taller than Viv, perhaps five foot seven. She had a long and elegant nose, a head of thick, curly, salt-and-pepper hair that seemed intent on escaping its bun, tanned skin that made Viv think of strong tea or ancient parchment, and fanlike creases in the corners of her large brown eyes and full lips.

Watching quietly as Giordano scrutinized her application, Viv had a fleeting thought that with a bit of lipstick, rouge, and a good jar of face cream to soften the wrinkles, the doctor might be beautiful. This was followed quickly by another thought that said no, this would only serve to make the physician look like everyone else, ordinary. And if Dr. Francesca Elena Giordano was anything, it was not ordinary.

Viv knew women doctors existed, of course. There had been two at the hospital where she'd done her training, one who worked with pediatric polio victims and another who did research in one of the labs. But Viv had never been treated by a female physician and never would have imagined herself working for one.

What was Dr. Giordano's story? How had she ended up studying medicine? And what would it be like, working for a lady doctor?

Viv had reported to some female officers during the war, as all nurses did. Some were good eggs. But she'd sometimes found them to be rigid, humorless, and unnecessarily tough, women who acted as if they had something to prove. They weren't wrong about that. Leaders must always prove themselves.

The problem was that most of those women had no role models, no one to demonstrate that the formula for good leadership was nine parts discipline to one part mercy—and that the one part was equally as important as the nine. With no example to follow, some of the women Viv had served under relied on rank, inflexible adherence to regulations, and sheer meanness.

Would working for Dr. Giordano be anything like that? If so, Viv might need to rethink the idea of going back to work.

The doctor laid Viv's application down and looked across the desk.

"You live in Concordia?" she asked. "That's quite a commute. Why are you interested in taking a job so far from home?"

The truth was, she wasn't. But at this point, Viv was getting a little desperate—and something about the tone of the help-wanted ad she'd seen in the newspaper, which listed few requirements but promised "rewarding and meaningful" work in a busy DC practice for a nurse who could start immediately, gave her the impression that whoever placed the ad might be a little desperate too. But of course she couldn't say that.

Viv smiled. "Well, it sounded like such an interesting position. I'm someone who likes to keep busy," she said, which was entirely true, "and I was impressed that you talked about the job being personally rewarding." This, however, was stretching the truth. Viv had always been a terrible liar, and the look in the doctor's eyes told her nothing had changed. Viv sighed.

"Okay, I'll come clean. If I hadn't been turned down for seven other jobs closer to Concordia, I wouldn't have applied."

Dr. Giordano propped her elbows on her desk, resting her chin on her clasped hands.

"Seven interviews and not *one* offer?"

Irritated by the doctor's tone and feeling combative, Viv crossed her arms over her chest and lifted her chin.

"Not one. In fact, it's gotten so bad that I've stopped telling my family and friends when I have interviews just to spare myself the humiliation of having to admit I didn't get the job *again*. When my friend Bitsy called this morning, asked if I'd drop by and try some weird vegetarian recipe she wants to bring to book club, I made up a story about a dental emergency."

"Seven interviews . . ." The doctor sounded almost impressed. "What's wrong with you?"

"Nothing!" Viv said, then thumped her chest. "I am a terrific nurse! The best! Gunshot wounds, gangrene, cholera, compound fractures, viruses, infections, tropical diseases—I've seen it all and can handle it all. Nothing fazes me."

"Good to know," the doctor said. "Because in this neighborhood, we deal with it all. Maybe not tropical diseases but just about everything else. But look, if you're so star-spangled stunning, why hasn't anybody offered you a job?"

"Because I've been out of the field for eighteen years. And because I have six children."

"Six?"

"Six."

In her previous interviews, this was the moment when, no matter how well qualified and willing she might be, or how well things had gone up to that point, Viv had been informed she wasn't right for the job. Since it was undoubtedly about to happen again and she had nothing to lose, Viv decided she might as well lay all her cards on the table.

"*And* I'm expecting a seventh."

"When?" the doctor asked.

"Late October."

Dr. Giordano frowned, tilting her head to one side and doing a little mental math. "So you're about eight weeks along?"

"More like ten," Viv said.

"Huh. And you're absolutely sure you're pregnant? How old are you anyway?"

"Forty-one," Viv said. "And after six previous pregnancies, believe me, I'm sure."

The doctor shrugged. "Fair enough. Tell me about the other pregnancies. Any complications? Morning sickness? Varicose veins? Gestational diabetes? Fatigue?"

"Some nausea in the first two months," Viv said, "but nothing else. Easy deliveries. I'm one of those weird people who actually feels more energetic when she's pregnant."

"Good thing, with six kids at home." Dr. Giordano narrowed her eyes and tapped a finger against her lips. "So, assuming this pregnancy goes like the others, there really shouldn't be anything standing in the way of you doing the job. I'd have to find somebody to fill in for you come fall, assuming you'd want to come back. That's less than ideal, but if we—"

"Hang on a second," Viv interrupted, shaking her head as if trying to clear water from her ears. "Are you actually thinking about hiring me? Why?"

"Because you're an experienced and obviously capable nurse. Anybody who's spent as much time in a military field hospital as you did really can handle it all. Do I wish your service had been a little more recent?" the doctor asked, nodding to answer her own question. "Sure I do. But people who've practiced combat medicine tend to be fast learners and very resourceful. I'm sure it won't take you long to get back up to speed.

"Also, I like that you aren't afraid to stand up for yourself. My patients are good people, by and large, but they can be a little rough around the edges. I need a nurse who won't put up with any guff."

"Well, being a mom trains you for that," Viv said. "Kids are like horses. They can smell fear. You've got to know how to hold the line."

Dr. Giordano spread her hands out wide, as if thanking Viv for making her point for her.

"Now, since you were honest with me, I'll be honest with you. To be frank, nobody else seems to want this job. The salary is less than you could make working just about anywhere else. Because, in addition to being rough around the edges, most of my patients are poor. Very few have insurance, and most of those who do only have coverage for hospitalizations. I bill on a sliding scale, according to what the patient can afford. In most cases, it isn't much. And even then, they don't always pay."

Over two weeks of interviewing, Viv had met five doctors in private practice. Every one of them seemed to be doing very well financially, which begged the question.

"Why practice here then? Why not open an office in a different neighborhood and work for patients who can afford you?"

"You know, I ask myself that exact same question almost every day."

Francesca leaned back in her chair, looking weary but also more relaxed than before.

"I grew up here. The Brookland neighborhood has always been a soup of nationalities and races. My parents came to America in 1907, opened up a little Italian grocery about three blocks from here. It's a Laundromat now and my parents are gone, but I still live in the house I was born in on Kearny Street. People call Brookland 'Little Rome' because there are so many Catholic institutions here, and I'm a product of that. I went to church at St. Anthony of Padua and did my undergrad studies at Catholic University, a ten-minute walk from my front door.

"When I was accepted to medical school at Case Western Reserve, the homilies I'd heard and catechism I'd been taught growing up followed me to Cleveland. Every time I'd think about joining some nice, lucrative practice in a suburb and treating businessmen for gout or their wives for nerves and palpitations, I'd feel a prick of conscience and hear the voice of my sixth-grade teacher, Sister Immaculata, talking about how much was expected from those to whom much had been given.

"So why am I here? Damned if I know. Blame the nuns, I guess."

When Francesca turned out her hands and shrugged, Viv couldn't help but smile.

"We had a Sister Immaculata at my parochial school too. She taught eighth grade, not sixth, but the speeches about service and sacrifice were the same. If I had a nickel for every time the nuns told me to 'offer it up' after something bad happened, I wouldn't need to work for you or anybody else."

"Yes," the doctor said, gesturing toward the silver Sacred Heart of Jesus pendant Viv wore around her neck. "I pegged you for a former inmate the second you sat down."

Viv reached up to touch her necklace. "Mother Superior presented them to all the girls when we graduated. You know, I really did admire the sisters—most of them anyway. Till I was fifteen, I thought I might join the order. Then I discovered boys."

"Italian boys?"

"*One* Italian boy," Viv said. "Tony. We met during the war. He took some shrapnel and ended up in the hospital. He wasn't there long, but it was long enough."

"How did your parents feel about you marrying this Italian boy?" the doctor asked. "Because I'm pretty sure you weren't born a Buschetti. German? Polish?"

"Irish," Viv said. "My mother was a McCormack, and my father was a Donovan. I never asked them how they felt about my marrying Tony, but they were probably relieved. Anyway, it was over and done before they had a chance to weigh in. As soon as I turned up PWOP, a military chaplain helped us tie the knot and the army shipped me home."

"PWOP?"

"Pregnant without permission. The army is a lot like the sisters that way, demanding vows of celibacy. But those Italian boys . . ." Viv gave her head a helpless shake. "What are you gonna do?"

The doctor laughed. "I've got an Italian boy myself, Paul. And two kids, Carlo and Lucia."

Viv was surprised. She never would have imagined that a lady doctor could also be a wife and mother. Medicine was such a demanding field, requiring at least a decade of higher education. How had Dr. Giordano been able to do all that and raise a family?

"It wasn't easy," she said, answering Viv's questions. "I had to make some tough choices along the way. That's why I only have two children instead of six. I just did the best I could, juggled the balls, dropped a few now and then, picked them back up again. It's easier now that the kids are grown, but I managed as every woman has to. That's why I'm not scared that you have six children, or even seven," she said with a nod toward Viv's still flat stomach. "I know you'd be up to the job. That is, if you want it. Honestly, I can think of all kinds of reasons you might not. Long drive, long hours . . . In twelve years, I've never taken a lunch break or left the office before six. Most nights I'm here until seven or eight, trying to catch up on my case files."

She cast her gaze across the cluttered desk, then went on to tell Viv more about the considerable duties and caseload. The good doctor wasn't sugarcoating things, that was for sure. Viv almost wondered if Dr. Giordano really didn't want to hire her and was trying to make the job sound as terrible as possible so she'd turn it down.

"But there's a plus side." The doctor leaned forward, fixing Viv with her huge brown eyes. "This work is rewarding. If making a difference in the lives of people the rest of the world has forgotten is a currency you care about, then this might be the best-paying job in town. So? What do you say, Nurse Buschetti? Would you like to work here?"

When Viv failed to respond immediately, Dr. Giordano's smile dimmed. She pulled her hands from the desk and placed them in her lap.

"It's a big decision. Maybe you want to go home and discuss it with your husband?"

Viv knew she should. But she also knew that if she did, all the rational reasons for turning down the offer might swamp the rise of emotions that made her want to say yes. Viv *liked* Francesca Giordano. She respected her too.

Most importantly, she understood her.

After Pearl Harbor, Viv joined the service for the same reasons most people did—patriotism, a surge of righteous anger, a quiet but undeniable desire to see the world, and a fear of missing out. But unlike many young women who rushed to enlist, Viv had real skills. She'd completed her nurse training two years previously and worked in a busy hospital. She was one of the best nurses on the staff. All the doctors wanted Viv working their shift.

Before she enlisted, Viv couldn't begin to imagine the full carnage of war. But she knew the men and boys who would fight and be injured in it would need the help she was equipped to provide. This, together with everything her parents, her faith, and her life experience had taught her, told Viv that she should help, that she *must* help.

From those to whom much has been given, much is expected.

It wasn't just a case of the much-maligned, often-ridiculed Catholic guilt. Something else figured into Viv's decision, a solid sense of right and wrong that was as much a part of her makeup as her blue eyes and small feet. In Viv's mind, failing to use her skills in that dark hour would have been an act of supreme ingratitude, an affront to God, serving to make the world and her character smaller and meaner and crueler and less.

Viv had never been eloquent. But had she been able to translate those impulses into words, she felt certain that Dr. Giordano would have nodded as she spoke and murmured, *"Yes. Yes, I know."* Because she *did* know. What else would have compelled her to take the hard road, juggle the balls, and offer up the gifts she'd been given to serve her family *and* her patients, fulfilling her purpose? If Francesca Giordano could do it, Viv could too.

Would Tony agree?

Though he'd never say she *couldn't* take the job, if Tony knew she was pregnant . . .

But he didn't know.

If she was careful about what she wore and dropped a few plausible complaints about gaining weight, two or even three months might pass before her swelling waistline gave her away. By that time, she'd be well settled in the job and able to prove to him and everyone else that she could juggle all the balls—nursing, mothering, *and* gestating.

From those to whom much has been given . . .

Viv thought about the baby in the waiting room, those laughing brown eyes. She thought about the eyes of the very young mother too, who had smiled and whispered, "Thank you," when Viv walked past. Then she thought about her own children, including the one she was carrying. She had to consider them too, find a way to keep all the balls in the air.

"I can't work late hours. I have to be home in time to make dinner. I can't work full-time either. Two days a week, nine to four, is the best I can do."

Dr. Giordano drummed her fingers on the desk.

"How about three days a week, ten to three?"

Viv fiddled with her Sacred Heart medal. Shorter hours would make things easier, but there was still the commute to consider. It would cost her time as well as gas money.

"What's the salary?"

After a bit of wrangling, they agreed to fifteen cents an hour above the original offer. Dr. Giordano rose from her chair, smiling as she shook Viv's hand to seal the bargain.

"As long as you're already here, would you like to stick around for a bit? Shadow me while I see some patients?"

"I can't," Viv said. "The cookies for my daughter's scout troop arrive today, and I've got to sort out deliveries. Also, my book club meets tomorrow night, and I need to finish the book."

"What are you reading?"

"*The Feminine Mystique.*"

Dr. Giordano nodded. "I read it too. Very interesting. It's going to be a wakeup call for a lot of people. What did you think?"

"I've never been much of a reader," Viv admitted. "My friend Margaret kind of roped me into joining the club. Honestly, I had second thoughts once I started the book."

Francesca popped her eyebrows. Viv lifted her hands and started to clarify.

"Oh, don't get me wrong—it grew on me eventually. But I had a hard time relating at first. Being a wife and mother was always my dream, and I've found it very fulfilling."

Francesca tilted her head to one side.

"And yet here you are."

"Here I am," Viv said, more to herself than to the doctor. "I guess I just reached a point where I wanted something more—a new challenge, maybe a new way to contribute?" She lifted her eyes. "Does that sound selfish?"

"Not to me. When men find new mountains to climb, they get a pat on the back and a round of applause. People call them go-getters. Why should it be different for women? It's not like you're running off to join the circus, leaving your kids to fend for themselves. If anything, you're making more work for yourself, caring for your family *and* others. What's selfish about that? Plus, you've got skills. Seems to me the selfish thing would be to keep them to yourself, rest on your laurels, and spend the next forty years playing bridge."

Viv found herself nodding as the doctor talked. It felt good to meet someone who understood her motives, who could explain them almost better than she could herself.

"Kids don't stay kids forever," Viv said. "Then what are you supposed to do? Go to lunch with the girls, complain about your arthritis, nag your grown children because they never call or write? That's what my mom did. It made everybody miserable, especially her."

"Exactly," the doctor said, making a "there you have it" gesture with her hands. "You're making the most of this season of life while preparing for the next." She clasped her hands together. "And speaking of that, Nurse Buschetti, do you think you could be ready to start work next week?"

Viv grinned. "Perfect. I can't wait."

Francesca's smile radiated gratitude.

"Neither can I."

CHAPTER 10

A Highly Curated Collection

Edwin and Helen Babcock, the owners of Babcock's Best Books, met in a graduate-level modern American literature course at the University of Wisconsin in 1927 and bonded over Ernest Hemingway, though not for the reasons one might expect.

Edwin adored Hemingway, described his writing as "spare and muscular," and thought he had "magnificent insight into the human condition." Helen loathed Hemingway, found his themes repetitive—"No matter how terrible the male protagonist is, no matter how awful his choices, somehow it is always the woman's fault, *always*"—and his descriptions miserly—"Would it kill the man to use an adjective? Is he paying for them by the pound?"

The argument had endured through thirty-five years of marriage and the joint ownership of two bookstores.

Their first store, not exactly a going concern but profitable enough, had been located in Minneapolis. After thirty-one years, they sold the shop and retired to Virginia to be closer to their only daughter and three grandchildren. When their daughter started dropping the kids off at their house several times a week, they decided that retirement wasn't all it was cracked up to be and opened another bookstore.

"I love my grandkids as much as the next woman," Helen explained to Margaret when they first met, on the day Margaret bought her copy of *Gift from the Sea*. "But I've served my time. And if I'm going to work, then I'd like to get paid for it. Besides, we missed the books."

The way she'd said this a little wistfully, in the same tone someone else might have used while recalling the hometown of their childhood or a dearly departed pet, made Margaret fall instantly in love with the eccentric, opinionated, sixty-five-year-old bookstore owner. Margaret had always had a soft spot for characters, and Helen definitely qualified.

She was tall and tanned, wore her long white hair in two braids that twined into a crown around her head, and dressed in flowing, colorful skirts and embroidered blouses with a Southwestern flair. She'd been born in Sun Prairie, Wisconsin, hometown of Georgia O'Keeffe. O'Keefe was a good bit older, but the two somehow struck up a correspondence. While visiting the artist in New Mexico, Helen became enamored of the regional fashions.

The fact that Helen and Edwin had traveled and read so widely cemented Margaret's affection for the couple. Their collective knowledge bordered on encyclopedic, and their ongoing argument about Hemingway was earnest but collegial, and utterly endearing. So was their reverence for the written word. Babcock's was less a bookstore, Margaret decided, than a highly curated collection of books that Helen and Edwin passionately wanted others to read.

On the morning of the book club meeting, Margaret dropped by the store to get Helen's opinion on what the Bettys should read next. Unsurprisingly, she had multiple suggestions.

Though Helen thought Friedan's book was a clarion call to the current generation, unlike Charlotte, she didn't feel it quite qualified as groundbreaking.

"More like a refining of sod that others broke before—in some cases long before," Helen said, casting a meaningful glance over the top of her green-rimmed cat-eye glasses. She handed Margaret a copy of *A Vindication of the Rights of Woman*, penned by Mary Wollstonecraft in 1791. Margaret added it to the books Helen had already recommended, including *The Second Sex* by Simone de Beauvoir and *A Room of One's Own* by Virginia Woolf.

"Woolf discusses the social and economic barriers for women writers. But in a broader sense, it's about women trying to succeed in almost any profession. You should find it particularly appealing, now that you're a woman of letters," Helen said.

"Oh, but I'm not really," Margaret protested. "It's just a silly column in a women's magazine."

The intensity of Helen's gaze was flattering and embarrassing by turns and made Margaret regret telling her about the contest, Leonard Clement, and her trip to New York.

"It is a *start*," Helen said, laying a hand, pebbled with age spots and knots of arthritis, onto the smooth, suntanned skin of Margaret's forearm. "There's nothing silly about *that*."

After choosing her favorites from the nonfiction section, Helen led Margaret to the opposite side of the bookstore. "You need some novels in the mix," she said, teal skirt swishing as she navigated a valley of bookcases, pulling volumes deftly from the shelves without even breaking her stride or pausing to peruse the spines.

"Books sprung from an author's imagination can be just as meaningful as those based on facts, figures, and events, or even more meaningful. Novels force you to *think*—to make your own conclusions about characters and themes, and decide if they're valid or relevant or true or good, or the opposite, or maybe somewhere in between. My personal preference is for in between. I don't think I've ever met anybody who was all one thing or the other, have you? Most people are a walking bundle of contradictions."

Margaret, thinking about Charlotte, nodded her agreement.

"Take a look at this." Helen plucked a book with a red title and a decoration of white daisies from the shelf. "*The Group* by Mary

McCarthy. It came out a couple of months ago. Reviews were mixed, but I loved it. It's about eight women who become friends at Vassar and what happens to them in the seven years after graduation, which is *everything*—marriage, divorce, childbirth, heartbreak, madness, betrayal, retribution—you name it. The setting is primarily the 1930s, but the plot rings true today. Perhaps because so little has changed." Helen sighed. "Anyway, you really *should* consider it."

That was exactly what Helen said about the rest of the novels she recommended as potential book club picks, including *Herland*—written in 1915 by Charlotte Perkins Gilman about what happens when a society populated and run entirely by women is infiltrated by three male outsiders—as well as *A Town Like Alice* by Nevil Shute, a collection of short stories by Flannery O'Connor, *Babbitt* by Sinclair Lewis, and *Revolutionary Road* by Richard Yates.

"Not specifically focused on female protagonists," Helen said of the last two, "but they've got lots to say about the stifling nature of excess conformity, something the powers that be in Concordia cannot seem to get enough of."

Helen stepped behind the checkout counter. "Did I tell you? The association sent a letter saying we had to remove the terracotta flowerpots we had outside the shop door because orange isn't an approved color in the Concordia master plan, and phlox isn't on the list of approved plants. Ridiculous!"

Margaret put her books down on the counter. The stack nearly reached her nose.

"Oh, I know. Yesterday Charlotte went outside and found that somebody had planted an eastern white pine in her yard. She thought it was a mistake, but then the head of the landscaping department told her it's part of the master plan too. Charlotte is livid."

Helen gasped. "What? It's her house! How can they tell her what to plant?"

Though the bookstore was located in the town center, Helen

and Edwin didn't actually live in Concordia. Instead, they'd bought a small house on three-quarters of an acre about a mile from the farm where Margaret had bought her Christmas turkey, so Helen wasn't entirely up to speed on the community's regulations.

"Because every home buyer in Concordia signed papers saying they'd abide by the rules," Margaret said. "I guess there are pluses and minuses to it. If the association hadn't put in our landscaping, we wouldn't have anything but grass. But the irony is that they planted birch trees in my yard, and that's what Charlotte wanted in hers."

"Corrosive conformity. Conformity for the sake of it," Helen declared, silver and turquoise bracelets jangling as she stabbed a finger in Margaret's direction. "Tell Charlotte that she *must* read *Revolutionary Road*. It'll speak to her on multiple levels."

"All right. But . . ." Margaret cast her eyes toward the tower of books. "Helen, these are all wonderful suggestions, but I don't think I can—"

"Afford all this?" Helen flapped her hand before Margaret could answer. "Don't worry. You're borrowing, not buying. Look them all over when you get home, take your favorites to the meeting so the Bettys can vote, and bring back the rejects. All I ask is that you try not to break the spines or spill on the pages."

"But . . . what if we do?" Margaret asked anxiously, remembering a coffee splotch on page 28 of her once pristine copy of *Gift from the Sea*.

Helen shrugged. "Then the book goes to the discount table. Cost of doing business. If I wanted to get rich, I wouldn't have opened a bookstore."

"Are you sure I can't leave some sort of deposit?"

"Only if you're planning to commit a felony and skip town to stay one step ahead of the law. You don't seem like a woman bent on a life of crime, so I'm willing to take my chances. Oh, by the way, I've got a present for you."

Helen reached beneath the counter and pulled out a slim, somewhat worn volume with two rose petals on the cover.

"Anne Morrow Lindbergh's latest, *Dearly Beloved*. Came out last year. I've already read it three times, so it's a little beaten up. But I didn't think you'd mind."

Margaret picked up the book. "Helen, you're the best!"

"No. Just a book lover who enjoys sharing a good thing. Back in Minneapolis, the store had twenty book clubs. The Bettys are our first in Concordia. Hopefully it's the start of a trend."

Margaret hoped so too, and not just for Helen and Edwin's sake. She'd come to think of the bookstore as its own sort of club, a place to share conversation and companionship with people who were curious about the kinds of things she was curious about, an island of ideas amid a sea of conformity. Margaret couldn't imagine Concordia without Babcock's and didn't want to. The fact that she was the only customer in the store that morning was worrisome.

"So," Helen said after writing a list of the books Margaret was taking, "can I get anything else for you today? You have an itch that needs scratching? A curiosity that needs satisfying?"

It suddenly occurred to Margaret that she did.

"Do you have any books on modern art?"

"Shelves full," Helen said. "Are you looking for a specific artist?"

"Yes, Lawrence Ahlgren. I really don't know much about him."

Helen's frown indicated that she didn't either.

"I'll get Edwin. He's in back, trying to massage the accounts into profitability. A pointless exercise, I assure you. He'll be grateful for a distraction, and the art section is really his baby."

If Helen was an exotic bird of rare plumage, Edwin was as common as a crow.

He stood half a head shorter than his wife and wore wrinkled trousers, scuffed loafers, a pilled blue sweater vest over a blue shirt with frayed cuffs, and thick eyeglasses that needed cleaning. But Edwin, too, had a magnificent head of hair—thick, white, and a bit long. Margaret suspected he would rather spend his time reading than sitting in the barber's chair.

The art section of the bookstore was indeed Edwin's baby, and he knew every inch of it.

"No one has written a book specifically on Ahlgren," he informed her. "Though I suspect that will change in years to come. If I'm remembering correctly, he is mentioned somewhere in here . . ." Edwin paused, flipping through an oversized book with a black cover. "Yes! Here he is, page 314. It's only three pages though. I don't suppose you want to buy a whole book just for three pages, do you?"

"Umm . . . that depends. How much?"

Margaret winced involuntarily when he told her the price. Edwin sighed.

"Just put it back on the shelf when you're done," he said. "Try not to break the spine."

The defeat on his face made Margaret feel guilty. Helen and Edwin had spent an hour of their collective time helping her without making a sale. He placed the book in her hands, then turned to shuffle toward his office. Margaret couldn't stand it.

"Say, Edwin? Just one more thing. I've been thinking about getting my husband a gift."

As soon as she said it, she realized it might be a good idea.

In the weeks since the argument in the kitchen, Margaret and Walt's relationship had been . . . not chilly, exactly, but stagnant. They'd never gone this long without making love, and Margaret missed it, not just the release of passion but the emotional connection of physical touch. Margaret didn't feel that was Walt trying to punish her. Their home life was actually calmer than before, but only because they were talking less than before. Walt was spending more nights at the VFW. When he was home, he spent the evening staring at the television and drinking beer, polishing off a six-pack on most nights.

Though she was starting to think a fight might be less insufferable than this separation of silence, she couldn't bring herself to start one. Having stood witness to years of loud, unfiltered verbal battles between her parents, she considered arguments to be anathema. Perhaps a gift could help close the distance between them.

"When we were in college, Walt loved Hemingway. Can you recommend something?"

Edwin spun toward her like a top released of its string, beaming a smile.

"I've got just the thing! Scribner's published an anniversary edition of *The Old Man and the Sea*. Beautiful illustrations. And only five dollars."

"That sounds perfect," Margaret said.

"Wonderful choice! I'll leave it at the counter. I'll even gift wrap it for you."

Edwin walked away whistling, with a spring in his step. When he was gone, Margaret opened the art book and started reading about Lawrence Ahlgren. The entry told her only a little about his work, offering no clue as to how a rapidly rising abstract expressionist painter had come into contact with Charlotte— who, for all her interest in art, was obviously from a different world. But one thing did catch her eye.

According to the book, Ahlgren was Danish and had started to attract some notice while still living in Denmark. However, his star didn't truly begin to rise until he came to New York in 1959. But . . . hadn't Charlotte told her they'd met at a party in New York nearly a decade before?

That Charlotte might not have told her the whole truth bothered Margaret. Though she'd told herself repeatedly that it didn't concern her, she couldn't forget the raw, unguarded hunger in Charlotte's expression when she looked at Ahlgren's painting.

And Margaret was starting to form a theory.

Other women talked about their husbands. Charlotte almost never did. Apart from the fact that the move to Concordia had been his decision, and that Charlotte resented it, all Margaret knew about Howard was that he spent his time shuttling between New York and DC, where he was supposedly opening a new branch of the family brokerage firm. Margaret had yet to meet him; he seemed almost never to sleep at home.

Were Howard's absence, Charlotte's banishment to the suburbs, and her conspicuous failure to speak of her husband connected to Ahlgren? A jealous husband certainly might uproot his family to put a stop to a wife's infidelity, or even to an unwise infatuation. For all Charlotte's loose talk about "loaner husbands," Margaret had a hard time imagining she would actually cheat. But there was obviously tension in the marriage, which could explain so many things . . . the pills, the afternoon cocktails, and the vein of sadness and anger that sometimes cracked the veneer of Charlotte's frenetic energy and caustic humor.

Margaret wished she knew for sure, and that Charlotte trusted her enough to talk about her personal life. Talking wouldn't alter the circumstances, but it might help Charlotte feel less alone.

Still, unless Charlotte brought it up, it really was none of Margaret's business.

Margaret slid the book back into the vacant slot on the shelf and walked to the register to retrieve her books, including the gift she hadn't planned to buy. Helen was waiting for her, holding out a slim rectangle wrapped in forest-green paper and tied with a tan ribbon.

"Hemingway? Really?"

"It's a present for Walt. I just thought—"

Helen cut her off with an uplifted hand and a stony expression that said while she might forget Margaret's betrayal in time, they must never speak of this again. Margaret clamped her lips shut. Helen picked a small booklet up off the counter and held it out to her.

"Could you please give this to Bitsy when you see her tonight?"

"Sure," Margaret said, happy to change the subject. "What is it?"

"A pamphlet of vegetarian recipes from Loma Linda University. She came in asking for a vegetarian cookbook. Tell her I'm still digging, but this is all I've been able to find so far."

Margaret flipped through the pamphlet pages, perusing recipes for easy chili, tasty nut loaf, and cauliflower fritters. Most of them sounded truly unappetizing.

"Bitsy isn't going to eat meat anymore? Not even fish? Why?"

"Beats me," Helen replied. "All she said was something about hell freezing over before she ever cooked another steak for Kingsley Cobb."

CHAPTER II

Mothers and Daughters

At their first meeting, the Bettys had decided that future gatherings would be potluck affairs, easing the burden on the hostess. So Margaret baked two cakes, one for their second Bettys meeting and one for Walt and the kids, but mostly for Walt. German chocolate was his favorite, and she was hoping to avoid another cheese sandwich incident.

Margaret slid the first cake into her green Tupperware cake carrier, then raised the plastic edge a smidge to burp out the excess air. She looked toward Beth, who was sitting at the kitchen table playing Mouse Trap with Suzy and Bobby.

"The cake needs to cool for another half hour yet. Bring a slice out to Daddy in the TV room before you serve yourself, all right?"

Beth stopped moving her red plastic mouse along the board.

"Why can't he get it himself? Why do I have to be the waitress?"

"Because you're the oldest. And because I'm paying you a quarter to keep an eye on your brother and sister and make sure they get to bed on time."

"Mrs. Kimble pays me fifty cents when I babysit for her."

"Mrs. Kimble doesn't provide room and board."

Suzy moved her mouse to a build space and added a red plastic chute to the board. "I don't need a babysitter," she said. "Give me a quarter and I'll put myself to bed."

"Me too!" Bobby rolled the dice and stuck his tongue out at his big sister. "Why does she get paid and we don't?"

"Because she's the oldest."

"So what? That's not fair!"

"Life isn't fair," Margaret said.

Beth clawed her hands like a cat ready to pounce, leaning toward her brother. "Hear that, runt? I'm in charge."

"Daddy is in charge," Margaret said. "Beth? Be nice to them, I mean it. And everybody, wash your own dishes after you finish your cake. Don't leave them in the sink."

"What about Daddy?" Beth asked. "Does he have to wash his dishes?"

"Don't be fresh," Margaret said.

After warning them to be good one last time, she carried the cake to the foyer and left it on a chair near the door, then walked to the den. Walt was sitting on the couch with his shoes off, drinking Miller High Life and watching the news. Walter Cronkite finished telling America about the collision between a Soviet nuclear submarine and a Finnish merchant ship, then launched into the evening's top story.

"In Birmingham, Alabama, civil rights leaders Dr. Martin Luther King Jr., Ralph Abernathy, Fred Shuttlesworth, and fifty others were arrested for parading without a permit. Dr. King is being held in solitary confinement. A spokesman for the Kennedy administration said . . ."

"Walt? I'm heading out now."

Margaret came up behind the sofa and laid a hand on his shoulder.

"Hmm? Oh. Okay."

He nodded but didn't take his eyes from the television.

"I just wanted to get over to Charlotte's a little early," she said, "in case she needs any help. There's cake. Beth will bring you a piece and make sure the little guys go to bed on time. I'm sure she's got it under control, but maybe you could check in around eight, just to make sure, okay?" When he didn't respond, she squeezed his shoulder. "Okay, Walt?"

"Yes, okay."

Margaret bent down and kissed the top of his head.

"See you later then. Love you."

Walt took a drink of his beer. "Uh-huh. Me too."

Returning to the foyer to gather her things, Margaret noticed that the gift-wrapped book from Babcock's was still tucked inside her purse.

After glancing toward the den to make sure Walt wasn't looking, she ran upstairs to the bedroom, fished a black pen from the nightstand, and drew a heart on the green paper. She laid the book on Walt's pillow and trotted back down the stairs, collected the cake carrier, her purse, and the shopping bag with Helen's book recommendations, and opened the front door.

In the kitchen, Beth boomed, "Mouse trap!" Bobby immediately began to wail, howling about unfairness and summoning his mother to referee.

Margaret closed the door, pretending not to hear.

✳ ✳ ✳

Margaret was surprised when Denise opened the door.

"You're early." Her scowl said she was surprised too, and not in a good way.

Though shorter and less well endowed, Denise bore a striking resemblance to her mother. Her nose and chin were slightly too pointed, her shoulder-length hair was the same shade of maple-leaf-in-late-autumn-red, and her green eyes held the same keen intelligence.

But from what Margaret had seen, the similarities ended there.

For one thing, Denise didn't care one whit about clothes. Though she now attended the local public high school, she was dressed in the pleated plaid skirt and blue blazer with a gold crest on the pocket that had been the uniform of her old school in New York. According to Charlotte, this is what Denise wore every day, and it drove her crazy.

"After eleven years in private schools, wouldn't you think she'd be excited about *finally* being able to wear anything she wants?" the clearly exasperated Charlotte had said. "I don't get it. Is she *trying* to look like an oddball? Doesn't she want to make friends?"

Margaret doubted that, but who could say for sure?

"Sorry," Margaret said, responding to Denise's scowl. "I thought I'd come early to see if Charlotte needed help." She lifted up the cake carrier, as if to prove her good intentions. "I can come back later if—"

A voice floated from the upper regions of the house.

"Denise? Did you answer the door? Who is it, darling?"

Denise turned her head and shouted over her shoulder. "One of your friends!"

"Which one?"

Denise turned back to stare at Margaret. Though this was at least their third meeting and possibly their fourth, none of them seemed to have left an impression on the girl.

"Margaret. Mrs. Ryan."

Denise turned away again. "It's Mrs. Ryan!"

"Maggie's here? Well, let her in! I'll be right down."

Moments later, Charlotte floated down the wide staircase with a smile and a lifted hand, a gracious queen greeting the commoners. Wearing a sheath dress of gold-colored silk shantung, a single strand of pearls, and a pair of light tan pumps with a small gold buckle, she looked wonderful and seemed to be in a very good mood. She kissed Margaret on the cheek and told her she had indeed decided to serve sidecars as the cocktail du jour.

"I gave some thought to daiquiris," Charlotte said, her heels rap-tapping on the parquet floor as she led the way toward the living room. "And whiskey sours. But the sidecars seemed better for spring, sweet but not too sweet. Still, you can't—"

Crossing the threshold, Charlotte froze in midsentence, shocked into silence by the sight that greeted her. Margaret was shocked too. If the living room had been a mess during her last visit, today it was a disaster zone.

The expensive sofas and chairs were so piled with papers, books, and clothes that no one could sit on them. The coffee and side tables were littered with overflowing ashtrays, empty high-ball glasses, pencils, pens, paintbrushes, balls of crumpled paper, and silvery tubes of oil paint. One was missing a cap and had dribbled a yellow blob onto a walnut sideboard that was probably worth more than Margaret's car. Several unpainted canvases were leaning against the furniture. Three easels held canvases in progress, all abstract in style. The largest of the three, measuring about three feet by four, was thickly spattered with dozens of colors. Fortunately, much of the floor was covered with canvas drop cloths. Otherwise the hand-knotted oriental rugs might have suffered the same fate as the sideboard.

Charlotte's face turned red. She spun around to face Denise.

"I *asked* you to tidy things up before the Bettys got here!"

Denise clucked her tongue in the way only teenagers can, communicating her disdain with one short but eloquent tsk. "That's what I was doing!" she shouted, flinging an arm toward a bookcase in the corner, the only piece of furniture in the room that seemed to be fulfilling its intended purpose. A child's Radio Flyer red wagon, filled with boxes, was also stationed nearby. "It's not my fault that one of them showed up early! Why is this my problem anyway? It's *your* party, *your* friends. I've got more important things to do than spend the rest of my life cleaning up your messes. My writing sample for Oxford has to be mailed by the end of the week."

Charlotte planted a hand on her hip. "I am so sick of hearing about bloody Oxford. If you think that running off to England is going to magically change your life and turn you into something you can never be, you've got another—"

Charlotte was getting very red in the face. Margaret turned a bit red too. She felt like mumbling an apology, saying she'd come back later. Instead, sensing that mother and daughter were winding up to hurl the kind of words they'd live to regret, she stepped between them.

"Denise, I'm so sorry. I don't blame you for being upset. I hate it when guests show up early too. But since I'm already here, I might as well pitch in and help tidy up before the others arrive. You go work on your essay. Charlotte and I will finish cleaning up. Really," she said, responding to Denise's doubtful look. "Everything's under control."

Denise looked like she wanted to say something, but she pressed her lips together and slunk off toward the door. Just before she made her exit, Charlotte squared her shoulders and started to lunge forward. Margaret pulled her back.

"Don't," she said. "Just don't."

＊ ＊ ＊

Margaret shook her head inwardly, thinking about the day she'd offered to help Charlotte finish unpacking and how Charlotte had assured her it wasn't necessary.

"It's all but done. Shouldn't take more than two or three hours . . ."

Charlotte had been either lying or deluding herself. No person in her right mind could have believed such a mess could be sorted out in a few hours, and now it was even worse.

How was that possible? What had she been doing in here? And why?

"It *was* all but done," Charlotte said. "But that trip to the gallery was so inspiring. I woke up in the middle of the night, started painting, and just couldn't seem to stop."

Margaret found this explanation about as convincing as that of a car thief telling the judge he hadn't really *stolen* the vehicle but had merely gone for a joyride. With Bitsy and Viv due to arrive in forty minutes, there wasn't time to discuss Charlotte's dissembling, or to properly clean her living room. Glancing toward the box-laden Radio Flyer wagon, she realized Denise had been onto something.

"Charlotte, why don't you tow the wagon to the garage? We

can stow stuff there for the time being. I'll find more boxes so we can pack up everything and get it out of sight."

With Margaret in charge, things moved quickly.

Mountains of debris were stuffed into boxes and hauled to the garage. Unfolded laundry was piled in a basket and carted away to an upstairs bedroom. Dirty dishes and overflowing ashtrays were stacked onto a tray and transported to the kitchen. Then the ashtrays were emptied, washed, and stacked back onto the tray along with Margaret's cake and some clean cocktail glasses she discovered in a cupboard. Charlotte didn't seem to own a broom and dustpan, but she had enough martini and highball glasses to stock the Round Robin Bar at the Willard Hotel. Margaret carried the tray to the living room and laid everything out on the newly decluttered sideboard.

They worked quickly and as a team. With five minutes left on the clock, Charlotte's home was beginning to look, if not sparkling clean, at least presentable, so long as nobody opened a closet or wandered into the other rooms. As Margaret started gathering up the canvases, she told Charlotte to take a dustcloth to the tables. Charlotte got right to it.

It wasn't that Charlotte was lazy, Margaret decided—more that she genuinely had no idea of what to do.

"We had a maid in New York," Charlotte said, swiping a rag across the coffee table. "Renate Badenhorst, a German war bride who got off the boat, took one look at her fiancé, and changed her mind. Efficient, dour, and blunt as a hammer. Never thought I'd miss her, but I do."

"Pick up the ashtray," Margaret instructed. "Dust under it, not just around it."

"Dr. Barry won't let me hire a new maid. He thinks that doing housework is therapeutic and will help me 'adjust to my role.'" Charlotte made air quotes with her fingers, then gave the coffee table a final swipe. "Howard says he agrees, but I think he's just being cheap. Pretty funny, considering it's my trust that supplied the down payment for this bourgeois monstrosity of a house and my father's company that pays his salary. Anyway, he's never here, so what does he care?"

Charlotte took a seat on the sofa and lit up a cigarette. Margaret carried a stack of canvases off to the dining room, then started folding up the drop cloths.

"Don't forget the side tables. And the lamps. They're covered with dust."

"Right." Charlotte picked up the cloth. "Howard is somewhat more amenable to the idea of hiring a cook. Especially after this weekend. I made brunch—waffles with chicken liver gravy."

Margaret choked out a laugh. "What? You purposely made something inedible just so he'll let you hire a cook? Oh, Charlotte, you didn't."

"I don't *set out* to cook something inedible. It happens all on its own, believe me." Charlotte shrugged. "Probably won't come to anything. Even if Howard agreed to hire a cook, where would I find one here in the sticks? Good help is so hard to find these days."

Charlotte laughed and then kept laughing, choking on cigarette smoke and whatever else she found so hilarious. When she didn't stop, Margaret put aside the drop cloth, crossed quickly to the couch, and started pounding her on the back.

"I'm fine," Charlotte said in a raspy voice after Margaret offered to get her some water. "But did you hear me? I sounded *exactly* like my veil-wearing mother and all her mindless, mahjong-playing friends on Park Avenue." She took another puff and settled back into the sofa cushions, a wry smile curving her lips.

"Maybe the therapy is working. Maybe I'm finally adjusting to my role. God help me."

Charlotte let out one of those long sighs that acknowledges life's ironies, then swung her arm across her body and silently offered Margaret a drag. Margaret put the cigarette between her lips and inhaled, then rocked her head back and blew a smooth column of smoke toward the ceiling. Charlotte had not brought up the subject, not directly. But the camaraderie of the moment and Charlotte's mention of her old life made Margaret feel safe probing more deeply about potential entanglements with Ahlgren and the dangers he might pose. Margaret took a breath before giving voice to her concerns.

"Oh, Margaret. Sweet, earnest Margaret. Do you have any idea how provincial you sound?"

Margaret had no doubt that the answer was *very*. But some things were right, and some things were wrong. If believing that made her provincial, then she supposed she was—but there was more to it than that. There were children to consider. Margaret knew all about the collateral damage that could be caused if an unhappy woman made a rash and foolish mistake.

"Really, Margaret. Quit being so dramatic. Lawrence is an old friend, a brilliant, talented old friend who knows absolutely everybody in the art world."

Charlotte pushed herself out of the cushions and perched at the edge of the sofa.

"So what if he's got a teeny crush on me? So what if I encourage it? It's nothing serious. I'm just hoping he will put in a word for me at some of the galleries, open a door or two. And it's not like we're hurting anyone. Lawrence and Enid have an open marriage. He doesn't believe in being tied down."

Margaret's eyes went wide. "Do you?"

The doorbell rang.

Charlotte popped up from the sofa to answer it, leaving the question unanswered.

CHAPTER 12

Perfectly Normal

Here you go," Charlotte chirped, handing Margaret a sugar-rimmed cocktail glass.

If Charlotte felt the least bit upset about their conversation, nothing in her demeanor gave her away. She was the same Charlotte as always, breezy and bright, ready to laugh at anything, including herself.

When Viv tried to go into the kitchen to find a knife to cut the cake, Charlotte had thrown herself dramatically in front of the doorway, blocking her entrance.

"No! You can't! I'll die of humiliation if you even think of going in there. It's an absolute horror, Vivian! An utter disaster. Everything was until about an hour ago. If Margaret hadn't come over to help stash the debris, I'd have had to cancel the meeting for fear that you and Bitsy would take one look at the house and call the health department."

That was the funny thing about Charlotte; she was unabashed and surprisingly transparent, owning up to flaws that might have made Margaret blush.

Well, to a point.

When Charlotte jumped up to get the door, Margaret knew she'd never get an answer to her question. It was just as well. She didn't want to cast a pall over the evening, and she shouldn't have asked in the first place. Charlotte's glib reference to Ahlgren's open marriage, as if such things were commonplace, took her so by surprise that the words simply popped out of her mouth. But knowing Charlotte, that's probably what she'd intended all along. She loved shocking people and ribbing Margaret for being "sweet, earnest, and provincial."

Anyway, it was over and done. Margaret accepted the drink.

"Cheers," she said, taking a sip and then setting it down on the table. Like the vodka stingers from the first meeting, side-cars were tasty but potent, and Margaret wanted to pace herself. Charlotte took the tray around, offering drinks to the others.

"No, thanks," Viv said, pushing the glass away. "I still don't like the idea of drinking when I'm pregnant."

"I made yours a virgin," Charlotte said. "It's just apple cider, lemon juice, sugar, and bitters. But I have to say, you don't *look* pregnant. A little bloated maybe, but not pregnant."

"Well, believe me, I am. I've started locking the bathroom door so Tony won't see me getting dressed. But I'm pretty good at camouflaging it, and since I was chubby to start with, he probably won't notice for a few more weeks." Viv sipped her drink. "Ooh, this is good!"

"Don't be ridiculous," Charlotte said. "You're not chubby. You're zaftig."

"What's zaftig?" Bitsy asked.

"It means round, full-figured."

"So . . . chubby," Viv replied.

Charlotte shook her head. "No. It means sexy, succulent, sumptuous. It's Yiddish."

"Huh. Sounds like it ought to be Italian. Either way, I'll take it. Sexy and succulent sounds good to me. And obviously," she said, glancing at her waistline, "it hasn't hurt my love life. Tony loves a woman with a little meat on her bones."

Bitsy took a long drink of her sidecar, then looked up to Viv as if she'd just remembered something. "Hey, how was the dentist? Was it just a filling? Or did he end up pulling the tooth?"

"Ah, well . . . about that," Viv said, then cleared her throat and set down her glass. "I have an announcement. In fact, I have two. First, against all odds, I finished *The Feminine Mystique*. It was a struggle, but I did it."

She dipped her head, acknowledging the smattering of applause.

"Furthermore, I have taken its message to heart. Starting next week, I will be finding fulfillment both in *and* outside of the home. In short," she said, sitting taller, "I got a job."

The applause became louder as the Bettys voiced congratulations and questions. Where would Viv work? When would she start? Full-time or part-time? Viv flattened her hands and pressed them down on empty air, laughing.

"One at a time, people. One at a time. I will work three days a week, from ten to three, as a clinical nurse for Dr. Francesca Giordano. Her office is in DC."

"Where in DC?" Margaret asked.

"Brookland, near Catholic University. It's a hike, I know. And I never imagined I'd be working for a woman. But this doctor . . ." Viv tilted to one side, a thoughtful expression coming over her face. "She's something special, incredibly dedicated. Honestly, I'm so excited about working with her that I'd probably do it for lunch and gas money."

Charlotte rose from her green armchair to refill her drink.

"What did your husband say?"

"He was thrilled. But that's my Tony. If I'm happy, he's happy. The kids were happy too. Well, Nick just wanted to know if my working meant we could buy a color TV. But do you know what? Andrea gave me a hug and said she was proud of me. She even offered to get dinner started on the days I'm working. Isn't that sweet?"

Everyone agreed that it was.

"Did you tell Tony about the baby yet?" Bitsy asked. "Does the doctor know?"

"Yes, and she's fine with it. She has a family too. I'll wait awhile before telling Tony and the kids. No point in muddying the water, right? If I break the news after I'm settled into the job, he'll see it's no big deal and that I'm managing everything just fine."

Margaret doubted that Viv felt as comfortable about keeping Tony in the dark as her words indicated. But Bitsy, who normally nursed her drinks until they turned lukewarm, nodded with apparent approval as she poured another sidecar. And Charlotte clenched her cigarette between her teeth, freeing her hands to give a round of applause.

"Brava, Viv! Aunt Betty would be proud of you, of all of you! Everyone is now gainfully employed. The only dilettante left in the group is me."

"Oh, stop," Margaret said, frowning. "Charlotte, you know that's not true. You might not be getting paid, but that doesn't mean you're not working. No one can question your dedication to your art, or your talent. I mean, just look at this," she said, gesturing toward a large, paint-spattered canvas on the opposite side of the room.

As Margaret was putting the paintings away, she realized that the biggest canvas was still wet. Rather than risk smearing it, she'd carefully slid the easel off the carpet to a spot near the bookcase where everyone could admire it. Now she crossed the room to stand in front of it.

"It's wonderful!"

"It's not," Charlotte said, then tossed back the dregs of her drink.

Margaret turned around to face the others. "It is," she said. "It's vibrant and alive and full of energy. I realize that I still don't know much about modern art, but I know what I—"

"No, Margaret. You don't know much about modern art. If you did, you'd realize that there is nothing vibrant, alive, or the least bit original about this painting. It's a bad imitation of Pollock, nothing more."

There was a moment of shock, then awkward silence. Charlotte turned her head and pressed a fist against her mouth. The others looked at one another with wide eyes, not sure how to respond. Then Charlotte shook her head, turning back to Margaret.

"I'm sorry. That was inexcusably rude. It's just that . . . I want to be so, *so* good," she said, wincing and squeezing her eyes shut. "And I'm afraid I never will be."

Margaret's heart ached with a pang of recognition. She understood exactly what Charlotte meant.

Margaret's first column would be published in the next issue. She'd turned in her second column, about the faux from-scratch cake, and was working on the third. She'd lost count of the hours she'd invested in it and the number of drafts she'd gone through. Even so, after reading the pages that afternoon, she had decided they were rubbish and started over. Again.

It was a magazine column, not literature. But she desperately wanted it to be a *good* magazine column. Leonard Clement had made himself clear; her job was to write words that made women smile. She had no objection to that.

If she could help other women smile or laugh, let them know they weren't the only ones who got it wrong or cut corners, who used cake mix from a box, who secretly wolfed down candy bars in the closet, who forgot to pick her son up from Little League practice, who loathed defrosting freezers and waxing floors and engaging with her in-laws, who felt like screaming as she faced five o'clock and her ten thousandth frozen chicken . . .

Well, that wasn't nothing.

Because if Margaret had learned anything in the last few months, it was that most women were desperately in need of a laugh. But, if at all possible, she also wanted to write columns that made them pause or think or even change. She wanted it more than anything.

Nothing she'd written so far even came close. Would it ever?

"You've got nothing to be sorry for," Margaret said, walking back to the sofa and taking a seat near Charlotte. "For what it's worth, I wasn't just trying to be nice. I really do think it's wonderful."

"Thank you. Now, can we please talk about something else?" Charlotte laughed, then smiled just as brightly as before. Margaret was struck by how genuine that smile was, as if she'd somehow tripped a wire into a completely different frame of mind and mood. Was it real? It looked real.

"How's the writing going? And when will we finally get to see your name in print?"

"Any day now."

"Well, I cannot wait to read it," Bitsy said, her drawl a little more pronounced than usual. "We'll all be able to say we knew you when." Bitsy took another slurp from her glass, then leaned toward the table and picked up a bowl filled with lumpy, dirt-brown spheres. "Anybody want to try a pinto bean mushroom ball? They taste better than they look."

Margaret doubted that but put one on her plate anyway, just to be polite. Apparently Bitsy was serious about becoming a vegetarian. She'd been very excited when Margaret passed on Helen's recipe book.

Charlotte declined, saying she was still feeling a little full from the cake, then reached past Viv's crudités and onion soup dip to pick up her copy of *The Feminine Mystique*.

"So, does anybody want to talk about the book?"

"Oh, I do!"

Bitsy waved her arm like a third grader with the answer to a chalkboard math problem.

"But first, I have a question. Is it *normal* to hate your husband?"

* * *

Viv handed Bitsy another paper napkin. She blew her nose into it, snuffling.

"Better now?" Viv patted her shoulder. "Look, you don't need to feel so guilty. There's not a wife in the world who hasn't hated her husband at some point."

Charlotte twirled her cigarette above her head as if to second the motion. Margaret, who had a mouthful of carrots and onion dip, nodded.

"And it's not like you really mean it," Viv said. "It's just a momentary flare-up, like sparking a match. Poof! Then it's gone. You'll get past it."

Bitsy dabbed the napkin against her nose. "Do you really think so? I'm so angry. I don't think I've ever been this angry," she said, sounding genuinely surprised. "And the terrible part is, none of this is really King's fault."

Charlotte made a sputtering sound. "Don't be an idiot. Of course it is."

"Oh, come on," Viv said. "You can't blame one man for *all* of society's ills."

Charlotte lifted her copy of the book. "I thought you said you'd read it."

Bitsy shook her head. "I don't think this has anything to do with the book. It's something that goes way back." She sniffled again. "Did I ever tell you how King and I met? And how he proposed to me? Twice?"

There was a collective shaking of heads. Bitsy reached for her glass and took a gulp.

"I was a junior in college. The regular vet at the stud farm where my father was barn manager had a heart attack, so King was filling in for a few months. We ran into each other in the barn pretty often, and I liked him well enough, but we never really talked about anything besides horses and the weather. So when he asked me to marry him, I was shocked," she said, widening her eyes to underscore the point. "Really shocked. I thanked him and all but said I was too young, that I wanted to finish school before settling down."

Charlotte smirked and tilted her chin into the air, exhaling smoke from her cigarette. "Let me guess. That made him even more determined. He plied you with candy and flowers and insincere promises until you finally gave in. Typical. Men love a conquest."

"No, no. It wasn't like that," Bitsy said. "He was very nice about it, even a little sheepish. He said he understood and that he just figured he'd ask while he had the chance. It was really kind of sweet. But the old vet came back a week later, and I didn't see King for months."

Bitsy paused to take a somewhat smaller sip before continuing her story.

"What I hadn't told King—or anybody, because I knew the odds were long—was that I hoped to become a vet myself. In the fall of my senior year, I had an A-minus average and stood fourth in my class. Veterinary colleges are very selective, but with grades like that, I figured I had a chance of getting in. Maybe not to my first-pick school," Bitsy said, "but somewhere."

"But you didn't. All your applications were turned down because you're a woman."

Margaret swatted Charlotte's shoulder. "Let her finish, will you?"

Charlotte pressed her lips together. Bitsy did the same, then took a breath.

"I didn't apply," she said. "Not anywhere."

"What?" Viv asked, looking confused. "Why not?"

"Because my adviser, who was also the department head, refused to write me a letter of recommendation. Vet schools aren't producing enough graduates to keep up with demand, and he said that even though I was a good student, writing a letter on my behalf would be a waste of time. No school would take a spot that could be filled by a man and give it to a woman who would end up leaving the program or the profession once she got married."

Margaret and Viv were seething by this time, and Bitsy looked like she might start crying again. But Charlotte was the one who said, or rather shouted, what all of them were thinking.

"What an ass!"

"That's the word," Bitsy agreed.

"So that was it?" Viv asked, incredulous. "You just gave up?"

"Not right away," Bitsy said. "I tried to argue—told him I didn't plan to marry and had turned down a perfectly good proposal a few weeks before. He just patted me on the cheek, said, 'Don't you worry, honey. A pretty girl like you will have men lined up around the block. You'll find the right one eventually.' Then he got up and showed me the door."

Margaret's fists were clutched so tightly that her knuckles hurt. Had Bitsy's professor been in the room, she'd have punched him in the nose. "So he thought you'd broken up with a boyfriend and that vet school was just a backup plan to keep you from being an old maid?"

"Pretty much," Bitsy said.

Margaret growled and called the arrogant academic the same name Charlotte had used. Viv scooped onion dip onto a celery stick, shaking her head.

"The guy in charge of admissions at my nursing program was just the same. Made me jump through all kinds of hoops, kept asking why I'd want to work instead of finding a man to support me. Then he had the nerve to ask me out on a date! He was disgusting. And *married*." Viv crunched her celery and looked at Bitsy. "Then what happened?"

"I pled my case to a few more of my professors," Bitsy said, "but they all said the same thing. They wouldn't write me the required recommendation. And then . . . Then my father died. He was up on the barn roof where he had no business being, trying to nail down some loose shingles. He slipped and broke his neck."

Bitsy fell silent for a moment, squeezing the wad of damp napkins in her fist.

"Of course we were devastated. But there was also a lot going on. Prescott Farms had a house for the barn manager; that's where I grew up and where we lived. But we knew they'd have to hire a new manager. So, in addition to grief and funeral arrangements, Mom and I worried about where and how we were going to live. Mom had always been a housewife. I had one semester left of school and no job prospects. It was scary." Bitsy picked up her cocktail glass, took a sip and another breath. "Then King came to Dad's funeral."

Charlotte dropped her jaw. "To propose? Like Rhett Butler? Wow! That's ballsy."

Bitsy shook her head. "He didn't propose until the next day. As soon as I saw his car drive through the gate, I knew why he'd come. And I won't lie. A part of me was relieved. He seemed like the answer to everything. I didn't say yes right away because I knew it meant closing the door on becoming a vet. But it looked like that was never going to happen anyway. By denying me the opportunity to study on grounds that I'd eventually end up getting married, they boxed me in and made sure I couldn't do anything else.

"King said he knew I didn't love him, but he promised that I'd learn to and said he'd work hard to make me happy. Then he started talking about opening a practice in Virginia. He made it sound like we'd be doing it together, as partners."

"And that's what a good marriage should be," Viv said, "a partnership. And at least you were able to finish college. That's bound to come in handy one of these days."

Bitsy paused, twisting her lips as if weighing the wisdom of saying something more, but then only shrugged, stretching her hand to Charlotte and wiggling her fingers. Charlotte passed over her cigarette. Bitsy took a drag, then sighed out the smoke.

"I guess I *do* help," she said at last. "In my way. If I wasn't taking care of the house, King couldn't work as many hours as he does. Building a practice from scratch isn't easy. You can't make a living treating a horse here and a horse there. You need connections with the folks who keep a full stable and can afford the best care. Mrs. Graham has just the one horse, but she knows everybody. King is taking care of Delilah now, and he's hoping it'll open some doors."

Viv spread her hands. "There, you see? And none of it would

have happened if you hadn't taken that job at the stables and introduced King to Mrs. Graham. So you are partners."

Though Bitsy nodded, she didn't look entirely convinced.

"I guess. When he proposed, he told me how much he admired that I had goals and wanted to finish my studies—said he was impressed by the way I handled horses too. 'You've got the touch,' he said. 'Just like your daddy.' The way he talked made me think we'd be working side by side, getting our hands dirty. But . . ." Her voice trailed off. "Maybe that's just what I wanted to hear. Either way, it hasn't worked out like I thought it would."

"What about his promise?" Margaret asked. "Did you learn to love him?"

"Well, not today, obviously," Bitsy said with a small smile. "Most of the time we get along, though the age difference can get in the way. He's so anxious to start a family. Though I can understand why, it's a lot of pressure. But yes, I do love him. King's not a bad man."

Charlotte dabbed imaginary tears from her eyes. "Gosh. 'Not a bad man.' Kind of gets you right here, doesn't it?" She thumped her chest.

"Well, he's not! He can really be very sweet. Did you know he brings me flowers on the fifth of every month to celebrate another month of marriage? He never forgets," Bitsy said, her expression softening. "He's good to me. And he really does try to make me happy."

"Then why do you hate him?" Charlotte asked.

Bitsy laughed nervously. "I don't *really* hate him. I think the book just kind of . . . set me off, stirred up bad memories. Up until now, you see, I thought it was just me. And even though the professors said they couldn't recommend me because I'm a woman, a part of me thought there was more to it, that they said no because I just wasn't good enough.

"So when I read about how many women are denied the chance to pursue certain professions because it's assumed they'll quit after marriage, or how colleges alter the curriculum so women are only learning what they'll need to know as wives and mothers, or that psychology classes are teaching girls that having ambitions beyond homemaking is a sign of neurosis—"

"Oh, do *not* get me started on psychiatrists," Charlotte said, her cocktail sloshing over the rim of her glass as her arm swept through the air. "Especially Dr. Barry. He's the worst."

"That bothered me too," Margaret said. "You know, I had to take one of those marriage and family courses in college—all the women did, but none of the men. There weren't any textbooks, just a lot of role-playing and lectures on how to support our future husbands.

"Once we were asked to role-play how a fictional fiancé would react if he found out we had a job that paid more than his, to imagine how it might damage his ego and jeopardize the relationship. I didn't think of it as indoctrination at the time, but it was."

"Exactly!" Bitsy cried. "The more I read, the more I started thinking about what happened to me, and the madder I got! Logically, I realize none of it was King's fault. He didn't get in the way of my becoming a vet. All he did was marry me. But . . . it's all mixed up in my mind somehow. Whenever I think about my horrible adviser, I end up picturing King's face."

"Hmm," Charlotte murmured. "Wonder what Dr. Barry would have to say about that?"

Viv reached for Margaret's sidecar and took a tiny sip. "Okay, but help me understand something. What does all that have to do with you turning vegetarian?"

"Oh," Bitsy said, turning a bit pink. "Well . . . it doesn't. Not really. The thing I said to Helen about hell freezing over before I'd cook another steak for King was just me boiling over after reading the book. The thought of eating animals has always bothered me. I wish King felt the same, but I guess we're just different," she said, shrugging. "Doesn't make me think less of him."

Bitsy took another puff of Charlotte's cigarette, frowning as she exhaled the smoke.

"Although," she said slowly, as if reexamining her earlier statement. "It does seem a little cruel, doesn't it? I mean, how can you say you love animals and devote your life to taking care of them but still feel absolutely no compunction about eating them?"

CHAPTER 13

Wee Small Hours of the Morning

By the time Margaret came home, the house was still and everyone was asleep. Instead of going upstairs right away, she slipped her shoes off in the foyer and padded to the kitchen in her stocking feet.

She washed the cake carrier and set it upside down in the dish rack to dry, then sat down at the kitchen table. She stared out the window toward the empty street and the blocky black silhouettes of their neighbor's hedges and the evenly spaced circles of light that shone down from the streetlamps onto the sidewalks, thinking about Viv's comment that every wife hates her husband at some point.

She had said it so casually, as if occasionally loathing one's spouse was just an unpleasant but unavoidable consequence of adulthood, as inescapable as death, taxes, and crow's-feet.

Was it? Should it be? And how did that happen?

They weren't living in the Middle Ages, after all. Not one woman in that room had been forced into marriage. Yes, Bitsy had been facing tough circumstances, but she'd still had choices—to marry, not to marry, to marry later, to marry someone else. All of them had been given and made a choice, had chosen one particular person from all of humanity as *the* one.

So what had happened?

How did one go from being the girl in the white dress—giving and receiving promises to eternally love, honor, and cherish—to the wife who shrugs her shoulders and nods her head when a newlywed asks if it's normal for her to hate her husband? Surely it wasn't meant to be that way. Yet here they all were.

Bitsy was starting to wonder if King might be a bit cruel. Charlotte had not one good word to say about Howard. Viv was keeping secrets from Tony. And Margaret and Walt didn't talk anymore—just exchanged information about kids, chores, budgets, schedules, and obligations.

How could things have gone so wrong? For all of them?

Margaret couldn't understand it, so she wrote about it.

The clack of the typewriter might have woken the family, so she left Sylvia in the closet and got out a notebook and pen. At first she just spilled her thoughts and questions onto the paper, scribbling impressions of the things she'd read, thought, heard, witnessed, and experienced, looking for connections that might bring answers. Then she took all that and tried crafting a scene: a book club meeting with characters who felt familiar but, ultimately, too familiar. Next she wrote about a neighborhood party where, instead of selling Tupperware or Avon, the exuberant hostess was trying to sell her guests a husband, attempting to make it funny.

But it wasn't funny. Just sad. She closed the notebook, put down the pen, and went upstairs. Walt was sound asleep, lying on his side and curled into himself, fisted hands tucked under his chin, breathing softly, steadily, innocently. Next to him an alarm clock ticked away seconds of a day that would never come again, casting a greenish glow over the copy of *The Old Man and the Sea* that was open to the middle and lying face down on the nightstand.

Margaret leaned down and pressed her lips lightly to his forehead.

"I don't hate you," she whispered.

CHAPTER 14

Most Important Meal of the Day

Bitsy was typically a light sleeper and an early riser. But she hadn't moved when the sun and King rose to greet the new day. She stirred herself only after Buster—one of their four cats, an overweight calico with an outsized personality—jumped onto the bed, unsheathed his claws, and began scratching her on the forehead, lightly at first but then with increasing pressure, until she groaned and opened her eyes.

"Buster, you are a fiend."

The cat made a chittering sound and butted her shoulder with his head. Bitsy yawned, scooting herself into a half-sitting, half-reclining position against the green tufted velvet headboard and pillows. Noises coming from the kitchen, the low twang of the country music station on the radio, Johnny Cash singing "Ring of Fire," punctuated with the occasional clank of a pot, pan, or silverware, told her King hadn't left for work yet and was probably making himself breakfast. She knew she should probably get up and cook it for him, but she couldn't quite bring herself to leave the bed. For one thing, her head was still hurting from too many sidecars the night before. For another, she knew King would want to talk. He was always chatty and cheerful in the morning. Normally she didn't mind. But today . . . she wasn't ready.

Bitsy was still sorting through all the things she'd shared with the Bettys, her feelings, and their reactions. She still felt a little funny about it, wondered if she'd been wrong, even disloyal, to speak so openly about her marriage. The tightness she'd been carrying in her chest for weeks seemed to lessen as she'd relayed her story, and her shoulders seemed looser than usual this morning, not nearly as tense as they often felt when she woke up. But Bitsy knew King would have been hurt had he overheard their conversation, and so—even though he couldn't possibly know what she'd said to the Bettys—she didn't feel ready to look him in the eye. Not yet.

Instead, she snuggled back down under the covers, pushed aside the insistently purring Buster, and picked up the copy of *Herland* she'd left on the nightstand, opening to the first chapter. Though the book was older, Bitsy was pleased that the Bettys had chosen it. She'd always enjoyed fantasy stories, so a tale about a utopian society run by women was intriguing.

As she started reading, Bitsy grew a little disappointed to find the book was narrated by Van—one of three men who went off in search of the mythical Herland. But the first few pages pulled her in just the same, dropping hints of adventure yet to come. She would have liked to read more, but Buster kept headbutting her and would not be put off, and she knew she really should get up and see her husband off to work. As far as her reluctance to look King in the eye . . . well, she was being silly. He couldn't know what she'd said to the Bettys any more than he could read her mind. Besides, she couldn't just hide in the bedroom forever, now, could she?

She put the book aside, put on her white terry cloth bathrobe and slippers, and shuffled into the kitchen with the cat in her arms.

King was standing at the stove. He was dressed in scuffed leather boots, dark blue jeans, and an indigo-colored shirt. A stethoscope peeked out from the pocket of his brown barn jacket. All this, combined with his broad shoulders, ruddy complexion, and touch of gray at the temples, made him look just like a horse vet ought to—strong, rugged, and trustworthy.

King cracked eggs into the pan. The other cats—Lilith, Oscar, and Bob—and the dog, a deaf and arthritic coonhound named Zeke, sat in a hopeful ring around his feet, eyes alert to King's every move, ready to spring into action should any food drop to the floor.

After Bitsy set him down on the floor, Buster went to join his comrades in fur. King flipped two eggs over in the hot pan, making them sizzle and pop.

"Good morning, li'l bit." He gave her a peck on the lips. "Sleep good?"

Bitsy yawned, nodding with her mouth partially open. "Too good. If Buster hadn't woken me up, I'd still be in bed."

Bitsy looked down at the cat. Buster collapsed on the ground next to her feet, then stretched and rolled his body over the top of her fluffy pink slippers.

"Fiend," she said, then squatted down to scratch him between the ears.

"Yep. You were dead to the world when I got up. That's why I thought I'd make you some breakfast." King pulled a plate from the cupboard and gave her a sly smile. "You know, just in case you had a reason for being so tired."

Bitsy felt her jaw clench. He was worse than her mother. If she *was* pregnant, did he honestly think she'd keep it a secret? She'd have been thrilled to tell him she was expecting, if for no other reason than to keep him from constantly dropping hints about it. Bitsy poured herself some coffee.

"Nope. Just a late night and one too many sidecars."

"Yeah, I figured."

Though his tone was casual, disappointment registered in his eyes, making them seem a little less blue than they had a moment before. King slipped a spatula beneath the eggs and slid them onto a plate alongside a slice of buttered toast, then set the plate on the counter.

"Here you go."

"Thanks. Aren't you eating?"

King grabbed his coffee cup and took a slurp, shaking his head. "Already did."

Bitsy carried her plate to the table, feeling even worse about the things she'd confessed to the Bettys. It was unfair of her to reveal so much, and only one side of the story. King really was kind, much more considerate than most men. Her failure to conceive was a thorn in their relationship, but that would change once she gave him the thing he wanted most: a child to carry on his name. And since the fertility doctor had found nothing that would eliminate the possibility of her becoming pregnant, apart from anxiety and somewhat irregular periods, it was only a matter of time.

"You're young and strong and healthy," the doctor had assured her. "Mix up a pitcher of martinis, put some Nat King Cole on the stereo, and let nature take its course."

"My friend Viv suggested Chianti and Sinatra. She's got six kids with one on the way."

"Well, there you go. Apart from her taste in music, I couldn't agree more." The doctor reached out and patted her knee. "Mrs. Cobb, half of my patients are just like you, women who've taken a little longer to conceive than whatever their mother or sister or husband or girlfriend says is 'normal.' They get themselves so worked up that it makes a perfectly natural process a whole lot harder than it needs to be.

"So I'm telling you what I tell them: Take care of yourself, eat healthy meals, get enough sleep and a moderate amount of exercise, and take some long, relaxing bubble baths. Especially right before your husband is due home from work." He winked. "Do all that, and you'll be picking out nursery wallpaper before you know it."

Bitsy could have done without the wink and didn't much care for having her knee patted, especially while wearing nothing but a thin cotton gown that barely covered her thighs. But his words were reassuring, and she felt certain he meant well.

And King meant well too. It wasn't fair of her to transfer her resentment about the world's injustices to him. All he'd done was love her, offer her a home and his hand. What more could she have asked for?

When Bitsy was a little girl, she'd sometimes dreamed of getting married. Every summer, she and her parents would drive to Tennessee for a week of vacation, staying with family. She and the girl cousins would play bride, using one of Aunt Naomi's old lace tablecloths as a veil and topping it with chains of daisies they picked from the yard. They played house too, sometimes, but bride was their favorite.

Then one summer, after Bitsy shot up so suddenly, growing a full five inches in one year, the cousins said she had to be the groom from then on because she was too tall to be the bride. "The girl *has* to be shorter than the boy," they insisted. Around that same time, she was coming to the kitchen to get a cookie and overheard a conversation between her mother and Aunt Naomi. "I don't know what to do about Bitsy," her mother said, sighing. "Tall, gangly, clumsy, shy as all get-out. How will she ever find a husband?"

After that, Bitsy told the cousins she didn't want to play bride anymore and talked them into playing Black Beauty instead, galloping through the field and leaping over logs, having races and adventures. It was a lot more interesting.

Bitsy did get married, of course. As did the girl cousins. But King was so much nicer than the men they married. Becky's husband stepped out on her every chance he got. Cindy's husband was bone lazy and dull as dirt. King, on the other hand, was loving, hardworking, and solicitous, doing everything he could think of to make Bitsy happy, from bringing her flowers to frying her eggs. All he needed to make him happy was a baby, preferably a son.

Once she had the baby, they would be happy, the both of them. The tension would disappear and everything would be fine. She was sure of it.

King brought the coffeepot to the table and topped up her cup. "You heading over to the stables this morning?"

Bitsy nodded. "Mrs. Graham is planning to ride this afternoon. The farrier was supposed to get Delilah shoed yesterday, and I want to make sure he did before Mrs. Graham arrives. Then I need to muck out some stalls and take Bitterroot out for a ride. Congressman Clancy hasn't ridden him in over a week, so he needs some exercise. Busy day," she said, unfolding her napkin.

"Same here." He gulped down the rest of his coffee, then bent down to kiss the top of Bitsy's head. "Wish I could stay, but I gotta go see a guy about a horse."

Bitsy smiled as she always did at his traditional exit line. She picked up her fork, ready to dig into the eggs, but stopped after taking a sniff.

"King? What did you cook these eggs in?"

"Just the bacon grease that was left after I made my breakfast." Bitsy put down her fork, and King rolled his eyes. "Oh, for heaven's sake, Bits. Don't look at me like that."

"But I told you, I don't want to eat meat anymore."

"I understand that," he said, in a tone that suggested he didn't understand at all. "That's why I didn't make any bacon for you. But a little grease won't kill you, and the pig's already dead. Why let it go to waste? Two weeks ago you wouldn't have batted an eye."

"I know. But I told you before that this is something I've been thinking about for a while now, and I feel very strongly—"

King cut her off by flinging his arms as if he was throwing her words to the four winds.

"I swear, I can't win for losing around here. I just wanted to do something nice for my wife. But you act like I'm trying to poison you. Or compromise your morals!"

"Honey, I'm not. It's just that—"

"No matter what I do or how hard I try, it's never enough for you."

King wasn't listening. Bitsy pushed back her chair and went to stand beside him.

"I'm sorry," she said, resting her hand on his chest. "You were just trying to be kind."

"I was." He slumped his shoulders, pouting.

"I know," she said. "I'm sorry."

When Bitsy pushed herself up onto her toes to give him a conciliatory peck, King twined his arms around her body, pulling her close, kissing her deeply, seeming to forget what he'd said earlier about his busy day. Bitsy had not forgotten. She didn't have time for this. She didn't want it either. But she didn't feel she could push him away, not after she'd hurt his feelings. Just as Bitsy was thinking she had no choice but to acquiesce, King groaned and pulled back.

"You are a temptress," he said, sighing. "But I really do have to see a guy about a horse."

Bitsy took a step back. "I understand. Me too."

"Bitsy? Sorry about breakfast. Next time I'll use butter."

She shrugged. "It's all right. Like you said, it won't kill me, and the pig's already dead."

Bitsy walked him to the door and stood on the porch, waving as he backed his battered green 1954 Willys Jeep Station Wagon out of the driveway.

When the car was out of sight, she went back into the kitchen and scooped one of the eggs into the dog bowl. Zeke gulped it down in two bites. Then she cut the other egg into tiny pieces, left the plate on the table where Zeke wouldn't get it, and called the cats.

* * *

The alarm jangled promptly at six. Margaret pulled the pillow over her head and nearly went back to sleep. But when Bobby started pounding on the door of the hallway bathroom, demanding Beth give somebody else a turn, she rolled over reluctantly and pushed herself into a sitting position. She felt like she'd been hit by a bus. There was a reason she never stayed up past eleven on weeknights.

By the time she came downstairs to make breakfast, Walt was on his way out the door. He had a cup of coffee in one hand and his briefcase in the other, but he stopped to give her a kiss good-bye and to thank her for the book. He looked into her eyes when he spoke, something he didn't do nearly as often as he used to, and sounded as if he meant it.

"You're welcome. I remembered you used to like Hemingway."

Walt nodded. "Can't believe I missed this one. Maybe because it was published in '52 and we were already married with a baby by then. Never enough time, you know?" He looked at his wrist-watch. "Anyway, thanks. Love you, Maggie."

Margaret stood on the stoop to watch him drive away. She didn't feel tired anymore.

They were all out of frozen orange juice, so she mixed up a pitcher of Tang, scrambled half a dozen eggs, and toasted English muffins before packing the kids' bag lunches. The childish argument over the bathroom made its way downstairs, and the bickering was so intense that Margaret threatened to revoke their TV privileges. Finally, they wolfed down their eggs, grabbed their brown bags, and ran out the door just in time to avoid missing the bus.

Once they were gone, Margaret had a second cup of coffee and a slice of leftover German chocolate cake.

Her plan for the day was to take the books she'd borrowed back to Babcock's—except the copy of *Herland*, which Bitsy had taken home with her—then come home and write. But first she walked out to the mailbox. Her copy of *A Woman's Place* normally arrived on Saturday, but she'd been checking first thing in the morning all week, hoping the issue with her first column might show up a few days early.

Margaret thrust her arm into the maw of the mailbox and pulled out a pile of letters, bills, and advertising circulars. Her heart beat a little faster when she spotted two magazines in the pile, but sank when she saw they were *Good Housekeeping* and *McCall's*.

Then, under the magazines, she saw a manila envelope with a New York postmark and was so excited that she let go of the rest of the mail. It fell from her hands and landed in a heap at her feet. She bent back the envelope's metal clasp and tore open the flap, feeling the thrum of her pulse in her eardrums as she slid the magazine from the manila sleeve, flipping to the pages that someone had bookmarked for her. The first was the letter from the editor, which made mention of her column and her name. David Miles had written a brief note on the page—"Welcome to *A Woman's Place*, Margaret!"—signed in his own hand.

The second bookmark brought her to an article that sounded like a Cinderella story: the tale of an ordinary housewife who had been plucked from obscurity to become the newest columnist at *A Woman's Place*. It included photographs taken during Margaret's tour of the magazine—one of her posing with Mr. Miles, one of her shaking hands with the "Selma Says" columnist, and one of Margaret leaning over the shoulders of an editor working on a layout. The final photo was a setup shot of her sitting at a typewriter with a pencil tucked behind her ear, pretending to write. It was, as Mr. Miles had said, a great angle.

On the opposite page, topped by a cartoon illustration of a smiling woman who looked a lot like Margaret but not quite, was her column.

Margaret had read it so many times before that she could recite it by heart. But she stood there in the street, a pile of litter at her feet, and read it again, savoring an emotion she hadn't experienced in a very long time—pride.

It was *her* name in the byline, *her* words on the page, *her* work that had accomplished this. And when she flipped to the third bookmark near the back of the magazine, she found a windowpane business envelope containing a twenty-five-dollar check.

Pay to the order of Margaret Ryan.

And no one else.

Margaret didn't hear the sedan approaching or realize it had stopped until Barb Fredericks rolled down her window and called out, "Margaret? Margaret, are you all right?"

"Hmm?" She looked up. "Oh yes. Fine. How are you, Barb? How're the kids?"

Barb frowned, looking confused.

"We haven't seen you at the coffee klatch recently."

"I've been busy. I've got a part-time job now."

"Oh." She nodded toward the envelope Margaret was holding. "Bad news?"

"What? Oh no. Not at all."

Margaret slipped the envelope and check into her jacket pocket and smiled. Barb looked more confused than ever.

"But . . . Margaret, you're standing in the street, so absorbed in whatever you're reading that you didn't even hear me drive up. Are you sure you're all right? Because if you have a need to talk to someone . . ."

Margaret gave an inward eye roll. Were she in distress, Barb Fredericks would've been the last person she'd confide in. Everybody in Concordia knew that the fastest way to spread neighborhood gossip was to telephone, telegraph, or tell Barb.

"I'm fine, really." Margaret lifted the magazine so Barb could see it. "I started reading a magazine column and got a little caught up, that's all."

Barb gave her an incredulous look. "Must be some terrific column."

Margaret grinned.

"It is."

CHAPTER 15

Slammed Doors

The late morning sky was a flat, dull gray. Even so, Bitsy felt her spirits lift as she got out of her car and walked to the stables, dressed in a pair of light tan, well-worn riding breeches, a black turtleneck, and a khaki-colored barn coat.

It was the same every day. No matter how gloomy the weather or her mood, the second she got out of the car and breathed in the scent of hay, manure, wet grass, and worn leather that was the perfume of barns everywhere, she felt happier, calmer, and more confident.

Bitsy liked the house King had bought for her. And since getting to know Margaret, Viv, and Charlotte, she was starting to like Concordia too. But it still didn't feel like home. The only place that felt like home to Bitsy, that had ever felt like home, was a barn. The house was where she lived; the barn was where she belonged, the only place she never second-guessed herself.

Striding toward the stables, she was pleased to see that Lydia Bee, a ten-year-old palomino, was being saddled up by her owner for a ride on one of the park's many trails. Lydia Bee was sweet-tempered but a little on the lazy side; the exercise would do her good. Three of the younger mares, Crystal, Dancer, and Gracie, had been turned out to the paddock. When they spotted Bitsy approaching, they perked up their ears and trotted to the fence.

Dancer got there first, lifted her nose to Bitsy's face, and greeted her with a warm whoosh of breath from her nostrils. Bitsy reached into her pocket and pulled out a piece of carrot, feeding it to the horse and stroking her neck. She was feeding carrots to Crystal and Gracie when she saw Joey, one of the other stable hands, coming out of the barns.

Bitsy raised her hand to greet him, and Gracie nosed her shoulder, looking for another carrot. "Don't be such a hog. You'll end up as fat as Lydia Bee if you don't watch it," she said to the horse, then turned toward Joey.

Joey had grown up in DC and graduated from high school the previous year. He'd never worked with horses before, but he loved animals and was a hard worker, arriving at the stables at six every morning.

"How's everybody doing?" she asked as he approached. "Did the farrier come yesterday?"

Joey nodded. "Yes, and I just finished cleaning out the ladies' stalls," he said, tilting his head toward the three mares. "But Mrs. Graham might want to postpone her ride today. I just looked in on Delilah. Seems like her arthritis is acting up. Either that or her new shoes don't feel quite right."

Bitsy frowned. "What do you mean?"

In horse years, Delilah was definitely a senior citizen and did have some arthritis. But she'd been fine when Bitsy saw her the day before yesterday, and a new pair of shoes shouldn't have caused her any discomfort.

"I don't know . . . She's just kind of standing funny," Joey said.

"Funny how?"

Joey scratched his nose, trying to come up with a description.

"Well, she's sort of shifting her weight to her back legs and stretching out her forelegs a little bit. I think the shoes don't—"

Alarm bells went off in Bitsy's head. She started toward the barn.

"Shit!"

Joey's eyes went wide. "What's wrong?" he asked, falling into step behind her.

"Shit!" Bitsy shouted, and broke into a run.

❋ ❋ ❋

The situation was just as Joey had described it. Delilah was favoring her back legs and stretching out her front legs, trying to keep the weight off them to alleviate her discomfort. The difference in her stance was subtle and might have gone unnoticed by someone with a less experienced eye. Bitsy gave Joey credit for recognizing that something wasn't right, but she knew it wasn't the result of arthritis or ill-fitting shoes. Even before she started her examination, the look in Delilah's eyes told Bitsy this was something more serious.

Bitsy took a deep breath, taking a moment to calm herself before approaching the horse, murmuring softly as she did. Delilah's nostrils flared and her ears twitched back, displaying her anxiety. But she stood perfectly still when Bitsy ran her hands down her leg to check her digital pulse at the back of her knee and feel for heat in the hoof, and she willingly raised her right leg when Bitsy nudged her.

Bitsy examined the bottom of Delilah's foot and shook her head.

"This isn't good."

She lowered the horse's leg and took a moment to stroke Delilah's muzzle, murmuring comforting words before sliding back the door of the stall. Joey followed her with his eyes.

"Where are you going?"

"We need to call Mrs. Graham right away. And my husband."

❋ ❋ ❋

Four hours later, Bitsy and Mrs. Graham stood in a corner of Delilah's stall, watching King with anxious eyes.

It had taken Bitsy some time to track down Mrs. Graham, who had been on a shuttle flight from New York when Bitsy reached her secretary. She'd come directly from the airport to the stables, still dressed in a pink suit she'd worn to a fundraising luncheon. Getting ahold of King, who'd been all the way out in Centreville, had been even more difficult. Thankfully, he checked in with the answering service before leaving the farm and drove right to the stables.

The two women barely moved as he conducted his examination, which was nearly identical to the one Bitsy had performed earlier. Bitsy was terribly worried about the horse and almost as concerned for her owner.

Mrs. Graham and Bitsy had developed a good, even warm relationship in the previous months. And although Katharine Graham wasn't the sort of woman who bared her soul, Bitsy had come to understand that being the socially well-connected wife of an important newspaper publisher wasn't always easy. She knew how much Delilah meant to her and what a source of comfort the horse was to a woman who must have felt very alone sometimes. There was more loneliness going around than people would have guessed. If Mrs. Graham lived in Concordia, Bitsy would have invited her to become a Betty.

As it was, all she could do was stand by Katharine's side and pray that her assessment of Delilah's condition had been incorrect. Never in her life had Bitsy so longed to be wrong.

It was possible, wasn't it? For all the time she'd spent with horses, she'd never gone to vet school. King had. Maybe he would lower Delilah's leg, look up with twinkling blue eyes and a patronizing smile, and say, "Aw, it's nothing, Bitsy. You're making mountains out of molehills. Joey was right. She's just getting used to the new shoes."

The ensuing embarrassment would be worth it, a small price to pay if it meant that Delilah, and her devoted owner, would be spared pain. Bitsy clamped her eyes shut and pressed her hands together.

Please, God. Please let me be wrong.

King released his hold on Delilah's foot and shook his head.

"Laminitis," he said, nodding toward Bitsy. "Just like you thought."

Mrs. Graham furrowed her brow. "Laminitis?"

"It's an inflammation of the tissue between the hoof and the coffin bone. That's why she's shifting her weight onto her back legs—because the front feet are sore."

Mrs. Graham nodded, acknowledging the diagnosis, then crossed the stall and stood next to Delilah, stroking her muzzle and looking into her eyes.

"Is she in terrible pain?"

"Not yet," King said. "But if it goes on for very long, if the coffin bone separates from the hoof and rotates . . ." He sighed heavily. "I know this is hard to hear, ma'am, but I think you should put her down. I can do it for you, if you'd like."

Bitsy let out a little gasp. She couldn't help herself. King shot her a look, but Mrs. Graham didn't seem to notice. Her eyes filled with tears.

"But surely there's something you can do? Some kind of treatment?"

King shook his head. "I'm sorry, Mrs. Graham, but laminitis can't be treated."

"Oh yes it can!" Bitsy cried, the words popping from her lips almost before she knew she'd said them. She couldn't help herself.

King shot her a furious scowl, the glare in his eyes asking how dare she contradict him. Bitsy avoided his gaze, speaking directly to Mrs. Graham.

"It is a serious condition," she said. "And if it gets worse, the horse can experience real pain, be lame for life. But if you catch it early, it can be treated. Back in Kentucky, my father treated four different horses with laminitis. Three out of the four got better."

"For how long?" King asked, sneering. "Laminitis is chronic. There's no cure for it."

"He's right," Bitsy said, dipping her head but keeping her gaze fixed on Katharine's face. "There is no cure. And no guarantee. But with the right kind of care, it *can* be managed."

Mrs. Graham was listening intently, her brown eyes solemn, her tears banished.

"And you know what to do? How to treat it?"

Bitsy hesitated, interrupted by doubt and uncertainty. But then, after looking into Delilah's patient, soulful brown eyes, eyes that would be certainly and forever closed if she stood back and let King take the lead, she squared her shoulders and spoke again.

"I watched my father treat those four horses. I know what to do."

"Your *father*?" King said. "And what vet school did he go to? Same one as you?"

King's laugh was loud and cruel, like the boom of a cannon. Delilah startled at the sound of it, flaring her nostrils and tossing her head. King paid her no mind.

"Mrs. Graham, I have been a practicing veterinarian for fifteen years. And I'm telling you what any good vet would say in this situation: This animal should be put down. If you'd rather take advice from a woman who picked up what little she knows about equine medicine from hanging around the barn when she was a teenager in pigtails . . . Well, I guess that's your prerogative. But if the horse had a say in the matter, I'm pretty sure she'd ask you to think twice before putting her into the hands of a college dropout."

Doubt flickered in Mrs. Graham's eyes. King swung his gaze toward Bitsy. Had this been a fencing match, he'd have shouted, "Touché!"

The night before, at the book club meeting, a slightly inebriated Bitsy had asked her friends if it was normal for a wife to hate her husband. Now, sober in a way she'd never been before, she realized that she'd never hated King, not really. In fact, she'd never truly known what hatred felt like.

She did now.

Bitsy lifted her chin, speaking in a steady, low, and deliberate tone. "Once again, my husband is right. I wanted to become a vet. I worked hard and was fourth in the undergraduate biology program. But because I'm a woman, none of the professors would write me a letter of recommendation to vet school, so I was unable to apply.

"Around that same time, my father died and King proposed. I wanted to stay in Kentucky to finish my final semester of college, but King had just opened his practice here. He was adamant that the wedding take place right away and that I move to Virginia as soon as we were married. In retrospect, I should have insisted he let me complete my education, told him that if he loved me as much as he claimed to, he would want that for me."

For the briefest of seconds, Bitsy looked directly at King, accusing him with her eyes.

"But I didn't. Instead, I went along with what he wanted and forgot about what I wanted. I can't say exactly why, but I was tired, grieving, and discouraged. And since the doors to a career had slammed shut, finishing that final semester didn't seem important anymore.

"So yes, Mrs. Graham, I am a college dropout. It's a huge embarrassment to me, something I've kept secret from everyone, even friends. King is an experienced equine veterinarian, and I'm not. But there's one thing I know how to do that he doesn't: heal a horse with laminitis. I know because I've seen it done successfully. King never has."

Bitsy stepped forward, next to Delilah, and laid her hand gently on the horse's neck as she looked into Mrs. Graham's eyes. "I can't give you a guarantee," she said, speaking in a gentle tone. "But if you let me, I can give Delilah a chance. And with all due respect to Dr. Cobb, that's more than he is offering."

Bitsy fell silent. Though King was standing behind her, she was sure she could feel the heat of his glare on her back. But she didn't flinch, just stood quietly, waiting. Mrs. Graham took two long, even breaths. Then her head began to nod, slowly and almost painfully, as if her neck was a rusty hinge that had just been touched with a drop of oil.

"Yes," she said, then nodded more firmly, locking eyes with Bitsy and reaching out to grab her hands. "Yes. Yes, let's try it. Let's give her a chance. She deserves a chance."

King turned away, sliding open the door of the stall and slamming it closed with such force that the metal railing clanged like a bell when it hit the stop. Delilah startled at the noise, but Bitsy didn't move a muscle or turn to watch him leave.

Her mind was already racing, thinking about what she must do next and who could help her do it.

CHAPTER 16

Three-Donut Day

As she fixed her hair and makeup, Margaret couldn't stop grinning, as if some out-of-frame photographer had commanded her to "say cheese" but then wandered away and forgot to snap the picture. But her joyous anticipation was genuine, and it continued as she got dressed to go to town, sorting through her options and deciding how to spend her paycheck.

Her first thought was to cash it and buy every single one of the books Helen had recommended. Margaret had wanted to read them all, and a collection like that would really dress up her mostly empty bookcase.

But thinking about the bookcase got her thinking about furniture in general. She'd wanted a new sofa forever. And a proper dining room set, Danish modern, a teak table and chairs and maybe even a matching sideboard. The sofa she had in mind cost nearly two hundred dollars. Buying just one of the dining chairs she wanted would take her whole check. But if she saved up for a few months, or even a year . . .

She dropped by the bookstore first. Helen was out running her own errands, so Margaret left the books she was returning with Edwin, using the money Bitsy had given her to pay for the copy of *Herland* that Margaret had brought to the meeting. She then asked him to order three more copies for the Bettys. He was happy to oblige and delighted to hear that Walt was enjoying *The Old Man and the Sea*.

"Have him call me when he's finished. Maybe we can go out for a beer and discuss it."

Margaret couldn't picture Walt joining a book club, even if it was just him and Edwin and beer was involved, but she promised she would. Still smiling, she got back into the car and drove to the bank, the same one that had gifted them with the coffee percolator when she and Walt opened their checking account.

The young woman sitting at the new accounts desk, Rhonda, a doe-eyed brunette who seemed to have doused herself in Wind Song perfume before leaving for work, couldn't have been more than twenty. When Margaret said she wanted to open a savings account, Rhonda pulled a form from her desk drawer and picked up a pen.

"Of course. I'd be happy to help. Miss?"

"Mrs. Margaret Ruth Ryan."

"Oh, I see. Is Mr. Ryan with you? We'll need his signature to open an account."

Margaret shook her head. "This account will be just for me. I've started a new job."

Rhonda put down the pen. "I'm sorry, Mrs. Ryan, but you won't be able to open an account without your husband. We'll need his signature—"

"Yes, you said that already. But this isn't his account. It's mine. I need an account where I can deposit and save my paychecks." Rhonda blinked her doe eyes. Margaret reached into her pocket, pulled out the check, and pointed. "See? It says right there, Margaret Ryan."

"Yes, I understand. But we still need your husband's signa—"

"May I please speak to the manager?"

The manager, Mr. Carlyle, a portly, red-faced man in his middle forties with halitosis and an officious manner, was no more help than Rhonda.

"Yes, Mrs. Ryan," he said with an exaggerated nod. "I understand that the money is being paid to you and not your husband. But bank policy requires a married woman to have signed approval from her husband to open an account."

"But it's *my* name on the check!"

Carlyle stared at Margaret the same way he might had she been speaking a foreign language, blankly and without a hint of comprehension. Margaret sighed and tried again.

"Let me ask you this. If my husband came in and wanted to open an account with a check in his name, would bank policy require him to get a signature from me first?"

He blinked twice. "Well, no. Of course not."

Margaret threw her arms out wide, waiting for Carlyle to connect the dots. It didn't happen. He reached into a drawer and pulled out a beige index card.

"If your husband doesn't have time to come to the bank during business hours, you can simply ask him to sign this signature card. Bring them back once he does, and we'll be more than happy to open your account."

He smiled a thin smile and held out the card. Quietly seething but seeing no alternative, Margaret took it, then walked out the door and around the corner to a nearby bakery.

Margaret ordered three jelly donuts, carried them to a bench down the block, and ate all three while she filled out the form and forged Walt's signature on the index card.

Less than thirty minutes after making her exit, she marched back into the bank and handed the card and her endorsed paycheck to Rhonda, who looked surprised and a little nervous to see her again.

"Oh. That was quick."

"My husband's office isn't far."

This was true. It didn't seem necessary to mention that she hadn't actually gone there.

Rhonda looked the form over to make sure everything had been filled out correctly. "Is that . . ." She lowered her head, squinting at a purple smear. "Jelly?"

Margaret folded her hands in her lap.

"He was on a coffee break."

* * *

For the most part, Margaret had given up door-slamming in late adolescence. But the humiliation she'd been forced to endure, the lie she'd been forced to tell, and the machinations she'd been forced to undertake simply to get access to money she'd earned through her own labor were all more than she could take.

She climbed behind the wheel of the station wagon and slammed the heavy door as hard as she could, not once but three times. Even that wasn't enough to quell her anger. She felt the same way she had when she was eight years old and one of the older boys in the neighborhood, Skip Halloran, who was thirteen, treated her to a cone from the ice cream truck, then reached out and smashed the cone in her face as she tried to take the first lick: furious, frustrated, and ill-used, the butt of a very unfunny joke.

She let out an aggravated shout and smacked the heel of her hand against the car horn. A couple of pedestrians shot her a strange look, but it helped a little. So did peeling out of the bank parking lot as fast as she could, spitting a small shower of loose gravel from her tires.

As she drove, Margaret mentally composed a letter to her congressman protesting the policies and laws that prevented women from being able to engage in simple financial transactions and demanding legislation to address the problem. She remembered what her mother, who had marched with the suffragettes as a teenager, had once said about the importance of civic engagement: "Had we waited for men to give us the vote, it never would have happened. We had to demand it for ourselves and do the work to see it through."

Margaret was under no illusions that her letter would be enough to send a senator scurrying, but she had to do something.

Maybe she could get some of the other women in Concordia to write letters too? The coffee klatch crowd would be no help, but she was sure she could get the Bettys on board. And possibly Helen.

By the time she pulled through the brick columns marking Concordia's entrance, Margaret had worked out a response, which left her feeling calmer and a little less helpless. As soon as she got home, she would take Sylvia out of the closet and start typing a draft letter, something she could show to the others. If she hurried, she could finish before the school bus arrived. That was the plan.

But the plan changed when Margaret pulled into the driveway and saw a girl dressed in a pleated plaid skirt, white blouse, and blue blazer sitting on the front steps.

Margaret turned off the ignition and got out of the car.

"Denise? What are you doing here? Shouldn't you be in school?"

"I told the gym teacher I had cramps." She stood. "Can I talk to you? It's kind of important."

CHAPTER 17

Simple Requests

Denise sat silently at the Ryans' kitchen table without touching her slice of cake or glass of milk, waiting for Margaret to finish reading. After doing so a second time, Margaret lowered the papers and looked at the girl for a long moment.

"Denise, this is . . ."

When Margaret had invited the girl into the house and asked what she wanted to talk about, she'd been surprised and a little flattered when Denise asked if she would read the writing sample she planned to send to Oxford. "Mom told me you write a magazine column. Since you're a professional writer, I thought you'd have ideas about how I can improve it."

Hearing the phrase "professional writer" applied to herself made Margaret uncomfortable. Her knee-jerk response was to deny it. Then she remembered the check and that someone had, in fact, paid her to write. Wasn't that the definition of professional?

She told Denise she'd be happy to read her essay.

Now that she had, she didn't quite know what to say.

"This is very, *very* good."

Margaret wasn't being kind. Denise's writing was extraordinary. The girl had penned a sort of tragic fairy tale about a woman who lived in an overregulated suburban community called Harmony. Upon moving there, the woman had made great, even grandiose plans for the installation of a lavish garden. After many years, because the woman never followed through with her plans, a crew of workers came and planted shrubs and trees that were identical to those of her neighbors and nothing like the garden she had imagined. The woman, now enraged, continued to possess a plan, as well as the tools and means to execute it. Rather than do so, she bought a watering can and a bottle of poison. Every day for many months, she mixed a few drops of poison in a full can of water and poured it on the roots of the shrubs and trees, killing them slowly but surely, leaving the garden bare and the ground so tainted that nothing would ever grow there again.

The fact that the main character was a thinly disguised version of Charlotte made Margaret squirm initially, but the story was so skillfully wrought that she soon moved past that. Denise's writing was sharp and precise. The woman's every action served a purpose, shining a light on the flaws, motives, and misbeliefs that lay beneath her behaviors. Each word was carefully chosen, each adjective ideal, creating descriptions that illuminated without embellishing.

And yet, for all that, there was a luminous quality to the writing, and a strange intimacy. Margaret felt like she was watching a scene through the thinnest of veils, witnessing every action and hearing every word, but never looking the character full in the face. That quality allowed the reader to insert anyone into the story, even herself. Especially herself.

"Denise, it's better than good. It's remarkable. And insightful . . ."

She had been about to say "especially for a girl of seventeen" but stopped herself. Adding an age qualifier was unnecessary. The work was remarkable and insightful. Period.

"If I had anything to suggest, I would. But I don't. You're an excellent writer."

"Thank you."

Another girl might have blushed, broken eye contact, or made a self-deprecating comment denying her talent while simultaneously fishing for another compliment to mitigate her own insecurity. That's what Margaret would have done at that age, and what she still did sometimes. But Denise simply thanked her, acknowledging the truth of Margaret's words with a quiet confidence that was not the least bit unseemly.

Charlotte always said Denise was an odd duck. If the definition meant a person who didn't fit in with her peers, then Denise was that. But if your peers were ordinary people destined to lead ordinary lives and you understood that you were the opposite, why would you waste time trying to fit in? You wouldn't. Instead, you'd be desperately searching for a place where you did fit in. So what Denise had to say didn't come as too much of a surprise, not initially.

"Mrs. Ryan, I have to go to Oxford. I just have to! If I don't, I . . ."

For the first time that day, Denise looked like what she still was: an anxious teenager teetering uncertainly on the cusp of womanhood, as desperate for transformation as Margaret had been at that age. Margaret reached across the table and clasped her hand.

"It's going to be all right. According to your mother, your grades are excellent. And you're obviously an exceptional writer. I don't doubt that there's a lot of competition, but with talent like yours, I'm sure your chances are better than most. And if Oxford doesn't work out for some reason, there will be a dozen other colleges that would be thrilled to have you."

Denise screwed her eyes shut as she spoke, nodding impatiently, as if pushing back the urge to interrupt her elder required focused effort.

"Thank you, yes. I do have a couple of fallback options, just in case. But I think my chances are good. I'm not as worried about getting admitted as I am about the things that could stop me from going *after* I am admitted."

Denise opened her eyes. "I appreciate you reading my story. And I am glad you liked it. But what I really came to talk about is my mother. You care about her, don't you?"

The curiosity in her voice, the way she tipped her head sideways, as if she couldn't quite believe it, took Margaret by surprise.

"Of course. Charlotte is my friend."

Denise nodded. "Yes. I realized that when you came over last night and pitched in to help so she wouldn't be embarrassed. I'm not sure Mom's ever had a friend like you before. But it made me wonder how much you know about her. I'm sure you've heard rumors."

"People gossip. Doesn't make it true."

"No. Unless it is."

Denise took a drink of her milk before going on.

"Last year Mom took an overdose of sleeping pills and spent a month in a psychiatric hospital. My deeply sensitive classmates, who never miss an opportunity to whisper about it if I'm in earshot, prefer to call it the 'loony bin.' But the point is, the rumors *are* true," she said, before going on to share a confession that Margaret found both sad and shocking.

Margaret felt a genuine pang of sympathy for all this very young and very odd duck had endured. Still, she wasn't sure that becoming privy to Denise's secrets was a good idea for either of them. After all, she barely knew the girl. But Denise didn't seem to believe in secrets. She was clear-eyed and frank, speaking plainly about things another teenage girl might strive to ignore, or hide, or try to forget. It occurred to Margaret that this might be part of what made her such a good writer.

Denise moved her fork, lining it up evenly next to the untouched cake plate.

"Mom can have a somewhat . . . casual relationship with the truth. But she swears the overdose was accidental, that she woke up and couldn't get back to sleep, and was so groggy she didn't realize she'd already taken her sleeping pills. I don't always believe what Mom says, but I do this time.

"She goes through these cycles," Denise continued, "getting incredibly excited about a project, like she did this week with her paintings. When it happens, she can stay up all night in a kind of exuberant rampage, creating chaos wherever she goes until, inevitably, she crashes. It has always been like that. I almost get it. When a story idea comes into my head, I'll sometimes stay up all night writing. The hours fly by so fast that I barely notice. The difference is, eventually I get worn out and go to bed. Not Mom. Even when she's exhausted, she can't always sleep, so the doctor gave her some pills. The doctors give her *a lot* of pills."

"Miltown?" Margaret asked.

"Among others. But I do believe the overdose was an accident. My mother may be crazy, but she's not that kind of crazy. She can be so stubborn and so incredibly contrary that sometimes I just want to—argh!" Denise clawed her hands in frustration.

"But Mom would never take her own life. She loves her kids too much, even me. And I drive her crazier than the other three put together."

Margaret smiled, remembering her own mother. Oh, the arguments they'd had! It was a complicated thing, the relationship between a mother and a nearly grown daughter. But then, as she reflected on how young Denise was, and how naive, Margaret's expression became somber. The girl might well be a literary prodigy, but when it came to her personal life, she could not yet imagine the unimaginable, that even a mother who loves you can let you down, even leave you. Who can at that age? Who should ever have to?

Denise went on with the story.

"Howard was skiing in Vermont when it happened. When I went into Mom's room, she wouldn't wake up, so I called an ambulance. After I explained the situation, the doctor said they'd probably just keep her overnight and then release her. Then Howard showed up, playing the role of concerned husband," Denise said, a bitter edge coming into her voice.

"He told them some lies about how erratic and unstable she was, and how supposedly worried he'd been. Well, if he was so worried about her, why did he run off to Vermont to ski? He wasn't there. He's never there. I was," she said, pressing her fist against her chest. "But once he showed up, the doctors wouldn't listen to me. They sent Mom to a psychiatric hospital and kept her there for a month. They only let her go after she agreed to leave New York and move here."

Denise picked up her fork and stabbed her slice of cake with a ferocity that would have qualified as attempted murder had the cake been animate, tearing into it but not taking a bite.

"Mom had no choice. Banishment to the suburbs was the price of her freedom. Theoretically, we moved to Concordia because a small town would be better for Mom's nerves and because Howard is opening the DC office, but that's an excuse. He spends most of his time in New York. If these were medieval times, he'd have shipped her off to a nunnery or locked her up in a tower. If he was king, maybe he'd just chop off her head. Thankfully, the world is somewhat more civilized now. But not much."

For all the angst that existed between them, Denise was clearly Charlotte's champion. That was wonderful. But teenage girls aren't always the best judges of what is really going on in the adult world, and Margaret was having a hard time accepting Denise's accusations at face value.

"I know you're angry. But is it possible that Howard really was trying to act in your mom's best interests? I mean, why would he do that?" Margaret asked, turning out her hands.

Denise put down her fork and coughed out a sarcastic laugh. "Why do you think? Because he wanted to get her out of the way. Because he's got a girlfriend in New York. And in Vermont. And another in Connecticut, for all I know. He's got a lot of girl-friends. Always has."

This time Margaret had no problem believing the girl. It made such sense and explained so much. Poor Charlotte.

"Does she know?"

"Sure. But there's knowing and there's *knowing*. I guess look-ing away makes it sting a little less. I do think Mom tried to make it work, at least early on. But he's despised her for years, and by now the feeling is mutual." Denise turned her fork backward and smashed the cake with the tines. "He's a bastard."

Though she understood the impulse, Margaret chided the girl gently, saying she shouldn't talk that way.

"You're right," Denise said. "I shouldn't. Anyway, he's not the bastard. I am." When Margaret frowned, Denise's eyebrows arched with surprise. "Wow. She hasn't told you much, has she?"

"About?"

"About why she married Howard? About me?"

"Charlotte told me they met on a blind date and married two weeks later, but nothing else."

Denise's lips twisted into a cynical smile. "Technically, that's true. But there's more to it. I assume she's told you about what a hell-raiser she was as a girl, right?"

Margaret nodded.

"All evidence to the contrary, I don't think Mom is quite as unconventional as she claims. I'm convinced that a lot of her behavior was an attempt to get the attention of my grandfather, who never forgave her for not being a boy. Whatever the reason, she took up with a country club caddy when she was twenty-one and ended up pregnant.

"After she refused to 'take care of the problem,'" Denise said, making air quotes with her fingers, "the problem being me, Grandfather got involved. He reached down into the firm, found an ambitious and unscrupulous but socially acceptable lower-level manager, Howard Gustafson, who was willing to marry his pregnant daughter and keep the secret in exchange for a promotion to director with the promise of more to come. An elopement was arranged, an announcement was placed in the *Times*, face was saved, and the problem was solved."

Denise squashed more crumbs.

"As far as Grandfather was concerned, things couldn't have turned out better. Though he ignores Mom, he's crazy about Howard, says he's the son he never had, a chip off the old block." She shrugged. "Makes sense. Grandfather has always had a lot going on the side too."

Margaret sat there for a moment, trying to absorb all she'd heard. It seemed unbelievable, and yet she did believe it. No girl Denise's age could make up a story like that, especially about herself.

"Denise, I'm so sorry."

Denise stared at the plate of crumbs. "Not your fault."

"Or yours," Margaret said. "I'm still sorry. But there's something I don't understand. Your mother is obviously unhappy. From what you say, your father—" Denise gave her a pointed look, and Margaret amended her statement. "Sorry. I mean, Howard is too. Why don't they just get a divorce?"

Denise laughed. "Money, of course! Howard won't ask for a divorce because he's afraid that if he did, my grandfather might oust him from the company and the will. Mom will never seek a divorce because she's afraid she'd be on the outs but that Howard would keep his job and everything that goes with it, that my grandfather would choose him over her—again."

"Over his own daughter? Would he really do that?"

Denise lowered her chin and looked directly into Margaret's eyes.

"In a heartbeat. You don't know these people like I do, Mrs. Ryan. When I was informed that the family was moving to Concordia, my grandparents said I could stay in New York and live with them to finish out my senior year. I said no for two reasons. First, because people who live with barracudas get devoured eventually. Second, somebody needed to look out for Mom. Nobody else was going to do it.

"But I can't stay here, Mrs. Ryan. I've got to get away and start living my life. If I don't . . ." Denise lifted her eyes to the ceiling, blinking. Margaret stayed silent until she collected herself.

"When you and the other Bettys left last night, I came back downstairs and borrowed Mom's copy of the book. I stayed up all night finishing it."

Margaret's eyes went wide. "What? Are you saying you read *The Feminine Mystique* in just one night? And that you haven't been to bed at all?"

Denise shrugged off Margaret's questions. "I told you, once I get interested in something, it's hard to stop. And now I see why Mom got so excited about it. Since the day she was born, her family, teachers, psychiatrists, the magazines she reads, and the whole of society have been sending the message that something is wrong with her, that the things making her unique—intelligence, stubbornness, creativity, and drive—are really neuroses that make her sick and unfeminine, even unlovable. The book made me realize we have more in common than I thought, because I've been getting those same messages all my life too. Sometimes Mom has been the messenger. She doesn't see that, but it's true."

Margaret sighed to herself. She wished she could tell Denise she was wrong. But those comments about the girl's disinterest in clothes or making friends, calling her an odd duck . . . Why did Charlotte do that?

"It doesn't make sense," Denise said. "But in a twisted way, she does it because she loves me. That feeling of always being wrong and never fitting in has caused her nothing but pain. She'd like to spare me that, even as she rails against it. Look, I'd love to be normal too, if I could. Who wouldn't? But it's no use. I'm just as much of an oddball as she is."

The flicker of Denise's smile sputtered, replaced by a worried frown.

"Did you read Friedan's interviews with those college girls who said they didn't want to talk about ideas or abstract things, only boys? And how girls who were too enthusiastic about their studies were considered peculiar and unfeminine? What about the girl who loved bacteriology but switched her major to home economics just to fit in?"

Denise set her jaw. "I felt like giving her a good slap! But at the same time, I got it. Everybody wants to fit in, don't they? That's why I have to get away," she said, a pleading edge coming into her voice. "Because if I end up at a school with those kinds of girls, the same thing could happen to me."

"But what makes you think things will be different there?" Margaret asked. "There must be vapid girls in England too. They can't all be scholars."

"Not all. But Dorothy Sayers went to Oxford. So did Vera Brittain and Elizabeth Anscombe. She's a philosopher," Denise said, responding to Margaret's blank look. "So there must be a few, don't you think?"

Denise's expression was so hopeful. Margaret felt like kissing her on the forehead.

"Yes. I'm sure you're right."

"I know it's so far away, but I can't stay here with my finger stuck in the dike forever. That's the real reason I wanted to talk to you, Mrs. Ryan." Denise tensed her body and clutched the edge of the table, leaning in to make her request.

"When I go, will you keep an eye out for Mom? Be her friend? Make sure she's okay?"

In a simple world, Margaret's answer should have been a straightforward, resounding yes. Had Denise asked anyone else, it probably would have been. But Denise couldn't appreciate the magnitude of her request—couldn't fathom the reality that no one can ever guarantee the welfare of another.

She didn't know what she was asking Margaret to do. She couldn't possibly. But . . . Charlotte was her friend. And Denise deserved her chance. Margaret took in a breath, let it out slowly.

"I'll try," she said at last. "I'll do my best."

Denise's smile of relief seemed to spread through her whole body.

"Thank you, Mrs. Ryan! You don't know what this means to me, really. Thank you so much. And I promise I'll—"

Margaret interrupted, saying it was nothing and that no thanks were necessary. But she was interrupted by the ringing telephone. Bitsy was calling. Her voice sounded strange.

"Margaret, do you have a sewing machine?"

"Not anymore. I gave it to Walt's sister when we moved. But I think Viv does."

"Can you call her and ask if I can borrow it? Also, would you be able to go to my house later and feed the pets? I won't be coming home tonight, and King isn't answering his messages. There's a key under the flowerpot."

Margaret frowned, shifting the phone to her other ear.

"Of course, but . . . what's going on? And where are you?"

CHAPTER 18

Dropping Bombs

The old green camping cooler Margaret had dug out of the garage weighed at least ten pounds all on its own. Filled to the brim with ice, it probably tipped the scales closer to forty. Margaret hefted it from the back of the station wagon with a groan.

"Let me help," Viv said. "You can't carry that monster all by yourself."

Margaret tightened her grip on the handle. "Hands off, pregnant lady. I've got this. You and Charlotte bring the other stuff. Charlotte? Don't let her carry anything heavy."

"Aye, aye, Captain."

Charlotte touched the fingers that held her cigarette lightly to her forehead before tossing the butt to the gravel and grinding it out with the toe of her alligator pump. Margaret rolled her eyes. Only Charlotte would wear high heels and a mink coat to a horse barn.

Bitsy's car was the only one in the lot. The paddocks were empty, and the horses were closed up in their stalls for the night. Margaret lugged the cooler to the last stall on the right, the only one with a light on, then set down her burden and slid the door open so the others could pass.

Viv entered first, toting a wadded armload of olive-green

canvas. Charlotte came next, tottering along in her heels with the handle of a wicker picnic basket looped over one arm and a blue wool blanket and pillow in the other. Spotting the horse, Charlotte pressed her back to the stall's rough boards, skittering sideways into the corner like a startled crab, keeping as much distance between Delilah and herself as possible. Once the others were inside, Margaret carted the cooler through the door and set it down with a thud, then slid the gate closed and reached out to envelop Bitsy in a hug.

"We brought everything you asked for," Margaret said, "plus a blanket and pillow and some food—cheese sandwiches, bananas, apples, and a can of peanuts. Sorry it's nothing more exotic. When it comes to vegetarian food, I'm a little out of my league."

"That's perfect," Bitsy said, returning Margaret's hug. "You gals are the best."

Charlotte called out from the corner: "I made a thermos of hot toddies." She pulled the mink closer around her body, shivering. "Do you want one? It's freezing in here!"

"Thanks," Bitsy said. "Maybe later."

"How's she doing?" Margaret asked, looking toward the horse.

She didn't know much about horses, but even Margaret could tell that Delilah, who was standing on a bed of sand with her hips pushed slightly back, was experiencing some pain.

"About the same," Bitsy said. "We just brought the sand in. That will help support the sole of the foot and should take some pressure off. I'm changing her diet too, putting her on grass hay that's been soaked in water to help leach out the sugars, mixed with some herbs—dandelion, rose hips, and comfrey—to increase circulation. It'll take some time to know if it's working. But we need to reduce the inflammation if we can. That's where the ice comes in."

Bitsy opened the lid of the cooler, then smiled up at them. "Thanks so much for doing this, really."

Viv dropped the armload of canvas to the ground. "I've done a lot of sewing over the years. But I have never sewn socks for a horse before. How's this supposed to work anyway?"

Bitsy squatted down next to the green pile and grabbed one of the "socks" Viv had sewn according to her instructions, using fabric from an old pup tent. It looked a bit like a concave canvas bucket, narrow at the top and wide at the bottom, with long ties sewn a few inches above the opening. In theory the canvas was waterproof. But Viv had melted down some old candles and brushed the inside with beeswax, just to make sure.

"It's a system my dad came up with," Bitsy said. "We'll put her feet in the socks, fill them with ice, and tie the top closed to keep them secure. We could use regular buckets, but the socks cool the foot more quickly and don't require as much ice. Ice is hard to come by in a barn, so less is definitely more."

Charlotte wedged herself even more deeply into the corner, looking alarmed. "What do you mean 'we'? Look, I was perfectly happy to come along and be a good scout, help support you in your hour of need and all that. But I'm not getting within ten feet of that horse. Certainly not close enough to help put on her socks."

Bitsy grinned. "Charlotte, don't tell me you're afraid of horses."

"Of course I am! You would be too if you had any sense. Just look at her! She's huge!"

"And gentle as a kitten. There's not a mean bone in her body," Bitsy said, walking to Delilah and stroking her nose. "Which, present company excepted, is a lot more than I can say about most of the people I know."

Viv moved closer and ran her hand down Delilah's neck. "She's beautiful. If Charlotte won't help you, I will. What do we need to do here?"

"Once a nurse, always a nurse. But I think it might be better if Margaret helps me," Bitsy said, glancing toward Viv's waistline. "Delilah is gentle, but she's also hurting. She won't understand what we're doing and why, so it's better not to take any chances. Margaret, do you mind?"

Margaret picked up one of the canvas socks and stepped

forward. The horse made a sputtering sound and tossed her head as she approached, but after Bitsy let her give the canvas a good sniff, murmuring comforting words in a low voice, Delilah calmed down. Bitsy leaned down and nudged Delilah's left front leg behind the knee, and the horse picked up her foot long enough for Margaret to slip the sock over her hoof. Viv scooped ice into a metal pail. Charlotte extricated herself from the corner and carried the pail across the stall to Margaret and Bitsy, who packed the ice into the sock and tied it closed. They then repeated the process with the right leg.

The whole thing took less than ten minutes. Not long after they finished, Delilah seemed to relax, shifting her body forward slightly and half closing her eyes. Bitsy patted her on the neck. "Feels better already, doesn't it, girl? Hopefully it'll ease the inflammation too."

Charlotte took a step out of the corner. "How long do you need to keep the ice on?"

"Seventy-two hours," Bitsy said. "That's what Dad always did, so that's what I'll do."

"You're not really going to sleep here, are you?" Charlotte clutched the blanket to her chest and looked around at the stall, eyes landing on a pile of hay that would presumably serve as Bitsy's bed. She wrinkled her nose. "It's cold. And it smells."

"I doubt I'll get much sleep. The ice needs to be replaced as it melts. But yes, I'll be here all night. And for as many nights as it takes until I know she's improving. As far as the smell," Bitsy said, "nothing wrong with a little good clean manure."

"Why isn't anyone here to help you?" Viv asked. "You're not the only stable hand around here, are you? What about Mrs. Graham? It's her horse. Why isn't she here?"

"She wanted to stay, but she couldn't. She's got some family problems right now. I'll be fine." Bitsy squatted down next to the picnic basket, chose one of the cheese sandwiches Margaret had packed, and took a big bite. "Thanks, Margaret. This is really good."

"It's Kraft slices on white bread with mayo. I'm not even sure it's real cheese."

"Well, it tastes good to me. I haven't eaten since breakfast."

As Bitsy ate, Margaret decided to address the elephant that was not in the room.

"Where is King?"

"Don't know. Don't care."

Bitsy's delivery was taut, clipped, and utterly un-Bitsy-like. She unwrapped another sandwich and took a bite. "We had a fight. He said some horrible things, embarrassed me in front of Mrs. Graham. I returned the favor. Then he got mad and left."

Margaret shot a brief but meaningful glance toward Viv and Charlotte, then sank down next to Bitsy, sitting cross-legged on the hay. Charlotte offered a hand to help Viv, who was a bit more unwieldy than she had been only a week before. Then she lowered herself to the ground as well, smoothed out her skirt, and rolled onto one hip, knees pressed together and angled to the right, as if riding sidesaddle.

Bitsy devoured the second sandwich, tearing off bites and gulping them down with a ferocity that wasn't necessarily linked to filling her empty stomach. When she reached for an apple, Viv dipped her head, trying to catch Bitsy's gaze.

"Do you want to talk about it?"

"No, I do not."

Bitsy bit into the apple. Charlotte sucked in an enormous breath, pressing her shoulders up to her ears, then let it out in one dramatic *whoosh*.

"Well, thank heaven for that! Is there anything as boring as listening to the transcript of somebody else's marital squabbles? Or as pointless? Besides, in situations like this, there's really only one sensible thing to do."

Charlotte reached into the basket to pull out the thermos, poured a glug of warm whiskey and lemon-scented liquid into paper cups, and passed them to the others. Bitsy tossed back her drink in one big gulp, then crushed the cup in her hands, closed her eyes, and hung her head.

Margaret reached out, resting a hand on her stooped shoulder. "This is about more than arguing with King, isn't it? Come on, Bits. What is it? You can tell us."

"Nothing. It's just . . ."

She lifted her head, looked at her friends with wide, anxious eyes. "I saw Dad treat laminitis, but I've never done it myself. What if I didn't catch everything he did? Or misunderstood it somehow? I could end up making Delilah suffer even more, and Mrs. Graham too. She's been so kind to me, and I want to help, but . . . what if I'm just making things worse by giving her false hope?"

Bitsy looked around at the three of them as if she genuinely expected answers. Margaret had none to offer. Charlotte was quiet too. But Viv leaned forward, pushed Margaret's hand away so she could place her own two hands on Bitsy's shoulders, and looked her in the eye.

"Bitsy Cobb, this is no time to start doubting yourself. You can do this."

"But what if King's right?" Bitsy asked. "What if I don't know what I'm doing?"

"Did I ever tell you about the time I had to perform a tracheotomy during the war?" Bitsy shook her head. "One of the patients started to choke and turn blue because his windpipe was blocked. We were up to our armpits in wounded that day. No doctor was available to do the trach, and time was running out. I'd seen the procedure performed but never done one myself. The thought of picking up a scalpel and cutting that man's throat was terrifying. I was so scared of making a mistake, afraid he might end up dying. But if I stood by and did nothing, I knew he *would* die. So I had no choice.

"That's where you are right now, Bitsy. If you'd done nothing, kept silent and let King have his way, Delilah would already be dead. But I know you. You couldn't stand by and let that happen any more than I could have let that poor man choke to death. We're a lot alike that way. If there's a chance we can help, that's what we do. That's what we have to do."

Bitsy's gaze had become more detached as Viv told her story—not in a way that made Margaret think she wasn't listening, but in a way that indicated she was turning inward, weighing Viv's words and measuring them against her own beliefs and experience. When Viv spoke of their common urge to help, Bitsy started to nod. Margaret did too.

"And it's not like you're in this all alone," Margaret said. "We're all behind you and will pitch in however we can."

"That's right," Viv said. "My sewing machine is at your service day or night."

"I'll get your mail and take care of your pets for as long as you need me to," Margaret said. "And if you need help icing Delilah's feet or doing anything else, say the word and I'll drive right down."

Charlotte cocked an eyebrow. "Hmm. I'm afraid I draw the line at anything that involves actually touching the horse. But if you want more ice, more blankets, more food, more liquor—especially more liquor—just whistle."

"Thank you," Bitsy said softly, a gentle smile bowing her lips. "Sorry for getting so emotional. I'm tired and a little overwhelmed. It's been a crazy day, for all kinds of reasons. But . . . you're right. I can do this. I have to. For Delilah, for Mrs. Graham, for myself . . . and for King," she said, her gentle smile now more of a grin, the kind that anticipates a comeuppance. "I'd sleep in a barn for a month for the chance to prove him wrong. The way I'm feeling today, I might end up doing it anyway. What do you say, Delilah? How would you feel about having a roommate?"

The horse sputtered and gave her head a small toss, as if to say she loved the idea. Charlotte pulled another paper cup from the basket, handing it to Bitsy. "Well, that settles it. There's only one thing that needs to be said."

Charlotte opened the thermos and filled Bitsy's cup to brimming before topping off the others and raising her own cup into the air.

"To Kingsley Cobb. And the horse he rode in on," she said, capping off her toast with a suggestion of what Kingsley could go do to himself, which included a word that Margaret had heard but rarely in her life, and never, ever from the mouth of a woman.

Bitsy gasped when Charlotte uttered the forbidden word. So did Margaret and Viv.

But then, after an instant of stunned silence, Bitsy giggled nervously. Soon they were all giggling, then laughing, at themselves and at the fact that releasing a single word into the air—and a short one at that, just four letters—should be so shocking yet *so* satisfying.

Bitsy laughed harder than anyone, until she gasped for breath and tears started to seep from the corners of her eyes. Her friends moved closer, wrapping arms around her shoulders, still laughing, knowing Bitsy was all right.

Because sometimes a woman needs a good cry. Because sometimes there truly is only one thing that needs to be said, and Charlotte had said it. When the tears and laughter subsided, Bitsy said it again, hoisting her cup into the air like a triumphant athlete with a trophy.

"And the horse he rode in on!"

* * *

Viv, who only drank a little of her toddy, drove Margaret's station wagon back to Concordia. They dropped Charlotte off first, then drove to Margaret's, arriving a little after eleven. Viv whispered good night as she crossed the street to her own house, relishing the softness of the air and the perfect silence of the night.

Tony was still awake when Viv entered the bedroom, lying in bed and reading the baseball scores from the newspaper. He looked up and smiled.

"You're late. Must have been some party. Did you have fun?"

"Not exactly. Poor Bitsy was kind of a mess. I'm glad we went because she needed cheering up. But boy, am I tired. So if you were waiting up, thinking you'd have your way with me, think again."

Tony snapped his fingers and pulled a face. "Sheesh! First the brass ordered a report on combat readiness in the Aleutian Islands that will take two months to write and never be read by anybody. Then the Mets lost to the Phillies by two runs, and now my wife refuses my bed. Talk about a disappointing day!"

Viv smiled and shook her head. "How'd I marry such a hound dog?"

"Dunno. Just lucky, I guess."

Viv opened the bureau drawers and pulled out her nightgown, thinking that Tony was right about being lucky. The gift of a good marriage to a good man shouldn't be taken for granted. She turned around, clutching the nightgown to her chest.

"Honey, can we talk before you head to the office in the morning? There's something I need to tell you."

He put his newspaper aside, frowning. "What is it? Something going on with the kids? Something about the new job?"

"Sort of. But not really. Don't worry, it's nothing bad. Promise."

"You're going to do fine," he said. "You know that, right? I know you've been out of the game awhile, but you're a terrific nurse. It'll all come back to you, you'll see."

"Let's talk in the morning, okay? I'm just too tired right now."

She went into the bathroom, removed her false eyelashes, washed off her makeup, brushed her teeth, and got undressed, fiddling with the safety pin she'd stuck into the waistband of her slacks because her zippers wouldn't close anymore.

After finally coaxing the pin to pop open, Viv shed her clothes. At the same moment she removed her bra, she heard the doorknob rattle and felt a jolt of panic, realizing she'd forgotten to lock it. She grabbed a towel, trying to cover herself before Tony could see her.

It was too late. The door was already open.

Tony's eyes traveled up and down the length of her naked body, bulging when he saw the swell in what had formerly been Vivian's waistline. For a moment, he said nothing. Then he let out the same expletive Charlotte had uttered earlier that evening, the word that had launched the Bettys into a wave of hilarity.

This time nobody laughed.

CHAPTER 19

Dearly Beloved

June 1963

June was a busy month, so the Bettys chose Anne Morrow Lindbergh's *Dearly Beloved*—which was fairly short—as their first read of the summer, and decided to hold their meeting at the soda fountain in Mayer's Drugstore.

Margaret, Viv, and Bitsy had to run an errand at Babcock's first. When they were done, they walked to Mayer's and took three stools at the counter. Bitsy ordered a strawberry shake, Margaret a cherry cola, Viv a banana split. The soda jerk went off to prepare their orders.

"Hope he makes it quick," Viv said. "I'm famished."

Bitsy pulled a box from her Babcock's shopping bag and lifted the lid, revealing a gold pen and pencil set that glimmered like jewelry against the box's black velvet lining.

"It doesn't seem very original. Maybe we should have gone with books after all?"

"She'll love it," Margaret said. "A good pen is the perfect gift for a budding writer."

"I suppose." Bitsy slipped the pen set back in the shopping bag and glanced at her watch. "Where's Charlotte? I thought she was going to meet us."

Margaret put the water she'd been sipping down on the counter. "Forgot to tell you. She called this morning and said she can't make it. Some crisis with the florist, another in the series," she said, giving her head a small but sympathetic shake.

"Sounds like this party is really getting out of hand. Howard invited his entire office, plus a bunch of clients and potential clients. Charlotte's parents are coming down too. What started out as a party for family and friends has turned into a corporate happening with all the trimmings—caterers, tents, flowers, photographers, and a dance band."

"Well, sure." Viv shrugged. "No point in throwing a gradua-tion party for your granddaughter unless you can write it off as a business expense, am I right? Did Charlotte say what we should wear? Because this is about as fancy as I get these days."

She glanced down at her pleated, yellow-checkered maternity smock. "You should see the looks I've been getting from the pa-tients. They've never seen a pregnant nurse before, and since I can't fit into my uniforms anymore, it's this topped with a lab coat. Yesterday one of the patients asked if I was the cleaning lady."

"Maybe you can sew a new maternity dress before the party," Bitsy suggested.

"And when would I do that?" Viv asked. "Between working, commuting, kids, and housework, I don't have enough time to change my mind, let alone sew. It's even busier now that school is out. The only reason I was able to come today is because Andrea took the whole crew to see a matinee of *The Nutty Professor*."

"I know what you mean," Margaret said as she picked up her water glass again. "Things were crazy enough before. The col-umn is taking more time than ever, but writing with three kids underfoot is—"

"Oh, stop," Bitsy said, tsking her tongue and rolling her eyes. "You know you love it. You both do! Kids, chaos, deadlines, sched-ules. Admit it—you two have never been happier."

Margaret smiled. She couldn't speak for Viv, of course. But yes, even on days when she felt like a piece of dough rolled too thin, she was happy, happier than she'd been in a long time.

The response to the initial column had been so positive that the magazine wanted her to write a piece in every issue, not just once a month. It was gratifying to know readers liked her work, and Margaret was delighted to put some extra money in her pocket. She was still saving up to buy furniture, but had decided to pay what she owed on Sylvia first. Doing so all but emptied her account, but marching out of the stationery store with a receipt marked "Paid in full" was something she'd never forget. That day she really did feel like a professional writer.

Thanks to the photo spread that accompanied her column debut, and Barb Fredericks's flapping tongue, word of her accomplishment had spread among the housewives of Concordia, turning her into a minor celebrity. Margaret couldn't say she didn't enjoy the attention. But it hadn't taken long to realize that attracting a certain notoriety also meant attracting a certain amount of jealousy.

The week before, while sitting on a lounge chair at the community pool and scribbling down possible ideas for columns while the kids swam, two women Margaret barely knew made a point of coming over to say how much they liked the column. It was flattering but also a little embarrassing, because once you say thank you, what else is there to say? Her embarrassment increased when they spread their towels out on chairs a few yards away and started talking about her, apparently unaware of how their voices carried.

"Will you look at her? Bringing a notebook to the pool of all places, just so everyone will know she's a writer. What a showboat."

"Well, you can't really call it writing, can you? Just silly little vignettes about the kinds of things every housewife deals with. I'm sure you or I could do it just as well, if we had the time."

"Oh, please. How much time could it possibly take to bang out one of those columns? I bet she just sits down at the typewriter and lets whatever's in her head spill out onto the keys."

Thankfully, some kids chose that moment to start playing

cannonball near the gossips, creating a splash that forced them to decamp to different chairs. If not, Margaret might have gone over and told them a thing or two about writing. But she did jot down some notes, just in case a future column might need a couple of gossipy, thinly veiled villains based on real people.

Producing two columns a month ate up nearly all of Margaret's free time. And though she wrote more quickly now than she had at first, she still spent hours on every piece. But the thing that really got to her, making her cheeks flush red, was the comment about her columns being silly, because she feared—no, she *knew*—it was true.

The world was changing, and so quickly.

June still had ten days to go, but so far that month a governor had been thwarted in his attempt to prevent two Black students from integrating the University of Alabama; a Russian cosmonaut named Valentina Tereshkova became the first woman to travel to outer space; the first human lung transplant had been performed; the president had signed the Equal Pay Act of 1963 into law; a Buddhist monk had died by self-immolation to protest the treatment of Buddhists in Vietnam, and horrifying photos of the monk engulfed in flames had appeared in newspapers across the globe; the pope had died, and the College of Cardinals had sequestered themselves to choose a new one; civil rights activist Medgar Evers had been shot and killed in his own driveway; and President Kennedy had gone on television to talk about a proposed civil rights bill, then sent the language for the bill to Congress just days later.

Earthshaking, society-altering change was happening all around, the kind of change Margaret felt was long overdue. As the three of them sat there at the counter waiting for their ice cream, she couldn't help but remember the Negro students who sat down at a segregated lunch counter only a few weeks before, and the pictures she'd seen of sneering young white men pouring ketchup, mustard, and sugar over the heads of the peaceful protesters.

What made those men so angry? Why did they feel so threatened? Margaret couldn't begin to understand it, but she didn't need to understand it to know it was wrong.

During his television address, President Kennedy had said that "the rights of every man are diminished when the rights of one man are threatened." She couldn't have agreed more. However, had she been writing the president's speech, she would have added "and woman" into the text. But it seemed things were changing on that front as well.

Charlotte didn't think the Equal Pay Act would amount to much. "Companies will find a way to worm out of it," she said. "As the daughter of a greedy, double-dealing captain of industry, you can trust me on this. There's always a loophole somewhere. Always."

Margaret wasn't as cynical as Charlotte, but she wasn't completely naive either. Change wasn't going to come overnight, but it had to start somewhere, didn't it? And when she thought about how many things were changing . . . Well, it was a pretty exciting time to be alive.

Yet, despite all that, the only thing Leonard Clement wanted from her was humorous, mostly made-up, and yes, *silly* columns. Bons mots about failed diets, dealing with a critical mother-in-law, or getting a flat on a lonely country road and trying to change a tire while wearing a dress and with two toddlers in the car.

Okay, that one *had* happened, back when they lived in Ohio. In retrospect it was pretty funny. But would it have been so terrible to throw a little *meaning* in along with the funny, to acknowledge the fact that the world, and women, were entering a new era?

Margaret didn't think so. But every time she tried to sneak something a little less trivial into her column, Clement put his red pencil to work, striking a line through the thing she wanted to say, or scrawling a few cryptic words to remind her of what she was being paid to write, hinting that the checks might stop coming if she didn't "stick to the script."

The fact that he used those exact words was discomforting

because Betty Friedan, who had worked at a few women's magazines, had said there actually was a script—that selling women on the idea of homemaking as the ultimate and only true path to feminine fulfillment also helped sell lucrative ad space for appliances, cleaning products, and foodstuffs. Until recently Margaret found Betty's theory a little hard to swallow, even conspiratorial. Then Mr. Clement called and asked her to come up with a column that involved diet gelatin.

"It should be funny, but the gelatin needs to be the hero, not the butt of the joke. We just brought D-Zerta on as an advertiser, and I think they'd eat it up."

The conversation had left a bad taste in her mouth for a day or two, a bitterness on par with that awful low-cal gelatin, making her wonder if Friedan's theory wasn't as far-fetched as she'd thought. If so, did Margaret's fluffy vignettes make her complicit in the conspiracy?

But that really did seem a little grandiose, didn't it?

After all, she was only one fairly new, fairly unimportant writer. It wasn't as if some brilliant young woman was going to read Margaret's column and decide to drop out of college because of it. And while Margaret might not appreciate his interference, at the end of the day, Clement was just doing his job. If Margaret wanted to keep *her* job, she had to play ball.

And she did want to keep her job, very much.

Margaret loved writing. And being paid to do it was the kind of validation that, strange as it sounded, money couldn't buy. Every paycheck felt like a declaration that her efforts and the workings of her mind had value. But having boundaries erected around those workings, limits on what she was permitted to say, took off some of the shine.

When the soda jerk set her banana split down on the counter, Viv dug right in. "Really, girls, what *am* I going to wear to the party? Pregnant or not, I don't want to look like a frump."

"I'll look through my old maternity dresses," Margaret said. "Bet I've got something that will do."

Margaret slipped the paper off a straw and took a sip of her soda.

"Charlotte sounded so frazzled when we talked. As if the party wasn't enough, she's also got to get Denise packed. She's taking three trunks on the ship, and two are just books."

"Must be exciting, don't you think?" Bitsy propped an elbow on the counter and rested her chin on her hand. "Sailing across the ocean? Spending the whole summer touring before she starts school? Viv, what was it like when you sailed to Europe?"

"Crowded," Viv said. "The bunks were stacked four high, and everybody was puking. I imagine accommodations on the *Queen Mary* will be a little more deluxe, but if you're prone to seasickness, it doesn't matter how nice your cabin is."

Bitsy sighed. "I envy her, being so young, having the whole world in front of her."

Viv and Margaret exchanged grins.

"Unlike you, you mean?" Viv asked. "Old, dried-up, and all of twenty-three? With your best years behind you and nothing to look forward to? And what *are* you up to these days anyway? Feels like ages since I've seen you. How're things at the barn? More importantly, how's the horse?"

"Doing great!" Bitsy beamed. "Since the condition is chronic, we still have to keep an eye on things. But I took Delilah out on the trail yesterday and she did just fine. King came to the barn last week, and even he had to admit that she looked practically good as new."

"Really." Margaret arched her eyebrows. "And was he willing to admit that you made the right call about Delilah?"

"Oh, well . . . not really. But we've been getting along better lately. Also . . ." Bitsy paused to take a sip of her milkshake, smiling a Cheshire cat smile. "I think maybe I finally do have something to look forward to."

Margaret gasped. "Oh, Bitsy! Are you? Are you really?"

Bitsy bobbed her head. "I think so. I'm ten days late and have been pretty tired. But it's still early and I don't want to jinx anything, so I'm not going to say anything to King until I've missed at least two cycles and seen the doctor. No rabbit tests for me, remember?"

"Well, don't wait too long," Viv said. "Prenatal care is important. In the meantime, get plenty of rest and watch your diet." She dug a spoon into her bowl, scooping out a chunk of banana with the ice cream, frowning thoughtfully. "You know, I'm not sure this vegetarian thing is a good idea during pregnancy. I'm worried about you getting enough protein."

"Oh, for heaven's sake!" Margaret laughed. "She's fine. Could you stop being a nurse for five minutes and congratulate her?"

"Sorry," Viv said. "Professional hazard. Congratulations, Bits. You must be thrilled."

"Oh, I am! It's such a relief. King will be over the moon once I tell him. You know, things were pretty tense between us for a while there."

Margaret sipped her soda, stunned by the magnitude of this understatement.

After the second hot toddy in the barn that night, Bitsy shared the whole story of King's terrible behavior—how he had revealed Bitsy's secret, implying she had dropped out of college due to academic failure, when nothing could have been further from the truth. Afterward, he had disappeared for days.

After leaving multiple messages with King's answering service, only to be told he wasn't picking them up, Bitsy got worried. When calls to his regular clients turned up nothing, she left Delilah in Joey's care and went to the police station. The smirking desk sergeant said husbands went off on benders all the time, but to come back if he was still missing after thirty days.

"Don't worry," he'd said. "He'll turn up. A man would have to be blind or crazy to leave a pretty filly like you alone and unprotected." Then he handed her a business card with his phone number on it. "In case you get *too* lonely."

It was awful. Bitsy felt furious, guilty, and terrified by turns. King might be a first-class jerk, but he was still her husband.

Finally, after five days, he showed up with an armload of red roses and a list of excuses, swearing it would never happen again. Bitsy had made him sleep on the couch for a while. Obviously, that hadn't lasted.

Margaret understood that forgiveness is an important part of any marriage. It wasn't easy, but sometimes you had to let things go, even if you were in the right.

Take Viv and Tony. Tony's discovery that Viv had concealed her condition from him for weeks had sparked an understandably heated argument, and her admission that the Bettys already knew made things worse. Viv had come over for coffee a couple of days later and given Margaret the play-by-play.

"How could you tell your girlfriends but not me?" he'd asked. "And when did I get to be the bad guy here, Vivian? We're a team, and you don't keep secrets from your teammates! If there are obstacles to overcome, we talk it out and make a plan—together. Just like we've always done. That's what being married means!"

Viv knew he was right and admitted it. Still, Tony wasn't quite ready to forgive her.

"Then I reminded him of the time he'd re-upped his enlistment without talking to me first," Viv told her. "That's the advantage of being married so long. I know all his weak spots."

Viv had meant that last part as a joke, but Margaret knew there was truth to it.

For good or for ill, no one knew her the way Walt did. He understood her history, hopes, fears, and vulnerabilities, the words that could cut her to the quick. He'd said some terribly cutting things in the last few months. But in all the years of their marriage, he'd never walked out the door and failed to come home, not even for one night, let alone five.

Forgiveness *was* important. But had Margaret been in Bitsy's shoes, she wasn't certain she could have forgiven King. Whether that made Bitsy the bigger person or the bigger fool wasn't for Margaret to say. If Bitsy was happy, well . . . she'd just be happy for her.

Margaret wiped her mouth with a paper napkin. "So? Who wants to talk about the book?"

Dearly Beloved was a novel centered on a wedding. Each chapter gave voice to the thoughts of a family member or wedding guest as they listened to the ceremony. Margaret hadn't enjoyed it in the way she'd enjoyed *Gift from the Sea*, but one scene had struck a chord.

Deborah, the mother of the bride, was thinking about her life and marriage, the years spent chauffeuring kids, buying groceries, making phone calls, and hosting dinner parties, when it suddenly occurred to her that it hadn't been a life at all—not *her* life, but only the scraps of other people's lives. With her daughter set to leave home, perhaps Deborah would finally have a chance to develop her own interests, become her own person.

The possibility that real life might be ahead of her was a comforting thought. But another, truly terrible thought came quickly on its heels. What if her real life was already behind her? What if she had missed her chance to be herself, to truly live?

The passage left Margaret on the verge of tears.

Deborah's thoughts, the sense of waste as she faced the impending departure of the child who had provided a veneer of purpose to her existence, reminded Margaret of the final months with her mom—the dark rooms and darker moods, the promise Margaret couldn't keep. If only her mother had lived until now, to the days of writers like Anne Morrow Lindbergh, Betty Friedan, and Mary McCarthy, when problems could be spoken of openly instead of hidden in the depths of lonely and unquiet minds, things might have been different.

Margaret felt a hand on her arm. Viv was looking at her, frowning.

"Are you okay?"

"Hmm? Oh yes. I'm fine. Just thinking about something I forgot to do." She took another sip of her soda. "Anyway, what did you think?"

Viv blinked. "You mean of the book? Oh, I loved it."

"Really? Huh. I didn't think you would."

"Well, you were wrong," Viv said, scooping equal amounts of chocolate, strawberry, and vanilla onto her spoon, assembling a perfect bite. "Loved it. Thought it was great."

Margaret was surprised. Viv *never* loved the book.

"What part did you like best?"

"The part with the wedding."

"The whole thing is the wedding. Which part—" Margaret stopped midsentence. "You didn't read it, did you?"

Viv tilted her chin, slipped the spoon daintily into her mouth.

"I did not."

Margaret tsked her tongue. Viv groaned and tossed out her hands.

"So I didn't read the book, big deal! I tried to read it. But it was just talk, talk, talk, talk, talk," Viv said, flapping her fingers together to mime a blabbing puppet. "And so depressing. So, no. I did not read the book. I did not like the book." She shrugged. "Sue me."

"Oh, please," Margaret said. "It's fine if you didn't read the book. All you had to do was say so." She turned to Bitsy. "What about you? How did you like it?"

Bitsy ducked her head and looked guilty.

"I didn't read it either."

CHAPTER 20

Absent Hosts

Although Charlotte's house was only a few blocks away, King insisted on driving to the party. Bitsy had new shoes, and he worried that walking would hurt her feet. Ever since he turned up with roses in his arms, King had been nothing but considerate and solicitous. So solicitous it sometimes set her teeth on edge, which didn't make sense. Maybe having nerves stretched like an overtuned guitar string was a symptom of early pregnancy. She'd have to ask Viv.

With so many people invited to the party, they'd had to park three blocks from the house anyway. That was all right. Bitsy's white patent leather peep-toe pumps didn't pinch at all and looked wonderful with her new dress—pink cotton linen with a scoop neck and bell sleeves, all trimmed with white bugle beads. Bitsy didn't normally spend much time thinking about clothes, but she had driven to Arlington and spent two hours sorting through the racks at Hecht's department store, trying on dress after dress until she found this perfect Goldilocks of a gown—not too loud, not too plain. Simple, elegant, and just right.

Or would have been . . .

As they were about to wade into the stream of people making their way up the sidewalk to Charlotte's open door, where two women in maid's uniforms were taking coats and directing people to the bar, King pulled a white cardboard box out from behind his back.

"This is for you."

Bitsy stared at the box, confused. It looked like something from a bakery.

"It's a corsage," he said, grinning as he opened the lid. "Here, let me pin it on for you."

Of course she let him. She couldn't very well say no, could she? King was trying so hard to make things right, too hard really. But she didn't like orchids, and she didn't want flowers.

What she wanted was an apology. Not just a blanket "I'm sorry," but a true apology, first for humiliating her in front of Mrs. Graham, then for deserting her and worrying her sick.

Bitsy had told Margaret she hadn't read *Dearly Beloved*, but that wasn't entirely true. She had read the first chapter and skimmed two more before closing the book. Like Viv, she'd found it depressing. However, not long before the Delilah incident, she had borrowed and read Margaret's copy of *Gift from the Sea*.

What a beautiful book *that* was! So lyrical and lovely, and so full of wisdom.

Morrow used different seashells as metaphors for stages of a woman's life. The chapter on the double sunrise shell—symbolizing the early marriage, the husband and wife in harmony, mirror image halves hinged at the center—spoke to her deeply. So did the oyster shell chapter, representing later years of marriage, when difficulties would create knobs on the shell surface. Bitsy found comfort in the thought that this ugly, bumpy, oyster shell stage of marriage was perfectly normal, especially when she reflected on how irritating bits of grit inside the oyster could become pearls with the fullness of time. Her marriage wasn't a mistake or failure; they were simply making pearls. What a relief!

Of course Morrow hadn't specifically mentioned pearls in that chapter, but Bitsy felt it was implied. How could one think of oysters and not think of pearls?

When King had returned home chagrined, Bitsy hadn't been thinking about oysters or pearls. She was almost too mad to think. She'd crossed her arms over her chest and stood in the doorway, told him she'd had enough. She meant it too. But he was so pathetic, saying he didn't deserve a second chance, begging for one anyway, that she started to feel sorry for him. When tears formed in his eyes, she couldn't take it anymore. She unfolded her arms and allowed him to come in the house but told him to sleep on the sofa.

King didn't protest. Over the next days, he was contrite and considerate. He made breakfast twice and did the dishes. He spent Saturday afternoon waxing her car. Every night, he kissed her lightly on the lips and carried his pillow and blanket to the couch without complaint. A week after his return, he came home with a pearl pendant on a gold chain.

Though he had neither specifically apologized for his behavior nor congratulated her for saving the horse, that pendant—the single pearl resting in a lining of midnight-blue silk—felt like a sign.

And so, remembering the oyster, she forgave him and let him back in her bed, resolving to accept as spoken the words he had never said, trusting that the hurtful grains of grit would be glossed over, layer upon layer and day by day, becoming beautiful in time.

But forgiving is hard. Despite her resolutions and attempts to gloss things over, she still wanted a real apology without excuses or amendments. She wanted him to admit that she'd been right, that she was smart, and that he knew this, knew *her*. And she wanted . . .

What else? Honestly, she didn't know. But that wasn't quite fair, was it? How could she be angry with him for failing to give her something she couldn't put a name to?

The corsage was composed of two purple blossoms tied with a lime-green bow. King pinned it to her dress.

"There!" he said, stepping back and smiling. "You're beautiful."

"Thank you."

King frowned. "You're not wearing your necklace?"

"There's already so much beading on the dress that I thought it might be too much."

"Oh. Suppose you're right. You look perfect now." He offered his arm. "Shall we?"

✳ ✳ ✳

The Gustafsons had one of the largest lots in Concordia, at least an acre, maybe more. It seemed as if every corner of it was teeming with guests. Some faces Margaret recognized, but most were unfamiliar.

She and Walt stood under a red maple tree chatting with Viv, Tony, and Edwin Babcock. Helen had been invited too, but someone had to mind the bookstore.

The men were talking baseball and Hemingway. Walt had enjoyed *The Old Man and the Sea* so much that he'd gone to Babcock's in search of more books, and he and Edwin had formed a book club of their own. They met in the VFW bar every second Thursday. So far it was just the two of them, but Edwin was trying mightily to recruit Tony. Viv was eating a mushroom stuffed with crab and pretending to listen. Margaret was taking in the scenery.

She had never been to a party like this. A chamber quartet played background music. Waiters circulated among the crowd, offering canapés from silver trays. Guests lined up to get cocktails from one of three bars—one in the house and two more outside. Honestly, it was like something out of a movie.

Margaret was glad she'd worn her best green suit, and that Viv was able to fit into the blue maternity dress Margaret loaned her. She'd have looked out of place and felt self-conscious in one of her plaid smocks. They weren't the best-dressed women at the party, but they looked like they belonged. The men were well turned out too, Walt looking handsome in his charcoal pinstripe suit, Edwin casual but dapper in a sport coat, and Tony, in his dress uniform, looking like a matinee idol in a war movie. No wonder Viv kept getting pregnant.

But Margaret's heart sank when she saw Bitsy exiting the back door of the house, holding King's arm, carrying a cocktail, and wearing what looked like . . . Was that a corsage?

She squinted to make sure.

Dear Lord, it was. An orchid corsage with a garish green ribbon that clashed with Bitsy's beautiful dress and made it look like she was running for prom queen. Judging from the look on Bitsy's face and the grin on King's, Margaret had no trouble guessing whose idea *that* had been.

With her lithe figure and long legs, Bitsy was one of those women who'd look stylish in a burlap sack. But she had been so excited about that dress, she'd dropped by Margaret's house to model it after her shopping trip in Arlington.

Oh, poor Bits. And poor King. He clearly had no clue. Well . . . men. What could you do?

Margaret waved. King saw her first and brought Bitsy over. The women exchanged hugs. The men exchanged handshakes. Tony, who seemed sincere, complimented Bitsy's corsage.

"King got it for me," she said, giving Viv and Margaret a side-eye.

Tony elbowed King. "Look at this guy, will you? Making the rest of us look bad."

King laughed and put a possessive arm around Bitsy's shoulders. For a few seconds, no one said anything—just shuffled their feet and sipped their drinks. In this setting, they weren't sure how to behave. And that was exactly the problem. They were behaving and not being, dressed in costume and playing parts but not quite sure of their lines. It didn't help that the men, apart from Walt and Edwin, didn't know each other well. Margaret finally broke the ice.

"Bitsy? What're you drinking? Looks pretty."

"Dubonnet on the rocks. Want to try it?"

Margaret took a sip. It was sweet and sour and herbal all at once. Viv, who was drinking iced tea, took a sniff when Bitsy moved the glass under her nose.

"Not for me, but it smells good. I heard somewhere that Queen Elizabeth drinks Dubonnet, so you're in good company. Hey, has anybody seen Charlotte?" Viv asked, turning her head to scan the crowd. "Or Denise?"

"Charlotte waved from the stairway when we came in," Margaret said. "She promised she'd be right down, but I haven't seen her since. Denise came by a little bit ago. She loved the pen and asked me to thank everybody."

Charlotte seemed almost too bright, too cheery, when she'd waved to them, twittering and overly alert, like a bird ready to take flight at the first hint of danger. It made Margaret nervous.

"I've got to get back to the store," Edwin said, "but I was hoping to see Denise and say goodbye. She's become a regular customer, has a fondness for George Sand and Edith Wharton and Virginia Woolf and . . . well, just about everybody." He chuckled. "I hate to miss her. Suppose she must be off somewhere with her friends."

Edwin looked around, as if trying to spot the other teenagers. But Margaret knew he wouldn't find them. Given her personality and the short duration of her residency in Concordia, Denise didn't have many friends. Besides, this party wasn't really about Denise. It was, as Viv had observed, a business expense.

Margaret saw Howard, dressed in a light gray suit, standing near the bars. He was schmoozing with clients, flirting with women, working the crowd. He hadn't said hello to any of them. Though he wasn't home much, he'd met the Bettys a couple of times. But Charlotte's friends were obviously of less interest to him than paying customers. Margaret turned toward Edwin, who was still scanning the party in hopes of spotting Denise.

"Her grandparents gave her a very nice camera for graduation," Margaret told him. "I bet she's off taking pictures."

Edwin nodded. There was another brief but awkward silence as people sipped their drinks. Then Tony—one of the nicest, most affable men Margaret had ever met—picked up the thread of dropped conversation, turning to Walt with a beaming smile.

"Viv tells me that Margaret's magazine column is a big success. You must be awfully proud," he said, tossing a wink in Margaret's direction, "having a celebrity writer in the family."

Walt twirled his highball glass, making the ice clink. "I mean, I don't think you can quite call her a celebrity. But it keeps her busy. Gives her a little pin money too. As long as it doesn't take away from the time she spends with the kids, I've got no problem with my wife having a jobette."

Margaret blinked and gave her head a shake. She surely hadn't heard that right.

"I'm sorry—what?"

Walt clinked his ice again, shifted his eyes deliberately away from hers. He spoke to Tony as if she wasn't there, as if Tony had asked the question instead of Margaret.

"Jobette. You know, a little job. A hobby that pays." He grinned. "So far, all she's been able to buy is a typewriter. So if you think about it, it's kind of a wash."

Margaret took in a short, shocked breath and held it, the way one might in the wake of an unexpected slap. And it did feel like a slap, the kind of blow the teenage Margaret had once received from her mother, sharp and cracking, an intentional humiliation. Margaret had never breached her private promise to never slap her own children. But oh, how powerful was the urge to strike her husband at that moment!

The fact that she couldn't because they were at a party only served to make her angrier. He had belittled her in a setting that made it impossible for her to respond.

She could only bite her tongue and seethe.

Viv, who was standing on the opposite side of the circle, gazed at Margaret with a look that suggested she knew exactly what her friend was thinking. Viv clapped her hands and said, "On second thought, I think I'd like to try a Dubonnet after all. Margaret, come help me. You too, Bitsy." She slipped her arm around Bitsy's waist.

"It's so warm. You'd better take off that beautiful corsage and put it in some water before it wilts. Then we can hit the ladies' room and look for Charlotte. She must be around here somewhere."

✳ ✳ ✳

Charlotte was still upstairs.

She'd been on the telephone extension in her bedroom, talking to Lawrence Ahlgren in soft whispers and low laughter, pretending not to understand the context of his leading questions, flirting for all she was worth.

Ahlgren was coming to town in a few weeks. The Washington Gallery of Modern Art would be mounting a new exhibit that winter, and the curator wanted to discuss which of his pieces to include. Lawrence proposed he and Charlotte meet for dinner and a night on the town after the meeting. Charlotte countered with lunch, which seemed safer. Then, as if the idea had just come to her, she suggested this might be an ideal opportunity for him to introduce her to the curator, and possibly recommend her work.

The negotiations were reaching a critical stage when Charlotte's mother, Patricia, a white-haired, rail-thin woman in her midsixties, whom no one ever dared to refer to as Pat, opened the door and gave her daughter a hard stare.

"Hang up the phone."

Charlotte did.

Her assurances that Ahlgren was simply a friend, not quite true, and that nothing had happened between them, which was true, held no sway with her mother.

"We're not fools, Charlotte. Your father knows what's going

on, and so do I. We've seen the photographs of you and this artist"—Patricia wrinkled her nose, as if encountering a bad smell—"this *bohemian*, during your last trip to the city."

"Photographs? Daddy had me followed? How could he! And how could you allow it?" Charlotte squared her shoulders. "This is a gross invasion of my—"

"Don't flare your nostrils. It makes you look like a camel. And don't strike attitudes—you're making yourself ridiculous. We had no choice, Charlotte. You brought this on yourself, as you always have."

"Mother, nothing is going on between me and Lawrence Ahlgren."

"The issue is how things look. Your father wants his position made clear. He will not stand idly by and allow you to embarrass yourself or the family. Neither will I."

"Daddy's worried that *my* behavior will stain the family honor?" Charlotte coughed out a laugh as she reached to the nightstand for her cigarettes. "Well, that's rich. Howard has at least two mistresses that I know of and has banged every cocktail waitress on the Eastern Seaboard. If Dad is worried about infidelities, maybe he should talk to my husband. Or perhaps look in the mirror? No one would know better than you. Am I right, Mother?"

Charlotte flicked open a silver lighter and ignited her cigarette. If her words stung, Patricia gave no sign of it.

"It's a man's world, Charlotte. If you could simply learn to accept that, as I have, perhaps you would finally become content to enjoy the highly privileged position you occupy within it."

Charlotte inhaled. "Oh, please."

Patricia inhaled too, then exhaled slowly, signaling the end of her patience.

"Whatever ill feelings you may harbor against your husband, justified or not, your father likes him. Howard is poised to take over the firm when the time comes. But make no mistake, Charlotte. If you embarrass the family with a scandal or divorce, you will lose everything—your reputation, your money, and your children. I doubt a judge will see someone with your history of instability as a fit mother."

"What?" Charlotte said in a voice that was more like a gasp. "You can't be serious. You'd take Howard's side over mine in a custody battle? What kind of parents are you?"

"The kind who will do what they must to keep their reckless, disappointing daughter from destroying the family."

Patricia crossed the room, passing so closely that Charlotte thought she intended to touch her. Instead, she picked Charlotte's martini up off the nightstand and drained the glass, then pulled a tissue from a box that sat on the dressing table.

"Wipe off that lipstick. That shade is terrible with your coloring."

Charlotte crumpled the tissue into her fist. Patricia turned to face her daughter once more before making her exit.

"Charlotte, you have guests. Pull yourself together and come downstairs, or people will start to talk. And where is Denise? This is her party, after all."

CHAPTER 21

Click

Denise was outside, avoiding people in general and her grandparents in particular.

It was bad enough that she'd have to drive to New York with them in the morning, then stay overnight in their apartment before boarding the *Queen Mary*. She saw no point in letting them parade her around as the supposed "guest of honor" at a party with a guest list primarily composed of people she barely knew.

Still, this party had some upsides, beginning with the gifts.

Nearly all those strangers had brought cards filled with cash. Denise didn't know what it added up to, but it was certainly enough to keep her in books for a good while. And her mother's friends had thrown in to get her that pen set. She had plenty of pens already, but getting one from Margaret and the Bettys felt like an affirmation, a vote of confidence that she really *would* become a writer. However, surprisingly, the best gift of all had come from her grandparents—an Olympus PEN-F camera and case plus two dozen rolls of film.

The camera had no end of features. Though she planned to read the manual and learn how to use them during her voyage, she couldn't resist trying it out right away. She'd spent the last hour slinking around the party, making herself as unobtrusive as possible in order to get candid shots of the guests. Since Denise was already skilled at making herself invisible, this wasn't too difficult.

Standing half-hidden behind the corner of the tent where lunch would be served, she'd already snapped shots of all the Bettys—Mrs. Buschetti eating a stuffed mushroom, pretty Mrs. Cobb wearing a hideous orchid corsage, and Mrs. Ryan staring at her husband with an expression Denise couldn't quite decipher.

She went into the house after that, hung around the fringes of the bar, and took pictures of people swilling too many cocktails, including her grandmother. Leaving the flash off, Denise had clicked a button on the camera just as Patricia—glassy-eyed and with an empty martini glass in hand—was sliding two cocktail onions off a toothpick with bared teeth. Denise couldn't wait to get that one developed. A picture like that might come in handy someday. She smiled to herself. This wasn't turning out to be such a bad day after all.

And it had been nice having all her siblings together under one roof for the weekend. Howard Jr.—Howie—was doing a summer semester at military school but had gotten a three-day leave to come to the party.

Mom had squealed with joy when Howie came through the door. She had hugged him tight for at least a minute before releasing him and rubbing the stubble of his crew cut, saying he was too skinny.

They'd gone on a trail ride in Rock Creek Park the next day, Bitsy having arranged everything. Then they ordered pizzas—Howie ate one all by himself—and had a picnic in their pajamas, the five of them sitting on Charlotte's bed and playing Stratego, just like a normal happy family. Charlotte was happiest of all, relaxed and laughing, sipping a Coke instead of a cocktail. Had life at home always been like that, Denise might have thought twice about England.

Of course, when Howard Sr. showed up, the atmosphere chilled considerably. Howie was in the attic above the garage right now, smoking pot and avoiding him. Denise understood, but she hoped he'd come down long enough so they could say goodbye. Strange to think she'd miss him—they'd always butted heads as kids—but she knew she would. And she would really miss Andrew and Laura.

They'd probably miss her too, but right now they were just excited about spending the rest of the summer swimming, boating, doing archery, and having fireside sing-alongs at a lakeside camp in Connecticut. It was their third year of going to camp, so Denise wasn't worried about them getting homesick.

Having them away from home would be much harder on her mother.

Had Mrs. Ryan not promised to keep an eye on her mother, Denise probably would have turned down the Oxford admission. Mrs. Ryan was such a kind woman, steady and intelligent. And Denise knew she cared about her mother; all the Bettys did. And all of them would watch out for her. Even so, this would be a hard adjustment, a lonely season.

Denise made a decision. Instead of spending her graduation cash on books, she would use it to telephone her mother once a month. No, once a *week*. Phoning internationally was terribly expensive, but they'd keep it short. They'd had their moments, and Denise knew they always would. They were just too different and, in some ways, too alike. Still, Denise knew her mother would be happy to hear her voice.

And then another, far more surprising thought came to her . . . She would be happy to hear her mother's voice too. She was going to miss her mother.

Denise pressed her hand against her mouth. In a week she would disembark at Cherbourg to spend a few weeks touring the Continent before settling into her Oxford rooms before the term began. An entire ocean would separate her from her mother. Such a long way. But . . . she could take a piece of her mother with her, couldn't she? A photograph?

Yes! She would take her mother's picture, frame it, and leave it near her bedside.

Denise searched the crowd for that familiar redhead, listened for that smoky laugh. Failing to find her, Denise took a quick loop through the house, pretending she didn't hear her grandfather saying there was someone he wanted her to meet. She slipped out the back door, twisting sideways to avoid a collision with a waiter, and padded across the grass to the far corner of the house. Perhaps Charlotte had snuck out too, escaped the crush to smoke a cigarette in peace and quiet.

The side yard was concealed by fencing. Charlotte had ignored Concordia's rules and installed the landscaping she'd wanted—a row of large and lush camellia bushes. If a person was trying to hide out, this would be the spot—the only place in the yard that offered privacy and a certain, albeit imperfect, amount of camouflage.

Approaching the hedge, Denise spotted a figure in the bushes. But it was another woman, not her mother.

And she wasn't alone.

Denise stopped short, took two slow steps to the right and the leafy cover of the camellias, doing what she did so naturally and so well, becoming invisible, observing keenly.

The woman had her head tilted back and her eyes closed. Howard's face was lowered into her décolletage, his features impossible to see. He raised her skirt to her waist, stroked her thighs, coaxed them apart, slipped his hand into the cleft.

Howard lifted his head. Denise lifted her camera. The woman moaned.

Click.

CHAPTER 22

Argument Interrupted

E ven though Margaret hated confrontations, everyone has their breaking point—and she had reached hers. Still, she couldn't pick a fight with her husband in public, especially not at a party, so she had no choice but to swallow her anger until they left.

As she and Walt were making their exit, Margaret stopped to thank Charlotte, who had finally come downstairs looking pale. When she'd said goodbye to Denise, Denise had gripped her hand so tightly that Margaret's wedding ring pressed painfully into the flesh of her fingers.

"You'll keep your promise?" Denise asked, her eyes dark and serious.

"I will. Don't worry. Everything will be fine."

Though Margaret still harbored some anxiety about making herself responsible for Charlotte, she was pleased to see that Denise recognized she would miss her mother. Some daughters didn't figure that out until it was too late. However, once she and Walt got into the car, Margaret's thoughts immediately turned to other matters. The moment Walt turned over the ignition, she let loose.

"What the hell was that?"

"What was what?"

"Don't you dare play innocent with me, Walter Ryan. You know what! That snarky comment about my 'jobette.' Look, I realize that nobody's going to nominate me for a Pulitzer, but I work very hard on my columns, and you know that. But you made it sound as if I'd taken up some cute little hobby, like doubles tennis or painting teacups!"

Walt rolled his eyes. "Oh, come on, Margaret. You know I didn't mean it that way. I was teasing, that's all. Why are you being so touchy? Can't you take a joke?"

"It wasn't funny. And you *weren't* joking."

During the drive, Walt refused to apologize or back off his claim that it was simply a joke. Arriving home, they sat in the driveway, snapping and snarling at one another, tossing barbs and dodging them. At some point, the argument inexplicably veered in a different direction, with Walt complaining about how ridiculous she was making him look and how ungrateful she supposedly was. "Whatever I do, no matter how hard I try, it's never enough for you!"—as if he were the injured party instead of her.

As Margaret was getting ready to storm into the house, she heard a knock on the car window. She looked and saw Beth standing there, staring at her parents through the glass.

How long had she been there? How much had she heard? Probably too much, judging from the somber look on her face. Margaret rolled down the window.

"You have to stop fighting and come inside," Beth said.

Margaret's face colored and she exchanged a glance with Walt, who frowned and licked his lips before trying to explain.

"We weren't fighting, honey. We were just—"

"Having a discussion," Margaret said. "You know, sometimes parents—"

Beth shook her head. "I don't care. You need to come inside. Grandma is on the phone, calling long-distance from Ohio. She told me to come out here and get you." Beth looked past Margaret, speaking directly to Walt. "Something happened."

✳ ✳ ✳

It was Walt's father, Jerry.

He'd collapsed while mowing the lawn and had been rushed to the hospital by ambulance. Walt held the phone out so Margaret could also hear the conversation with his mother, Bernice. The doctors were still conferring but thought it was a stroke.

"It looks bad," Bernice said, her voice hoarse. "Please come, won't you, Wally? I just . . . I don't know what to do."

"I'll come, Mom. Just as quick as I can. You just hang on, okay? Tell Dad to hang on too."

"I will. But hurry, son. Please, hurry."

Walt hung up the phone. The argument was forgotten.

While Walt called his boss at home to explain the situation, Margaret started ironing extra shirts and packing Walt's bag. Then they switched places, Walt taking over the packing and Margaret getting on the phone to Northwest Orient Airlines to check on flights between DC and Cleveland. Then she called to find out about train timetables. In either case, Walt wouldn't be able to leave until the morning, and the tickets were expensive. Margaret said they could use what was left of her savings to pay for a ticket, but Walt shook his head.

"Thanks. But if I can't leave until tomorrow, it makes more sense to drive. If I leave now and drive through the night, I'll be there by morning."

"Do you want us to come with you?" Margaret asked.

He furrowed his brow and made his lips into a line, considering her question. "Probably better for me to go alone. I don't know what's going to happen, and by the time we get the kids ready—"

"No, you're right," she said, lifting a hand to indicate he didn't need to explain. "You finish packing. I'll make sandwiches and a thermos of coffee for you to take along."

He nodded and turned as if to leave, but stopped short.

"Maggie? What I said at the party . . . I didn't mean to—"

"It's not important now," she said, shaking her head. "Just go. It's all right, really it is."

He reached for her hand. "I love you, Maggie."

"I know," she said, and she did. "I love you too."

＊ ＊ ＊

Walt called Margaret from a hospital pay phone to let her know he'd arrived.

"I'm not sure if he even knows I'm here," Walt said.

"He knows," Margaret told him, though she wasn't sure either.

Jerry hung on for two more days but never regained consciousness. Walt called again to let Margaret know what happened. They discussed the possibility of Margaret and the children driving to Ohio for the funeral but decided it would be too distressing for the kids. According to Walt, his mother was an emotional basket case, and his sisters were squabbling, which was nothing new.

"I miss you all, but I think it'll be easier for everybody if you stay home. I'll need another week to sort things out, and honestly, I've got my hands full."

He sounded tired and a little detached, almost numb. Margaret was worried about him. She felt guilty about not being there to support him and her mother-in-law but agreed this was probably the wisest course of action.

Naturally, the children were sad about their grandfather's death. Beth, who had spent more time with Jerry than the others and was one of the few people who could make him laugh, was upset about missing the funeral. Margaret suggested they plant some rosebushes in his honor—raising roses had been Jerry's only hobby—and that seemed to satisfy her.

Margaret had never had an especially affectionate relationship with her father-in-law—Jerry was gruff and often critical, and drank more than was good for him—but his sudden death was a reminder of how fragile life can be, and how brief.

For the last few months, writing the column had taken much of Margaret's time and focus. How could it not? Juggling deadlines and domestic duties wasn't easy, and trying to write with three boisterous, often bickering children in the house would try the patience of a saint—and Margaret wasn't a saint.

Still, before she knew it, the kids would go out on their own, flying the nest, just like Denise had done. Margaret wanted to savor this summer with her children, to create memories they would look back on fondly. She wanted to spend her days taking them to the pool, the park, and the library, playing board games and baking cookies, sitting on a lawn chair at dusk to watch them catch fireflies, or helping them chase down the ice cream truck, not hollering at them to shush because Mommy needed to work. Yet she *did* need to work. Mr. Clement and her deadlines didn't care if it was summer.

And so, she started doing something she truly despised: getting up very, *very* early.

When the alarm jangled at four thirty, she'd throw on some clothes, stumble groggily into the kitchen, brew some coffee, get Sylvia out of the closet, then sit down to write. Most days she'd get in three or four hours of writing before the kids wandered in, which was great.

Much as she despised having to rise so early to meet her deadlines, she knew she really couldn't complain. At least she didn't have to show up at an office.

Honestly, she didn't know how Viv did it, especially being pregnant and having such a long commute. Viv never complained. That was partly because she loved nursing so much, but also because, as Viv told her when she brought some of her kids over to play, she and Margaret really had no right to.

"You and I work because we want to, because we love it. But so many of the moms I meet at the clinic work jobs they hate because they have to. They'd give anything to have what we have, the choice to stay home and take care of their kids. If they don't work, those kids don't eat. Being a woman is never easy, but . . ." She took a breath and let it out with a sputter.

"Since I started at the clinic, I've thought a lot about Betty Friedan. Her book sparked a lot of conversations, but it's really only directed to people like us, isn't it? Women with choices. What if, in addition to all those Vassar coeds and suburban housewives, Betty had interviewed some of my patients? They're widows, divorcées, single women, married women whose husbands don't earn enough to pay the rent, women who never had a shot at college or didn't finish high school. They might look different than us, but they want the same things. It bothers me that Betty left them out of the conversation. I mean, don't they deserve choices too?"

Viv had a point. Dawn patrol or not, Margaret had no right to complain.

After a bit of nose-holding, she'd figured out a way to work diet gelatin into a column after all. Margaret still thought the piece was a ridiculous bit of fluff, but Clement was thrilled, and it was nice to finally be in his good graces. Though it felt a little odd to say so under the circumstances, all in all, things were going well.

She missed Walt but had decided that might be a good thing. Maybe the old adage about absence making the heart grow fonder was true. He seemed to be missing her too, because even though calling long-distance was expensive, he phoned nightly. The conversations weren't very long or deep; the phone was located in the foyer, and Bernice could overhear their calls. But it was good to hear his voice and know he was thinking of her, and Margaret was happy when, a week after the funeral, he said he was coming home.

"I've got to take Mom to run errands, then mow the lawn and do some chores before I go. Probably won't arrive until the wee hours, but definitely before breakfast."

"And I'll make a good one—eggs, bacon, the works. Then you

can go back to bed and catch up on your sleep. I'll tell the kids to keep quiet."

"Bacon and eggs sound great, but I need to go to the office tomorrow."

"After driving all that way? Oh, Walt, you must be joking."

"Wish I was. The boss called day before yesterday, ostensibly to offer his condolences but mostly to let me know he wants me back at my desk pronto." He lowered his voice, as if trying to make sure his mother couldn't hear him. "And since I may need to come back in a few weeks, I'd better get on his good side."

"You're going back?"

"I'm not sure yet, but probably. Mom is . . ." He sighed. "She's lost without Dad, and the girls are no help. I was hoping we'd be able to take the kids to Virginia Beach this summer, but it looks like I'll need to use what's left of my time off to come back here. Sorry, Maggie."

"It's okay. If she needs you, she does. Maybe we'll all go, take a vacation to Ohio."

"Doing yard work and teaching Mom how to light the pilot on the furnace doesn't sound like much of a vacation to me. But we'll see. Anyway, I'm just glad to be heading home. How are the kids? And you?"

"Everybody's fine."

"Everybody?" he asked, a smile coming into his voice. "Even Charlotte?"

"Yes," she said, stretching out the word to let him know she got the joke. "Even Charlotte. In fact, I got a note from Denise today, thanking the Bettys for the pen and saying she'd arrived in Paris. I wrote right back, told her that Charlotte's doing just great."

"Thank heaven for that," he said. "I hadn't been able to sleep for worrying."

Margaret didn't blame him for teasing her, but no one, not even Walt, could fully understand how seriously she'd taken her promise.

Thankfully, her worries seemed to be in vain.

Though the kids were keeping her busy, Margaret was still popping over to Charlotte's place when she had time, then calling her when she didn't. She phoned almost every day, and sometimes twice a day—so often that Charlotte told her to knock it off.

"Enough already! How am I supposed to get any painting done with you calling every five minutes? I'm fine," she said, laughing. "Really I am."

And she did seem fine. Better than fine.

If only Margaret could get herself to truly believe that and quit waiting for the other shoe to drop, maybe she'd quit having the dream.

* * *

It was the same every night.

Margaret walked through the front door of the house, the little bungalow on Cedar Street where she'd grown up, carrying a satchel. Usually it was stuffed with books, but sometimes it was food—apples, oranges, or loaves of bread. Once it was filled with baby bottles, another time with kittens. Who could say why?

In the dream, Margaret always set the satchel down on the worn brown sofa that sat near the window, then headed toward the kitchen. The house was strangely quiet. The only sound was the *tick-tick-tick* of a jade-green wall clock and the echo of her footsteps as she walked down the hall and into the empty kitchen.

The kitchen cabinets were pink. Shortly before the war, Margaret's mother had seen an article with cupboards just that shade in *Better Homes and Gardens*. She took the magazine to the hardware store and supervised the color matching personally, then brought the paint home and did the job herself. Everything looked the same as it always had, and yet not the same.

At first Margaret couldn't put her finger on what was different. Then it came to her.

Everything was clean.

The counters were clear of clutter, the sink devoid of dishes, the floor swept and mopped. Before and during the war, even when Mom worked long hours turning out airplane parts, it had always looked like that, tidy and organized. After the war, things changed. The kitchen, the house, the woman who had been told to turn in her tools and put on her apron, started looking unkempt and uncared for, sad.

Now, in Margaret's dream, everything was as bright as a new penny. It was oddly disquieting. Margaret called for her mother but received no reply. Where could she be?

The clock kept ticking. Margaret was hungry. She opened the refrigerator. The blast of cold air made her shiver. It, too, was clean and sparkling.

The gleaming metal racks and glass shelves were stacked with lidded glass containers of food—casseroles, soup, a meat loaf, a chicken. Each container had a note taped to the front with heating instructions and a day of the week, meals for the next seven days. It was the kind of thing the woman who once had been her mother—the woman she'd been before the war ended—might have done prior to leaving for a journey, making sure her family could manage without her once she left.

A tight, cold ball of fear lodged in Margaret's middle. Still shivering, she closed the door.

She walked through the pantry, living room, and dining room, then opened the door to the cellar, searching for her mother. Margaret approached the stairwell. The ticking clock became louder and faster, echoing the rising, rapid pulse of her heart.

As she climbed the stairs, dread fell upon her like a heavy blanket, suffocatingly close. She gripped the banister the way a mountain climber grips the rope that could save her life or cause her to lose it, making the slow, careful, painful ascent to the closed door of her parents' bedroom.

She pressed her ear against the dark wood, hoping to detect some sound from within, fear spreading through her like spilled ink. She wished the door would open, that her father would come home so she wouldn't have to be the one to turn the knob and see what was on the other side.

But her father was gone, and it was her responsibility. She had promised.

Margaret stretched trembling fingers to the doorknob, turned it, and cried out.

✳ ✳ ✳

"Maggie, wake up! Do you hear me? Wake up, sweetheart. It was only a dream, okay? Just a dream. You're safe now. I've got you."

Margaret was still gasping, sobbing. She always woke up before the door opened. But it was still terrifying, more frightening now than on the day it had actually happened.

Back then, a strange unsettled feeling had come over Margaret when she saw the contents of the refrigerator and the bizarre preparations her mother had made before taking her own life—as if the only thing they might miss later would be the absence of hot meals she would have provided. Margaret had not known what she would find when she opened the door that day. Now, she did.

It was a sight a seventeen-year-old girl could never unsee— she who had blithely promised her father to keep an eye on her mother while he was away was blissfully ignorant of what could happen if she failed in her duty. Though she had somehow learned to live with the guilt and fear, it would never leave her entirely. In her dreams it was even worse because now she knew what awaited her on the other side of the door.

"Come here," Walt said.

The room was dark. Walt was sitting on the edge of the bed and his suitcase was sitting on the floor, as if he'd only just come in. He pulled Margaret toward him, scooting so his back rested against the headboard, scooping her up and into his lap as if she'd been Beth or Suzy, holding her close. When her body quit shaking and her tears subsided, he kissed the top of her head. "Better?"

Margaret nodded, pressing her cheek against his chest.

"You take on too much, Maggie. You can't take care of everybody. You know that, don't you? But I do admire you for trying."

Margaret looked up at him. He kissed her again, on the lips this time, but lightly.

"Listen," he said, then cleared his throat, frowning. "About the party, and how I made fun of your writing. It's really been bothering me ever since I left, and—"

Margaret covered his mouth with her fingertips. "Not now. Not tonight."

He nodded. "Sorry. It's late. You're tired."

Looking into his eyes, Margaret shook her head and started to undo his shirt buttons.

"I'm not tired," she whispered, then pulled him down on the bed with her, wrapping her arms around his neck and melting into him like warm wax, thinking how much she missed this and how much, how very much, she missed him.

CHAPTER 23

The Way Things Are

July 1963

When the first light of dawn filtered through the bedroom curtains, Margaret slipped out from under the covers and crept down to the kitchen to cook Walt's breakfast—eggs, bacon, toast, orange juice, and coffee. She even made hash browns.

Walt walked in about forty minutes later, wearing a suit, tie, and surprised expression.

"Wow, Maggie! What got into you?"

"Nothing," she said, smiling as she took bacon slices from the pan and set them on a paper towel. "I promised you a proper homecoming breakfast, remember?"

He crossed the kitchen to stand next to her, took the tongs from her hand, and put his hands on her waist. Then he turned her body so they were facing one another.

"Not that. *That*," he said, tilting his head in the general direction of their bedroom. "You were a tiger last night. Seriously, what got into you?"

"Dunno," she said, twining her arms around his neck. "Guess I just missed you."

"Yeah? Maybe I should go out of town more often."

"Please don't. Not unless you have to." He bent his head as

if to kiss her. "Your eggs are getting cold," she reminded him. "Don't worry, I'll be here when you get home."

While Margaret filled their plates, Walt put the silverware on the table and poured the coffee. He pulled out her chair before she took her seat and then pushed it back in, as if they were kids on a prom date instead of an old married couple with a mortgage and three kids.

Margaret almost asked what had gotten into *him*, but the expression on Walt's face when he sat down told her the moment for teasing had passed. Though it seemed he didn't quite know how to begin, Walt clearly had things on his mind.

"My dad . . ."

Margaret locked her eyes on his and bobbed her head so he'd know she was listening. Instead of going on, he took a breath and swallowed hard, blinking back tears. She reached across the table to touch his hand.

"Such a shock," she said. "Jerry was still so young, not even sixty. You've been so busy helping Bernice that it's probably only now sinking in. But he was a good man, and I know he—"

"That's not true," Walt said, shaking off the threat of tears as he interrupted her. "My father was not a good man. You know it, and so do I. He was an angry, bitter, controlling, critical, miserable man who did his damnedest to make everyone around him miserable too."

Walt's lips pressed in a grim line. "And I'm turning out to be just like him."

"That's not true! Honey, you are *nothing* like your father—"

"Oh yes I am. Maybe not a carbon copy, but heading in that direction. Ironic, isn't it? Part of the reason I lied about my age and signed up to get shot at was because I wanted to get away from him. I figured the Germans couldn't be worse than my old man. Turned out I was wrong about that, but still . . . I promised myself I'd be nothing like him. Yet here I am."

He picked up his coffee cup. Margaret watched him drink, wishing she knew how to make him feel better, wishing she could truthfully say she had absolutely no idea what he was talking about. Walt wasn't *just* like his father. But he wasn't the same optimistic, buoyant man she had married either.

He put down his cup, looking at her.

"I really missed you, Maggie. But I'm kind of glad you didn't come to Ohio. Driving alone gave me time to think, to figure out where I went wrong and if there's a way to change direction before it's too late. To start with, I think I need to cut back on the booze. Dad got meaner when he drank too much, and I think it's doing the same thing to me."

Margaret couldn't say she hadn't been concerned about how much Walt had been drinking lately and how it impacted his mood. But it was hard to see him like this, sad and self-recriminating. She tightened her hold on his hand, hoping he felt love in her grasp.

"You're not mean, Walt. Never mean. More like . . . morose."

He smiled wryly, as if to say he appreciated the nuance but wasn't quite buying it.

"Well, maybe that's the difference between bourbon and beer. I still want to cut back. A couple help me relax. A six-pack makes me . . ." He lifted his eyebrows. "What was the word?"

She returned his smile. "Morose."

"Right. Also, I want to stop thinking about the stuff I don't have and be more grateful for what I do have, including three terrific kids and a smart, talented, gorgeous wife. I mean it," he said. "I love you, Maggie."

Margaret's eyes welled, not because Walt never said he loved her, but because it had been a long time since he'd said it quite like that.

"There's something else, Margaret. What I said that day at the party—"

"Oh, Walt." She swept her hand in the air as if to bat away his words. "That was almost two weeks ago. It's water under the bridge. Honestly. You don't need to say anything more."

"Yes, I do. Because I acted like an absolute jerk. And because

I knew *exactly* what I was doing. I wanted to bring you down a notch, embarrass you."

Though Walt's intentions that day came as no surprise, hearing him admit to them did.

"But why would you do that to me? Especially in front of other people?"

"Because I was jealous," he said. "I know how stupid it sounds, but I was. I'm sorry, Margaret. You didn't deserve that. I know how much the column means to you."

Walt sighed the kind of sigh that people do when they look in the mirror and are disappointed by the sight of the person who looks back. Margaret's eyes went wide.

"Jealous? Honey, that's crazy! Yes, I love writing, but nothing like the way I love you. Or the kids. You know that, don't you?"

"Not that kind of jealous," he explained. "'Jealous that you're so special, that you found a way to get paid for doing something you love and are so good at. As opposed to me, a mediocre man stuck in a mediocre job."

She stared at him. Mediocre? He didn't really believe that, did he? He couldn't.

In spite of everything, Walt was the love of her life. Didn't he know that? Margaret pressed her lips together, shaking her head inwardly. On the one hand, she wanted to wrap him in her arms and tell him he was her hero. On the other hand, she wanted to give him a good shake, slap some sense into him.

Walt was a lot of things, but mediocre was not one of them.

"Don't say that, Walter Ryan. Don't you ever say that. I had other offers. Don't forget. But I picked you. It was the best decision I ever made. You're the glue that holds this family together. Without you, we wouldn't *be* a family. You work so hard, taking care of everybody, making sure we have everything we need— food, clothes, Beth's braces, and our dream house."

"That's why I do it," he said. "Because I want you and the kids to have the things you want, the life you deserve. But there's nothing special about that. It's a man's responsibility to provide. If that means doing a job he hates . . . so be it."

Margaret felt pulled up short. "But . . . you don't really hate your job, do you?"

"Are you kidding?" He huffed out a laugh. "Of course I do. Anybody would. I spend my life filling in forms, calculating debits and credits. Now and again, I have a meeting with a client or some flunky from the IRS. Most of those guys are dull as dishwater, yet it's still the highlight of my week. The rest of the time, it's just me and the paperwork."

He took a bite of his bacon, then picked up his fork and started in on the eggs.

"The only good thing about my job is the paycheck. But what can you do?" he asked, shrugging before taking a sip of his coffee.

"Somebody has to pay the bills, Maggie. That's just how the world is."

✳ ✳ ✳

After Walt left for the office, Margaret cleared the table and washed the dishes, thinking about their conversation.

When she first met Walt, the handsome, bright-eyed young man who skipped meals so he could buy himself a guitar, the spark between them had been undeniable. Three dates in, she'd found herself writing *Mrs. Walter Ryan* in the margins of her notebook instead of listening to a sociology lecture, just to see how her future signature might look.

And yet despite their mutual attraction, she had concerns. Walt was good-looking, fun-loving, kind, and intelligent—the only man she knew who read books for pleasure. But he also seemed a little aimless, which worried her.

Many girls on campus set out to bag themselves a future doctor, lawyer, or banker in the way big-game hunters stalked their prey: stealthily and with a great deal of cunning. But that wasn't

Margaret's style. What did it matter what neighborhood she lived in or how nice a car she drove if she didn't love her husband? Love was important.

But love couldn't be the only criteria when choosing a mate. A girl needed to be practical, choosing a man of character who would be faithful, a good provider whom she and their future children could depend on. Despite her growing feelings for him, Margaret wasn't completely convinced Walt was that kind of man. Not only did he seem uncertain about his future profession; he couldn't even settle on a major.

When Eugene Buckman, a business major whom she'd been dating, surprised her with a proposal, Margaret said she needed time to think about it. Walt heard about it somehow. He tracked her down in the library, declared his love, and told her he'd decided to study accounting. "I know I haven't always been the most serious guy, but I'm serious about you. We might never be rich, but I *can* take care of you, Maggie. I swear I can. Just give me a little time to prove myself."

The following year they were married.

The early years hadn't been easy, but Walt had made good on his promise. Leaving Ohio had been hard. After all, they'd spent their whole lives there. But the salary for the new job was too good to pass up. Finally, they would be able to buy a house! And not just any house: a beautiful new house in Concordia with sidewalks, playgrounds, and a pool, near lots of families in the same stage of life as them.

After so many years of scrimping and saving, they were living the American dream. Until today Margaret hadn't fully appreciated just how expensive that dream was, or that the cost was measured in more than mere currency.

She'd always known Walt wasn't crazy about his job. His standard cocktail party joke poked fun at the dullness of the profession. "What's the best sleeping pill?" he'd ask the other guests before providing the answer himself. "An accountant discussing his work."

It always got a laugh, with Walt laughing hardest of all.

But Margaret hadn't realized he *hated* his job. She wanted nothing but good for Walt; the idea that he woke up every day and trudged off to a job he despised was painful to her.

Still, Walt was right. Somebody had to pay the bills.

She gladly would have turned over her paychecks if it could have eased his burden, but what difference would it make? Fifty dollars a month for writing two columns had seemed like a small fortune to Margaret, but it still wasn't enough to cover their monthly grocery budget.

Of course there was always the possibility of her going to work full-time. But apart from babysitting as a teenager and clerking part-time at Woolworth's in high school, Margaret had never worked. Any job she got now would likely pay the minimum wage of a dollar and a quarter. It wasn't much, especially after deducting expenses for clothes, commuting, and taxes. And what if one of the kids got sick? She'd either have to pay a babysitter or call in sick herself and run the risk of getting fired.

Margaret rinsed suds off the orange juice glasses and put them in the rack. No, she thought to herself, working full-time wasn't the answer. Maybe they should move?

Margaret loved this house, but there was no denying that buying it had stretched them financially. Still, they had to live somewhere, and the bills kept coming every month. Somebody had to pay them. The only one who earned enough to do that, who *could* earn enough to do that, was Walt.

It did indeed seem to be the way things were.

Margaret opened a drawer, so caught up in her thoughts that she didn't know she'd reached for the catchall drawer instead of the one where she stored the tea towels. Inside, among capless pens, tape dispensers, partially filled Green Stamp booklets, rubber bands, and ragged-edged recipes torn from magazines, Margaret saw her dog-eared copy of *The Feminine Mystique*. She flipped through the pages, remembering what Viv had said about people who'd been left out of the conversation, and wondering if husbands shouldn't be added to the list.

In a lot of ways, Walt was just as trapped as she was. The invisible fence of rules and mores that confined women to a small, carefully defined patch of human achievement impacted men as well, required them to carry the bulk of a family's financial burden, even if it meant doing work they disliked. It occurred to Margaret that Walt, too, must sometimes feel as if he were living a life that belonged to someone else—a life that was so much less than what Margaret wanted for him.

She put the glasses away in the cupboard, then stood statue-still in the middle of the kitchen, ears cocked for the sound of children. They hadn't come downstairs until eight thirty the day before. With any luck, today would be the same. If she hopped to it, she could still squeeze in at least an hour of work.

An idea floated into her mind, one with the potential to be just as funny as diet gelatin but far more meaningful—a column that might make people think as well as smile, one she could feel proud to have written.

She took Sylvia out of the closet. After feeding a sheet of paper into the roller, Margaret hovered her hands above the typewriter keys, wiggled her fingers to loosen up her knuckles, then started writing.

CHAPTER 24

Two Places at Once

Viv wrapped the blood pressure cuff around her patient's arm and pumped the inflation bulb, listening through the stethoscope as the cuff slowly deflated, too slowly to suit her.

Earlene Jackson was a tall woman with coffee-colored skin and intelligent brown eyes. According to the paperwork, she was forty-three years old, widowed, and had a seventeen-year-old daughter, but Viv knew nothing else about her.

Viv normally spent time chatting with new patients. People could be nervous when meeting a new doctor, and a little small talk often helped them calm down and open up. Sometimes they shared details that could help Dr. Fran find a more accurate diagnosis or a better course of treatment. Viv didn't have time for that today.

Andrea had been a brick this summer, keeping an eye on the younger kids while Viv was at work. She was going to a party in Potomac, Maryland, with some girlfriends that evening. Viv had promised to be home by four so Andrea would have time to get ready. It was twenty to three right now, and Earlene was her last patient of the day.

As Viv jotted her blood pressure results onto the chart, Earlene craned her neck and squinted, trying to decipher Viv's handwriting.

"I can read that the systolic is 135, but what's the diastolic? Looks like you wrote 57, but I *know* that can't be right."

"It's 81," Viv said, turning the chart around so Earlene could see.

"You sure you're not a doctor? You ought to be, with that chicken scratch."

Viv laughed. "Nope, just a plain old nurse. And a parochial school failure. The sisters tried their best to teach me proper penmanship, but it never took."

Earlene clucked her tongue. "Well, if the nuns can't give you good handwriting, nobody can. You must be a hopeless case."

"No question about it." Viv glanced quickly at her watch and got back to business. "Anyway, your blood pressure is elevated. Not terrible, but a little higher than normal. Sounds like you already know that, and that you might have some medical training?"

"I'm a nurse." Given the way Earlene tossed around terms like *systolic* and *diastolic*, this came as no surprise. But what Earlene said next got Viv's attention. "Twenty-two years. Got my training at a hospital in North Carolina, served in the Army Nurse Corps during the war."

"No kidding. Me too!"

Viv smiled broadly. She hadn't run into another army nurse in years, and she'd never met a Negro army nurse. The temptation to put down the clipboard and trade war stories was strong, but she resisted. She absolutely had to leave by three because she never knew about the traffic. She'd learned that lesson the hard way, missing the opening innings of two playoff games for Nick's baseball team. She couldn't let it happen again.

Viv picked up her pen. "What brings you in today, Mrs. Jackson?"

"Call me Earlene. We just moved from North Carolina, so I need a new doctor." She sat up straighter, beaming. "My daughter is starting at Howard University in the fall. My sister has a house here in Brookland, so we're living with her for now. It's nice being close to family."

"All my family is out west, so I know what you mean," Viv said. "My sisters and I fought like cats and dogs when we were kids, but I'd like to think we've outgrown that."

"Oh, don't be too sure," Earlene said, eyes twinkling. "Sondra and I can still go round and round. And let me tell you, getting two grown women to share the same kitchen takes some negotiating. Yesterday we almost got in a fistfight over the right way to cook a chicken."

Viv chuckled. She liked Earlene. Since there wasn't really anything wrong with her and Dr. Fran was still with another patient, she laid the chart on the counter and pulled up a stool.

"Tell me, where did you serve during the war? I was deployed with a field hospital, started in Tunisia and then went to Europe."

"North Carolina the whole time. None of the Negro nurses went overseas, though we all wanted to. After D-Day, thousands of us applied to the Army Nurse Corps, but every single one was turned down. In '41 they finally decided we could serve in segregated wards at Camp Livingston and Fort Bragg, taking care of injured Negro soldiers. They only took forty-eight nurses, and I was one of them. They upped the quotas later. By the end of the war, five hundred of us were serving, but only in the segregated wards or taking care of German POWs. They wouldn't let us anywhere near a field hospital."

"That's a shame. Because we sure could have used you."

"Yes, you could," Earlene said, lowering her chin. "Do you remember back in January of '45? President Roosevelt threatened to draft eighteen thousand nurses if they didn't get enough volunteers?"

Viv bobbed her head. "The army was desperate for nurses."

"They didn't have to be. Right at that moment, they were sitting on applications for nine thousand well-qualified Negro nurses who just wanted the chance to serve their country."

Viv's jaw dropped. Earlene nodded meaningfully, as if saying yes, Viv really could believe it. "I love my country. I could have served. In a war for freedom, segregation shouldn't win."

Viv thought back, remembering how she'd felt when she applied to the Army Nurse Corps. Though the call of adventure had certainly influenced her decision, a burning desire to serve her country had been her primary motivation. She had no doubt that the same fire had burned in Earlene and women like her.

Viv had been so excited when her application was accepted. How disappointed and angry would she have felt had she opened that envelope and learned that her willingness to sacrifice in service to her country was rejected because of the color of her skin? Viv frowned to think of the injustice and insult this woman had endured. And marveled that when the opportunity to serve finally did come her way—delayed and with limitations based on her race—Earlene had stepped up to the plate and done her part. Had Viv been forced to walk in Earlene's shoes, she couldn't say how she would have responded.

"For what it's worth, Earlene, I'd have been proud to serve along-side you. I don't know you, but I bet you're a really good nurse."

"No, I am a *great* nurse. Bet you are too."

Earlene's smile was replaced by a sigh. "I tell you, I do not understand this world sometimes. I surely do not. But at least things are starting to change. Have you heard about the march coming up at the end of August? Dr. King is going to speak."

Earlene didn't have to specify which Dr. King she was referring to. Everyone had heard about the young, charismatic civil rights leader, a minister who preached nonviolence and refused to back down despite the threats he received.

"I've signed up to volunteer at the march," Earlene said. "In the first aid station. If as many people show up as they predict, you can bet somebody will need a nurse."

"Gosh, that's great! Good for you."

"I'd invite you to come along, but I've got a feeling you might be busy then." She cocked an eyebrow at Viv's very round stomach. "When are you due?"

"October. I know it looks like sooner, but my babies are always big. Plus, my stomach muscles are shot." Viv patted her belly affectionately. "This is my seventh."

Earlene's eyes bulged. "Your seventh! God bless you. One was enough for me. How long are you planning to keep working?"

"As long as I can. Hopefully until October. I really do love this work."

"I know just what you mean," Earlene said. "Nothing more rewarding."

"I won't lie to you. It's hard some days. My feet are killing me right now. And with six kids at home . . ." Viv's smile faded a little. "I feel so torn sometimes. I want to be here with the patients, but I want to be with the kids too—"

"And you can't be in two places at once," Earlene said, finishing Viv's thought for her. "Oh, I know that feeling. My Joe was killed in a car wreck when Shirley was only three. I had to go back to work at the hospital after that. But I loved the job, and I was good at it too. Still, I missed so much when she was growing up. And we can't ever get those years back, can we?"

The door opened. Dr. Fran stepped into the exam room and greeted Earlene, then gave Viv a quizzical look. "Didn't you say you had to leave at three?"

Viv's eyes flew to her watch. It was three minutes to three.

Five minutes later, Viv climbed into her car. If the traffic gods were smiling, she could still be home by four. And indeed, it seemed they were. She sailed down Rhode Island Avenue and zipped around Scott Circle with no problem. At this rate, she might even be early.

But then she got to the Key Bridge.

Flashing lights of police cruisers and ambulances were everywhere. The brake lights from the stopped cars waiting to cross into Virginia were a mile-long necklace of glowing red.

"No!" Viv cried. "Dammit!"

She pressed the brake pedal, bringing the car to a stop, and slumped against the seat.

Earlene Jackson was right; no matter how hard she wished it were otherwise, a woman simply cannot be in two places at once.

✳ ✳ ✳

At the same time that Viv, resigned to her fate, was opening the copy of *A Room of One's Own* she'd stashed in the car for just such an emergency, Bitsy was leaning against a paddock fence, engaged in a conversation with a stranger that was turning out to be surprisingly personal.

Bitsy had arrived at the stables as Mrs. Graham and Delilah were returning from an afternoon ride. Another woman, midfifties with bright blue eyes and short ash-blond hair, was with her, mounted on Crystal. When Mrs. Graham waved, Bitsy waved back.

"How was she?" Bitsy asked as she approached, looking Delilah up and down, paying special attention to her gait, which seemed steady and comfortable.

"Perfect. As good as ever," Mrs. Graham answered, then turned to her friend. "Alice, this is Bitsy Cobb, the one I was telling you about."

The woman, Alice, smiled. "Ah! So you're the miracle worker!"

Bitsy's cheeks went pink. "Oh no. I wouldn't say that."

"No need to. Katharine already did." Alice pulled a leg from the stirrup and over the saddle, climbing nimbly down from the horse. "And I agree. I gave Delilah a once-over before we rode out, and she seemed perfectly sound, barely a hint of inflammation. I'm impressed. Treating laminitis isn't easy."

Mrs. Graham slid off her saddle, still holding Delilah's reins.

"Bitsy, meet Alice Brennan, an old friend who's in town for a conference." Mrs. Graham's smile spread. "Alice also happens to be a professor at the school of veterinary medicine at University of California, Davis."

Bitsy blinked her big brown eyes. "Really?"

Alice nodded. Mrs. Graham called to Joey, who was just coming out of the barn with shovel in hand. He put it down and jogged toward the women.

"Joey, could you give me a hand unsaddling? I'll take Delilah if you can take Crystal."

He said he'd be happy to, took hold of Crystal's reins, and led her toward the barn.

"Well, I shall leave you to it," Mrs. Graham said, looking to Alice and Bitsy in turn. "I imagine you two will have *lots* to talk about."

✳ ✳ ✳

At first Alice did most of the talking.

Like Bitsy, she'd grown up around animals and had a loving, supportive father whom she adored, who happened to be a veterinarian. Young Alice spent Saturdays and summers working in his hospital. She started out cleaning cages and filling water bowls, but it wasn't long before she was his assistant. Her father took pains to explain what he was doing and why, everything from how he reached a diagnosis to the safest way to vaccinate a temperamental terrier. And as he instructed her, he would say, "When you go to veterinary college . . ."

"Not *if* I went, but *when* I went." Alice thumped the fence with her closed fist for emphasis. "He acted like it was a given, and there was no question that I would grow up and become a vet. Because he believed it, I did too."

She leaned closer and stood taller, until she and Bitsy were practically nose to nose. Then she let her voice drop to almost a whisper, as if imparting some precious secret.

"Having faith in yourself," Alice said, "believing you have as much right to be in the room as anybody else, is half the battle."

She popped her eyebrows, giving Bitsy a meaningful look. Then she took a step back and clapped her hands together.

"So, Bitsy! Tell me about yourself. Who are you? Where did you grow up? How did you learn so much about horses? Why are you working as a stable hand? And how in the world," she said, tipping her head back, "did such a tall drink of water come to be called Bitsy?"

Bitsy answered her questions and supplied all the background information Alice requested, including the one item Bitsy found most embarrassing.

"Now, you listen to me, Theodora Leonora," Alice said, grinning as she employed Bitsy's given name, which they had agreed didn't suit her at all. "You have nothing to be ashamed of. Not one thing. You were under a lot of pressure. It's not like you're the first woman who put her education aside to get married. And it's not as if this was an irreversible decision. You're only short one semester. Go back to college, finish up those last few credits, and take a crack at getting into vet school. If you're worried about recommendations, I'd be willing to vouch for you. There are no guarantees, of course, but if you apply to our program at UC Davis, I feel confident that a recommendation from a faculty member would give you a good shot."

"Alice—I mean, Professor Brennan, you're so kind—"

"Alice is fine for now," she interrupted. "Once you're admitted, then you can call me Professor Brennan. And I'm not being kind. Veterinary medicine can be a lonely profession for a woman, and I'm out to change that.

"Everybody didn't have the opportunities I did—a father who believed in her and was already in the profession, and who also just happened to have donated to the college and done a bit of guest lecturing," Alice said, chuckling. "So when I see a bright, promising young woman with a desire to enter the field, I try to help pave the way for her, the way Dad did for me. Somewhere down the road, maybe you'll help pave the way for somebody else. That's how the world gets better, Bitsy. One generation helping the next."

Bitsy swallowed back the thick feeling in her throat. Mrs. Graham was only trying to help, but Bitsy wished she hadn't introduced her to Professor Brennan. She felt as if someone was dangling a jewel in front of her, the glimpse of a life she might have had but never would.

Bitsy tried to smile. "I appreciate your encouragement so much. And your willingness to recommend me. Truly, I do. But California is so far away—"

"You're right, you're right," Alice said, briefly raising both hands. "But there are other schools. A recommendation from me might not have the same clout at another institution as it would at Davis, but it would still count for something."

"Yes, I'm sure, but there aren't any veterinary colleges in this area, nothing within commuting distance. My husband has been working hard to build up his practice. He's not going to abandon it and move just so I can go to school."

"Yes, Katharine told me about your husband. He sounds like quite a guy." Alice twisted her lips and sniffed. "Well, far be it from me to tell you how to live your life. But if I were in—"

Bitsy lifted a hand. She didn't want to hear more. She couldn't.

"I'm pregnant."

The professor stopped midsentence. Her mouth hung open.

"Ah," she said at last. "I see."

"I'm not certain yet, and I haven't told my husband, but he's going to be so happy. I am too, obviously," she added. "We've been trying to start a family for over two years. Finally, after all this time . . . success!"

She flashed a smile, hoping Alice would read in it what she wasn't saying. Bitsy had made a commitment, taken a vow. Now, more than ever, she couldn't turn away from that.

"Well, that's wonderful. Congratulations."

"Thank you."

Alice gave her head a sort of "guess that's that" bob and started walking toward the barns. But then she stopped, retraced her steps, and pulled a business card from her pocket.

"Just in case. You're still young, and babies do have a way of growing up. Maybe someday?"

Bitsy took the card from politeness and slipped it into her pocket.

"Yes, of course. Maybe someday."

✳ ✳ ✳

Once the traffic started moving, Viv drove back to Concordia as fast as she could without risking a ticket, pulling into the driveway at twenty-five minutes after four. Before she'd even turned off the ignition, a wet-haired Andrea came flying around the corner of the house, waving her arms. Viv started apologizing while she was still getting out of the car.

"Honey, I am so sorry. The traffic was awful. But I'm here now, so go on and set your hair. Borrow my Lady Sunbeam," she said, referring to her new home hair dryer. "Just pull that plastic shower cap thing over the rollers and crank the blower to high. You'll be dry in no time."

Viv was using her "nurse voice," a reassuring tone that could calm the most anxious of patients. But Andrea still looked frazzled.

"Mom. It's not that. It's Jennifer. She climbed up on the roof and won't come down. She says she's going to jump!"

"What!" Viv slammed the car door and craned her neck, squinting in the sunlight as her eyes searched the roof. "Where is she? How did she get up there in the first place?"

"She's in the back," Andrea said, grabbing her mother's arm and pulling her around the corner of the house. "It's all my fault. The kids were complaining about the heat, so I set up the Slip 'N Slide. Mark grabbed the hose and ruined my hair, so I sprayed him back. Jenny must have gone inside during the water fight, then climbed out the bedroom window while I had my back turned. It was just for a minute, Mom. I swear!"

Andrea was on the verge of tears. Viv nodded reassuringly, said she believed her and that everything would be all right. Andrea sniffled and opened the gate to the backyard. Viv looked up.

Sure enough, five-year-old Jenny was standing on the roof with a white bath towel tied over her shoulders and a defiant expression on her face. Thankfully, she was standing on the lower of the split-level roofs. It wasn't that high, perhaps nine feet, but still high enough that she might break a bone if she fell.

The two youngest Buschetti boys, Nick and Mark, stood barefoot on the grass, their shorts and hair dripping wet, looking up at their baby sister and clucking like chickens.

"Come on, scaredy-cat!" Mark taunted, tucking his fists under his bony arms and flapping them like wings. "Scaredy-cat!"

"I'm not a scaredy-cat!" Jennifer cried.

"Then do it already!" Nick shouted. "Jump!"

Jennifer scooted closer to the edge. Viv broke into a run, pushing Andrea aside and calling out sharply to Jenny. Jennifer appeared startled, but her face split into a grin, revealing a gap left by recently lost baby teeth.

Jennifer waved. "Hi, Mommy!"

Viv, puffing from the effort of running, came to a stop near Nick and Mark, gave Jenny a half-hearted wave, then cuffed the boys' heads.

"What was that for?" Mark said, blinking with feigned innocence.

"Yeah," Nick said, sounding offended. "She wants to jump. We're just cheering her on."

"Not *jump*," Jenny said, shaking her head to correct him. "*Fly.*"

Viv gave the boys an "I'll deal with you later" glare, then looked up at her youngest and asked her to please come down. Jenny pushed her lips into a stubborn line and shook her head. Viv glared at the boys.

"You two knuckleheads get upstairs, climb through that window, and get your little sister off the roof. Now."

"We already tried," Andrea said. "The window's stuck. Vince and Mike might be able to fix it, but they went to the movies."

"Yeah," Nick said, scowling and kicking the grass. "And they wouldn't take us."

"Go to the garage," Viv said. "Bring the ladder."

"Nooo!" Jenny wailed. "No ladder! I want to come down by myself. I want to *fly* down!"

"I know," Viv said sympathetically. "But you can't, sweetie. People can't fly."

Doubt flickered across Jenny's face as she considered this information, but briefly. She crossed her arms, jutted out her chin, and stamped a bare foot on the gray shingles.

"Maybe *people* can't," she declared, "but that doesn't mean *I* can't."

Lord, but this child was stubborn! And oh, how Viv loved her for it. She pressed a hand against her mouth to cover her smile.

"Okay, Jenny. I'll make you a deal. If I let you fly into my arms this one time, do you promise never to do it again?" Viv asked, waving off Andrea's protests and keeping her eyes glued on Jenny. "You have to promise. Otherwise, we get the ladder."

Jenny seemed unhappy with these terms. But after a long moment, she sighed a disgruntled sigh and crossed her heart with her index finger.

"Oh, okay."

The little boys whooped with excitement and yelled at Jenny, reminding her not to forget to flap. Andrea bit her lip and looked anxious. After taking a moment to reassure her eldest daughter that all would be well, including the baby, and that she'd helped heave a two-hundred-pound patient off an exam table that very day, Viv took two steps backward and raised her arms high, ready to catch her youngest. Jenny crouched like a swimmer on a starting block.

"Ready?" Viv called. "One. Two. Three!"

Jenny thrust out her arms and leapt into the air. Andrea gasped. The boys cheered. Viv stumbled backward a bit, bending her knees to absorb the weight, but caught her easily.

"You did it!" Viv shouted, crushing Jenny to her breast. "You flew!"

"I flew!" Jenny cried.

"You did not," Nick groused. "You jumped."

"Yeah," Mark said. "You jumped and Mom caught you. That's all."

"I flew," Jenny said, sticking out her tongue at them. "Didn't I, Mommy?"

"You did," Viv agreed. "Like a little bird."

Jenny gave an exaggerated nod that her brothers couldn't miss, then wrapped her thin arms around her mother's neck and moved her lips to Viv's ear, voice dropping to a whisper.

"I flew a little," she said. "And you caught me a little. Didn't you, Mommy?"

"Yes," Viv said. "And I always will."

CHAPTER 25

Not Paid to Think

Nothing had really changed in the weeks since Walt had returned from his father's funeral, at least not in practical terms.

Margaret was still taking care of the kids and the house, getting up oh-so-early to squeeze in time for her writing. She read her book club picks before bed or in the car as she waited to pick Bobby up from Little League practice or the girls from swim lessons, feeling as if there was never as much time for any of it as she'd have wished. Walt was busy too, even more than before.

Although Walt was using his vacation time, his boss, Mr. Ackerman, had made it clear that he wasn't happy that Walt had gone to Ohio and was going back again to help his mom. Walt was getting up with Margaret and heading to the office earlier than ever to compensate, hoping to get back on Ackerman's good side. Walt and Edwin still met at the VFW to talk books every other Thursday evening—two more men had joined their book club— and now Walt was going to the bookstore on Saturday mornings to help Edwin with his bookkeeping. "Edwin's ledgers are as boring as anybody else's, but he pays better," Walt told her one Saturday, grinning and holding up a copy of *Ice Station Zebra* by Alistair MacLean.

So, yes, on the face of it, not much had changed. But the Walt who had dashed off to his father's deathbed was different from the Walt who'd returned from it.

He was drinking less but talking more, asking Margaret about her day when he got home, then telling her about his or sometimes sharing a highlight from the book he was reading. There was never any earth-shattering news to relate, but it was nice just to be talking again. The kids benefited from Walt's new leaf as well. Now, instead of plopping down in front of the TV when he came home from work, he often took them to the park or joined in a game of Go Fish. When Walt did watch television, he and Margaret watched together, sitting on the sofa after the kids were asleep, tuning in to *Bonanza* or *The Dick Van Dyke Show*, with his arm draped over her shoulders.

And when they went upstairs to bed and turned out the lights . . . That was nice too.

This week, however, Walt was back in Ohio, trying to help Bernice deal with probate, paperwork, home maintenance, and everything else. Walt had phoned Margaret the day before, speaking more frankly than usual because Bernice was at the beauty parlor.

"It's ridiculous, Maggie. Mom isn't stupid, but Dad kept her in the dark about so many things. She never knew how much money he made or how much they owed, or what bills were due and when. She didn't even know how to write a check until I showed her how to do it! Dad made so much noise about protecting her, but he's left her completely vulnerable. Did it never cross his mind that she might outlive him? Or she might have to take care of herself someday?"

"Poor Bernice," Margaret murmured, shifting the telephone receiver to her other ear. "She must feel so frightened about the future."

"Yes, and she's right to be," Walt said, sounding disgusted. "She'll get about seventy dollars a month from Social Security, and there's a little life insurance too, but they've still got a mortgage.

If Mom could get a job, it might be enough. But she doesn't have any real skills, and every time I bring it up, she starts to cry." He sighed. "She's going to have to sell the house."

"Oh, Walt," Margaret said, feeling a pang for her mother-in-law. "Are you sure?"

"I just can't see another way," he said, sighing again. "I'll tell you something, Maggie. I know I wasn't too thrilled when you started working for the magazine—"

"Excuse me, Mr. Ryan, are you referring to my 'jobette'?"

Walt chuckled, taking her teasing with good grace.

"Okay, okay. I deserved that. But seriously, this situation with Mom has opened my eyes to a lot of things. Even if it's only part-time, you're getting some real work experience. I hope you never have to work full-time unless you want to. But it makes me feel better to know you could take care of yourself if the worst did happen.

"You're smart," he said. "And capable. I guess what I'm trying to say is . . . I'm proud of you, honey."

Margaret thought it might be one of the nicest things he'd ever said to her. However, on this hot July day and with Walt still out of town, she wasn't feeling very capable. She'd come down to make breakfast and found a puddle of water on the kitchen floor. The freezer had gone on the fritz, and everything inside was defrosting.

This had happened once before. Walt had done something to fix it, but Margaret didn't know what to do, and the repairman couldn't come until Friday. She let the kids have chocolate ice cream for breakfast—they were thrilled—tossed a worryingly soft package of bacon into the trash can, made soup from once-frozen packages of peas and carrots and a pound of hamburger, and put two more pounds plus a box of fish sticks into the refrigerator to be cooked in the next couple of days. Later that day, when she drove the kids to the pool, the car made a funny rattling noise she'd never heard before. Or had she? Either way, she found herself mentally rehearsing what she should do if the station wagon suddenly broke down.

Thankfully, nothing of the kind had happened, because the thought of being stranded on the side of the road with three cranky kids on a hot, humid summer day in Virginia was almost too terrible to contemplate. They'd been bickering and picking on one another all week, and Margaret had finally run out of patience. When threats of docked allowances and the consequences that might ensue when Walt came home had no effect on their behavior, she sent all three to their rooms.

She could still hear them, even from the kitchen. Bobby was up there playing with his plastic popgun, which emitted an irritating *pop-click* every time he fired a round. Beth and Suzy, who shared a room, were arguing over troll dolls. No matter that they had a whole set of the ugly little things, both of them wanted to be the bride. As long as no blood was drawn, Margaret planned to stay out of it. She was tired of playing referee.

Margaret had just poured herself a glass of iced tea when the phone rang. Leonard Clement was calling to discuss the column she'd just sent in—the piece she'd written after realizing that Walt felt as hemmed in by societal mores and boundaries as she did.

She'd worked hard to keep the tone light, using winking references to Sadie Hawkins Day—an invented holiday made famous in the *Li'l Abner* comic strip, in which women were permitted to turn the tables and do the proposing—as the linchpin of the piece. Though she knew her between-the-lines comments about masculine and feminine roles wouldn't go unnoticed by her editor, she hoped tongue-in-cheek humor might win him over.

Mr. Clement was not amused. Not even a little.

"I don't care how many pictures they published of you or how great an angle it was to hire a housewife. Send in one more piece like that, and I will fire your ass! You got that?"

"Yes, all right, I'm sorry. I didn't mean to upset you. But with all the changes going on in the world, I just thought—"

"Lady, you're not paid to think! You're paid to write. And to write what I tell you to write! Obviously, Mrs. Ryan, you think you have something to say. You're wrong! And even if you weren't, *nobody* wants to hear it. So either get with the program, or I'll find somebody who will. Am I making myself clear?"

After another apology and more groveling, Margaret hung up the phone. She felt drained, like a wet dishcloth that had been wrung out. Margaret couldn't remember the last time someone had talked to her like that. Nor could she believe how close she had come to getting fired. The truth of it shook her.

Nothing drastic would have happened if Clement had fired her, not in the grand scheme of things. Yes, she liked getting a paycheck, but the loss of it wouldn't cause the family to go hungry or end up on the street. The real payday of writing was less tangible but somehow more meaningful—a sense of pride in an accomplishment that was hers alone.

A memory swam into her mind. What year had it been . . . 1946? Possibly '47? She wasn't sure, but not too long after the end of the war.

For years, Margaret and her mother had prayed for the day when the war would end, Dad would come home, and life would go back to normal. During that memorable, belated Christmas, it seemed their prayers had all been answered. But it hadn't taken long for things to begin fraying around the edges.

Margaret remembered standing at the top of the stairs, hesitant to come down because her parents were arguing—again. She sank down onto the top step, wrapping her arms around her knees, holding herself tight, feeling anxious and unsettled when her father began shouting.

"What the hell is wrong with you, Ruth? The war is over, the country is getting back to normal, we're healthy, rationing is finally over . . . I'm making good money at the factory, and you just got a new washing machine. So why can't you be happy? Why is it, no matter what I do or how hard I work, it's never enough for you?"

Her mother's laugh was acidic. "A new washer. You think I should be happy because you bought me an appliance that makes washing underwear and getting the stains off your shirt collars easier? That's your definition of happiness? Bill, this isn't about what you do or don't do. Why can't you understand that? It's about what *I* do. And what I do is precisely nothing, nothing that matters."

While her mother was still speaking, Margaret overheard footsteps, the clink of a glass, and the glug of liquid being poured from a bottle, and knew her father was pouring himself a drink.

"Oh, for Pete's sake. Are we back to this again? You take care of the house, the kids, and me. Don't we matter? Maybe you'd like to go back to working ten-hour shifts with grease on your hands, me getting shot at, and leaving our kids to fend for themselves because you're working late at the factory. Is that what you want? For the war to keep going just so you could feel like you *do* something?"

"Stop it. That's not fair. Of course I don't wish the war was still on. I just want—"

"What?" he shouted. "What can you possibly want that we don't already have? What?"

There was a pause, then the sound of a sob, choked with confusion and shame.

"I don't know. I don't know. Just . . . more."

Teenage Margaret was just as bewildered as her father. She leaned closer to the banister, ears straining for a retraction or an explanation of what it would take to make her mother happy again. Instead, she heard another sob, pounding footsteps, and a slammed door.

Though there would be similar arguments in the months to come, Margaret's mother never did find the words to define the meaning of *more*. In time she gave up trying. Gave up entirely. Discontent bloomed into depression and impenetrable silences.

Margaret had long ago ceased trying to understand why her mother decided to end her own life. She hadn't even left a note, only a full refrigerator. But now Margaret thought she understood what her mother had never been able to articulate. It was the sense that her labor made a difference, the satisfaction that came from setting herself to a hard task, something that truly challenged her, and coming to master it over time.

The work of Ruth's hands, like those of millions of other women, had literally helped to win the war. Margaret's work was completely different and infinitely less consequential. Even so, when a perfect turn of phrase popped into her mind, or when she opened the magazine and saw *her* name printed next to *her* words, or read a note from a subscriber complimenting her work, she felt important.

Or maybe alive?

Yes, that was it. *More* meant *alive*, knowing that her existence made ripples felt by others, that she was doing more than just sucking oxygen and taking up space, that she had something unique to offer.

And it felt good. Too good to risk losing.

Tomorrow she'd get up early and write a new column. Perhaps something about a harried housewife who sent the kids to their rooms and accidentally-on-purpose forgot to call them back down.

Yes, that could work. It was a scenario almost any mother could relate to, and one Mr. Clement would like. And since keeping Clement happy meant keeping her job . . .

The ice in Margaret's tea had melted while Clement was chewing her out. She poured the pale, diluted liquid down the drain, then sat down at the kitchen table to mentally map out a new column. A loud thump, followed by an even louder crash and a furious shriek, came from upstairs. A door opened. Two pairs of little feet pounded down the staircase, searching for retribution, bellowing for a referee.

"Mom! Mom! *Mom!*"

Margaret propped her elbows on the table and covered her face with her hands.

Could this day possibly get any worse?

CHAPTER 26

Truth-Telling

Margaret's day did get worse.

Around nine o'clock that night, just minutes after she finished talking to Walt, who would return the following day, the phone rang again.

Charlotte was calling, and she was drunk.

The background noise of clinking glasses, music, laughter, and the buzz of conversations punctuated by an occasional shout was so loud that Margaret had to repeat her question twice, practically yelling into the receiver.

"I said, *where are you?*"

"Ohhh," Charlotte said, stretching out the word, then laughing. "I thought you asked *how* I was. Not *where*," she slurred, tongue so thick she sounded like a dental patient whose novocaine injection hadn't worn off. "The answer to how I am is, absolutely hammered. Sloshed. Blotto. Three sheets to the howling wind."

"Yes, I figured that out. But *where* are you?"

"Well, yeah, that's kind of the problem. Someplace in the city? But I'm not sure. I can't find my car or my keys. If I could just figure out where they are, I'd drive myself home, but—"

"No, no. Don't do that, Charlotte. Just stay put. I'll come and get you. Is there a waiter around? Flag somebody down and let me talk to them."

After a bit more urging and repetition of instructions, Charlotte handed the phone off to a bartender, who gave Margaret an address in Georgetown and promised to exchange Charlotte's martini for strong black coffee and keep an eye on her until Margaret arrived.

It took Margaret well over an hour to change out of her pajamas, enlist Beth to babysit, consult a map to figure out where she was going, and find a parking spot in a decently lit location that wasn't too far away from the bar. Walt would have thrown a fit had he known she was traipsing around Georgetown at night by herself.

The bar was crowded, loud, and dimly lit, its walls paneled in dark wood. A piano player was pounding bravely away in a corner, but no one was listening. Cigarette smoke hung in the air like a summer haze, so thick it made Margaret's eyes sting. She blinked and squinted, trying to catch sight of Charlotte. After wading into the scrum of lushes standing three deep at the bar, a friendly man named Steve, the same bartender she'd talked to on the phone, pointed her in the right direction.

Charlotte was sitting at a corner table in the considerably quieter upper level, slumped in a chair and staring grimly into a coffee cup. When Margaret sat down, Charlotte lifted her head, looking sad but unsurprised to see her. Clearly, the buzz was beginning to wear off.

"I'm sorry," she said.

Margaret dismissed the apology with a quick shake of her head. "I'm glad you didn't try to drive home. You still don't remember where you left the car?"

Charlotte screwed her eyes shut for a moment, thinking. "Maybe the Willard?" She pulled a cigarette from a pack lying on the table.

"The Willard Hotel? Near the White House? How did you end up here?"

"Not sure. Guess I took a taxi? I don't remember now."

"What were you doing there in the first place?" Margaret asked. "We talked yesterday, and you didn't say a thing about coming to DC."

Charlotte lowered her eyes, lit the cigarette, took a drag, and blew out the smoke.

"I met up with Lawrence."

Margaret gasped. "Charlotte, you didn't. *Please* tell me you . . ."

"It's not like that. What do you take me for, Maggie?"

The intensity of Charlotte's glare and the accusation in her eyes pulled Margaret up short, left her feeling disloyal but also confused.

"Sorry. I shouldn't have . . . But will you tell me what happened?"

"There's to be a new exhibition of his work next year, and he had to come down for some meetings at the gallery," Charlotte said in a voice as glum as her expression. "He called and said we should meet up for dinner."

"Dinner? Just the two of you? Didn't it occur to you that—"

"Of course it did! I'm not stupid, Margaret!"

Charlotte grabbed the coffee cup, took a drink, and made a face before taking another furious puff on her cigarette. This time Margaret had the feeling her anger was directed inward.

"I said no to dinner but agreed to lunch. Then I suggested I go to the gallery with him afterward so he could introduce me to the curator. He's been promising to help pave the way for me for ages. Before the move, when we were still in New York, he invited me to come to a party in the Village that Clement Greenberg was hosting. He's a very important critic, and everybody who's anybody was supposed to be there. Lawrence said he wanted to introduce me to some people. But then I ended up in the hospital, and . . ."

Charlotte broke eye contact, paused to pick invisible lint from her sleeve.

"Anyway, that was that. Until today." She shifted backward in her chair and craned her neck, scanning the room. "Damn, but I need a drink. Do you see a waitress?"

Margaret pushed the coffee mug toward her. "Have some more of this."

Charlotte scowled. "It's cold."

Margaret fished three ice cubes from a nearby glass of water and plopped them into Charlotte's mug, one at a time.

"There you go. Iced coffee. Perfect summertime beverage when you're visiting a city that was built on a swamp. Very à la mode."

Charlotte's lips twisted into a wry smile. "You're an idiot."

Margaret nodded, conceding the point. "So," she prompted, "you were meeting Lawrence for lunch. And then?"

"We were supposed to meet at the Occidental, inside the hotel. When I arrived, the maître d' passed on a message. He told me Lawrence sent his apologies, but he had to take an unexpected but very important long-distance call from his agent—and if I wanted him to introduce us on the phone, I could meet him upstairs. Then he handed me a key to Lawrence's room."

Charlotte flicked ashes into a black plastic ashtray.

"Of course, when I came through the door, there was no phone call, no agent. Just a bed, a bucket of chilled champagne, and Lawrence, wearing nothing but a robe."

"So instead of lunch, he lured you to his hotel room on the pretext of some supposedly important call. And you believed that?"

"Not really. But I wanted to. Stupid. So, so stupid," Charlotte murmured, closing her eyes. "And it gets worse. For a moment, I honestly considered staying. I thought, *If I just go through with it, give him what he wants, maybe he will help me.* But in the end . . . I couldn't."

Charlotte swiped a tear from her cheek and opened her eyes once again, then took a breath, composing herself.

"My marriage is a sham, I know. Howard only married me for the money and has been serially unfaithful from day one. Though I've crossed plenty of lines in my life, that's one rule I've never broken. Not sure why," she said, shrugging. "Stubbornness, I suppose. Reverting so gloriously to type would give my parents too much satisfaction, would confirm their set-in-stone convictions about my lack of character."

Margaret had listened with a simmering irritation as Charlotte described the circumstances of her meeting with Lawrence. But when Charlotte started talking about her faithless husband and coldhearted parents, Margaret felt herself soften.

"Going up to that hotel room was a dumb, dumb move," she said. "But I'm glad you left. And no matter what Howard has done, I admire you for sticking by your convictions, and your vows. But Charlotte, there's something I don't understand. Why don't you just leave Howard and get a divorce? If all the things you've said about him are true, there never was a marriage. Not really. So why not free yourself from all that and go on with your life? If you did, maybe you could find someone else. Even if you didn't, at least your life would be your own."

Charlotte shook her head. "My parents have been very clear. Doesn't matter what Howard does. In the event of a divorce, they'd cut me off without a dime."

"I understand, but . . ." Margaret leaned in. "It's only money. Compared to your freedom and self-respect, how important can it—"

"Oh, don't be such a fool!"

Charlotte was sobering up now, and the look in her eyes was as sharp as her tongue.

"Honestly, Margaret. Idealism is all well and good in books or movies. But here in the real world, money matters. Even if it didn't, it's not the only thing they've threatened to cut me off from. They'll take the kids too."

"What?" For all she'd heard about Charlotte's parents, Margaret just couldn't believe they'd actually side with a cheating husband over their own daughter. "But they wouldn't do that. They couldn't!"

Charlotte leaned back, crossed one arm over her waist, and propped her elbow on her clenched fist, cigarette pinched between her fingers.

"They would. In a heartbeat."

"Well," Margaret said, blinking as she collected her thoughts. "Then you have to fight back, tell the judge about Howard's affairs. They're not going to grant custody to a man who's been cheating on his wife for years."

Charlotte arched her brows. "But you think they'll have no problem granting it to a mother who spent time in the nuthouse? Who sees a psychiatrist twice a week and has a prescription for Miltown? Oh, stop being so naive," Charlotte said, waving her cigarette through the air when Margaret began to protest. "Do you know why money matters? Because it buys power. Power to influence outcomes and break people, power to bend the world to your will. And who has the money? The power? The control?

"Men. Sure, every now and again, some clever girl manages to outlive her male relatives and get her hands on the inheritance, but the rest of us?" She shook her head. "We've got no choice but to dance to their tune, use our looks and wiles to convince those bastards to toss a few crumbs our direction. My mother is right. It is a man's world. And there's not a thing we can do about it."

Charlotte put the cigarette to her lips. She craned her neck to the right, eyes glittering with bitterness as they searched the room.

"Where is that damned waitress? I need another drink."

The defeatism in Charlotte's speech, her retreat into resignation, bitterness, and liquor took Margaret's irritation from simmer to boil.

"What a bullshit artist you are. What a fake."

Charlotte's head snapped toward Margaret, as if absorbing the shock of an invisible blow.

"What did you say?"

Margaret leaned in. "I *said* you're a fake. And a coward. All this bull you've been shoveling about women breaking free from societal roles, about confronting the myth of the mystique, about rights and equality and demanding the freedom to choose our destiny. It was just a bunch of talk, wasn't it? Your latest obsession, something for you to play at whenever the whim hits you, the same way you play at painting."

Charlotte ground out her cigarette, snatched the pack from the table, pulled out a fresh one with shaking hands.

"Knock it off, Maggie. If you value our friendship, stop right there." Charlotte clicked open her lighter. When it failed to ignite, she threw it onto the table. "Who the hell do you think you are anyway, Margaret Ryan? A housewife. A nobody from Ohio! What do you know about my painting, about art?"

"Next to nothing," Margaret said. "But enough to know you're not taking it seriously. You're always whining about the art world being a boys' club, about what a bad painter you are and how you've never produced anything really original. If that's true, then why don't you do something about it? Why don't you study or go back to school or do whatever it is real artists do to develop their own style? But I don't think you ever will, and you know why?" Margaret gripped the table edge. "Because you're a coward. Because deep down you're afraid you're not good enough—"

"I'm not good enough!"

"But how do you know that? How do you know if you don't try? If you'd put half as much effort into painting as you do into complaining, maybe you'd get better. And if not, at least you'd know the truth. At least you'd have the honor of hard work and honest effort."

"Oh, spare me," Charlotte said. "You sound like a Girl Scout. You can't change the way things are, Margaret."

Margaret shifted back in her seat. "You don't believe that. If you did, you wouldn't have started the book club. The Bettys wouldn't exist."

"If you'll recall," Charlotte countered, "I didn't start it. You banged on my door with your cookies and earnest eyes and said we should start a book club, to read *A Tree Grows in Brooklyn*, of all things. If it'd been up to you, the Bettys would've been named for Betty Smith. I joined for two reasons: because I was bored and because I felt sorry for you."

Charlotte's barb struck its intended target, but only barely. Margaret had known her long enough to recognize the tactic for what it was: an attempt to mask her own insecurities by pricking at the insecurities of others. When Margaret failed to take the bait, Charlotte sighed.

"Let's just go, all right? I don't want to talk about it anymore. It doesn't matter anyway."

"It does matter. It matters because you want it, Charlotte. So much that you went up to that hotel room, knowing what was waiting for you. And you came *that* close to doing it," she said, pinching two fingers together. "That close to compromising your morals by giving yourself to a man you don't love, trading on your sexuality instead of your talent. In exchange for what? The off chance that he might deign to introduce you to some 'somebody'? What does that have to do with getting what you really want, with becoming a good artist? Nothing. You know it, and so does Lawrence."

Margaret's voice was pleading. "Stop and think for a minute, Charlotte. How can you expect him or anybody else to take you seriously if you won't take yourself seriously?"

"Oh, that's rich! You lecturing me about taking myself seriously." Charlotte tipped her head back, barked out a single, sharp-edged laugh. "Did you plan this speech ahead of time, Maggie? Or are you making it up as you go? If so, you ought to give up that pathetic column and try for a career in fiction. Really, it's the best story you've ever come up with and probably ever will, the way you've been heading."

Charlotte laughed again and kept laughing. The barb worked its way in a little deeper. Margaret set her jaw and shoved her chair backward.

"It's late. We should get going."

Charlotte didn't move.

"As long as we're truth-telling, I'm not the only coward around here, am I, Margaret? You say you want to be a serious writer. But you never write anything serious, do you? Just mindless pabulum. Horseshit for housewives. And why is that? Because you're afraid to try anything else. Because it might prove, once and for all, that pabulum is all you *can* write."

"That's not fair," Margaret said. "You know I've tried to write other kinds of pieces, slip some meaning into my columns. My editor keeps rejecting them. That's not my fault."

"Slipping in some meaning," Charlotte deadpanned. "Not quite the same as actually writing something meaningful, is it? But you know, let's leave that aside for right now. Let's assume you do have the capability and courage to write something worthwhile, and that your editor really is what's standing in your way. What makes your roadblocks any different from mine? Why is it failure to get past the gatekeepers 'complaining and whining' when it comes to me but simply 'not your fault' when it comes to you?"

"I didn't say that."

Charlotte gave her a hard stare. "Yes, you did. And who knows? Maybe you're right. But if you are, then you're right about both of us. So before you start tossing out words like *fake* and *coward*, I suggest you look in the mirror. In the meantime . . ."

Charlotte stuffed her cigarettes into her purse and got to her feet.

"Where are you going?"

"To get another drink and call a cab."

Charlotte started toward the stairs. Margaret rose quickly and followed her.

"I'm sorry. I was out of line, and I apologize. Let's just drive home and forget about it, okay? Charlotte, stop. No cabdriver is going to take you all the way to Concordia at this hour."

Charlotte spun around to face her.

"I'd rather walk every step of the way than spend one more minute with you."

CHAPTER 27

Simultaneous Circumstances

August 1963

Three days after the incident in Georgetown, Margaret picked up the phone and dialed Charlotte's number, intending to apologize again, as abjectly as was necessary.

She'd gone too far, pushed too hard. Of course so had Charlotte. But somebody had to make the first move, didn't they? Now that they'd both had a chance to cool off, Margaret hoped that her regrets would be reciprocated and that she and Charlotte would put the whole thing behind them.

Seconds into the call, Charlotte had cut her off midapology.

"Yes, all right. But I really don't have time to talk now, Margaret."

"Oh. Well, what are you doing tomorrow? Maybe we could meet for lunch at the drugstore? My treat."

"Thanks, but I don't have time. I'm just very busy."

"Anything I can help you with?"

"No. But thank you."

"Okay, then . . . I guess I'll see you at book club?"

"Not sure. Depends on how things go."

And that was that. After thanking Margaret for calling, Charlotte said she had to run and hung up without saying goodbye.

Two weeks passed, and Margaret hadn't talked to Charlotte since. Viv and Bitsy hadn't heard from her either, not a peep.

"Quit worrying," Viv said when Margaret called. "She's probably immersed in some new project, decided to start a painting or wallpaper the dining room. You know how she gets."

Margaret did. By this time they all did. But this felt different. Normally, when Charlotte went off on a tear, she sounded upbeat and full of energy, almost giddy.

"How did she sound this time?" Viv asked.

"Intense. I wish I knew she was all right," she said, biting her lip and thinking of her promise to Denise.

"She is all right," Viv assured her. "Just yesterday I saw her driving out the gate when I was driving in. She waved and smiled and seemed perfectly fine."

Margaret nodded. She'd altered the route of her evening walk to go by Charlotte's house over the last few days and had seen lights in the windows. She'd seen Howard's car in the driveway a couple of times too. Physically, Charlotte was fine.

"She's probably still mad," Viv said. "She'll get over it. Give it some time, and try to think about something else."

Easier said than done. Margaret wasn't just worried about Charlotte; she missed her too. She was hoping beyond hope that Charlotte would show up for the book club meeting at Bitsy's later that evening. This afternoon, however, she had other fish to fry.

Margaret lowered herself into a too-small, too-low, engineered-for-discomfort hard chair that was stationed directly in front of a black-and-gold desk plaque reading "David K. MacGruber, Assistant Principal."

Concordia Junior High was less than two years old, yet the air was already permeated with the odors of floor wax, hamburger grease, chalk, rubber, and sweat. The junior high school she'd attended as a child in Dayton had smelled exactly the same. When the office door opened and David K. MacGruber entered the room, Margaret wondered if public school assistant principals were standard-issue too.

With beady eyes, a striped bow tie, a cheap gray suit, and a crew cut that made his already blocky head look even bigger, Mr. MacGruber looked so much like her old assistant principal,

Mr. Fosdick, that Margaret did a double take. The resemblance was uncanny. Hopefully Mr. MacGruber would turn out to be a little less rigid.

MacGruber sat down and folded his hands on the desk.

"Good afternoon, uh . . ." He flipped open a manila file folder, glancing at the form inside. "Mrs. Ryan. I understand you want to talk with me?"

"Yes, I do. It's about my daughter."

He glanced down again.

"Elizabeth. She'll be joining us in September?"

"Beth," Margaret corrected. "Yes. She's already enrolled in her classes, including band."

MacGruber's thin lips drew back, revealing nicotine-stained teeth. "Wonderful! I'm pleased to hear it! This will be our first year offering band, but we're expecting big things. I interviewed and hired Mr. Hoover personally. He'll be a fine band teacher."

"Yes, I'm sure. He's the reason I'm here. He said I had to talk to you."

MacGruber tugged at his tie. "I see. About what?"

"When the children came to pick up their instruments so they could start practicing over the summer, Mr. Hoover said Beth could choose a flute, piccolo, clarinet, or oboe."

"That's right. Is there a problem?"

Margaret scooted forward in the chair, which was making her lower back hurt, and smoothed her skirt over her knees. "There is. Beth doesn't want to play any of those instruments. She wants to play the trombone."

"She wants to play the trombone?" Mr. MacGruber widened his eyes. "Why?"

"We saw The Music Man at the movies, and Beth fell in love with the trombone." MacGruber stared blankly. Margaret lifted her eyebrows. "You know, 'Seventy-Six Trombones'? The Music Man? Robert Preston played the bandleader? Shirley Jones was Marian the librarian?"

"Mrs. MacGruber and I don't go to the movies," he said, his

tone of voice and facial expression suggesting that not only did he and his wife not go to the movies, but also they disapproved of those who did.

Apparently assistant principals *were* standard-issue.

"Ah. Well, it was excellent. And because of it, Beth wants to play the trombone."

"So you said, but . . . why? Why would a girl want to play the trombone?"

Margaret tilted her head to one side. "Well, why would a girl want to play the flute? Or the clarinet? Because she does. Because she likes the sound, or the music, or Robert Preston. I don't know. What difference does it make?"

"It's just very unusual. We've never had a girl trombone player before."

"You've never had a band before either. Guess there's a first time for everything."

He clasped his hands together more tightly, shook his head, and leaned forward. His black glasses slid to the midway point on his nose.

"Mrs. Ryan, I'm concerned about how this will impact Beth from a social standpoint. Conformity is important at this age. Don't you want your daughter to fit in with the other girls?"

Margaret paused, thinking about roles, roadblocks, and the Bettys.

"Believe me, Mr. MacGruber. When it comes to my daughter, fitting in with the other girls is the last thing I'm concerned about."

* * *

At the same time as Margaret was exiting Concordia Junior High School, having gained Mr. MacGruber's reluctant approval for Beth to play the trombone—obtained only after a painstaking search of district policies turned up no rules or guidelines prohibiting it—Viv popped her head through the door of Dr. Fran's office.

"Just wanted to say goodbye."

The doctor looked up from the stack of charts she'd been perusing and pulled a sad face, blinking her brown eyes like a dejected basset hound. "Is there nothing I can do to convince you to stay till the baby's born? Give you a raise? A lifetime supply of tongue depressors? A longer lunch break?"

"I've never had a lunch break. Neither have you." Viv stepped inside the room. "You'll be fine. I'm leaving you in good hands, the patients too."

"You're right," Fran said, getting to her feet. "Earlene was a find. She's a good nurse."

"The best," Viv agreed. "Smart, efficient, dedicated, and friendly. The patients have warmed right up to her. I'm so glad I had the chance to work with you, Doc. It's meant more than you'll ever know. But Earlene lives right in the neighborhood and can work full-time. Let's face it—she's the nurse you hoped to find in the first place."

Viv tilted her head sideways, as if daring the doctor to deny it. They both knew she couldn't. When Fran came out from behind her desk, Viv put out her hand.

"Feels weird," Fran said, "just shaking hands and walking away. Maybe we could run up to the coffee shop for a donut before you go?"

"You don't have time. Mr. Agosti is in exam room 2. His ulcer is acting up again, and I've got to get going too. My book club is meeting tonight."

"Ah yes. The infamous Bettys. What are you reading this month?"

"Virginia Woolf's *A Room of One's Own*."

"Did you like it?"

"More than I thought I would. For one thing, it's short. Definitely a plus." Viv laughed. "I probably would have related to it better if I was a writer like Margaret. But the idea that a woman needs something of her own, the chance to shine a little . . ."

Viv bobbed her head but didn't finish the sentence. Fran nodded too, signaling her understanding of the things left unsaid.

"Well. I should probably get going."

Fran opened her arms and took a step forward to give her as much of a hug as was possible in consideration of Viv's blooming belly.

"I'm going to miss you, Nurse Buschetti."

"I'm going to miss you, Dr. Giordano. I'm going to miss *this*."

Viv sniffled. Fran took a step back and ducked her head so she could look her in the eye.

"I'm serious. If you want to stay on for a few more weeks, it's fine with me."

Viv shook her head. "You can't afford to pay two nurses. Besides, I'm excited about getting ready for this little one," she said, stroking the curve of her belly affectionately. "And getting to spend more time with my kids. Vince is planning to enlist right after high school, so this'll be our last summer together. I don't want to miss it."

Fran reached out to rest her hand on Viv's shoulder.

"I think you're making the right decision, at least for now. You're a terrific nurse, Viv. I've got a feeling you'll be back someday."

"We'll see. At mass on Sunday, Father Valenti quoted a verse from the book of Ecclesiastes in his homily. He said, 'There is an appointed time for everything, and a time for every affair under the heavens.'" Viv patted her stomach. "Maybe it sounds silly, but I couldn't help but think it was a message just for me."

Dr. Fran smiled. "I think you might be right."

✳ ✳ ✳

And as Viv left the clinic for the last time, Charlotte walked out of Union Station, carrying a leather portfolio with two paintings and three sketches, returning from a day trip to Philadelphia, her second visit there in as many years.

Two years before, having received no interest or encouragement from the New York galleries, Charlotte had decided to try her luck in Philly, with only marginally better results.

Most gallery owners had dismissed her work with barely a glance. But Mr. Nikolai Fedorov—a tall, elderly man with a Russian accent and an economy of words, who owned a small gallery occupying two floors of a brick building in a less-than-fashionable neighborhood— gave her portfolio serious consideration. He took his time, flipped back and forth, murmuring and squinting, lowering his head to get a closer look.

Charlotte had watched his face, practically holding her breath, trying to interpret his expressions and decipher his murmurs. She couldn't. But taking so long to examine her work had to mean something, didn't it? If he hated it, wouldn't he have closed the portfolio by now, told her she was wasting her time and his, as so many others had before?

Finally, he looked up, squinting again, this time at Charlotte. His silence and the feeling that she was being sized up made her heart pound. When she couldn't bear it anymore, Charlotte reached into her purse, pulled out a cigarette, and asked the question.

"Well?"

Mr. Fedorov frowned and raised his index finger, moved it back and forth. Charlotte slid the cigarette back into the pack, then snapped her purse closed and sat up straighter, waiting.

"I think . . ." The old man worked his lips. "I think not yet. I think you are not ready."

Charlotte's heart plummeted, but briefly. "Not yet" wasn't what she had hoped to hear, but it wasn't the same as "no," was it? And since "no" was all she'd heard up to this point . . .

"But you think I could be ready? Someday?"

"Maybe someday. Also, maybe never. I cannot tell for certain. But I think . . ." Mr. Fedorov frowned more deeply, drawing together the shaggy white caterpillars of his eyebrows. "I think perhaps you are not serious—"

Charlotte interrupted him, contradicted him. The old man lifted his hand.

"I think you are afraid to be serious. Perhaps this will change.

But today?" He closed her portfolio, resting his gnarled hand on the brown leather. "No. Not yet."

He stood up and walked away.

Charlotte followed him, arguing and entreating. It did no good. He raised his finger once again, as if to say he would hear no more, then walked through a door and closed it.

Charlotte shed a few furious tears, took a taxi to the train station, downed three martinis and some Miltown during the trip to New York, woke up with a blinding headache the next morning, and tried never to think of that painful day ever again.

On the whole, she'd been successful in this. But when Margaret accused her of the same thing, of not being serious, she remembered the old man with the accent. Mr. Fedorov was a total stranger. Yet he'd seemed to have a strange insight into her. And Margaret?

Well, Margaret was as annoying as all get-out, especially when she got all white-bread, golly-gee-whiz Girl Scout. How had she picked such a Pollyanna as a friend? But Charlotte knew Margaret *was* her friend, and that friends sometimes know us better than we know ourselves.

After leaving the bar in Georgetown on the night of their argument, Charlotte found her car and checked into the Madison, not the Occidental, lest she run into Lawrence. In the morning, she drove back to Concordia and got to work—*serious* work.

Howie was at summer school, and the younger kids were still at camp. And so, day after day, she did nothing but paint.

Occasionally she was interrupted. Margaret called once, nibbling around the edges of their argument, obviously hoping to clear the air. There was no need.

If things turned out the way Charlotte hoped, she might well end up thanking Margaret for kicking the hornet's nest. Charlotte would explain it later, at the next Bettys meeting. Right now she needed to maintain her focus. The fact that Howard was sleeping at the house three or four nights a week didn't help. Charlotte didn't understand the sudden change; maybe he was between girlfriends? She didn't ask. She couldn't waste energy on scenes and dramas.

Instead, she fed him dinner—out of necessity and with Margaret's help, she had learned to make spaghetti and a passable meat loaf—mixed his evening Manhattan, and pretended to listen when he talked. When he walked up behind her and unzipped her dress one night, then unhooked her bra, she let him.

Lying on her back in the darkened room, waiting for him to finish, she appraised her own anger and degradation—observing herself as she might a model, memorizing the pose, the line, the cutting edge of hatred hewn from raw humiliation. If she could bear it, she could use it. And using it would mean she was in control, not him.

She worked as much and as hard as she could. But thoughtfully and steadily, not frantically. She eschewed coffee entirely, then limited her liquor consumption. She cut her Miltown dosage by a quarter, then a half, and stretched herself in ways she never had before. Clear-eyed, she examined hidden thoughts and unvarnished emotions, and did her best to transform her discoveries into something original and eloquent—into art.

When her first attempts didn't satisfy, she started again. And again. And again. Until she *was* satisfied, until she knew she had tapped the best that was in her. Was it enough?

When she entered the gallery, Mr. Fedorov turned toward her.

"Ah, you are back," he said, as if Charlotte had been gone two minutes instead of two years. Seeing the portfolio tucked under her arm, he wiggled his fingers, beckoning.

"Come. Now we will see."

It was the same as last time, yet not.

Fedorov took his time as before, murmured and squinted and nodded to himself. But this time he included Charlotte in the conversation too, brought her attention to the things she had done well, as well as the ways she had missed the mark. It was enlightening, but in ways she never would have expected. When, at last, Fedorov lifted his gaze from the paintings to her eyes, placing his two heavy hands on her shoulders, Charlotte already knew what he would say.

"*Now*, you are serious," he said, nodding his leonine head slowly, almost deferentially. "Be proud. You have worked hard, with great honesty, great passion."

"But not great talent," Charlotte said.

He smiled sadly. When he spoke his voice was tender, almost fatherly.

"No."

The pronouncement sank in—short, frank, and final. Charlotte was caught up in a swirl of emotions—disappointment, frustration, loss, resignation, and an odd, surprising sense of relief, like a patient finally receiving the diagnosis of an ailment she'd suspected all along.

There it was, at last.

At least she knew now. And at least she was able to separate those emotions, confront them one by one, feel them without feeling destroyed by them or giving in to the urge to run away from them or from herself. This was a new skill for her, acquired over these last weeks as she'd undertaken the hard work of looking inward. It wasn't easy, but it could be learned. And if she kept at it, she'd get even better at it.

Talent was different. You could hone it, but you couldn't learn it. Either you had it or you didn't. To be great, you needed a lot of it. Charlotte had some but not enough.

Now she knew. But deep down, hadn't she always?

Fedorov gripped her shoulders once more with his strong hands.

"Come!" he said. "I will make tea and show you the gallery. Then we will talk."

The tea was fragrant with cloves and sweetened with honey, served in an elegant glass teacup. Each cup was nestled into a sterling silver holder, emblazoned with a double-headed eagle clutching a scepter and orb in its talons. Charlotte cupped the brew in both hands as they traversed the gallery, pausing before each of the paintings. She had never heard of any of the three artists on exhibit, but the work was remarkable. Fedorov's eye was unquestionable.

"Thank you." He bowed his head briefly. "Like you, I had passion for painting. But not talent. But," he said, raising a finger, "I see talent in others, sometimes more than they see in themselves. That is my gift. Because I love art, I am sharing this gift. I am helping these artists."

He turned his eyes to a painting, nodding slowly, speaking more to himself than to her.

"It is a good life."

Fedorov's English was imperfect, but he had no trouble making himself understood, at least to Charlotte. Strange to find she had so much in common with an elderly Russian émigré who was very probably descended from royalty and had somehow ended up in Philadelphia, but there it was.

They talked for over an hour. If not for her train, Charlotte would have stayed longer.

She was still thinking about him as she drove back to Concordia, recalling the intensity of his gaze, the clarity of his vision, the certainty that, though possessed of only modest personal talent, he brought something meaningful and needed to the world of art. There was much to mull over, but one sentence kept playing over and over in her mind.

"It is a good life."

What would it feel like to say that and mean it? To have a purpose and know you had lived to fulfill it? Was *this* something that could be learned? Something *she* could learn?

Charlotte opened the garage and was relieved to find it empty.

She'd told Howard the book club was meeting tonight and led him to believe she was hosting, knowing he'd be less inclined to come home if the house was full of women. It looked like her ruse had worked.

Entering the house, she called his name to make sure he was gone, grateful for the silence and the chance to kick off her heels.

She would change into a cotton blouse, black cigarette slacks, and ballet flats before going to Bitsy's, maybe take a cool bath if she had time. But first she wanted to check the mail.

Though Charlotte hadn't been enthusiastic about Oxford, she was starting to understand Denise's choice.

In these last weeks, Charlotte had devoted nearly all her mental energy into husbanding her own creativity. But the leftover space—small gaps with more volume than one might guess at first glance, like a full pail of pebbles with room for half again as much water in the crannies and crevices—was reserved for thoughts of Denise, and Virginia Woolf.

Insomnia had driven Charlotte to pick up *A Room of One's Own*. It was a compact book, perhaps a hundred pages. But like that pail of pebbles, there was more inside than met the eye. In speeches delivered in 1928, Woolf reflected upon the thin literary contributions of female authors up to that point, saying it would ever be thus until women writers laid hold of two advantages their most talented male counterparts had long enjoyed: money and privacy.

Charlotte knew Woolf was right. She also knew that Denise had the kind of talent she could only dream of, and was determined to see she had the opportunity to develop it. As Mr. Fedorov said, supporting the talents of others was a gift too, a calling that mustn't be ignored.

Howard was less generous toward Denise than the other children, but Charlotte made sure she got her fair share. If Howard got control of the company after her father died, that might get trickier. But for now, money wasn't an issue. Denise had plenty.

She also needed privacy, that "room of one's own" with space to be her own person and think her own thoughts, think *bigger* thoughts, the kind that lesser mortals could never conjure. Though young, Denise was aware of her gifts. Fostering them meant removing herself from distraction, walking off the stage and into the wings to become an interpreter of the drama rather than a participant or—if you were born a Gustafson—a combatant. One thing was sure: having been raised by Charlotte, with cameo appearances by Howard and the Machiavellian grandparents, Denise would never lack for material.

Charlotte smiled at this last thought, committed the sentence to memory for inclusion in her next letter to Denise. They were corresponding regularly now. Strangely, it was easier to communicate by letter. Their exchanges were more open and less fraught than before. Being separated from her child by an ocean was hard, but it was for the best. Denise needed distance and privacy, at least for now.

But that wasn't all she needed.

Charlotte was acutely aware of her maternal failings, deeds done and left undone, words she should and shouldn't have said. She couldn't change the past, but she could give her daughter what she had been denied: freedom, acceptance, and encouragement. If a talented woman had all that plus that room of her own, who knew what she might accomplish?

Charlotte padded toward the front door in her bare feet. A pile of envelopes that had been stuffed through the mail slot by the postman was lying on the blue oriental foyer rug. The largest of them, made of rigid cardboard and big enough to hold photographs, displayed international stamps and an Oxford return address. Charlotte smiled when she picked it up, pleased that Denise was making good use of her camera.

She slit the envelope with her fingernail and pulled out a large, glossy photograph, expecting an image of the Vatican, the Eiffel Tower, or a Venetian canal.

Instead, she saw a backdrop of familiar shrubs, a woman she remembered, a head arched back in an expression that could have been pain or ecstasy, a high-raised hem, bare thighs, an unzipped fly, an exploring hand . . .

And an ice-clear image of her husband's leering face.

CHAPTER 28

A Shell of a Man

Hearing words isn't necessarily the same as understanding them, or believing them.

Bitsy, feeling bewildered and strangely numb, asked King to repeat himself. Instead, he laid his hat down on the bed and took a step toward her.

"I'm sorry, li'l bit. I know you weren't expecting this."

No, she wasn't. That wasn't the point. Bitsy took two steps back, avoiding his embrace.

"Say it again," she demanded.

King stuffed his hands into the pockets of his blue jeans and hung his head.

"I'm leaving you, Bitsy. I'm sorry, honey. But I . . . I just don't have a choice."

Bitsy blinked her eyes. Her bewilderment eased but only slightly. He was serious. This wasn't a joke. King lifted his head. The look on his face made her think he might cry.

"It's my fault," he said. "Nothing to do with you. I know we've had our differences, but you couldn't have tried any harder to make this work."

No, she couldn't have. Bitsy had bent over backward and turned herself inside out to make this marriage work, bitten her tongue and sublimated her own desires, convinced that if she did, the grit of their personalities would be smoothed over with the passage of time, producing a pearl, a work well done, a family and life they would one day look upon with pride.

She was wrong. She had been from day one.

King was an imposter, a shell of the man she'd believed him to be.

"When I came home that day," he said, referring to the aftermath of his disappearance, "and told you how sorry I was and swore it would never happen again, I meant every word." King lifted his hand as if taking an oath. "But when you asked me where I'd gone and what I'd been doing, I . . ." He faltered. "Well, I didn't tell you the whole truth.

"I did go off to think things over, to try and figure out if we had a future. But I ended up doing my thinking in a bar. There was this waitress, Sally Ann. And she . . ."

He hung his head again for a moment, then gave Bitsy a side-eye, as if hoping she'd feel sorry for him. She didn't.

"It was getting late, and I was a little worse for wear," he continued. "When the time came for last call, Sally Ann asked if I wanted to come over to her place to get some coffee and sober up. Well . . . one thing led to another, and I ended up staying with her. When I got my head screwed on straight, decided to come home and forgive you—"

Bitsy's eyes went wide at this last statement, but King didn't seem to notice.

"I figured that was the end of it. That we'd pick up where we left off and forget the whole thing. But Sally Ann got in touch with me today, and it seems . . ."

He paused, sniffed, pressed his lips together momentarily.

"Well, it seems she's going to have a baby. My baby."

He fisted his hands more deeply into his pockets, drooped his shoulders, and ducked his head—a posture of contrition belied by the tug of a smile at the corner of his mouth.

"Congratulations," Bitsy said.

King's head popped up, his eyes bright and smiling for the

briefest of moments, as if he actually thought she was sincere. Then he saw the look on her face.

"I don't blame you for being mad, Bits. But you know it hasn't been good with us for a long time. And . . . there's a baby coming." He shrugged. "I'm just trying to do the right thing."

Bitsy's eyes bulged. The right thing? Was he serious? He'd had an opportunity to do the right thing some months ago but galloped right past it and into some floozy's bed. Honestly, could he hear himself?

King opened the closet, pulled a battered brown suitcase from the shelf, and started piling his clothes into it. Apparently, when he said he was leaving, he meant immediately.

"Doesn't make sense to drag things out," he said, glancing up as if feeling the heat of her gaze. "And Sally Ann needs me. She's had a rough time of it, terrible morning sickness."

"Has she now? The poor thing."

"Oh, don't be like that, Bits. You're going to be fine. You're still young, and pretty as all get-out," he said, smiling in a way that suggested he expected she'd relish the compliment. "You'll find somebody else in no time. Even if it takes a while, the practice is pretty well established now, so I can afford to be generous. Well, within reason.

"It'll be a whole lot easier on everybody if we just try to act like adults here. You can stay here for now, get yourself sorted out before we sell the place. There's no rush. And no point in spending a bunch of money on divorce lawyers if we can avoid it, am I right?"

The doorbell rang. King, who had been piling underwear into his suitcase, looked toward the sound, frowning and clutching a pair of Fruit of the Looms in his hand.

"Who's ringing the bell at this time of night?"

"The Bettys," Bitsy said. "It's book club night."

"Book club night? Well, you'd better go and let them know it's canceled. Make an excuse. Tell them you've got a headache."

King dropped the briefs into the suitcase, then grabbed a half dozen pairs of black socks from the dresser. Bitsy stood there for a moment, watching him pack. The bell rang again. King looked up with an expression that suggested he was surprised she hadn't moved.

"You know . . . I don't think so. I'm going to go let my friends in. This is my house now." She started to walk away, then hesitated and turned to face him.

"By the way, the days when you get to tell me what to do? They're over."

CHAPTER 29

Day of Jubilee

Margaret slid some fish sticks into the oven for the kids, then opened the refrigerator door and studied its contents, trying to decide what she should bring to book club.

There wasn't much to work with, but she didn't have time to go to the market. Nor was she willing to subject herself to another of Bitsy's experiments in vegetarian cooking; the memory of cauliflower and kidney bean croquettes still made her gag. Finally, she pulled out a couple of apples and a block of slightly green cheddar that, once cleared of its moldy spots, would work just fine for a fruit and cheese platter.

She was washing the apples when she heard Walt's car in the driveway. The kids were thrilled he'd come home early and practically knocked him over when he walked in the door.

"Daddy! Daddy! Dad!"

Bobby flung himself onto Walt's leg like an offensive lineman going after a tackle dummy, begging him to come outside to play catch and help break in his new baseball glove. Suzy jumped into his arms, kissed him, and said she'd baked brownies in her Easy-Bake Oven. Did he want one? Beth tugged his arm to get his attention, telling him about how Margaret had "told off Mr. MacGruber."

Walt shifted Suzy to his hip and pulled Beth into a one-armed hug. "Oh, did she now?" he said, and tossed Margaret a wink.

"You're early," she said.

It wasn't that Margaret wasn't glad to see him, but Walt never came home from work early, *never*. She worried something bad had happened. Mr. Ackerman had been piling on even more work since Walt's return from Ohio, punishing him for the sin of taking time off. Had Ackerman decided to inflict the ultimate punishment? Had Walt been fired? Or maybe Walt just wasn't feeling well. He did look a little flushed.

"You're not coming down with something, are you?"

"Nope. Ackerman is out with a gout attack, so I snuck out a little early." He leaned forward to give her a kiss. "I've been thinking about you all day."

The kids were talking all at once, clamoring for his attention. Walt shushed them.

"Guess what, sports fans? I've got four tickets for the Senators game tonight. Don't worry about dinner. We'll get some hot dogs at the stadium." The kids cheered, and Walt set Suzy down. "You kids go get ready, okay? I just need to talk to Mommy alone. Honey?"

He jerked his head, indicating that Margaret should follow him. As they climbed the stairs, the sick, sinking feeling in her stomach sloshed and swelled. She could think of only one reason he would need to talk to her alone.

He *had* lost his job. How much did they have in savings? Enough to pay the mortgage? How long would it take him to find work? What if they lost the house? What then?

Walt opened the bedroom door to let her pass, followed Margaret inside, and clicked the lock. She turned to face him.

"What happened? Is it Ackerman? Did he—"

He stopped her questions with a kiss, then scooped her up in his arms. Margaret let out a whoop of surprise and a gale of giggles as he carried her across the room to the bed.

"I told you," he said, grinning and stretching out next to her, "I've been thinking about you all day."

* * *

Thankfully, Beth pulled the fish sticks out of the oven before they burned. By the time Margaret showered and dressed again, there wasn't time to make a cheese platter. She trotted down the sidewalk with a copy of *A Room of One's Own* tucked under her arm, smiling broadly. When she arrived at Bitsy's, Viv was standing on the stoop.

"Charlotte's not here?"

Viv shook her head, and Margaret felt a blip of disappointment. She'd really hoped Charlotte would come to the meeting so they'd be able to put the argument behind them.

"She might just be late," Viv said. "Or already be inside. Although I'm starting to wonder if anybody is in there. I rang twice already, but nothing. Are we sure this is the right night?"

Viv pushed the bell again. Finally, a grim-faced Bitsy opened the door. But she didn't invite them in or say a word. She just stood there, looking pale, almost stunned.

Before they could ask what was wrong, King came tromping down the hall with boots on his feet, a hat on his head, and a suitcase in his hand. He pushed past the three women without speaking, tossed the suitcase into his Jeep, and climbed in after it.

"He's gone," Bitsy said as he drove away. "For good. We're getting a divorce."

Margaret and Viv gasped simultaneously.

"What? Bits, you're kidding!"

"Oh, sweetheart. Are you all right? What happened?"

"He walked into the house, said he was leaving me, and packed his suitcase," Bitsy said, her voice and manner so detached and devoid of emotion that Margaret thought she must still be in shock. "There's another woman, a cocktail waitress. You remember when he disappeared? While I was staying at the barn, taking care of Delilah?"

Viv and Margaret nodded. How could they forget?

"Apparently he went to drown his sorrows after he stormed off, and met Sally Ann. Now she's pregnant, and King's going to 'do the right thing,' as he put it, by divorcing me and marrying her, preferably before the baby is born."

"Baby!" Viv exclaimed. "What about your baby? Didn't you tell him you're pregnant too?" Bitsy shook her head, and Viv gave her an indignant look. "Why not? You were here first!"

"Because I'm not pregnant anymore," Bitsy said softly, then shrugged. "Who knows? Maybe I never was. Apart from being late and feeling a little worn out, I really didn't have any other symptoms. Either way, my period came this morning."

Bitsy stared into the middle distance, her gaze dull and un-focused, her tone musing. "Weird, isn't it? How your whole life and your whole perception of yourself can change in a few hours. Yesterday I was a wife and an expectant mother. And today I'm . . ."

Bitsy's voice trailed off. Margaret exchanged a worried glance with Viv.

Poor Bitsy. Not only had King walked out, but she'd lost a baby too. Or maybe just the idea of a baby. Either way, it had obviously come as a shock. Just as Margaret was about to suggest she sit down, have a glass of water, Bitsy gave herself a shake and looked at her two friends. The color came back to her cheeks.

"Today I'm . . . free," she said slowly, in a tone that mingled disbelief with wonder. "As of this minute, I'm nobody's wife or mother or anything. I'm just . . . me!"

Bitsy's mouth split into an enormous, delighted grin.

"Isn't that wonderful?"

* * *

Though the Bettys had already been through a number of col-lective highs and lows, they'd never experienced one quite so pronounced—a roller-coaster plunge into a potential crisis that, seconds later, became a jubilant celebration of emancipation. Bitsy let out a whoop and hugged her friends, then marched into the living room and threw open the doors of a well-stocked bar that had been King's but now, presumably, belonged to Bitsy.

"Now, where did he put the vodka? I'm making stingers for everybody!"

After that, the party was on.

Viv mixed the drinks. Margaret went into the kitchen, found bread, cheese, mustard, and Worcestershire sauce, and made Welsh rarebit. Bitsy turned the radio up as loud as it would go and danced around the kitchen, twisting and gyrating to "Wipe Out." She grabbed Viv's hands and pulled Margaret away from the stove, insisting they join her. If Margaret lived to be a hundred, she would never forget the sight of a very pregnant Viv bopping around Bitsy's kitchen floor, jerking her arms up and down, doing the monkey.

They did settle down and talk about the book eventually. Everyone liked it, but for very different and very personal reasons. The discussion was lively.

Not surprisingly, Margaret identified with Woolf's arguments about the hurdles that make it harder for women writers to fulfill their potential. The chapter about Judith Shakespeare, an imaginary sister of William, really struck a chord. There was no question about it; had a writer with talent and drive equal to William's been born a woman, the world would have been robbed of one of its greatest literary voices.

Viv agreed but had a bone to pick when it came to the imaginary Judith's ultimate fate.

"Just because she got pregnant, did that mean she couldn't write anything? Not ever? I'm not saying it would be easy. But I don't buy the idea that suicide was her only option."

"Remember," Bitsy said, lifting a hand to signal her entry into the conversation, "Judith was forced into marriage at a very young age. That's a lot to deal with all by itself. But then to find out you're going to be a mother? That must have been over-whelming, especially if she thought motherhood would mean the end of her writing.

"I'll be honest," Bitsy said. "Realizing I wasn't pregnant after all was a big disappointment. But it was also a big relief. I really would like to have kids and a family someday, when the time is right. But right now?" She shook her head.

"And I'm not arguing with that," Viv said, leaning in. "A woman should have an opportunity to chart her own course. When it comes to career and family, there will always be some trade-offs. But that's not the same as having no choices, is it? Okay, sure. Motherhood might not have left Judith time to finish all the plays. But at least she could have written the sonnets, don't you think? That ain't nothing, am I right?"

Viv reached for her cranberry juice and started to laugh.

"Oh, for the love of Mike. Will you listen to me? Getting all worked up over an imaginary character. I'm starting to sound as crazy as the rest of you bookworms. Ha!"

❋ ❋ ❋

Margaret and Viv walked home together.

Though it was past nine, the summer sun had only just dipped below the horizon, streaking the twilight sky with shadows of pink, orange, umber, and violet. The children of Concordia were still outside jumping rope, riding bikes, playing freeze tag, and roller-skating.

When the streetlights flickered on, it was as if a factory whistle had blown that only they could hear, signaling the end of the shift. The games came to an abrupt halt. Children turned on their heels and headed home, running across spongy green grass or hard cement sidewalks and disappearing through doors. Within moments the streets were empty and quiet.

Viv looped her arm through Margaret's.

"That was fun," she said.

"It was. But it does make me sad knowing Bitsy will probably be moving away."

Viv frowned. "Oh, gosh. I hadn't thought of that. But not right away, do you think?"

"No, probably not. But eventually. Concordia's not really designed for singletons."

"Guess not. Hey, what if we fix her up? I mean, somebody around here must be getting a divorce. We could scoop up a rejected husband and hand him off to Bitsy so she'd stay."

Margaret gave her a side-eye. "Umm . . . weren't you the one who was just making a speech about letting people chart their own course?"

"Fine," said Viv. "You're right. Change is inevitable, I guess. Even if Bitsy moves away, I think we'll always be friends, don't you?"

"Always."

They walked in silence for a time, hearing only the chirrup of crickets and their own footsteps.

"I wish Charlotte had come," Margaret said as they reached the corner. "She'd have loved tonight. Maybe we should drop by. Tell her about Bitsy and King, and what we're reading next month."

Viv stopped walking and turned to face her. "It's time to let it go, Maggie. Charlotte will either come around in her own good time or she won't."

❋ ❋ ❋

Walt and the kids were still at the baseball game when Margaret entered the unlocked door and went into the kitchen to get some water. As she was filling her glass, the phone rang.

There was a lot of static on the line. After a moment, an operator said she had an international call for Mrs. Margaret Ryan from Miss Denise Gustafson and asked if she could connect it. Margaret stood by as the operator performed whatever magic was required to let two people separated by an ocean talk to one another.

Margaret had never received an international call before but knew they were expensive. Why would Denise spend that kind of money to phone her, especially at this hour? It must have been two in the morning there. Or three?

Finally, the call was connected. Though Margaret could tell Denise was practically shouting, she still sounded very far away.

"Mrs. Ryan? It's Denise. Can you hear me?"

The line still crackled with static. Margaret pressed the receiver more tightly to her ear.

"Yes. Can you hear me?"

"Yes, barely. Have you seen my mom today? I've been calling all day and all night. She isn't answering."

"No," Margaret said, raising her voice, hoping Denise would be able to hear. "Not today. I saw her car in the driveway a couple of days—" Margaret stopped. Though it might just have been more static, it sounded like Denise was breathing heavily or even crying.

"Denise, are you all right? Did something happen?"

"No. I mean, yes. I'm fine. But something did happen. I took some photographs at my party. I sent Mom a picture of Howard and a woman. They were alone in the bushes and . . ."

Denise didn't finish her sentence, but she didn't have to. The girl's anguished tone of voice and the memory of the way Howard had been flirting with the women at the party was enough to help Margaret fill in the blanks.

"Denise! Why would you do something like that?"

"I don't know. I just—I thought if she was confronted with hard evidence, maybe she'd stop looking the other way and find the guts to finally leave him. But I shouldn't have done it. It was a stupid idea. So stupid! Now I keep getting a busy signal and she's not answering the phone and . . . Oh, Mrs. Ryan! What have I done?"

CHAPTER 30

Something Rash

Margaret didn't wait for Denise to ask her to go check on Charlotte. She said she'd call later, hung up without waiting for a response, then ran out her front door and down the dark, still street. When she got to Charlotte's corner, her feet and head were pounding. All traces of her book club buzz had vanished, expelled from her body by a one-two punch of fear and adrenaline.

She raced up the walkway to Charlotte's front door. The lights were on, but the drapes were closed. Margaret rang the bell three times in succession, then hammered her fist on the dark wood as hard as she could, so hard her hand hurt. Still there was no answer, no sound or sign of life coming from inside. Margaret reached for the doorknob. It was unlocked.

When teenage Margaret opened the family refrigerator all those years before and found it uncharacteristically organized and filled with meals prepared by her mother, she didn't understand what it signified. Why would a woman determined to take her own life spend her final hours engaged in something so small, so trivial?

Now she knew.

After a lifetime of cleaning up other people's messes, most wives and mothers are loath to leave loose ends that someone else will have to tie up. Even in moments of despair, that hard-wired, hard-learned hatred of inconveniencing others isn't easily pushed aside.

And that was why, after walking through Charlotte's unlocked front door and finding the normally cluttered home in a state of perfect order—paint canvases stacked neatly in a corner, paintbrushes smelling faintly of mineral spirits placed ends up in a mason jar and left to dry on a sill, like a bouquet of field-gathered pussy willows, tubes of tempera oils carefully capped and lined up on the table, carpet devoid of drop cloths and marked with fresh vacuum tracks, throw pillows arranged just so on the sofa, kitchen floor mopped—Margaret was flooded with a terrible dread that grew as she circled through the still and empty house, silent except for the dull buzz of the telephone in the foyer, which had been left off the hook.

Margaret set the phone back in its cradle.

"Charlotte? Where are you? Denise has been trying to call. She got worried when you didn't answer and asked me to come check on you. Charlotte?"

She circled back to the foyer, stood at the bottom of the stairway, frozen with fear.

Please, Charlotte, open the door and come out. Please, God, oh, please. Not again.

Every cell of Margaret's being resisted climbing those stairs. But someone had to. *She* had to. She'd promised Denise. She grabbed the handrail and pulled herself upward, anxious breath coming in short, labored puffs, until she reached the top and Charlotte's bedroom door.

"Charlotte? Charlotte, are you in there?"

Margaret pushed the door open. The room was empty. But evidence of Charlotte's presence and intentions was everywhere.

The tallest of the two dressers stood with the empty drawers opened like gaping mouths. A half dozen suitcases, mounded with piles of unfolded clothing, lay open on the bed. Atop one of the piles, Margaret saw three large black-and-white photographs of Howard and a woman Margaret remembered seeing at the party. They were every bit as graphic as Denise had said, so lurid that Margaret turned her head away in disgust, and pity.

Poor Charlotte.

Opening an envelope from her daughter, only to find those humiliating pictures, must have been horrible. Thankfully, the sight had only jolted Charlotte into taking her leave, not her life.

Margaret sighed, feeling suddenly drained, awash with the relief that follows narrow escapes and dodged danger. She crossed the room to a side chair and started to sink down.

"Ack! Oh my G—"

Margaret's startled shriek came directly upon the heels of Charlotte's and was just as loud. Leaping from the chair and spinning toward the sound, she saw Charlotte, wrapped in a bath towel, with damp hair and no makeup, standing in the open bathroom door with her hand pressed to her chest.

"Good Lord, Margaret! You scared me half to death! I thought you were a burglar. Or Howard! Which, come to think of it, would have been worse. What are you doing, sneaking in here like that? I damn near had a heart attack. Didn't anybody ever teach you to knock?"

"I did knock. And rang the doorbell. And walked through the house screaming at the top of my lungs. You didn't hear me at all?"

"Not over the shower. Hang on a second."

Charlotte went to her closet and emerged a moment later wrapped in a robe of shimmering silk the color of a sun-blushed peach, wet hair turbaned in a towel.

"What are you doing here anyway? Did something happen? Some sort of book club emergency?"

"Not an emergency. Something did happen at the Bettys meeting, but I'll tell you about that later. Denise phoned and asked me to come check on you. Seems she had second thoughts about the wisdom of sending the pictures," Margaret said, shifting her gaze to the pile of photos. "She's been calling and calling. When you didn't answer, she started to worry you'd done something . . . well, something rash."

"As you can see," Charlotte replied, cracking a sardonic smile that made her eyes glitter, and sweeping a hand toward the clothing-strewn bed, "I did do something rash. Or rather, I'm in the process of doing something rash. It'll take a while to get everything packed."

Margaret nodded, her spirits drooping as relief made way for regret.

Charlotte was safe, she reminded herself, which was the important thing. Still, knowing that both Bitsy and Charlotte would be leaving Concordia was a hard pill to swallow. Viv said they'd stay friends no matter what happened. But would they? With Bitsy and Charlotte leaving, what would happen to the Bettys?

"Have you decided when you're going?"

Charlotte's eyebrows, thinner without benefit of brow pencil, popped with surprise. "Oh, I'm not going anywhere." She picked up her cigarettes and lighter. "However, in a final act of domestic devotion, I am graciously packing Howard's bags for him."

"Howard has decided to move out?"

Charlotte lit her cigarette, shaking her head. "I decided for him. As you may have noticed, I'm cleaning house." She took a short but clearly satisfying drag. "The first thing to go is Howard."

Charlotte placed her cigarette in an ashtray and started scooping mounds of Howard's unfolded clothes into the nearest suitcase, squashing them down so they would fit, and wrinkling them mightily in the process. When the first suitcase was full, she slammed the lid closed, leaning hard to keep it from popping open, and snapped the locks with a flourish.

"And that's just the beginning. From here on out, you're going to see a whole new Charlotte, a Charlotte who has her act together, a Charlotte who finally starts living her own life. I don't know exactly what that will look like at the moment . . ."

She paused to take another puff before attacking the next suitcase, tossing shirts, pants, jackets, and jockey shorts into its maw. "But one thing it will not include is Dr. Ernest Barry. First thing tomorrow, I'm calling to inform him that his services are no longer required. My head's been shrunk enough, thank you very much."

"Yes, but . . . Charlotte . . ." Margaret bit her lip. "Are you sure that's a good idea?"

Charlotte straightened and planted her hands on her hips, giving Margaret a hard stare.

"This is not a manic phase, if that's what you're thinking." Frowning, she grabbed some undershirts and tossed them onto the pile. "I don't know what it is exactly, but trust me, not that. I know the difference.

"Look," Charlotte said, her expression softening somewhat. "I understand that I still need help, just not from that man. Maybe not from any man." She paused briefly, eyes narrowing. "Now there's an idea. Maybe I could find a female analyst. Are there such things? Honestly, I'm not particular. Anybody who isn't a Freudian and a jerk and who will let me smoke during sessions would be fine."

She snapped the locks on the second suitcase.

"Hey, can you give me a hand? This thing is heavy."

Margaret helped haul the suitcases off the bed, then turned to Charlotte.

"You know what I think? I think you're happy. Not manic, just happy."

So it seemed. Margaret had witnessed more than one of Charlotte's frenetic phases. Charlotte was right; this was not that. Despite her initial misgivings, what Margaret now saw was a woman in control of herself and her circumstances, who had made up her mind to take charge and make choices, choices that were right for her.

"You think so?" Charlotte's smile reached her eyes. "Well, if it's true, then you're part of the reason. You're a good friend, Maggie."

Margaret cocked an eyebrow. "I thought I was a Pollyanna. And a pain in the butt."

"Oh, you absolutely are," Charlotte said. "But you're also a good, sometimes infuriatingly honest friend, and braver than you think you are. The kind of friend who doesn't hold back from speaking the hard truths that people don't want to hear but need to."

When Margaret's eyes started to fill, Charlotte waved a hand in the air.

"Oh no. No, no, no. Just stop right there. Because if you start crying, then I will too, and there's no time for that. Come on, give me a hand with the rest of this crap. We can evict Howard and catch up at the same time. I've got so much to tell you."

"Me too," Margaret said. "Wait till you hear what happened with Bitsy and King. Unbelievable, but all for the best, I think."

She picked up a pair of men's oxfords and dumped them into the next suitcase.

"But first, tell me something. What changed? You always knew Howard was cheating, so what's different now? Was it the pictures?"

"Yes and no."

Charlotte took one of the photos from the bed, pinching the edges gingerly between two fingers, as if afraid of smudging it.

"There was a lot leading up to it, other things that made me realize I couldn't keep going on this way. Still," she said, her tone philosophical, "an eight-by-ten glossy of your husband with his fly unzipped and his hand up a woman's skirt *will* get your attention."

She laid the photo down on the nightstand, then picked up a cigarette with one hand and one of Howard's crisp white dress shirts with the other. She held the shirt up close to her face, squinting.

"Well, will you look at that? I do believe this collar has a lipstick stain. And in a very unattractive shade of mauve I wouldn't be caught dead wearing," she said, and tsked her tongue. "That's a shame. You know, I'll just have to see if I can get it out."

Charlotte gripped the cigarette in her fingers, holding it like a stylus, and pressed the lit end against the shirt collar for a long moment, curling the fabric and leaving a charred hole.

Margaret gasped, then laughed.

"Charlotte! That's a nice shirt! It must have cost ten dollars!"

"Don't be ridiculous. This shirt is from Saks. It cost twenty. Probably more."

"Charlotte! You're terrible!"

"I am," she said, eyes sparkling as she tossed the burned shirt aside. "Thanks to Denise, I plan to go on being terrible. Those pictures aren't just pictures. They're my ticket to freedom."

The blue princess phone on the nightstand started to ring. Margaret's eyes went wide.

"Denise! I promised to call and let her know you're okay. She must be worried sick."

"I'll tell her myself." Charlotte picked up the telephone and perched on the edge of the bed, waiting for the call to be connected, lips bowing to a smile when she finally heard her daughter's voice.

"Hello, baby. How is Oxford? No, no, I know. Margaret told me. I'm so sorry, I didn't mean to worry you. I must have knocked the phone off the hook while I was dusting."

Charlotte puffed her cigarette and grinned, listening to Denise's reaction.

"Yes, dusting. Yes, me. No, I'm not lying! Ask Margaret if you don't believe me."

Charlotte laughed. Margaret took a step backward, then another, inching toward the door. Charlotte and Denise needed to talk, and Margaret needed to go home. She had things to do, including a task she'd put off for far too long and which suddenly felt very urgent.

Margaret slipped out the door, catching a final snippet of conversation.

"Oh, darling. Darling, please don't cry. I'm all right, Denise, truly I am. From here on out, everything will be."

CHAPTER 31

Being Brave

Walt was pulling into the driveway when Margaret returned from Charlotte's.

Suzy had fallen asleep on the ride back from the ballpark and couldn't be roused, so Walt carried her into the house and put her to bed. Beth and Bobby were still wide-awake and insisted on giving Margaret a play-by-play of the game. The Senators came through in the clutch, scoring two runs in the final inning. But the highlight occurred in the fourth, when Beth caught a foul ball with her bare hands.

"Bobby was so jealous!" Beth said, smirking at her little brother. "I tortured him for a while. But then he started to cry, so I let him have it."

"I did not cry! There was something in my eye." Bobby held out the ball so Margaret could see. "Look! Three of the players signed it! Dad said he'll get me a case to put it in."

"Wonderful," Margaret said, ruffling his hair. "I'm glad you had fun. Head up to bed now, and don't forget to brush your teeth. Bobby, give me that shirt. I need to get the mustard stains out before they set."

By the time Margaret dealt with the laundry and made sure the kids were in bed, it was too late to do any writing. But she was up before the sun, feeling not the least bit groggy, brain buzzing with thoughts about what she wanted to say and how to say it as she sat down at the kitchen table and fed a clean sheet of paper into Sylvia's roller.

If Charlotte could be brave, then so could she.

Women of the 1960s are living through the Age of Advertising, an era with one sole purpose: to sell products to ladies like you and like me. And how do those marketing geniuses of Madison Avenue accomplish that purpose?

Easy. By convincing us that the products they peddle will "change your life." As a reader of this magazine, you know just what I'm talking about.

Sandwiched between the catnip of entertaining articles and columns, we find endless pages of slickly written advertisements for time-saving appliances, mild-tasting cigarettes, comfortable girdles, perfumes to make us irresistible, face cream to erase wrinkles, depilatories to remove unwanted hair, shampoos to make the hair we do want look shiny and more manageable.

Some claims they make seem plausible, others impossibly far-fetched. There is no such thing as a comfortable girdle. We know this. Yet we continue to buy them, and so much else, because what we're really buying is a subliminal promise that a product will change our lives for the better.

Why do we fall for such obvious fiction? That's easy too. Because so many of us long for . . . something. We're not sure what exactly. But something.

Something different. Something better. Something to change our lives. Or perhaps make us feel alive.

We don't admit this publicly because we know we should be happy. After all, everyone else seems to be. Open a magazine or turn on the television, and you'll find yourself bombarded by images of perfect, perfectly satisfied women.

Which means the problem must lie with us, mustn't it? Perhaps we are weak, neurotic, selfish, or ungrateful. Or simply lacking . . . something.

And so we buy the product, hoping it will fill the void or dull the ache. It never does.

I know, because I've been as susceptible to snake oil as anyone. I've bought all of it over the years: face cream, soaps, toasters, perfumes, instant mashed potatoes, no-calorie gelatin, and yes, girdles. None of it changed my life.

Then I bought a book.

"The Feminine Mystique" by Betty Friedan has changed my life.

Maybe you've heard about this book? If you have, it wasn't here.

The editors of "A Woman's Place" would rather you didn't know about books like this, or anything else that might make you think. If you did, you might start to question exactly what and where a woman's place is. Or should be. And that might make it harder for them to sell you soap, depilatories, and girdles.

Maybe you've heard that Mrs. Friedan's book is dangerous, that she herself is a shrewish hysteric bent on wrecking homes, emasculating men, and fomenting feminine dissatisfaction.

Don't believe it.

After reading her book myself, I'm happy to report that my home has not been wrecked. My children continue to thrive, and my marriage is rock-solid. In fact, my husband and I are happier than ever before. Some of the credit goes to him. He's a good man, the kind who not only can admit his mistakes but take steps to correct them—a rare bird indeed.

But much of the credit must also be attributed to the journey I began by reading Mrs. Friedan's book, a journey that is leading me to a more satisfying life that makes the most of my unique experiences, education, and personality. And isn't that better for everyone? Wives, husbands, children? How can a home be happy if the homemaker isn't?

I'm not suggesting that every housewife is discontented. Many intelligent, energetic women find joy and sacred purpose in tending to home and hearth. It's an important task, and the women who choose to make it their career deserve our appreciation and respect. But as I discovered while reading Mrs. Friedan's book, there are countless good and right ways to be a woman and only two wrong.

The first is to insist that your way is "the" way, the only way. The second is to buy into that nonsense and to spend your life limping along an aimless path in shoes that will never fit.

Another lesson I've learned in these last months is that the longing for something more, even when I couldn't put a name to it, didn't mean I was crazy or selfish or—most important—alone.

When the members of my "Betty Friedan Book Club," "the Bettys," for short, met for the first time, some of us were strangers. Now we are inseparable friends, sister travelers on parallel roads with differing destinations. Some of us found new careers, and others found their way back home. Every one of us, cheered and challenged by the others, tapped into wells of courage and strength we never knew we had.

The Bettys' adventures are not finished. Perhaps they never will be. There may be many destinations in a woman's journey, many seasons in her life. Time alone will reveal where our roads will lead, whether our paths will diverge or cross again. But wherever we go, our hearts will remain close, connected by an invisible but unbreakable bond.

Now that I think of it, that has been the true change.

And so I amend my earlier statement. Betty Friedan's book didn't change my life. But it did send me in search of a better life, a life that truly fits, and gave me companions for the journey. For that, I am forever grateful.

And forever changed.

As Margaret was typing the final sentence, Walt entered the kitchen, yawning.

"Is there coffee?"

She lifted a flat hand, signaling the intensity of her concentration and a request for silence. Walt walked to the percolator, poured himself some coffee, then came to stand near Margaret, watching with a curious frown. After reading the piece one more time, she pulled the paper from Sylvia's roller, added it to those she'd already proofed, then handed the stack to Walt.

He set down his cup to read. Margaret waited, clenching and unclenching her fists, until he flipped to the last page.

"Well?"

Walt lifted his hand. "Hang on. Let me finish."

Margaret hugged herself, arms wrapped tight against her middle, trying to be patient. Finally, his eyes tracked to the bottom of the page.

"Well?" she asked again. "What do you think?"

He sniffed and flipped back to the first page.

"Not bad. The stuff about your husband seems a little overblown, but other than that—"

Margaret scuffed her foot in his direction, giving his shoe a chastising little kick.

"Be serious. What do you think?"

He lowered the papers and looked her in the eye.

"I think it's excellent, Maggie. It may be the best thing you've ever written."

Margaret cocked her head to one side and let out a small, bemused laugh.

"How would you know?"

His smile spread slowly. "Because, Margaret Ruth Ryan, I have read every single one of your columns. Even the early ones, back when I was still acting like an ass and being jealous of your job. Every other Thursday, I stop by Mayer's Drugstore on my way to work and buy three copies of the new issue. I keep one for myself and give the others to the women in my office."

"Only the women?"

"Yeah, well." He shrugged. "I doubt most of those guys know how to read. But to the secretarial pool, you are a celebrity. Catfights over who gets first dibs on the issue have been known to break out."

"Okay, now you're lying."

"More like exaggerating," he said, pinching two fingers together. "A little. But the girls really do love your columns. So do I. But this?" He lifted the typewritten pages. "This is terrific. And do you know why? Because it's honest and real, something you really believe."

Margaret murmured a thank-you. She knew he was right. Hearing him say it out loud felt good, but it added to her conundrum.

"So, do you think I should send it in? Because if I do . . ." She let her sentence go unfinished. Walt had heard her complain about Leonard Clement for months now, so he knew all about his threats.

"It really is good," she said, lifting her hand toward her mouth and biting the edge of her thumbnail. "I mean, I can see why he cut the other pieces. I wasn't really committed to anything, more like nibbling around the corners of what I wanted to say without actually saying it. But *this*, this is different. I'd have to take out the snarky reference to *A Woman's Place*, of course. And soften gibes about women's magazines in general. He'd never go for that.

"But maybe I can work around it," she said, a hopeful note creeping into her tone. "What matters is that the ideas are clear and meaningful. The piece could resonate with a lot of readers, I just know it. Surely Mr. Clement will see that too. He has to, don't you think?"

Margaret lifted her head and looked up at Walt.

"Maybe," he said. "But maybe not. You'd be taking a chance."

Yes. Yes, she would.

Margaret bit her lip, thinking about how she'd feel if Clement followed through on his threat to fire her if she didn't toe the line. Then she thought about how she'd feel if she backed away from what she'd written, or if this piece, her best work to date, never saw the light of day. Both outcomes felt potentially devastating, though in different ways. She looked at Walt again.

"What do you think I should do?"

"Well, I—" He stopped, clamped his lips together, gave his head a shake. "You don't need me to tell you what to do. You're a smart woman with good instincts. Whatever decision you make will be the right one. And whatever you do, whatever happens, I'm proud of you."

He bent low to kiss her. Margaret lifted her arms, twined them around his shoulders, and kissed him back. A shuffling noise, the *wiff-wiff* of slippers on wood floors, came from the hallway.

"Mom? Can you make waffles?"

They released their hold on each other. Margaret looked toward the door. Bobby, still in his blue striped pajamas, was staring at them.

"How about pancakes?"

"Okay."

Margaret got to her feet. Walt gave her a peck, then grabbed his coffee cup and headed for the door. Margaret took a mixing bowl from the cupboard, calling after him.

"Honey? Just one thing. The part you thought was overblown, about the husband? I'm leaving it in. From here on out, I only want to write what I truly believe."

CHAPTER 32

Calling the Shots

Mrs. Gustafson?"

The receptionist at Gilbert Partners was new on the job and as thick as cold oatmeal. She was also doe-eyed, busty, brunette, twenty, and just Howard's type. If he hadn't slept with her yet, he'd surely try before long.

"The one and only," Charlotte said. "At least this week."

The girl blushed a deep shade of pink and blinked her doe eyes, looking flustered.

Oh yes, Charlotte thought. Howard was *definitely* sleeping with her.

"Oh gosh. Um, I don't think he's expecting you." The girl reached for the telephone. "Let me just call back and—"

Charlotte, dressed in an off-white Chanel suit with navy trim, the same ensemble she'd worn to the first book club meeting, waved an arm through the air, cutting the girl off as she breezed past the reception desk.

"No need. I'd like to surprise him."

The girl popped up from her chair, stuttering protests. Charlotte ignored her, striding through the bullpen of desks with the flustered receptionist dogging her heels. Charlotte beamed smiles and nodded acknowledgments to the wide-eyed employees watching the parade, making her way toward the dark walnut doors that distinguished Howard's office from those of lesser rank. His sanctuary was guarded by another doe-eyed woman, a few years older than the receptionist and not quite as dumb, but even better endowed and also a brunette.

Good Lord, Howard was predictable! But oh my, how Charlotte had been looking forward to this moment.

As Charlotte approached, the dark-haired guardian rose from her chair, moving out from behind her desk and taking a stance in front of the office door.

"You can't go in there. He's in a meeting."

Charlotte flashed a brilliant smile and practically purred her greeting.

"Brenda, darling! How are you? Haven't seen you since the party. I hope you had a nice time. You know, I'm sorry we didn't have a chance to chat that day," Charlotte said in a regretful tone that sounded almost genuine, touching fingers lightly to her pearls. "I looked everywhere, but you were nowhere to be found. Must have been hiding someplace. However, I understand Howard gave you a personal tour of the gardens. So considerate of him. Most of the plants are still taking hold, but the camellias are so lovely and lush, don't you think?"

Brenda said nothing but blushed even more deeply than her colleague from reception, who had given up the chase but was standing within eavesdropping distance. Charlotte's green eyes glittered like those of a cat preparing to pounce. She took two slow, stalking steps toward her prey.

"Of course those bushes can be something of an attractive nuisance, a tempting spot for couples bent on sneaking off to engage in dirty, illicit deeds."

Brenda's lip started to quiver. Charlotte leaned in as if about to share a secret, speaking in a stage whisper that could easily be overheard by those listening in—including the eavesdropping receptionist, whose expression suggested she was waking up to the fact that her relationship with Howard was less than exclusive.

Charlotte pressed her fingers to her cheek and let her eyes go wide.

"And do you know something? I actually think someone did. The day after the party, my gardener found an abandoned pair of panties in the bushes! Can you imagine? Whoever it was must have been a real tramp. I mean, honestly. How cheap can you get?"

Brenda let out a sob, covered her face with her hands, and ran toward the ladies' room. The other receptionist gasped, did an about-face, and fled. Charlotte smirked to herself.

"Oh, that was almost too easy."

She entered Howard's office without knocking. He had a guest.

"Daddy! What a convenient surprise. Saves me the trouble of a trip to New York to explain my demands."

With his sharklike smile, steely eyes that missed nothing, a full head of platinum hair, and even fuller lips, George Beverly Gilbert III—known as G.G. by those who pretended to like him—had the air of an elder statesman when in a good mood, a dictator when not. Charlotte referred to those as his "Il Duce days" and could tell this was one of them.

G.G. removed his cigar from his mouth. "Demands? What the hell are you talking about? And what are you doing here? Can't you see we're in the middle of a meeting?"

"I know. But this won't take five minutes, Daddy. And it really can't wait. Or perhaps it's just that I can't wait. Either way . . ."

Charlotte stripped off her gloves and laid them atop the inlaid walnut conference table at which her father and a very agitated-looking Howard were seated. Howard stood.

"Charlotte, you can't just barge in here without an appointment—"

"Ah, but it seems I can," she said. "I don't know what got into your secretary, Howard. A few cordial words from me and a mention of our camellia bushes, and she went scurrying off to the bathroom in a torrent of tears, leaving her desk unmanned and you unprotected. Same thing happened with the receptionist."

Charlotte tsked her tongue. "Next time, try to find a bimbo with a thicker skin. And an IQ not measured in single digits."

Howard's lip curled into a sneer. He started to say something cutting but stopped when G.G. lifted his hand. Howard sank back down into his chair like the yes-man he was, yielding the floor to his father-in-law. G.G. picked up his cigar.

"Quit playing games, Charlotte. If you have something to say, then say it so we can get back to work. But if you've come to ask for an increase in your allowance, the answer is no. You cost more than you're worth as it is."

"Not quite an increase in my allowance," Charlotte said. "More like a settlement. To be blunt, this is a shakedown."

G.G. chomped the end of his cigar, observing his only child with the wary expression of a soldier who has just stumbled upon a cache of unexploded ordnance. Charlotte folded her hands demurely in her lap.

"My demands are as follows. All proceeds from the sale of the house, a onetime payment equal to twenty years' worth of Howard's current salary, including bonuses, and an equal amount put into an irrevocable trust for Denise. Of course Howard will also be paying child support and college tuition for all of the children, but I want to make sure the baby born on the wrong side of the blanket won't be cut out of the will after you die, Daddy." She flashed a serene smile. "Oh, and as I'm sure you've already guessed, I want a divorce and full custody of the children."

Howard raised his eyebrows and coughed out a laugh. "Isn't it a little early in the day to be drinking, Charlotte? Even for you?"

"I am stone-cold sober, Howard. And deadly serious."

"Nobody is getting a divorce." G.G. waved his cigar, leaving a trail of smoke that smelled like burnt mushrooms soaked in whiskey. "My great-grandfather founded this firm in 1822. The reason we've managed to survive while others failed is by keeping things in the family, guarding our image, and avoiding scandal. Nobody is going to entrust their money to a family firm that can't keep its members under control.

"So let me say again, nobody is getting a divorce. Not now, not ever," he said, glaring in Charlotte's direction. "I thought your mother made the consequences that would ensue, should you embark on such a reckless course of action, perfectly clear. Do not test me on this, Charlotte. I meant every word of what I said."

He wedged his cigar between his teeth and gave Charlotte a look that, in former days, would have withered her spirit as well as her resolve. Those days were over.

"I don't doubt it. But I can be ruthless too, Daddy. After all, I learned from the best. And thanks to your generous graduation gift to Denise, the tables have turned somewhat."

Charlotte pulled out the manila envelope containing Denise's photographs, a typewritten list of names and addresses, and a business card from her handbag, and laid the contents on the conference table.

"Not Howard's best side, I'll admit," she said, fanning the photos out like a croupier dealing a hand of blackjack. "But nobody will have any trouble recognizing his face. Or his anatomy. The newspapers would have to crop out some of the more explicit bits, but the facial expressions of you and the tramp will be more than enough to pique people's interest. And certain things are even more lurid if left to the imagination, don't you agree?"

Charlotte rubbed her thumb over the smooth veneer of her manicured fingernails with a sly smile and studied nonchalance. "Oh, just in case you were wondering about the list, it includes the names and addresses of reporters covering the financial beat of every major newspaper. Gossip columnists too, including Walter Winchell and Suzy Knickerbocker.

"Envelopes with copies of the pictures and a note explaining the circumstances are all addressed and ready to go," she said. "I haven't decided if I should start with the gossip columnists or just send them out all at once, more of a rifle shot. But I'm leaning toward the latter. Best to cover my bases, don't you think, Daddy? Even you won't be able to buy off that many journalists, not for a story with artwork as juicy as this one."

"You cheap, vindictive little . . ."

Howard, whose face had turned an angry shade of red the instant he laid eyes on the photos, sputtered and stood, clawing his hands as if preparing to lunge. His father-in-law placed a firm hand on his shoulder and pushed him back into the chair.

"Sit down, you idiot. You've already done enough damage for one day!"

G.G. turned a soul-shriveling scowl upon his son-in-law, the kind of look that, up until now, he had only bestowed upon his disappointing daughter. Though Howard blinked with momentary confusion, Charlotte could see realization of his demoted status breaking over him, a layer of tarnish that the former golden boy would find hard, perhaps impossible, to remove. She almost felt sorry for him.

Almost.

"If those pictures get out in the press," G.G. said, almost growling at the still stunned Howard, "we'll lose every client we've got. Since you're obviously too stupid to be discreet, at least have the brains to know when you've lost."

Howard slumped in his chair. G.G. turned toward Charlotte.

"All right, Charlotte. You win. You can have your divorce. Honestly," he said, taking a puff on his cigar and giving her an appraising look that held a hint of admiration, "I didn't know you had it in you. You're tougher than I thought. But you've got to be reasonable. You and I are going to have to sit down and work out a—"

Charlotte interrupted him with a shake of her head. "No negotiations, Daddy. Under the circumstances, my offer is more than reasonable. That's a business card for my lawyer," she said, nodding toward the table as she picked up her gloves. "He's drawing up papers as we speak, spelling out the details of my demands. There will be some administrative hoops, and we'll both have to appear before a judge at some point, but I'd like to move quickly. No point in dragging things out. I'm sure Howard agrees."

Howard shot her a look of unadulterated loathing. "I can't wait to be rid of you."

"Excellent! We're all on the same page."

She slipped on her gloves and walked to the door.

"Oh, just a couple of housekeeping items before I go. Daddy, I'm sure this goes without saying, but I expect you to pay the lawyer and court costs."

Charlotte looked toward her soon-to-be ex-husband. "And Howard, not that you'd want to come home, but in case you were thinking of it? The locks on the house have already been changed. Don't worry about your clothes. I made you a reservation at the Willard and left six suitcases of your things with the bellman. They were awfully heavy, so do be sure to leave him a nice tip." She looped her handbag over her arm. "Well, I think that's everything. Bye, all."

She gave them a wave and swept out of the room, making her way through the canyon of metal desks with a confident stride, walking in rhythm with the clacking of adding machines and clattering of typewriters. Approaching the lobby, she ran into Edna Green, the friendly, middle-aged manager of the typing pool and one of the few people on the company payroll Charlotte actually liked.

"Mrs. Gustafson! I didn't know you were coming into the office today. So good to see you." Edna looked her up and down. "My goodness, Mrs. Gustafson. That is a beautiful suit. So stylish. And you look so happy. What are you up to today?"

Charlotte smiled.

"Calling the shots. And I have to tell you, Edna. It feels good."

CHAPTER 33

Choices and Consequences

One day, when Margaret was thirteen going on fourteen, basically a selfish bundle of raging hormones and contradictions encased in a sack of skin, she had deliberately goaded her mother into action, purposely crossing the line—curious, perhaps, to see if there truly was a line, wondering just how far she could go.

The war was still on, and her mother was working long days and frequent overtime shifts at the factory. Margaret wanted to have a big sleepover for her birthday, inviting fourteen of her "closest" girlfriends, not one of whom she was in contact with anymore. Even if her mother hadn't been working all the hours God gave her or struggling to stretch ration points to keep the family fed, it was a big and, quite frankly, unreasonable request. Her mother countered with permission for two girls to stay over, finally upping the number to three, saying that was as much as she could cope with, and the negotiations were closed.

Margaret would not be deterred. She broached the subject again when Mom was chatting with other women in the vestibule after church, hoping the presence of an audience would make it harder to deny her request. But her mother's response was emphatic.

Still, Margaret asked again and again and again, until her mother lost patience and spun toward her. "That is enough, Margaret Ruth. I'm warning you. One more word and I'll—"

Margaret didn't listen. The word came. So did the slap.

It shouldn't have been a surprise. She'd been warned. Had Margaret been in her mother's shoes, she might have done the same thing. But young Margaret couldn't make herself believe her mother would make good on the threat, not in such a public setting. When the blow fell, Margaret was shocked, embarrassed, and chastised. She wished she could take it back, but it was too late. The deed was done, the promised consequence delivered.

Hanging up the phone after Mr. Clement fired her, Margaret felt the same way. Humiliated and shocked. She shouldn't have been; he'd warned her. But, as with her mother's threats so many years before, Margaret hadn't truly believed he'd follow through.

After softening her criticism of advertisers and polishing the piece until her points rang clear as a bell and the writing was as tight as possible, Margaret had convinced herself that the column had at least a fifty-fifty chance of being published. Because even Clement would be forced to acknowledge how well it had turned out. Worst-case scenario, she figured, was that Clement would yell at her again, kill the piece, and, as punishment, force her to write a column about daytime soap operas, visiting mothers-in-law, floor wax, or some equally mind-numbing topic—basically a return to status quo.

But she could not convince herself that he'd really fire her, just for the sin of writing something that was actually good. Yet he had.

Margaret buried her head in her hands and sank down on the sofa, so upset she forgot where she was and sat on the cushion with the sprung coil, taking a sharp poke in her bottom as a rebuke. A few more months of writing and she'd have saved up enough for a new couch. But now . . .

She'd poured everything she had into crafting a piece she felt proud of, a column readers might actually think about, act upon.

To what end? If nobody got to read it, or anything else she might have written in the future, what did it matter?

"Stupid, stupid, stupid," she said, murmuring into the mask of her hands.

But if Margaret was angry with herself, Walt—who had wandered into the kitchen in search of a snack, seen the distressed look on Margaret's face, and ended up eavesdropping on her phone call—was furious. Not with Margaret, but with Leonard Clement.

"How could he just fire you? For writing something good? Isn't that your job? That was the best column you've ever written, Margaret. By far."

"And if you were my editor instead of him, things would be different. As it is . . ." Margaret closed her eyes and sighed. "What an idiot I am. A first-class idiot. It's one thing for Betty Friedan to climb up on her soapbox, but I'm just a housewife. What made me think I could pull this off?"

Walt, who had been pacing like a captive lion in a small enclosure, stopped and stabbed a finger in Margaret's direction. "You are not *just* a housewife. You're *my* wife. And one of the smartest, most talented people I've ever met!" He growled with frustration and smacked his fist into his palm. "That man calls himself an editor? Clement wouldn't know good writing if it walked in the door and bit him in the ass. If he was here, I'd—"

Margaret moaned. Walt turned toward the sound, scowling.

"You're not going to take this lying down, are you, Maggie?"

"What else can I do? Writers write, but editors decide if people get to read it." She turned out her hands. "That's just the way things are."

"Well, that's stupid. And wrong." Walt snatched a battered issue of *A Woman's Place* from the coffee table, the same copy he had filched from the dentist's office and passed off as Margaret's Christmas gift all those months ago, rolled it up, and whacked it against his leg. "It's worse than wrong. It's censorship. It's un-American!"

"It's really not," Margaret said, shaking her head. "Not if you're getting paid. Magazine publishing is a business. And as far as publishers are concerned, writing is a product like any other. If they don't think they can sell it, they don't want to print it."

He stared at her. "So you're saying it's all about dollars and cents with these people?"

"Well . . . yes." Margaret let out a sardonic laugh, surprised he even had to ask. "The only thing they really care about is selling magazines and advertising space."

Walt narrowed his eyes and made a sucking sound with his teeth. Margaret tilted her head to the side; she could practically see the wheels turning inside his head.

"Walt? What is it?"

Instead of answering her question, he unrolled the magazine and started flipping furiously through the pages of ads, editorials, columns, and articles. "There it is!" he cried, stabbing his finger against one of the pages as he started toward the hallway. Margaret popped up from the couch and followed him.

"There what is? Walt? Where are you going? What are you doing?"

He looked over his shoulder. "To call the advertising department!"

CHAPTER 34

The Group

When Margaret phoned Viv to tell her she'd been fired, doing her best to swallow the catch in her voice, Viv cut her off.

"Don't say another word, Maggie. Just hang tight, okay? I'll be right over."

Twenty minutes later, Viv was standing on Margaret's doorstep, flanked by Charlotte and Bitsy and holding a cake plate in her hands. Judging from the beads of moisture still clinging to the Saran wrap covering, it was still warm.

"You baked a Bundt?"

"Cherry chocolate chip," Viv told her. "It was just about done, so I figured I'd bring it along and call the others, save you from having to tell the story three times." She looked down at the platter and shrugged. "I've got more time for baking now that I'm not working."

"Well, looks like I'll be dusting off my oven mitts and joining you." Margaret sighed, waving the group inside. They ended up in the kitchen. Margaret sliced the cake and poured iced tea. Charlotte accepted the glass and the ice but filled hers with Dubonnet.

"Yes, it's early," she said, responding to Margaret's raised eyebrows, "but Dubonnet practically is tea, infused with herbs and all that."

Bitsy picked up the bottle and looked at the label.

"And alcohol. Nineteen percent by volume."

"Oh, don't be a spoilsport," Charlotte said. "Independence Day came late this year, and I'm still celebrating."

"Come to think of it," Bitsy said, her countenance brightening, "so am I."

Bitsy poured her untasted tea back into the pitcher, filled the glass with the last of the Dubonnet, and clinked her rim on Charlotte's. Margaret tossed the empty bottle in the trash.

"Looks like I'll have to make a run to the liquor store."

"Later," Viv said. "Right now, tell us the rest of the story."

"What's to tell? Clement fired me. My brief, ignominious writing career is over." Margaret shrugged. "Anyway, I really don't want to talk about it."

Viv clucked her tongue. "Don't be ridiculous. Of course you do."

Viv had a point. Though it didn't alter the circumstances, relating the story to her friends after the gathering moved into the living room—watching their heads nod in support or wag with indignation—made Margaret feel a little better.

But the best part, and also the most heartbreaking, was their response after she gave in to their demands and read the column aloud—not the watered-down version she'd submitted to Mr. Clement, but a well-polished rendering that featured all her original points, even the bits that blasted the magazine by name. When she finished, the Bettys were silent.

But not for long.

"Margaret, that's . . . well, it's just brilliant."

"Brilliant. I mean, I always knew you were a good writer. But . . . wow."

"It's as if you put my thoughts into words, even before I knew I was thinking them. How do you do that?"

In short, they loved it. Not just because she was their friend, Margaret could tell, but because her words rang true for them. Margaret felt certain that other women would have had a similar reaction and that her essay could help them know they weren't alone, perhaps even given them courage to band together to assert some influence. But since nobody besides Walt and the Bettys would ever get to read it . . .

"It's insane," Charlotte said, exhaling an indignant column of cigarette smoke. "Absolutely insane! I understand that you failed to follow your editor's orders, but how could he fire you? Can't he see how talented you are? This column is ten times better than the rest of that drivel you wrote."

"Well, gee," Margaret said, cracking a half smile. "Thanks. I think."

Charlotte flapped her hand. "Oh, you know what I meant. None of it was bad, and some of it was really funny. But at the end of the day, it was just . . . fluff."

Margaret nodded. "And now I don't even get to write fluff. I really blew it, didn't I?"

She reached toward the cigarette pack Charlotte had left on the coffee table, arching her eyebrows in a silent request. Charlotte nodded to let her know she could help herself. Margaret smoked only rarely, and never enough to bother buying cigarettes for herself. But she was in such a rotten mood, and the Dubonnet was gone.

"What about Walt's idea of publishing it yourself as an advertisement?" Bitsy asked.

"Too expensive," Margaret replied after lighting up. "We'd need at least two-thirds of a page. A full page would be better. But the price for an ad that large is . . ." Margaret took a drag from her cigarette, shaking her head as she exhaled. "Well, let's put it this way. If I'd known how much the magazine made on advertising, I'd have asked for more money."

"Quit being so coy," Viv said, pushing the heel of her hand against her very prominent belly, as if urging the baby to shift to a more comfortable spot. "How much are we talking?"

Margaret named the figure. Viv let out a low whistle.

"Sheesh. You could buy a car for that. A used one, but still . . . I had no idea."

"Neither did we," Margaret said. "I used some of the money I made from the column to pay for my typewriter. But even if I'd saved every dime, it wouldn't come close to what we'd need to buy a full-page ad in *A Woman's Place*, or any national magazine. For about ten seconds, Walt made some noise about tapping our savings to pay for it—though that wouldn't have done it either—or even taking out a loan. Thankfully, I was able to talk sense to him. The way his boss has been acting, we shouldn't be taking any financial risks."

"But it's sweet that he wanted to," Bitsy said, breaking a piece of Viv's Bundt cake off with her fingers before popping it into her mouth. "If I ever get married again, I'd want it to be to somebody like Walt. Or Tony. A knight in shining armor type."

Margaret smiled to herself, thinking about Walt. In terms of knighthood, he might be more Don Quixote than Sir Lancelot, tilting at windmills in a nobly fruitless attempt to defend her honor. But Bitsy was right; it was sweet that he'd tried. Margaret loved that about him.

However, despite the rocky patch they'd endured over the last months—no, come to think of it, *because* of that rocky patch— what she'd come to love most about Walt were the things she'd written in the column. Not many men were brave enough to admit their mistakes; fewer still had the strength of character to change their ways. Jerry hadn't been strong enough to do that. But Walt was a better man than his father. Not a perfect man, but a good one.

Viv leaned forward to cut herself another slice of cake, bumping Margaret's arm as she did and nudging her from her reverie.

"Oh, you'll marry again," Viv said, nodding sagely in Bitsy's direction. "You're only twenty-three, and biology is a powerful thing. For about three days every month, Tony Buschetti looks like Rock Hudson."

Margaret sputtered out a laugh along with her cigarette smoke. "But Tony does look like Rock Hudson. Always."

"I know." Viv sighed heavily. "I'm doomed."

Charlotte, who had been leaning back against the sofa, legs stretched out, slim ankles extending from the cuffs of her black stirrup pants, smoking steadily and listening to the conversation with uncharacteristic silence and lidded eyes, abruptly changed the subject.

"Who's started reading the book?"

The other three exchanged curious glances. They weren't due to start discussing Mary McCarthy's novel *The Group* until the official Bettys meeting, which was still more than two weeks off. Margaret lifted her hand tentatively, like a student who thinks she might know the answer to the teacher's question but isn't entirely sure.

"I'm about six or seven chapters in," she said. "It's good so far."

"I've read about half," Bitsy said. "With King gone, I can read as late as I want now."

"I've only read the first chapter," Viv admitted. "The wedding. Interesting characters. But I already have a feeling that things aren't going to end well for them."

"They don't." Charlotte pulled her legs in and sat up. "I won't go into detail because I don't want to give the plot away, but I've read the whole thing, and nearly all of them end up suffering. It's really been bothering me."

Charlotte stubbed her cigarette butt out in the ashtray, then reached for the pack.

"I mean, here they are, eight smart, attractive, well-educated women from good families, promising in every possible respect. Yet not a one of them ends up fulfilling their promise. Not even close," she said, sliding a fresh smoke from the pack. "If women like that can't manage it, what hope is there for the rest of us?"

Charlotte stopped talking long enough to light her cigarette, leaving her question hanging. Viv drew her brows together, frowning.

"Well, how are we supposed to know? You're the one who finished the book, not us."

Bitsy turned to Viv. "I think she's speaking rhetorically."

"I've been giving this a lot of thought," Charlotte said, "and I think I've figured it out. The reason the girls in the group end up failing—not only to live up to their potential, but failing in almost every sense of the word—is that they stopped *being* the group. Once they graduated and it was every woman for herself, things started to go horribly downhill."

"And you think things would have gone better for them if they'd stayed together?" Margaret asked.

"Absolutely. No question. Viv, you know exactly what I mean. You're always talking about the war and how all the nurses pulled together in unimaginably tough circumstances."

Viv nodded. "The worse things got, the closer we got. The only way we were able to get through it and do the job was as a team. But war is different. You can't expect women to act like that in regular life. You can't stay in the barracks forever, or the dorm."

"True. But you can always be part of the group."

Charlotte swiveled her head in Margaret's direction. "Maggie, how much did you say the ad would cost? And how much do you have left from your savings?"

Margaret ground her cigarette into the ashtray, shaking her head. "No, Charlotte. No. I appreciate the thought, but no. You can't buy that ad for me."

"Of course I can!" Charlotte cried, throwing her arms wide. "Weren't you listening when I told you about the showdown with my father? As of this week, I am a woman of independent means. And I can spend those means on any damned thing I want. Now . . . how much?"

Margaret clamped her lips shut. Charlotte gave her an impatient look.

"You really are the most exasperating woman, Margaret Ryan. Either you tell me how much the ad costs or I will phone the magazine and find out for myself. What's it going to be?"

Realizing Charlotte wouldn't be swayed, Margaret reluctantly repeated the figure. After further prodding from Charlotte, she also revealed how much she had in her savings account.

"There, was that so hard?" Charlotte asked. "Now look, I don't have my checkbook with me, but I can drop a check off tomorrow. When is the deadline for placing the ad?"

"The end of the week," Margaret replied. "But I can't let you do this. It's too much."

"You're not *letting* me do it," Charlotte countered. "I am *doing* it. Period. End of story. Because I want to. Because you'd do the same for me. Because you're my group."

"Charlotte's right," Viv said, setting her iced tea down with a decisive thump. "A lot of my nursing money went to pay for gas and pizza on the nights I didn't have energy to cook. But there's a good chunk left, and you're welcome to all of it."

"No!" Margaret said. "Viv, you can't. You need money for the baby."

Viv threw out her hands. "To buy what? I've got six kids' worth of hand-me-downs and a crib in the attic."

"I want to help too," Bitsy said. "King's trying to absolve his guilt through generosity, so I'm doing fine financially. Plus, I'm still working at the barn. Whatever Viv puts in, I'll match."

Margaret got to her feet, held her hands out flat, and screwed her eyes shut.

"Stop! Everybody, just stop!"

When she opened her eyes again, all three Bettys were staring at her.

"Sorry," she said, taking a breath. "But there's no way I'm taking your money, especially not to fix a problem that can't be fixed and that I created myself. It's a crazy idea. Crazy!"

Charlotte stood.

"It's not. It's *smart*. It's what men do. Why do you think they join all those clubs—the Elks? The VFW? The Masons? Congress!" she cried. "To support one another, that's why. Why do you think they call them booster clubs? Because they're trying to boost each other over the wall or bend the rules in their favor, help the group. If women stuck up for one another the way men do, this would be a very different world."

She crossed her arms, as if daring Margaret to find fault in this argument. She couldn't.

"Ask Aunt Betty if you don't believe me," Charlotte said. "I can't tell you what chapter, but I'm sure she wrote about it somewhere."

When Margaret smiled, Charlotte smiled back.

"Accepting help is hard. I understand that. But talent like yours is a gift that's meant to be shared. You're in church every Sunday, Maggie. In all those visits, didn't you ever hear the one about not hiding your light under a bushel? Even I know that one."

Viv bobbed her head. "She's got a point, Margaret."

"She does," Bitsy agreed.

"I think you're taking that verse out of context," Margaret said. "But even if you weren't, what would be the point? One little column isn't going to change the world or convince Leonard to give me my job back. And for all that money—"

"True," Charlotte said. "One column won't change the world. But it might change somebody's world, the way Betty's book changed ours. And you never know; someone who reads it might like it and decide to offer you a new job, a better job."

Charlotte stepped closer. "Think of it this way, Maggie. If you let us give you a boost today, then someday maybe you'll be in a position to do the same for someone else. We've got to start someplace. If we don't, how is anything ever going to change?"

CHAPTER 35

Fan Mail

September 1963

S ummer was over. But what a consequential summer it had
been—a season all four Bettys would remember as among
the most pivotal in their lives.

And it wasn't just them.

Across the globe, the tides of change were bringing tumult and
transformation that would push and eliminate boundaries, altering
the landscape of society in ways that wouldn't be fully apparent
for years, decades, or even generations to come. August alone had
been replete with events that would shake the world with the
passage of time.

In that month, the United States, United Kingdom, and Soviet
Union signed the first Nuclear Test Ban Treaty.

Lee Harvey Oswald got into a scuffle with three men while
distributing flyers for the Fair Play for Cuba Committee. He was
arrested in New Orleans but released the next day.

Vietnamese President Ngô Đình Diệm declared martial law,
then ordered armed government forces to raid Buddhist pagodas
and arrest fourteen hundred monks.

Washington Post publisher Philip Graham took his life, making
Katharine Graham a widow at forty-seven and the twentieth century's first female publisher of a major newspaper.

And on August 28, at least 250,000 people gathered to attend the March on Washington for Jobs and Freedom, and to hear the Reverend Martin Luther King Jr. speak from the steps of the Lincoln Memorial.

Like millions of people, the Buschettis watched Dr. King's speech live on television.

Viv sat rapt as King spoke, finding his words profoundly moving but also profoundly commonsensical. Because if America really was the land of the free, surely freedom should extend to everyone. Almost as thrilling as the speech was the moment when the television cameras panned the crowd and Viv caught a glimpse of Earlene standing in the audience, not thirty feet from the stage. She squealed and rocked forward, pointing to the television screen.

"Look! There she is!" Viv pressed her hand to her chest, beaming. "Isn't that something? It's history in the making, and Earlene is right there in the middle of it. She said she was going to go, and she did. Good for her!"

Later that day, after finishing her work at the stables, Bitsy drove to the post office to mail a condolence letter to Mrs. Graham and then to the campus of American University to register for classes. The deadline for fall semester admissions had come and gone, but after Alice Brennan placed a phone call to a former colleague who worked at American, Bitsy was informed they'd make room for one more student.

The next day, Margaret stopped into Mayer's Drugstore and bought six copies of the latest issue of *A Woman's Place*—two to keep, one for each of the Bettys, and one for Helen and Edwin Babcock, who had also insisted on contributing to the cause.

"There it is!" Helen said, beaming and tapping her fingers on page 46, where Margaret's column appeared opposite a recipe for deviled lettuce. "Right there in black-and-white! It's wonderful, Margaret! I'm so proud!"

"Thank you. But you know, I couldn't have done it without you. From the very first day, even when I was just writing fluff, you couldn't have been more encouraging."

"And what did I tell you?" Helen said, the half dozen bangles on her wrist jangling as she wagged her finger at Margaret. "What did I say on the day you published your 'silly little column in a silly little women's magazine'?"

Margaret smiled. "That it was a start."

"That's right," Helen said, nodding sagely. "Starting is the hardest part. Today you're making another start, and not just for you. Mark my words, Margaret. This piece will start a conversation. Good things will come from it. Big things! Wait and see if I'm not right."

* * *

Two weeks later, it did seem Helen's prediction was coming true.

Margaret had been amazed by the number of women from the neighborhood who'd told her they'd read her essay and planned to read *The Feminine Mystique* because of it. Helen reported quite an uptick in orders for the book, so it seemed they were serious. Iris Rasmussen and Dorothy Fisher, her old friends from coffee klatch, had even knocked on Margaret's door holding a copy of the magazine and asked for her autograph, an experience she'd found simultaneously embarrassing and flattering.

Of course, not everyone was pleased by what she'd written.

Barb Fredericks deliberately snubbed her in the grocery store, steering her shopping cart right past when Margaret greeted her in the produce aisle. And two women she encountered when dropping Bobby and Suzy off at school, the same two who'd talked behind her back at the pool, felt no compunction about criticizing her once again, this time to her face.

"That book is dangerous," the first one said. "A threat to the American way of life! If you can't see that, you're either a radical, an idiot, or both!" The second, echoing the opinion because it saved her the effort of forming her own, nodded vigorously. "Exactly!"

Though Margaret could not have cared less what they thought of her, the vehemence and personal nature of their criticism flustered her. Why would somebody go so far out of their way to be so nasty just because somebody held a differing opinion? Margaret doubted they'd even read the book. Regardless, wasn't the right to free speech and differing opinions an important part of "the American way of life"? Maybe the most important part?

But on the whole, she received much more positive feedback than negative. In fact, that very morning, the mailman had knocked on the door and handed her a large, fat manila envelope that was too big to fit in the mailbox. Inside, Margaret found twenty-one smaller envelopes, all addressed to her in care of *A Woman's Place* magazine, and a note that read:

Dear Mrs. Ryan,

You don't know me, but I work in the magazine mail room and noticed a lot of letters coming in addressed to you. My supervisor said I could just mark them all "Return to Sender" because you don't work here anymore.

But I read the magazine myself and know you took out an ad so you could get your article about your book club published, so I figured all these letters were probably about that. Since I still remembered your address from the other times you got mail, I decided to send them to you myself. (Don't tell my boss.)

I'm very sorry you won't be writing for the magazine anymore. Your columns always made me smile. I liked that you were a regular housewife who got a chance to be a real writer.

I've been working in the mail room for eight years now, never missed a day of work. But I've only ever gotten one raise in all that time and never a promotion, of course. The men who work in the mail room get promoted or find better jobs and leave, but it seems like the women who start here stay here forever. My supervisor started working here just three years ago, right after high school, just like me. I trained him, and now he's my boss.

I hope I don't sound like I'm complaining too much. But I just wanted you to know that I thought it was great that you had a chance to write for the magazine, and that I always liked your column. This last one wasn't as funny, but if you thought so much of that book, then I figure it must be worth reading.

There's a long list to check it out from the library, so I will have to wait my turn. I guess a lot of other people read your article and decided they should read the book too. Next time you recommend a book, can you write me a note beforehand so I can be first in line? Ha!

Anyway, thank you again. I hope you get this note and enjoy reading your "fan mail."
Very truly yours,
Carla Hennessy

It was gratifying to know her columns had put a smile on the face of Carla Hennessy, but that smile couldn't have begun to match the smile that spread over Margaret's face when reading Carla's note and the letters she had so kindly forwarded.

Not all of the letters could be considered fan mail. Three were similar in tone to the criticism she'd received from the pool gossips—one letter writer called her a communist, among other less savory names. However, the remaining eighteen letters were very positive. Five writers said they were forming Betty Friedan book clubs of their own. Five!

Those five letters filled Margaret with a tingle-all-over anticipation she hadn't felt for a long time, like the thrill a child gets while making a wish and blowing out the candles. Charlotte was right; you never knew what would happen.

Margaret sent letters and clippings from her column to editors at two dozen magazines and had yet to receive so much as a "thanks but no thanks" for her trouble. She wasn't really surprised; unsolicited letters like hers probably went into the trash unread. But her essay about the Bettys had been read by so many and had elicited such strong reactions—was it a stretch to think at least one of those readers might be someone of influence? Someone who could offer her a *real* writing job, an opportunity to write truth instead of fluff?

Margaret felt certain something *was* going to happen, something good. But she didn't share that with the Bettys. Feeling certain wasn't the same thing as being certain. Besides, today was all about Charlotte, who apparently had big news. She'd phoned the Bettys the day before and told them to be ready at ten thirty.

"Time for another field trip," she'd said. "I've got something amazing to show you!"

CHAPTER 36

"I'm Afraid Our Time Is Up"

Since marching out of Howard's office as a soon-to-be free woman, it seemed to Charlotte that each day was better than the one before.

Which was not to say that her life was utterly free of stress.

Despite her declarations about there being no room for negotiation, some back-and-forth between the lawyers had taken place. However, after informing her father that she would release the photos to the press if no agreement was reached by Labor Day, G.G. backed down. The legalities would take a little time, but half of the cash had already been deposited into Charlotte's account, and the paperwork for Denise's trust was being reviewed by her attorney.

Things were tougher on the domestic front.

Upon learning of his parents' impending divorce, Howie's only response had been to ask if Charlotte having full custody meant he could leave the military academy and move home. As far as Charlotte was concerned, the answer was yes. Howard disagreed vehemently, so that would have to wait until the divorce was final. Denise was fine; England agreed with her. But Charlotte was concerned about the younger children.

Laura was very clingy and whiny these days, and Andrew was sulky. And though Charlotte was convinced that Howard had picked the most bourgeois monstrosity in Concordia just to spite her, she had decided to stay where she was for the time being. Another big change was the last thing the kids needed right now. Keeping the house meant learning how to maintain it—dealing with gardeners, insurance, tax bills, and repairmen. Howard's secretary had always handled it before; now it was Charlotte's responsibility. The learning curve was steep, forcing Charlotte to buy filing folders and ask Viv what to put in them.

There were other, more existential problems too. On the days when she allowed herself to dream of such things, Charlotte's imagination always brought her back to New York and a career as a professional artist. With those doors shut, what was she to do with her life?

The answer appeared, as such answers often do, in the last place she expected.

"Well?" Charlotte asked her friends, spreading her arms wide, as if trying to embrace not only the exterior of the town house they stood in front of but the entire block. "What do you think?"

Bitsy frowned. "You're renting in Alexandria? I thought you planned to stay in Concordia for the time being."

"It is nice," Margaret said, craning her neck back to take in the full three and a half stories of red brick. "Tons of character. But are you sure this is a good idea? You said you didn't want to move the kids right now."

"It's an awfully busy street," Viv said, turning her attention to a placard listing of the building's occupants. "And aren't these offices? How can you rent an apartment here?"

"Because I'm not a renter," Charlotte said, beaming and pulling a key from her pocket. "As of yesterday, the entire building belongs to me. Come on. I want you to see the inside."

Charlotte unlocked the door and waved the others into the foyer, which was really more of a long hallway. Three office doors lined the wall on the right. A steep, narrow stairway, which presumably led to more offices, hugged the wall on the left. Once everyone was inside, Charlotte closed the door.

"The tenants have thirty days to move out, so I can't show you much more today. But I've hired an architect, and he's got some wonderful ideas. To start, we'll knock out the walls on the first floor, creating one big space," she said, squeezing past her friends and moving to the staircase.

"Obviously, the stairs have to go. We'll replace them with something wider, much more open and modern. We're thinking about stair treads of very thick glass, so the people climbing them would appear to be floating. We may even take out the ceiling between the first two floors. A tall, soaring ceiling would be very dramatic, especially in such an old building. The architect thinks installing beams will mitigate any structural issues, but we'll have to see what the engineer says."

"Well. Sounds like a plan," Viv said when Charlotte finished. "But you may have left out one teeny, inconsequential detail. After you rip out the walls, ceiling, and stairs, what are you going to do with it?"

"Sorry! I got so excited that I skipped that part."

She took a breath, declaring her intention in a measured, confident tone, as if it were less an aspiration than a thing already done.

"I am opening an art gallery."

Margaret's face lit up. "Charlotte, that's a wonderful idea!"

"To show your paintings?" Bitsy asked.

"No," Charlotte said. "I've finally come to terms with reality. Though I'm not a bad artist, I'm not a very good one either."

"So you plan to sell other people's paintings?" Viv asked.

"That's the idea. I want to focus on the work of promising but unknown artists who need a champion. Women in particular. I may not have the talent to create great art myself, but I know it when I see it. That's a talent of a different sort. And since I now have the means to give those talented female artists a leg up, why wouldn't I?" she said, turning her hands out to underscore the validity of her point. "I can't afford to lose money indefinitely, but thanks to the settlement, I won't have to show a profit for a while. We'll see how it goes. But it seems like a pretty good way to spend a life, don't you think?"

Viv, who had been nodding while Charlotte was speaking, had a question.

"Do you know anything about running a gallery?"

"Oh, next to nothing!" Charlotte said, laughing and making her eyes go wide. "But why should that stop me? Just look at all the skills I've picked up lately. With Margaret's help, I have enough cooking skills to keep the kids from starving. Bitsy showed me how to balance a checkbook. Viv helped me organize my files. I even learned to clean the house!"

Charlotte tilted her chin upward, striking a brief "ta-da" pose.

"Of course, I don't actually intend to keep doing my own cleaning. With Howard and my psychiatrist both out of the picture, I've decided that adjusting to my role is vastly overrated. I don't care how much it costs," she said. "I'm getting a housekeeper. I'd have done it anyway, but between working and commuting and the kids, I really am going to need some help."

"Send her over to my place when she's done with yours," Viv said.

"We've all learned a lot in the last few months," Margaret said, then hesitated, frowning, as if reluctant to be the bearer of bad news. "But running a business is a lot more complicated than making a meat loaf, don't you think?"

"Believe me," Charlotte said stoutly, "I'm under no illusions about how much I need to learn. Thankfully, I've got an adviser. I'm taking the train to Philadelphia to talk with him at his gallery next week. Then he'll come here to help me once the renovations are done. I called him yesterday, after I got the keys. I think Nicky is almost as excited as I am.

"Before you even ask," Charlotte said, reading the intrigue in Bitsy's arched eyebrows, "Nicky is short for Nikolai. He's seventy years old, speaks better Russian than English, and has no more romantic interest in me than I do in him. We love art but not each other."

"Can't blame a girl for being curious," Bitsy said.

"I'm curious about something else," Margaret said, glancing around at the cramped quarters and creaky staircase. "Why this place? It's got character and a good location, but you're going to have to put so much money into the renovations. Couldn't you have bought another building that didn't need quite so much work?"

Before Charlotte could explain, a key turned in the lock and the entry door opened. A white-bearded, stoop-shouldered man in a brown tweed jacket stepped into the foyer. Charlotte's eyes sparked with the same green fire they'd had on the day she marched into Howard's office and fanned the photos out on the conference table.

"Dr. Barry! I see you're back from lunch." Charlotte smiled, glancing at her diamond wristwatch. "Right on time, as always. I was hoping we'd run into each other."

The look on the doctor's face suggested the feeling was not mutual. Charlotte turned toward the Bettys.

"Ladies, this is Dr. Ernest Barry. I believe you've heard me mention him."

Three sets of eyes registered recognition, but no one spoke.

"Anyway," Charlotte said, flapping her hand, "that's how I came to buy the building. Last month I came to tell Dr. Barry I'd found a new doctor, Dr. Louisa Bernstein—turns out there are women psychiatrists—and that his services were no longer required. As I was leaving, it occurred to me that this building might make a wonderful gallery. I did some sleuthing, found the owner, and made him an offer. And voilà!" Charlotte exclaimed, striking another pose. "Here we are!"

Dr. Barry let out a derisive-sounding snort. "I see that your new doctor doesn't seem to be making any more progress with you than I did. This infantile need for revenge against authority is yet further evidence of your neurosis."

"Possibly," Charlotte replied sweetly. "Then again, Dr. Barry, you've accused me of so many things—repression, depression, sublimation, regression, denial . . . They can't all be true, can they? And I do question your authority in this and so many areas." Charlotte took a step closer to the disgruntled doctor, fixing her eyes on his. "One thing I do want you to know. No woman, including me, has *ever* been envious of the male organ.

"By the way, how is your search for a new premises going? Only twenty-nine days left. *Tick, tick, tick,*" she said, tapping the face of her watch. "Then our time really will be up."

Charlotte stepped back again, her lips bowing into a slow smile.

"Now, if you'll excuse me, I'm taking my friends out to lunch."

✳ ✳ ✳

Fifteen minutes later, the Bettys were sitting around a table at The Majestic café. Viv, who asked for a glass of water before they were even seated, was too big to squeeze into a booth.

"This is getting ridiculous," she grumbled when the waiter returned with water and menus. "Baby's not due for five weeks, but I can't walk three blocks without getting winded."

"You'll love this place," Charlotte informed them, opening her menu. "It's one of the oldest restaurants in Alexandria. The food is excellent, and so is the service." She smiled at the waiter. "I'd like the chicken salad, please. And a glass of iced tea. Ladies, what's your pleasure? We're celebrating, so this is my treat."

Bitsy looked up with a hopeful expression.

"I don't suppose the French onion soup is made with vegetable broth?" The waiter shook his head. "Then I'll have the Caesar salad. No anchovies, please."

Margaret asked for a club sandwich with sliced tomatoes instead of fries. The waiter jotted down her order, then looked to Viv, who was frowning deeply and studying the menu, apparently unable to make up her mind. After a minute, the waiter softly cleared his throat.

"Viv?" Charlotte prompted. "Do you know what you'd like?"

"Yes. How about a ride to the hospital?" Viv closed her menu. "Sorry to break up the party, girls, but I'm in labor."

✳ ✳ ✳

Charlotte drove like a madwoman, weaving in and out of traffic and shouting, "Move it! Move it! Move it! Lady with a baby!" at the other drivers. She got them to the hospital in record time. Margaret was clutching the door handle so tightly that her knuckles were literally white, but the guttural noises coming from Viv's mouth as they screeched around the final corner made her grateful Charlotte had learned to drive on the mean streets of New York.

Bitsy bailed out even before the car came to a complete stop, then ran inside to commandeer a wheelchair. Charlotte jammed on the brake and leapt from the car to help Margaret extricate an unwieldy Viv from the vehicle. Viv was groaning, wincing so hard that her flushed red face resembled a shriveled apple.

"Don't push!" Margaret shouted as they pulled Viv from the back seat. "Whatever you do, don't push!"

Viv groaned again, indecipherably, but the look in her eyes told Margaret exactly what Viv thought of this unsolicited advice, and that it had something to do with the horse she'd rode in on. Bitsy and a nurse with a wheelchair arrived on the scene. A writhing Viv was piled into the chair. The nurse pointed to a nearby waiting room and whisked Viv away to the maternity ward, breaking into a run when Viv shouted, "Hurry it up, will ya? This baby won't wait!"

Viv's little girl, whom she named Betty, was born twenty minutes later, even before Tony arrived from his Pentagon office. She weighed just four and a half pounds and was placed in an incubator immediately after birth. The doctor declared her small but healthy and said both she and Viv would be released from the hospital once Betty put on some weight.

As the three friends stood with their faces pressed against the window of the hospital nursery, gazing on Viv's beautiful, tiny, absolutely perfect baby with a mixture of elation and awe, Margaret couldn't stop smiling. Her sense that very good things were about to happen seemed spot-on.

In many ways, it was.

CHAPTER 37

Timing Is Everything

October 1963

V iv and the baby came home from the hospital in early October, and little Betty was thriving. The architectural plans for Charlotte's gallery were nearing completion, with renovations slated to begin in November. Bitsy and King seemed well on their way to an amicable divorce, and Bitsy was doing well in her classes at American University.

Then there was Margaret.

A month after reading those eighteen pieces of fan mail, letters she felt sure were the first ripples in a movement that would certainly swell to a tide of change for the women who read her essay and perhaps for Margaret herself, nothing had changed.

Margaret was embarrassed. Embarrassed, disappointed, and despondent.

Had she left her friends out of it, kept her whole mistaken adventure under wraps, it wouldn't have been so bad. Nobody would have known what a failure she turned out to be. But because she had allowed them to invest in her foolish, fruitless quest, her failure was not only public but expensive. The return on her and her friends' money was nothing more than a few fan letters and a quickly forgotten flash of neighborhood celebrity.

To make her humiliation complete, earlier that week Margaret had opened the most recent issue of *A Woman's Place* and discovered that her column had been taken over by a woman named Margie Reynolds. The fact that Margie shared her facial characteristics as well as her initials told Margaret that the magazine publishers thought readers wouldn't know the difference. They were probably right.

Thus, her embarrassment. And her despondency.

She didn't feel like seeing anybody or going anywhere. But Bitsy had shown up on her doorstep that morning, insisting that it was a beautiful day for a ride. She pulled a pair of dungarees and a short-sleeved cotton blouse from Margaret's bureau and all but stood guard while she changed.

Now here Margaret was, mounted on Lydia Bee—a placid, slightly rotund horse—clip-clopping down the bridle path beside Bitsy, who was riding the younger, more spirited Crystal.

The air was warm but not sultry, freshened by a gentle breeze that stirred the red, orange, and golden leaves of the trees lining the path. They rode side by side in silence for several minutes, which was a relief. Margaret didn't need anyone telling her what she'd already said to herself a hundred times, which was that she had endless reasons to be grateful. Though true, it didn't make her feel better.

But it was a beautiful day for a ride.

Rounding a bend in the trail, they met another rider coming in the opposite direction. Margaret recognized the horse. Bitsy pulled back on Crystal's reins as the woman approached, stopping in the middle of the path.

"Mrs. Graham! It's been so long! Oh, I'm so glad to see you."

The woman returned Bitsy's smile.

"Bitsy! I was hoping to run into you today. I know I've been neglecting poor Delilah, but between the funeral and the family and the business . . ." Mrs. Graham's smile faded. "Well, I'm sure you understand. There hasn't been time for riding."

"Of course not. But Delilah is fine. I check on her every day."

"That's why I was hoping to see you. We've had a lovely ride today. Considering her age and all she's been through recently, she seems to be in fine shape. I suppose we're a bit alike in that respect." Mrs. Graham smiled again. "Anyway, I wanted to thank you for that, and for your note. It was kind of you to write, and it means so much to know you were praying for me."

"I still am," Bitsy said. "Every day."

"Well, don't stop. Stepping into Phil's shoes at the paper hasn't been easy. I'll take every prayer I can get."

Delilah snuffled and gave her head a small toss that said she was anxious to be on her way. Mrs. Graham reached down and patted her neck, as if urging her to be patient.

"And how are you, Bitsy? Alice told me you've gone back to school. Are you enjoying your classes?"

"So far. I need to make straight As to be accepted to vet school next year, but I'm on track at the moment. Fingers crossed."

"Good for you!" Mrs. Graham turned toward Margaret. "I'm sorry, I'm not sure we've met? I'm Katharine Graham."

As Margaret was introducing herself, Lydia Bee shifted her weight a bit and stamped a foot. Margaret clutched at the saddle horn. "I'd shake your hand, Mrs. Graham, but I haven't been on horseback since I was about ten years old. If I let go, I'll probably fall off."

"Margaret's a writer," Bitsy informed Mrs. Graham. "A magazine columnist."

"Is that so?" Mrs. Graham said, with what Margaret was certain could only be polite interest.

"Yes," Bitsy said quickly. "Margaret used to write a humor column, but she recently published an essay about how we formed a book club to read *The Feminine Mystique*, and how it changed our lives and turned us into close friends."

Halfway through Bitsy's speech, a spark of recognition flickered across Mrs. Graham's face. She turned her gaze from Bitsy to Margaret and back again.

"Wait a moment . . . I read that piece. You're the Bettys?"

Margaret's jaw went slack. Katharine Graham, publisher of the *Washington Post*, had read her essay. She couldn't believe it. In her shock, Margaret loosened her grip on the saddle horn. But when Lydia Bee stamped her foot once more, she grabbed it again.

"Not just us," Bitsy explained. "There are two more Bettys in the book club, Viv and Charlotte. And they all pitched in to help when Delilah had laminitis, brought me food and ice and kept me company. I never could have managed without them."

"Then I owe you a debt of gratitude for helping to save my horse," Katharine said to Margaret. "And my congratulations on producing such a fine piece of writing." She narrowed her eyes a little. "If I'm remembering correctly, you actually had to pay to get it published. Isn't that right? You bought advertising space in the magazine?"

"Yes," Margaret replied. "After my editor refused to publish it, everybody pitched in to buy the ad—the Bettys, my husband and I, and the couple who own our local bookstore."

"Well, I think that is admirable," Mrs. Graham said in a hearty voice that made Margaret believe her. "If you're not too busy, I'd love to get together for lunch. I'm sure we'd have lots to talk about. Can you give me your business card?"

"Oh, gosh," Margaret said, blushing. "I'm afraid I don't have one. I'm not writing for the magazine anymore. They fired me after I turned in that piece."

"That's right, how silly of me." Mrs. Graham reached into her pocket, pulled out a small gold pen and a card of her own, and handed both to Margaret. "Jot down your number, and I'll give you a call."

Margaret still couldn't believe this was happening. Writing legibly on a small business card while mounted on an increasingly restless horse was a challenge, but she complied. Mrs. Graham slipped the pen and card back into her pocket. Delilah tossed her head and sputtered.

"I'd better get going," Mrs. Graham said, sitting straighter in the saddle and loosening her grip on the reins. "But I'm so glad I ran into the two of you today. Bitsy, I'll give Alice a full report on your progress.

"And Margaret? You'll be hearing from me very soon."

CHAPTER 38

Women Worth Knowing

November 1963

Margaret did not hear from Katharine Graham very soon.

In fact, she never heard from her at all.

But during the drive back to Concordia, Margaret felt like a bottle of pop that had been shaken hard and uncapped, practically fizzing with happiness. She rolled the windows down and turned the radio up as she and Bitsy sang along with the Chiffons, belting out the lyrics to "He's So Fine" as they sped along the parkway, dancing in their seats and tapping the car horn every time they got to the word *fine*.

Relating the story to Walt that evening, Margaret deliberately downplayed her hopes, saying that while it was gratifying to know that Mrs. Graham liked her work, she didn't imagine much would come of it.

In truth, she spent much of the next week imagining no end of wonderful things that might come of it, anticipation bubbling on the back burner of her mind as she cooked, vacuumed, and did laundry, one ear continually cocked for the sound of a ringing phone.

By the end of the week, the bubble became more of a simmer. But she didn't lose hope, reassured by Bitsy's reminder that Katharine Graham was one of the busiest women in DC. Viv,

Charlotte, and Walt all agreed and said she should try to stay busy to keep her mind off it.

Margaret took their advice to heart and spent the second week reading *Joy in the Morning* by Betty Smith, making chicken cordon bleu, and sewing Halloween costumes on a machine she borrowed from Viv—a marching band outfit for Beth, a ballerina tutu for Suzy, and an astronaut costume for Bobby, complete with a silver spray-painted, papier-mâché helmet.

Walt praised the chicken, and Bitsy said Mrs. Graham always kept her word.

During the third week, Margaret read *The Girls of Slender Means* by Muriel Spark, stripped and waxed the floors, penciled out menus for Thanksgiving, let down the hems on all Bobby's pants, reorganized the closets, cleaned the oven, and helped Viv wallpaper her kitchen.

Walt said the house looked fantastic. Bitsy said "very soon" probably meant different things to different people.

In the fourth week, Margaret made applesauce and tried to read *The Bell Jar* by Sylvia Plath, but she put it down because it was too depressing. Viv suggested they join the bridge club, and Margaret said she'd rather put a fork in her eye. Then she drove to the drugstore, bought a sampler of Whitman's chocolates, and ate a third of them while sitting in the car.

Walt said that even if Mrs. Graham never called, he still thought she was a terrific writer. Margaret and Bitsy stopped talking about it.

But then, in the middle of the fifth week, the phone rang.

"Hello, Mrs. Ryan? I'm Gloria Sizemore, Katharine Graham's social secretary. Mrs. Graham wonders if you could join her at home for luncheon on Thursday?"

Bitsy was right. Even if it took time, Katharine Graham was a woman who kept her word.

❊ ❊ ❊

Georgetown, one of the oldest neighborhoods in DC, was home to a number of large, elegant, architecturally impressive houses. But Mrs. Graham's home was in a class all its own. Sitting on more than an acre, the white brick, three-storied structure was an exquisite example of Federal-style architecture, surrounded by tall trees and manicured lawns. Seeing it brought words like *palatial* and *opulent* to Margaret's mind and made her wish she'd raided Charlotte's closet for a nicer outfit.

Margaret climbed the stone steps to the black-painted front door with a finish so shiny it almost looked wet. After taking a moment to screw up her courage and pick imaginary lint from her green suit jacket, she rang the doorbell.

A middle-aged woman wearing a black dress and white apron greeted her with a pleasant smile, beckoning her into a foyer bigger than Margaret's living room. There was a huge, richly colored oriental rug on the floor and a three-tiered brass chandelier hanging from the ceiling. A marble-topped table with an enormous bouquet of calla lilies stood directly beneath it.

As the pleasant woman helped Margaret with her coat, a somewhat younger woman, wearing cat-eye glasses and a conservative but elegant dress of blue wool, appeared.

"Mrs. Ryan? I'm Gloria Sizemore. A pleasure to meet you. Mrs. Graham apologizes for the short notice, but she is so pleased you were able to come."

"Thank you. I hope I'm not late. I had a bit of trouble finding the address."

Margaret followed Miss Sizemore across the foyer and into a hallway with paneled doors on one side and tall, thick-paned windows facing a lovely winter garden on the other.

"Not to worry, Mrs. Ryan. There are a few stragglers, but most of the others are already in the library."

Margaret stopped short.

"Others?"

* * *

The library was as elegant as the rest of the house. Three of the four walls were lined with built-in wooden bookcases painted a soft green color, the shelves so full there didn't appear to be space to squeeze in even one more volume. Scores of framed photographs hung on the remaining wall, black-and-white prints of Mrs. Graham and the late Mr. Graham posing with presidents, politicians, and celebrities. The room was filled with groupings of comfortably elegant sofas and chairs and the hum of female voices.

Margaret didn't take a head count but estimated about fifteen to be present, ranging in age from midtwenties to late sixties. Some of the women sat; some stood. Some smoked cigarettes; some sipped small glasses of sherry. All were deeply engaged in conversations and paid not the least attention when Margaret entered the room. She hung near the doorway, feeling very out of place.

The room smelled of coffee, cigarettes, and Shalimar, the same scents that perfumed the air of Concordia coffee klatches. In that situation, Margaret would have established eye contact with the nearest bored-looking woman, then walked up and introduced herself.

But none of these women looked bored, and Margaret couldn't summon the courage to insert herself into a conversation. Instead, she wandered toward one of the bookcases, tilting her head sideways to read the spines, feigning interest in an entire shelf of books written by current or former members of the Supreme Court. Justice John Jay had published not one but three volumes of his papers and correspondence. Who knew?

As Margaret was sliding volume three from the shelf, a pocket door in the middle of the picture wall slid open. Mrs. Graham entered, looking elegant in a pale pink shantung suit.

"Sorry! Sorry! Sorry!" Katharine said, lifting her arms and bringing all conversation to a temporary halt. "Telling the office that I'm not to be disturbed invariably triggers an avalanche of editorial emergencies. But I'm all yours now, at least until the next crisis. How are you all? Does everyone have everything they want?"

A blunt-featured woman with dark auburn hair waved her hand. "I'd like an exclusive with the attorney general, if you can arrange it."

"Oh, Helen, wouldn't we all?" Mrs. Graham laughed and the others joined in. "We're still waiting on one more, so lunch is a little delayed. In the meantime, anyone who isn't on deadline can help themselves to more sherry."

There was another round of laughter. Mrs. Graham's eyes brightened with recognition when she spotted Margaret standing near the bookcase.

"Ah, you made it! Ladies, I want to introduce you to a new friend of mine," she said, crossing the room. "This is Margaret Ryan, a freelancer. She recently wrote an essay about her neighborhood book club, the Bettys, and how reading *The Feminine Mystique* impacted them. If you haven't read it yet, you should."

The women murmured collective greetings. Margaret smiled and nodded politely, certain she was blushing.

Freelancer? If Margaret had ever qualified for the title, she sure didn't now. *Fired freelancer* might be closer to the mark. Or *poser.* Though Margaret didn't know these women, the fact that they all seemed to know one another, and Katharine Graham, was an indication that they were serious writers, journalists, whereas Margaret—

Mrs. Graham touched Margaret's shoulder and began speaking to her in a low, almost conspiratorial tone, just loud enough to be heard over the hum of resumed conversations.

"Let me give you a quick who's who. That's Nancy Dickerson over there." Mrs. Graham gestured discreetly to a slim woman with light brown hair and a face a movie star might envy. "You may recognize her. She's a correspondent at NBC television. First woman to report from the floor of a political convention.

"And the woman she's talking with?" Mrs. Graham nodded toward a much older lady with salt-and-pepper hair. "After a long career as a reporter, Bess Furman is now in charge of the press office of the Department of Health, Education, and Welfare. The redhead who wants an exclusive with Bobby Kennedy?" Margaret's gaze shifted to the other side of the room. "That's Helen Thomas, White House correspondent and president of the Women's National Press Club."

As Katharine continued, Margaret scanned the faces of the other guests, feeling a mixture of awe, gratitude, and disappointment. She was amazed to be standing amid such an accomplished group. And of course, she was honored that Mrs. Graham had included her. Even so, she had hoped this day would turn out differently. Mrs. Graham seemed to pick up on that.

She tilted her chin downward and looked Margaret directly in the eye. "I can't give you a job at the paper," she said. "Executive editors get very testy when publishers interfere with hiring. Also, you're just not ready. One good piece of writing doesn't entitle you to a job in a major newsroom, and I'm not sure hard journalism would play to your strengths anyway.

"But this town is all about connections, Margaret, and there's not a woman in this room who isn't worth knowing. Just remember one thing. A friend can give you a leg up to see what's on the other side of the wall, but you've got to pull yourself over the top. Understand?"

Margaret nodded.

"Good girl," Katharine said. "Now, get out there and mingle."

✳ ✳ ✳

That was easier said than done.

The other women were friendly, but they already knew one another well. Because Margaret knew so little about journalism and wasn't nearly as up to speed on current events as they were, she found herself hanging on the fringes of the conversation, clutching her sherry and feeling superfluous—and hungry.

If she'd known lunch would be late, she'd have eaten before she came. Who were they waiting for anyway? And when would she deign to grace them with her presence?

Feeling a tap on her shoulder, Margaret turned around. A younger woman, perhaps twenty-five, with intelligent slate-gray eyes and thick, dark hair cut in a pageboy style, stuck out her hand.

"I'm Susan Stamberg. You look like you could use rescuing, or a stronger drink."

"Is it that obvious?" Margaret shook her hand. "I'm Margaret Ryan. What do you do, Susan?"

Margaret had already figured out that women journalists had little patience for small talk. They jumped in and got to the point, no preambles, no nonsense.

"I work at WAMU, a public radio station located on the American University campus. I'm the program director. I know, I know," Susan said, shrugging. "I don't look old enough. But the good thing about working for such a small station—it's just four thousand watts and we've only been on the air two years—is that you can learn a lot, move up quickly, and do some of everything. In my case, that means program directing and reporting. I also cohost a show called *Kaleidoscope*. It's like a magazine," she explained, "but for radio."

"I've listened to your show!" Margaret exclaimed. "I heard it in the car one day, a story on the history of the Hope Diamond before it was donated to the Smithsonian. So interesting,"

Margaret's admiration was genuine. Small station or not, she was impressed that Susan had carved a career for herself at such a young age.

"Thanks," Susan said. "And I read your piece. You definitely know how to write."

Margaret was pleased but surprised. A smart, busy young career woman like Susan Stamberg didn't seem to fit the readership profile for *A Woman's Place*.

"A friend clipped it out and sent it to me because we'd been discussing *The Feminine Mystique*," Susan explained. "She thought you had some good insights, and I agree. But I'm curious. Katharine said you're a freelancer, but you bought ad space to publish that piece, didn't you? Don't take this the wrong way," she said, looking Margaret up and down, "but you don't strike me as the kind of person who goes around writing big checks."

"Trust me, I'm not. It was kind of a group project," Margaret said, going on to give a condensed explanation of the events that had brought her to this point.

"That is a great story," Susan said when she was finished. "There's not a writer in the world who hasn't dreamed of making an end run around her editor. But you actually did it!"

"Yes, for all the good it did. Months later I'm as unemployed as ever."

Susan frowned sympathetically. "It's a hard business to break into, especially for women. Getting the column was a lucky break, but you need more credentials. Have you thought about going back to school? WAMU offers internships for journalism students. It's a great way to get experience."

"Oh. Well . . ." Margaret shifted her shoulders. "We couldn't afford it. Like you said, I'm not the kind that goes around writing big checks. And with three kids at home—"

The door opened again. An unsmiling man in a dark suit stepped inside, scanning the room and bringing all conversation to an abrupt halt. He glanced over his shoulder and nodded to an unseen someone, then flattened himself against the wall like a sentry at a battlement.

Margaret looked toward Susan, thinking she might explain what was going on. But she was staring at the open door just like everyone else.

An elegantly dressed, dark-haired woman with a willowy figure and a light step entered the room. The jolt Margaret felt upon seeing her was so electric that she pressed her hand against her mouth to keep from gasping. The woman scanned the assembly with smiling brown eyes before turning to their hostess, speaking in a familiar, slightly breathless voice.

"I'm terribly sorry to be so late. Katharine, can you ever forgive me?"

Mrs. Graham stepped forward, taking the woman's delicate hands between her own. "There's nothing to forgive, Mrs. Kennedy. We're so pleased you were able to come."

The First Lady's laugh was bright and fluid, like liquid gold.

"Oh, none of that now, not among so many familiar faces. Today I'm just Jackie. But I'm warning you, girls. From here on out, everything is off the record."

She took a seat in a cream-colored chair and pulled a pack of cigarettes from her purse.

"Does anyone have a light?"

* * *

The sideboard buffet of salad, crustless sandwiches, and petit fours went largely untouched. As soon as the stories started flowing, everyone, including Margaret, forgot their hunger.

It seemed that the First Lady and many of those present really did know each other—had traveled in each other's orbits well before she became Mrs. Kennedy, back when she truly was "just Jackie," an ambitious and talented young woman who wanted to be a journalist.

As Susan had observed, it was a hard business to break into, even for a woman as socially well connected as Jacqueline Bouvier. Those connections opened the door to a secretarial job at the *Washington Times-Herald*, but getting her boss to take her seriously, and eventually give her a byline, took hard work, ingenuity, and more than a little nerve.

When Princess Elizabeth of England came to Washington in 1951, the uncredentialed Jackie crashed an invitation-only press event, hoping to land an interview—or even just a quote—that she could craft into a career-catapulting story. She failed on all counts, earning a loud lecture from her boss, who reminded her in no uncertain terms that she was "not a reporter!"

Even so, when a freelance stringer quit and no one else wanted to take over the unbylined "Inquiring Photographer" column—a man-on-the-street feature requiring the reporter to take photos and pose questions to random citizens—the assignment went to Miss Bouvier. The question for her first column was, "Is Princess Elizabeth as pretty as her picture?"

"I was paid twenty-five dollars a week to take photographs and write interviews with six different people, six days a week—144 interviews a month. I ran all over Washington lugging a huge Graflex camera and accosting perfect strangers on the street."

Everyone laughed. Mrs. Kennedy lit a second cigarette.

"Nobody wanted that column, but I threw everything I had into making it the kind of feature people looked forward to reading, and it worked. They changed the name to 'Inquiring Camera Girl,' gave me a byline, and raised my pay to a whopping $42.50 a week."

There it was again, that self-deprecating, liquid gold laugh. But something in Mrs. Kennedy's eyes told Margaret that despite all she'd seen and done since, the First Lady looked back on her stint as the Inquiring Camera Girl with fondness and not a little pride.

Nearly every woman there had a story about seizing some meager opportunity that came her way and turning it into a ladder to get from where she was to where she wanted to be.

Veteran political reporter Mary McGrory spent years writing book reviews and "dog stories"—human interest features that male reporters dismissed as puff pieces—before finally getting a chance to cover the McCarthy hearings, referring to the junior senator from Wisconsin as "an Irish bully" and making a name for herself in the process.

After spending years writing for Midwestern papers, Bess Furman was offered a job in the DC offices of the Associated Press covering political wives. The most prominent was then First

Lady Lou Hoover, who "loathed reporters." Masquerading as a troop leader at a White House reception for the Girl Scouts, Bess charmed Mrs. Hoover. Soon a legitimate invitation was extended to her, kicking off a decades-long career spent reporting on presidential wives.

Their stories were incredibly inspiring. But what Margaret loved most about the women was the way they talked to one another—sharing advice, counsel, and camaraderie, along with the occasional snarky comment. Their exchanges felt comfortable to Margaret, and familiar.

Oh yes, she thought to herself, *they could be Bettys.*

The party went by much too quickly. As Mrs. Kennedy was telling the story of how, in 1952, still seeking opportunities to write features in addition to her column, she bluffed her way into Griffith Stadium and stationed herself right next to the locker room in hopes of scoring an interview with Ted Williams, the door opened. The man in the dark suit stepped into the library. Mrs. Kennedy crushed out her cigarette.

"Ladies, this has been lovely, but I'm afraid I have to go. There's a judicial reception this evening, and then I've got to pack."

She stood and gathered her things. Mrs. Graham walked her to the door. As the two women passed by, Margaret heard the First Lady's promise to Mrs. Graham.

"Let's get together soon, Katharine. Maybe we can sneak in lunch before Thanksgiving. I'll call you on Saturday as soon as Jack and I get back from Dallas."

CHAPTER 39

Before and After

November 1963

F rom the bird's-eye vantage point of ivory towers, scientists, theologians, and academics take the long view of human history, measuring existential change in eras or epochs.

Change looks and feels different at the ground level of lived life, more jarring, measured in moments rather than ages. Nearly every generation can point to an unanticipated event that divided time into before and after, a day after which the world would never be the same, when the markets crashed, or bombs dropped, or wars began, or towers fell.

For the generation cognizant in the early 1960s, the demarcation of the time before and after was a collective shock, a recollection indelibly etched, a shared trauma that would be retriggered by the question they would ask one another for the rest of their lives: "Where were you when Kennedy was shot?"

Margaret was at the market.

Hoping to get a jump on Thanksgiving preparations, she had filled her shopping cart with canned cranberry sauce, pumpkin, and sweet potatoes, bags of miniature marshmallows, and day-old bread for stuffing. When she wheeled the cart to the register, she saw two clerks, the produce manager, and a box boy clustered around a transistor radio. The box boy looked pale. One of the clerks was crying openly.

"What's happened?" Margaret asked.

The weeping, red-eyed clerk looked toward her.

"Somebody shot the president."

Margaret abandoned her shopping cart where it stood and drove directly to the elementary school. It seemed imperative that she collect her children so the family could be together. She wasn't the only one who felt that way; scores of parents had come to take their children home early.

As Margaret, Bobby, and Suzy were driving to the junior high school, a decision to dismiss early was made. Beth was lining up to board the bus when they arrived. Margaret spotted her and waved her over to the station wagon. Blunt as always, Beth voiced the question Margaret had been silently asking herself since leaving the supermarket.

"Is the president going to die?"

"Oh no. No, I'm sure he'll be fine," Margaret said, not because she was dissembling but because she found it impossible to imagine otherwise.

President Kennedy was so young and charismatic, full of life, vitality, and the desire to do good. And Margaret had only just met Mrs. Kennedy, spent substantial time in the same room with this lovely and elegant young wife and mother, a First Lady of legend who was remarkably relatable and even more admirable in person.

They were Jack and Jackie, the golden couple, two halves of a perfectly matched set. Providence could not be so cruel as to separate them.

Oh no. Surely not.

Even after Walter Cronkite, the stoic, rock-solid news anchor on whom Americans counted in times of crisis, confirmed the president's death in a voice choked with emotion, Margaret couldn't make herself believe it. She kept waiting for a retraction, for the moment a sheepish but relieved-looking Cronkite would admit his mistake.

Later that night, when the plane carrying the president's body arrived at Andrews Air Force Base, and Margaret saw Mrs. Kennedy, dressed in the pretty pink suit she had donned for a Dallas parade, now stained with her husband's blood, being helped into the ambulance that carried the president's flag-draped coffin, it all became real.

"But I know her," Margaret said, collapsing onto Walt's shoulder in tears. "I just saw her two days ago. How can he be dead? How? What will she do without him?"

* * *

Four days later, one million people lined the street to watch the caisson carrying the fallen president's coffin pass by on its way toward the Capitol. Tony Buschetti, wearing his dress uniform, and the four older Buschetti children were among them. Millions more watched the procession on television, including Helen and Edwin, Bitsy, Charlotte, and Viv and her younger children, who were gathered in Walt and Margaret's home.

Though there had been no discussion of it beforehand, the adults all dressed in black. The women brought food, too much food, as is customary in gatherings of grief. Only the children had appetite for it. The little ones sat cross-legged on the floor, the adults on sofas and chairs, observing the ceremonies in silence. Even baby Betty, swaddled in a pink blanket and held in her mother's arms, was quiet, stirring only when she wanted a bottle.

Margaret had wept on and off for days. But today, as the coffin with the president's remains was removed from the cathedral for the journey to his final resting place in Arlington National Cemetery, she had no tears left, only dull acceptance of the heretofore unimaginable.

When the honor guard loaded the casket onto the caisson, passing near the former First Family, Mrs. Kennedy leaned down and whispered into the ear of her youngest, John Kennedy Jr., a chubby-cheeked boy barely out of toddlerhood, who had turned three that very day. After a second whisper, little John-John stepped forward and touched the fingertips of his right hand smartly to his forehead, saluting his father's casket.

It was a wrenching moment and a picture the world would never forget, a day that stirred up a vast range of unexpected emotions, regrets, and fears.

Bitsy pressed a hand hard against her lips. Charlotte squeezed her eyes shut and clutched the neck of her black dress. Viv murmured, "Oh, that precious baby," pulling her own baby closer to her breast. Walt rose from the sofa, leaving the room so abruptly that everyone turned away from the television. Beth frowned with concern and turned to Margaret.

"Is Daddy okay?"

Margaret assured her that he was, then got to her feet and followed him to the kitchen.

"I'm fine," he said, lifting a hand but not his eyes. "Just needed a break. You go on back, and I'll be there in a minute."

Walt was gone longer than a minute, but he did return looking composed and took a seat next to Margaret. When the funeral was over, Walt found Edwin's hat and helped Helen into her coat, then walked them to their car. Margaret stayed inside to say goodbye to the Bettys, hugging each woman in turn.

"I'm glad we could be together today," Bitsy said, her brown eyes filling. "You know, I'm starting to have second thoughts about applying to vet school. California is so far away. What am I going to do without you three?"

"Live and thrive," Viv said, taking hold of Bitsy's chin like a gently chiding schoolmarm. "We'll miss you just as much as you'll miss us, but you're going to be fine. Promise."

Charlotte nodded. "You know what Eleanor Roosevelt used to say: 'A woman is like a tea bag. You never know how strong it is until it's in hot water.'"

Bitsy swiped at her eyes and twisted her lips. "I know. But . . . couldn't I start with warm water and work my way up?"

"Are you kidding? What kind of water do you think you've been in lately?" Margaret asked, clicking her tongue. "You're one tough tea bag, Bitsy. And so are you, and so are you," she said, looking at Charlotte and Viv in turn. "And so am I. Think of all we've gone through in the last few months and all we've learned about ourselves, starting with the fact that we're all a lot stronger and more capable than we ever realized."

Charlotte nodded. "Good point. Maybe we should start calling ourselves the Tea Bags?"

Margaret rolled her eyes, then shook her head.

"We're the Bettys. And we always will be. Always."

* * *

Margaret had a hard time falling asleep that night. So did Walt. He lay in the dark, staring at the ceiling, holding his arms arrow-straight and tucked tight against his sides. Margaret turned on the bedside lamp.

"Are you sure you're all right?"

After thirteen years of marriage, Margaret thought she'd seen every side of her husband, but this was a Walt she didn't recognize, a man whose inner thoughts and body language were a mystery to her.

"I had to get out of there," he said, shaking his head but still staring at the ceiling. "I didn't want to start crying in front of people."

Margaret nodded. She thought she understood. Walt was more softhearted than most people would have guessed, but he didn't like to display that side of himself. She'd seen him shed tears only rarely and never in public.

She moved nearer, lifted his arm, and draped it over her shoulder, nestling closer.

"No one would have thought less of you. Everybody was on the verge of tears. That poor, sweet, fatherless boy. And little Caroline. You'd have to be made of stone not to cry for those kids. And poor Mrs. Kennedy," she said, her voice dropping as she recalled the bright-eyed woman of the week before, now made a widow.

"Every time I think of her, I feel like bursting into tears. But sometimes I wonder if I'm not crying for myself as much as for her."

Margaret looked up into her husband's eyes.

"If anything happened to you, I don't know how I'd find the strength to go on. Maybe it sounds selfish, but meeting Mrs. Kennedy, understanding that she's a real, flesh-and-blood woman, not so different from me, and knowing that something so unimaginably terrible could happen, and so unexpectedly, has taken the lid off things that frighten me most."

Walt rolled toward her. "If that makes you selfish, we're both guilty. I'm sad for the Kennedys, but I'm sad for myself too. When John-John saluted the casket . . ."

Walt paused, took a breath.

"I know the president wasn't perfect, but I admired him. He was so full of energy and vision and plans—the Peace Corps, civil rights, the space program. If he'd lived, who knows what he might have accomplished? But then, just like that—" Walt snapped his fingers. "All that promise, all those plans. Gone."

"He was so young," Margaret said, her voice almost a whisper.

"But that's the thing, isn't it? Nobody knows if today will be their last day. It all goes so fast. At least Kennedy did something with his life. Whereas I—" He shifted his eyes abruptly from hers. "Never mind. Guess I'm just feeling sorry for myself. Or ashamed of myself."

He tried to turn away, but Margaret put her hand on his shoulder.

"Ashamed? Why? No, really," she said when he tried to dismiss her. "Why do you feel ashamed, honey? I want to understand."

Walt hesitated, as if weighing how much he wanted to reveal.

"You remember how I was back in college? I wanted to do everything. Now here I am, thirty-six years old. And what have I done with my life? Nothing."

Though Margaret flinched inwardly, she knew he didn't mean it the way it sounded. After all, she'd experienced some of those same feelings recently, the sense that her life didn't amount to much. And so rather than remind him of his children and her, she bit her tongue.

As it turned out, he didn't need reminding.

"No, no," he said. "I take that back. I wanted to marry you. That was the only thing I was certain of back then, the one decision I never second-guessed. I was willing to do whatever I had to do to make it happen, and I've never regretted it, not for one minute."

His words made Margaret flinch again, but for a different reason. She pushed herself to a sitting position.

"Well, I regret it," she said. "Not that we got married. Only the hoops I made you jump through to get me to say yes. You only went into accounting because of me."

Walt sat up too. "Yes, because I wanted a life and a family with *you*. If studying accounting was what it took to make it happen, I was fine with that. I still am. You and the kids are everything to me. And I had to figure out some way to support you, didn't I? You may not realize this, Maggie, but nobody who lives in Concordia majored in philosophy."

Walt smiled, trying to lighten her mood. Margaret hugged her knees to her chest, thinking back to the day he'd proposed, how relieved she'd been that Walt had finally come to his senses and settled on a profession that could support a family, that could support her. But shouldn't she have supported him as well? Considered his happiness along with her own?

Walt ducked his head so he could see her eyes.

"Maggie, don't be so hard on yourself. Remember how young we were. We were just trying to figure everything out, doing what we thought we were supposed to do."

True. They had been raised to believe that the road to a happy, successful adulthood was well defined but extremely narrow, and that deviating from the path was not only irresponsible but also wrong, a quick route to certain disaster.

Margaret thought back to the words she'd written months before, that there were a million good and right ways to be a woman, and only two wrong ways. First, to insist that your way was the *only* way. Second, to allow your unique, square-peg soul to be deformed and misshapen, pounded into the round hole of someone else's ideal.

If that was true for women, shouldn't it be true for men as well?

She sat up straighter, replaying Walt's words in her mind.

"But honey? We're *not* young anymore."

"No," he said, chuckling. "We are not."

"So if that's true," Margaret said slowly, brow creasing as she gathered her thoughts, "why are we still acting like it? No one knows what we want out of our lives more than we do. So why are we still following a script somebody else wrote?"

She spun around to face Walt, sitting cross-legged and looking into his face with an intent, expectant expression.

"All right," she said in a tone that was simultaneously elated and practical. "Certain things are givens. We're married and we have three kids, so that's always going to be part of the equation. But beyond that, if we could do anything we wanted to do, live however and wherever we wanted to live, what would that look like?"

Walt narrowed his eyes. "Margaret, am I supposed to believe you're serious?"

"I am serious."

Walt frowned and fell silent.

"I don't know," he said after a moment, turning out his hands. "Honestly, Maggie, I don't have any more clue now than I did in college."

"Exactly! Neither do I. And that's the problem!" She leaned toward him, grabbed his hand. "It's like you said—we were still trying to figure everything out back then. But the thing is, we never did figure it out, did we? Instead, we just did what we thought we were supposed to do, kept following the rules like everyone else.

"But here's the good news," she said, squeezing his hand because she just couldn't contain her excitement. "It's not too late to do something about it! And I think we should, together. Maybe we're not as young as we used to be, but we're still young. Let's quit wasting time and figure this out.

"So, I ask you again, Mr. Ryan, if we could do anything we wanted with our lives—no boundaries, no buts, and no shoulds—what would it be?"

Margaret squared her shoulders and folded her hands in her lap, awaiting his response with an alert expression. Walt smiled, the warmth of his affection spreading over his face and into his eyes.

"I love you, Maggie."

"I love you too. Now answer the question. Oh, wait!" she cried just as Walt opened his mouth to speak. "Hold that thought!"

Margaret sprang from the bed and started digging frantically through the nightstand.

Walt shook his head, laughing. "What are you doing?"

"I always think better if I write things down," Margaret said, pulling a pen and notepad from the drawer and brandishing them with a triumphant gesture before climbing back into bed. "We should probably make a list. Or a few? I have a feeling this might take a while."

* * *

It was the start of a long conversation—one that would stretch on for months, and that they would revisit year upon year, decade upon decade.

However, that first round of talks reached its apex in early June of the following year.

Walt, carrying a rubber mallet with a long wooden handle, exited the garage and called to Margaret through the front door of the house, which stood partly ajar.

"Honey? I found it!"

Margaret emerged a moment later, holding a red and white "For Sale" sign in her hands.

They walked down the driveway together and across the lawn to a spot near the curb. Margaret knelt on the grass and pushed the pointed end of the wooden stake into the turf as far as it would go, steadying the sign with her hands.

Walt raised the mallet above his shoulders, preparing to swing.

"You're sure you're ready for this? Because if you're not . . ."

Margaret shifted her weight back, sitting on her haunches and taking in her surroundings—the peaceful neighborhood, the white house with the forest-green shutters, the tidy yard, the two birch trees.

She thought about unlocking the door for the very first time, walking through the vacant rooms, breathing in the scent of paint, sawdust, and new beginnings. It had been her dream house, back before she understood that dreams could change. For a season she had loved it.

The trees, on the other hand, Margaret had *never* loved. Though they really were quite lovely now, with spreading branches and a wealth of bright green leaves, she still didn't.

But someone else would. And that was just as it should be.

Margaret rocked forward again, tightened her hold on the sign, and smiled up at Walt.

"I'm sure."

CHAPTER 40

Who Were, Are, and Will Be

October 2006

Margaret, wearing a champagne-colored silk sheath dress, came out of the bathroom at the same time Walt entered the bedroom. He carried a wicker basket wrapped in a cellophane bag and topped with a big blue ribbon.

"This just came for you," he said. "Probably from the kids."

Indeed, it was. A card had been signed by all three, but the touching note expressing congratulations for Margaret's award and regrets that they couldn't be there to see her receive it had clearly been penned by Suzy, who had become a fine writer herself. Bobby had probably picked out the champagne, and Margaret had no doubt about who had insisted on including the hideous orchid corsage with the neon-green ribbons. Walt grinned when he spotted it.

"Let me guess. Beth?"

"Once a smart-ass, always a smart-ass," she laughed, then turned her back toward Walt. She pushed her hair up off her neck. "Can you zip me? I can't reach."

"I can't get the doohickey at the top to hook," he said after a few seconds of fiddling.

"It's fine. Just as long as the zipper is up."

Margaret walked to the bed and slipped on the jacket she'd laid out for herself. It was new, purchased just for tonight, made of an elegant chocolate-brown and gold-flecked wool-silk blend and trimmed with gold buttons. She turned to face Walt, extending her arms from her sides.

"What do you think?"

His eyes traveled up and down her frame, from the tips of her tan Stuart Weitzman pumps to the top of her shining and sleekly styled hair, which Margaret's hairdresser had lightened to a color more platinum than gray.

"Beautiful. As always."

"You're sure? Not too mother-of-the-bride?"

"Nope, you look great." He tilted his head to one side. "Have you lost weight?"

Margaret shook her head and retrieved her evening clutch from the top of the dresser.

"It's the Spanx."

"Spanx?"

"Shapewear," she explained. She touched up her lipstick, then slipped the tube and a few extra business cards into her bag. "A sort of one-piece undergarment made of spandex or elastic or some such thing. It holds you in. Smooths out the rolls and bumps."

"So, a girdle."

"Well, now that you mention it . . ." Margaret paused to think. "Yes."

"Ha! Guess what goes around comes around."

It does indeed. And never more than tonight.

* * *

Betty Friedan's book had been the catalyst to a life Margaret could scarcely have imagined when she first knocked on Charlotte's door. Forty-three years later, a piece she had written in the wake of Ms. Friedan's death in February would mark, though not the end of Margaret's career, probably its pinnacle. At seventy-six, she realized this award would likely be her last.

Margaret was fine with that. She took pride in not just accepting change but embracing it. And Walt? Well, he practically chased it with a lasso.

They'd obtained three advanced degrees between them, taking turns as primary breadwinner when the other was in school, and sharing the load the rest of the time. Collectively, they'd held more than a dozen job titles, working for themselves but also for others at companies as small as Babcock's Best Books and as large as the *Washington Post*. Unsurprisingly, Walt had changed careers more frequently than Margaret, but eventually landed his dream job as a research librarian at the Library of Congress, specializing in prerevolutionary American history of the Virginia Tidewater region.

"Pretty specific for a guy who could never make up his mind," Walt joked after he got the job. True, but he'd finally found his niche and worked at the library until his retirement.

They'd changed addresses often too. Their most recent move had taken place two years before. Margaret had liked their house in Arlington, so her first response to Walt's suggestion was a firm no.

"I know you love this place, Maggie. So do I. But the upkeep is harder every year. Those condos on D Street Northwest are brand-new and in a great location, two blocks from the mall and a metro station. We'd be able to get rid of the car—"

Margaret raised both hands, signaling he should stop right there.

"Hang on. You want to sell the house *and* the car?"

"Walking is better for you," he said. "Keeps you young. Besides, you're always complaining about the traffic. And at our age, is it really a good idea to keep driving?"

"Hey, you're the one who pushes the yellow lights, buster. I am an excellent driver."

"Yes, you are. An excellent driver," he said, tilting his head and tucking his chin in a perfect imitation of Dustin Hoffman's character from *Rain Man*. "An excellent driver."

Margaret crossed her arms. "If you think you're going to joke me into moving, think again. I like this house," she said, repeating her primary argument. "And those condos are so small. What are they? Maybe half the size of our current house?"

"Probably less," Walt admitted. "Look, all I'm asking you to do is take a tour and keep an open mind. Yes, it would be a big change. But it could also be a big adventure. At this stage of life, how many more of those are we going to get?"

Moving to downtown DC had been an adventure. Shops, restaurants, museums, theaters, and a subway station that would take them anywhere in the city were just a stone's throw from their building. Weekly happy hours had made it easy to meet the neighbors, people in every stage and walk of life. With Walt volunteering as a docent at the Smithsonian and Margaret still writing every morning, they were as busy as they'd ever been, and as happy.

The condo *was* small, and paring down their possessions was hard. But Margaret knew that an adventurous life required trade-offs. As Betty Friedan once said, "You can have it all, just not all at the same time." People often cited that quote in reference to women. As far as Margaret was concerned, it applied to any person of any gender at any stage of life.

* * *

Walt's hair was white and a bit thinner, but he was still a handsome man, especially in a tuxedo. He stood in the foyer, holding Margaret's coat as she exited the bedroom.

"It's ten blocks. Do you want to walk or hail a cab?"

"Oh, let's walk. It's a nice evening."

"You sure? Ten blocks," he reminded her, casting a doubtful glance at her new shoes.

"I'll be fine," she said, sliding one arm into her coat. "Oh, wait! I forgot my earrings!"

"If you don't hurry up, there won't be time to walk," he called as she scurried away.

Margaret pretended not to hear him. The earring backs were a bit fiddly, but she finally got them on and crossed the room to the bureau to check herself in the mirror one more time.

Not bad, she thought.

Turning to leave, she caught sight of the shelf where she displayed her most important mementos: two previous awards, a notebook of her clippings, framed photographs of the Bettys, and photos with various colleagues, including Mrs. Graham. Katharine had died in 2001, but not a week went by without Margaret thinking of her old boss, the woman who had opened so many doors for her. Margaret reached for the photo.

"Thanks for inviting me into the room, Katharine. That lunch changed everything."

Sylvia, a bit worse for wear but still functional, also had a spot on the shelf. Every now and again, Margaret typed out a letter or two, just for the pleasure of striking the keys and hearing the cheerful ding of the roller return. Today Sylvia sat atop Margaret's 1963 copy of *The Feminine Mystique*, near a snapshot of Margaret and the author.

They'd met at a fundraiser in 1971. Margaret had found Friedan prickly, defensive, and a bit arrogant, nothing like the Aunt Betty of her imagination. But that was beside the point. It wasn't the woman herself who had altered Margaret's path, but the words she had written. Prickly or not, Friedan had produced a work that cast ripples through generations of women, including many who had never heard her name or read her book.

"Margaret Ruth Ryan," Walt shouted from the foyer, "if you don't shake a leg, you're going to miss your own party!"

"Coming!" Margaret placed Mrs. Graham's picture back on the shelf, then scanned the photo gallery once again. "Thanks, girls. Thanks for everything."

✳ ✳ ✳

Though the Lafayette Ballroom was beginning to fill as they entered, Margaret and Walt were the first of their party to arrive. Margaret saw plenty of familiar faces milling around the reception area, people she had worked with over the years. They offered congratulations on her award, complimented her outfit, and said they needed to get together soon. Margaret took note so she could follow up later. What Mrs. Graham had said all those years ago was still true—Washington was all about connections. Margaret was always intentional about maintaining hers.

At the check-in table, a young woman who introduced herself as the "honoree wrangler" escorted them to their seats. "You're right here," she said, gesturing toward a round table at the front of the room. "Number 5. We put all the award recipients near the stage to help move things along. Remember, everyone only gets three minutes for their remarks."

"What happens if I go over? Do you play music over the speech? Bring out the hook?" At the wrangler's alarmed expression, Margaret laughed. "Don't worry," she said. "I'll be brief."

When the woman left, Walt gave Margaret a look that was half reproving and half admiring. "That wasn't very nice, Margaret. You scared that poor girl."

Margaret gave him an impish smile. "Well, I'm not as sweet as I used to be."

"But a helluva lot more fun." He gave her a peck and pulled out her chair. "Why do all hotel ballrooms look the same? And why, even with all these people around, can you never flag down a server? I want a drink."

"Me too. Can you go to the bar?"

"What would you like?"

"Oh, I don't know," Margaret said distractedly. "Surprise me."

Walt set off on his mission. Margaret picked up a copy of the program that was sitting on the plate. Her award was thirteenth of twenty. It was going to be a long night.

"There she is! The woman of the hour! My famous friend!"

"Nurse Buschetti!"

Margaret leapt to her feet, embracing Viv with genuine joy, as if it had been years instead of a week since they'd last seen each other.

Viv and Tony had stayed in Concordia longer than any of the Bettys. All but one of their brood had graduated from Concordia High, where Viv began working as a school nurse. After Jenny flew the nest, Viv, Tony, and thirteen-year-old Betty set off on a new adventure.

For ten years the Buschettis lived on a hospital ship that sailed the globe, providing medical care to people in impoverished nations. Viv was on the medical team, and Tony worked in operations. When Tony passed away, Viv returned to Virginia. She and Margaret saw each other often and talked on the telephone most days.

After a long, hard hug, Margaret released her grip on her old friend.

"Thanks for coming. How are you? How's the new knee?"

"Fantastic. Look! No cane!" Viv exclaimed, throwing out her hands. "And after only two months. Impressive, right? My doctor says I'm doing great. Isn't that right, Doc?"

Viv beamed at her petite companion. Margaret smiled too and gave her a hug.

"Good to see you, Betty. Thanks for coming."

All seven of the Buschetti children had done well for themselves. Jenny was a pilot for Delta. Betty was an obstetrician at Sibley Memorial Hospital. Viv lived with Betty and her husband and their three children. Whenever their paths crossed, Margaret couldn't help but recall that tiny baby in the incubator. What an impressive woman she'd grown up to be.

"Hopefully I'll be able to stay for the whole thing," Betty said. "None of my patients are due this week, but I'm still on call, and babies tend to show up when they feel like it."

"Don't I know it," Viv said with an exaggerated roll of her

eyes. "Hey, Maggie, if Betty's pager goes off and she has to leave, can Walt help me hail a taxi?"

"Why don't you just stay over at our place? The guest room is already made up, and we were going to invite everybody over for a drink after anyway."

"Are you sure? That would be great!" Viv exclaimed. "I'd love the chance to catch up. It's been so long. Say, where is Bitsy? I thought she'd be here by now. And Walt?"

"He went to the bar," Margaret said, looking across the rapidly filling ballroom and smiling when she spotted a tall, willowy figure near the entrance. "Bitsy and Kyle just came in."

Margaret and Viv turned toward the back of the room, yoo-hooing and waving their arms over their heads. Bitsy's face lit up when she saw them. She grabbed the hand of the very tall, very handsome man next to her and started wending her way through the crowd. Moments later, the three Bettys were hugging and squealing and telling one another they looked fantastic and hadn't aged a bit. In Bitsy's case, it was almost true.

There were creases at the corners of her eyes and touches of gray at her temples, but Bitsy was lean, lithe, and as lovely as ever. She wasn't the same shy, uncertain girl that Viv and Margaret had first met, and her childhood dreams had all come true. Besides a long and successful career as an equine vet, Bitsy had two grown daughters with Kyle and a beautiful home on a California vineyard—Kyle was a vintner—with a stable for Bitsy's horses. Three were already in residence, and a fourth, another rescue, would be arriving shortly.

A photographer approached, asking if she could take a picture of Margaret's table.

"Not yet. My husband seems to have gone missing, and we're waiting on one more."

Margaret felt a tap on her shoulder and turned around.

"If you're talking about me, I'm here."

"Denise!" Margaret's eyes started to fill, but the tears were happy ones. "Oh, Denise. I am so, *so* glad to see you, and honored that you've come so far to be here."

"Well, it wasn't just because of you," Denise said in the blunt manner and tone Margaret remembered well, now tinged with a British accent. "I had to fly over for the annual family meeting with the trustee anyway, and I thought I'd spend time with Laura, see how things are going at the gallery. Your invitation arrived at the right time, you see? And I thought—" Denise ducked her head. "Well, I thought Mom would have wanted me to come."

"Yes, I see," Margaret replied. "And I think you're right."

Ten years had passed since Charlotte's death from congestive heart failure, and Margaret still missed her. But she had lived fully and left a remarkable legacy, incubating the careers of scores of women artists, several of whom had risen to prominence. Laura ran the gallery now. Charlotte would have been proud of her, and of Denise, who never left Oxford. Denise was still an odd duck, but those were generally the ducks worth knowing.

"Whatever the reason, I'm glad you came. Here," Margaret said, pulling out a chair. "Sit next to me. I'd love to hear about your new book. Number seven, isn't it?"

"Yes. I'll begin the eighth soon," Denise said, frowning while taking her seat. "What does a girl have to do to get a drink around here?"

Walt appeared as if on cue, balancing a tray of seven cocktail glasses brimming with bright green liquid. "Slipping twenty bucks to the bartender helps."

When he set the first glass down on the table, Margaret, Viv, and Bitsy squealed simultaneously. Margaret clapped her hands, jumped to her feet, and kissed her husband.

"I don't believe it! You are the dearest man!"

"Well," he said, grinning and distributing the drinks, "you told me to surprise you."

Denise eyed her drink suspiciously. "What is it?"

"Truth serum!" Viv said, lifting her glass to salute her friends. Bitsy leaned toward Denise. "An old family recipe."

"No, but really," Denise said. "What is it?"

"Vodka stingers," Margaret said. "The ideal drink to cement new friendships. Or to celebrate old ones."

* * *

The program hadn't been as lengthy as Margaret feared. Except for one or two windbags, the acceptance speeches had been entertaining and blessedly brief. Margaret kept her remarks short as well, expressing gratitude for her husband, her children, the association, and the Bettys—"Those who were, those who are, and those who will be in the years to come"—before walking away with her plaque. The bulk of the audience likely had no clue what she meant, but her friends knew and she knew. That was what mattered.

Margaret was anxious to get home and open the wine before people arrived at the condo. While waiting for Walt to retrieve their coats, a young woman with curly black hair and a nervous expression approached, said she was a reporter, and asked for an interview.

"You want to interview me? Why?"

Margaret's question was a request for clarification, not an attempt at false modesty. There were several prominent journalists in the room, people whose status bordered on celebrity. Though proud of her accomplishments, Margaret knew she was not among them.

The woman flashed a wide, excited smile, as if Margaret actually was a celebrity. "I read your piece about Betty Friedan—my modern history professor assigned it—and decided to read *The Feminine Mystique* because of it. So interesting! We're still a long way from true equality, but what women were up against in the sixties was so unbelievably unfair. I mean, really! I got some of my girlfriends to read it too, and your article, and—"

"Hang on," Margaret said, interrupting the woman's torrent of words. "You're a reporter? What's your name? You never said."

"Oh, right." Some color drained from the woman's face. "My name is Emma Quinn. I'm not exactly a reporter, more of an intern. I thought if I could get an interview with you, or even a quote, I could write it up and maybe my editor would publish it."

Margaret smiled inside, remembering the story of young, uncredentialed Jackie Bouvier bluffing her way into an audience with Princess Elizabeth, hoping for a scoop or just a quote. Guts were a journalistic job requirement. Emma Quinn was green, but she had guts.

"Nothing wrong with being an intern. At what publication?"

"*Washington City Paper*," she said, sounding a bit sheepish. "It's only a weekly. They give it away at newsstands."

"I've read it," Margaret said. "Good publication. It might not be the *Post*, but it's a start. So don't ever apologize for working there."

Emma nodded. Margaret looked across the room. Walt was coming, carrying the coats. "Listen, Emma, I would love to talk to you, but—"

"Really? That's great!" Emma started to pull out a pocket recorder.

Margaret shook her head. "No, no, you didn't give me a chance to finish. But," she said, "I don't have time now. Do you have a business card?"

"Interns don't—"

"No, of course not. How silly of me."

Margaret opened her clutch and offered one of her own cards. Emma took it with both hands, as if afraid she might drop it. She lifted her head, giving Margaret a questioning look.

"Call me tomorrow, and we'll pick a day to have lunch." Margaret smiled. "I'm sure you and I will have lots to talk about."

A Letter to Readers

Dear Reader,

The longer I live, the more aware I am of the finite nature of time and how quickly it passes. That you've chosen to spend some of your precious, finite store of time with me and my "troublesome women" is an honor that I don't take lightly. Thank you.

Though the novels I've published for the last decade or so have all had contemporary settings, I began my career writing historical fiction. It's been a real pleasure, and something of a homecoming, for me to write a story set in an earlier time period, particularly the early 1960s, which was marked by such profound societal change.

A story set in such a pivotal moment of American history, featuring an ensemble of characters with widely different personalities, backgrounds, and destinies, gave me a lot to work with as a writer, and lots to mull over as well. I think readers, especially book club members, will agree.

Discussion questions to help book clubs get the conversation rolling can be found in the back of the book. But for those clubs who'd like to kick things up a notch, an online book club party kit with book-inspired recipes, recommendations for additional reading, playlists, and more can be found at my author website, www.mariebostwick.com. (That's also the place to go if you want to drop me an email.)

Whenever I read historical fiction, I always wonder which parts of the story were born of the writer's imagination and which were based on actual people or events.

If you read the dedication, you already know that this book was inspired by a conversation with my then eighty-nine-year-old mother, who told me that reading *The Feminine Mystique* had changed her life. As my research quickly revealed, she wasn't alone in this.

Coming face-to-face with the rules, attitudes, and indignities that confined and constricted women of my mother's generation often moved me to anger—and deep admiration. The opportunities I take for granted were paid for by the generation of fearless, dauntless, troublesome women who came before.

Naming my main character after my mother was an homage to her, but the character of Margaret Ryan is entirely fictional. So are the rest of the Bettys and most of the secondary characters. However, some pivotal secondary characters were based upon real people.

Even before her husband's death made her the twentieth century's first female publisher of a major newspaper, Katharine Graham was a storied society hostess and one of the most influential women in Washington. In those roles, she would certainly have known and socialized with important political figures and members of the press. However, the luncheon in her home for members of the Women's National Press Club and Mrs. Kennedy is invented. Although Mrs. Graham rode from an early age, Delilah is an invention and there is no indication that she kept horses at the stables in Rock Creek Park. Having her do so in the story provided an avenue for her to connect with Bitsy and later with Margaret.

First Lady Jacqueline Kennedy was, of course, a real person. The events surrounding the assassination of President Kennedy on November 22, 1963, are well documented. The details of her life prior to her marriage, including her early career in journalism and stint as the Inquiring Camera Girl, are less well known. The stories she relates about those days, during the fictional luncheon at Katharine Graham's home, reflect actual events. If you wish to learn more, I recommend reading *Camera Girl* by Carl Sferrazza Anthony. It's a fascinating book.

Other characters present during the luncheon in the book, including Helen Thomas, Bess Furman, Nancy Dickerson, and Susan Stamberg, were real women who worked as journalists during that period. Helen Thomas was a White House correspondent for nearly fifty years and the only member of the press corps to have her own seat in the White House Briefing Room. When the National Press Club voted to admit women in 1971, Thomas became its first female officer. Susan Stamberg, one of National Public Radio's "founding mothers," worked as a program director at WAMU radio in the early sixties and produced and cohosted *Kaleidoscope*.

The situations that some characters find themselves in over the course of the story—Viv's doctor refusing to prescribe birth control without Tony's consent, Margaret's inability to open a bank account unless Walt was a cosignatory, Bitsy's professors refusing to recommend a woman for vet school—were entirely products of my imagination but based upon my research into the kinds of obstacles women may have faced in the period.

In the 1960s, the type and degree of discrimination any given woman encountered could differ widely depending on her location and individual circumstances. Laws impacting women's rights differed from state to state. However, it wasn't until the 1965 US Supreme Court's ruling in Griswold v. Connecticut that married couples were guaranteed a right to contraception. In 1972, another ruling in the case of Eisenstadt v. Baird legalized birth control access for unmarried people. And it wasn't until 1974 and the passage of the Equal Credit Opportunity Act that married women through the United States were guaranteed the right to open their own bank accounts.

So, yes, actual people, events, and societal norms influenced the book.

But what really made me fall in love with this story was the characters—Margaret, Charlotte, Viv, and Bitsy—and how the books they read, the sisterhood they discover, and the risks they take transform their lives and sense of self. Chapter by chapter, book by book, secret by secret, four lives come together to illuminate a unique moment in history, a story crafted to sound a chord of truth with readers of every generation.

You know, as much as I love to write, it's never been easy for me. I'm incredibly slow, one of those authors who has to write her way into the plot and characters. Every published page generally represents three or four that were deleted.

But this time it was . . . different. Special.

While writing *The Book Club for Troublesome Women*, I felt imbued with peace and purpose, a sense that I was crafting the book of my life, and that I wasn't doing so alone. I stood on the shoulders of my mother and all the women like her, telling their stories, tapping their strength.

And as the deadline approached, I found myself dragging my feet, putting off writing the final chapter because I just didn't want the story or my time with these characters to end.

I hope that readers—that *you*—feel just the same.

Thank you again for reading *The Book Club for Troublesome Women*. Readers are the reason I get to do this work I love. I am grateful for that, and for you.

Sincerely,
Marie Bostwick

Acknowledgments

A thousand thanks to . . .

Laura Wheeler, a talented, patient, and enormously insightful editor. I am grateful for your faith in my troublesome women, for the way you saw what others couldn't, and for the acumen and experience you used to help shape the story and bring them so vividly to life.

Liza Dawson, my intrepid literary agent, who never gives up, pushes me to reach for the best that's in me, and never lets me settle for anything less. I couldn't ask for a better partner or champion.

My Bettys: Robyn Carr, Jane Green, Rachel Linden, Adriana Trigiani, Debbie Macomber, Rachel McMillan, Katherine Reay, Sheila Roberts, and Karen White. Tales of women supporting women aren't just stories I make up. It's my lived experience, demonstrated in your incredible generosity, encouragement, and steadfast support. The sisterhood of authors is one of the biggest perks of this job. I love and appreciate you all.

Brad Skinner, the world's best, most supportive husband/cheerleader. I know you don't like to be acknowledged publicly, but too bad. I'm doing it anyway. (Love you to the moon and back BBS.)

Betty and John Walsh, for encouragement and superior first-round editing skills. How lucky was I to get two sharp-eyed grammar nerds for relatives? You're the best!

Amanda Bostic, Caitlin Halstead, Savannah Breedlove, Nekasha Pratt, Margaret Kercher, Kerri Potts, Jere Warren, Taylor Ward, and the entire Harper Muse Team. Book publishing truly is a team sport, and I'm so lucky to have all of you on mine.

Linda McDonough, Adam Kortekaas, Ashley Hayes, Kathie Bennett, Kylie Balstad, and the entire behind-the-scenes team who helps me connect with readers in person and online. I don't know what I'd do without you!

Faithful readers, who are always in my thoughts as I write, and without whom I wouldn't have the opportunity to do this work I love.

Discussion Questions

1. Describe Margaret's encounter with Betty Friedan's book, *The Feminine Mystique*. How did it reframe her life as a wife and a mother? What did the book give voice to that she'd never heard expressed before? Likewise, how did it affect Charlotte, Bitsy, and Viv in different ways?

2. If possible, describe a book you've read that has completely altered your outlook on the world. What has been the book's lasting impact on your thinking or your actions?

3. Of the four Bettys—Margaret, Bitsy, Charlotte, and Viv— which woman resonates with you the most and why?

4. Discuss the marriages in this novel. Whose were most successful? The most frustrating? Whose outcomes surprised you the most?

5. What particular struggles did the Bettys endure that women still experience today? How much has changed for American women of all stripes since the 1960s? What steps forward— and what steps backward—have been taken?

6. Did Walt's transformation by the novel's end surprise you? If so, what were you expecting of him and his story?

7. What held Charlotte back from pursuing her art, and what eventually set her free? Describe how she was able to find contentment and purpose in something she loved despite several disappointments along the way.

8. What factors led to Margaret's success as a writer? What qualities did she embody, and how crucial was her proverbial "village"?

9. For decades, women have debated the possibility or impossibility of their "having it all." In your opinion, what does having it all look like? Can having it all be attained? And how might each of the Bettys answer this question?

10. Think over some of the other women who came alongside the Bettys and broadened their horizons (such as Dr. Fran and Katharine Graham). How do the women of this novel take opportunities to "pay it forward," and how can women today do the same?

11. Which do you think was more transformative for the Bettys: the books they read together or the sisterhood and camaraderie they experienced?

12. Do you have a "village"? If so, how has the support of those friends made a difference in your life? Have you always gotten along well? Or, like the Bettys, did you experience some bumps, misunderstandings, or rifts along the way? How did you work through them?

MARIE BOSTWICK is the *New York Times* and *USA TODAY* bestselling author of more than twenty works of uplifting contemporary and historical fiction. Translated into a dozen languages, Marie's novels are beloved by readers across the globe. Her 2009 book, *A Thread of Truth*, was an "Indie Next Notable" pick. Three of her books were published as *Reader's Digest* "Select Editions." Marie lives in Washington state with her husband and a beautiful but moderately spoiled Cavalier King Charles spaniel.

* * *

Facebook: @mariebostwick
Instagram: @mariebostwick
Pinterest: @fiercelymarie